PARADISE INTERRUPTED

Brad Goodwin

PARADISE INTERRUPTED

Brad Goodwin

BRAD GOODWIN
An imprint and publication of
Brad Goodwin

Body Type set in 12 pt Times Roman Numeral

 A catalogue record for this
book is available from the
National Library of Australia

ISBN:- 978-0-6483593-8-8

National Library of Australia
Cataloguing in Publication
Author: *Brad Goodwin*
Title: *Paradise Interrupted...*
Subject: *Adventure Fiction*

For My Dad...

Dreams Can Come True

Rest_In_Peace

About The Author

Brad Goodwin currently lives in Brisbane, Queensland, Australia. His previous role saw him write and implement Queensland Government legislation, policy and finances for over a decade.

Brad's life changed dramatically in 2010 when he was diagnosed with a rare degrading incurable neurological condition. This severe debilitating condition saw him medically retire in 2014 at the peak of his public service career.

Writing has now become the cure Brad desperately sought out to keep his seizures at bay and he made a continual effort to prove medical science wrong.

This is Brad's legacy dedicated lovingly to his twin boys, Nicholas and Alexander.

Inspirational Quotes - Embraced

"We are all in the gutter but some of us are looking at the stars"
- Oscar Wilde

"Life would be tragic if it weren't funny"
- Stephen Hawking

"Do, Or Do Not.... There Is No Try..."
– Yoda

"Live your life like you mean to, for you"
- David Costello

ACKNOWLEDGEMENTS....

For those who by their wisdom, support and guiding presence ignited my passion and enlightened my soul:

Therefore, special thanks goes to —

Ronald Goodwin
– My father and biggest inspiration, R.I.P.

Carol Fitzpatrick
- Endless poof reading, helping me find my way back to life, et al...

Joanne & Anthony Jeffries
– For just being my big sis, brother and their encouragement

Simon Knowles
- Encouragement and daring me to actually start, he probably forgot...

Jim Lergessner
- My friend and editor

David Costello
– The nicest guy I've ever met, plus his hilarious sarcasm

Author's Thoughts:

The descent into one's psyche and soul may exude irrational fear. It is a journey not everyone is willing to undertake or confront. Such a voluntary honest exploration of your inner most exclusive foundations brings with it psychological challenges and raw acceptance. One cannot avoid resurfacing — Unchanged.

AUTHENTICITY:-

All literature, sciences, military and historical references in this novel are real.

'The World Monarch, Crown Council of Thirteen, Committee of Three Hundred and Think Tanks' are widely held New World Order conspiracy theories not conclusively proven to exist or to not exist...

'The Chimera' are myths, legends and espoused folklore. References are rarely documented.

CHAPTER ONE

ANOTHER DAY BEGINS...

Randall McCaw's bloodshot eyes opened slowly, with the realisation that he had once again been blessed with another shitty day in his self-imposed, chosen exile. It was 5:00am a-fucking-gain, but at least he was still breathing, a good sign given the previous week's events. The sun in all its glory had started to rise. 'Alive, breathing, bonus', he thought as he opened his eyes all the way to focus. It was the year 2055.

The unfenced caravan park wasn't far from the local and beautiful blue Hockalugie Bay. It was, however, closer to the thickly-scrubbed mountain range that surrounded it: Barraiya. This range was enormous, steeply grounded in indigenous culture and heritage, dating back into the Dreamtime. The park was now awakening to the sounds of the overflowing, overgrown creek as life was becoming reanimated. It had rained torrentially the night before. Water from the scrub-filled range had flowed into the creek and made it rise, in turn breaking its banks. There was a combination of fresh scummy water and filthy run off that drained over these banks and into the park. And it stank. The smell produced was reminiscent of putrid raw sewage. This was then combined with the wonderful pungent odour emanating from the fresh vomit regurgitated by local homeless drunks. These downcast lifeforms were lying on each side of the creek in their makeshift camps, sleeping among last night's empties and bowel movements.

Birds began rising for the dawn to feed their young in the various shrubbery and trees. Colourful water dragons were backstroking in one of two green scum-filled communal swimming pools. A dead possum was still lying on Darren's back porch between the red wine glasses and stale crackers. Darren had collapsed, still lying in his yellow-green easy chair as it decomposed around him. He was slumped backwards, his eight-pump shotgun still clenched in his right fist. It had been completely emptied except for one unfired cartridge, a habit Darren had adopted as a matter of self-preservation since the goanna incident. He had passed out and collapsed from an alcoholic-fuelled night of shooting. Another one of his "shoot anything that moved again evenings". This had become universally accepted by all, especially when he was pissed as a fart. He was overseeing the dead possum like some overzealous big game hunter, its head having been totally obliterated.

The dull dawn streaked through the deciduous trees which surrounded the park. The rays now highlighted a decomposing snake which had stupidly ventured into Randall's side yard the previous week. Here it had had the misfortune to tangle with the local feral cat, became lost and left to rot. The light breeze carried its fetid stench adrift throughout the park. As the sun's rays slowly broke through the trees that surrounded the creek, it appeared similar to an enchanted, haunted forest. It lit up the rubbish-ringed nests the bush rats were still hiding in, shaking and fearful of the local residents. Last night's drunken wild corroboree had made their numbers dwindle slightly, probably because they were the main food source for the oversized BBQ grill. The little old black boom box that Viktor had found still worked. It was sitting on top of the jagged, rusted-out, fluro orange, upturned forty four gallon oil drum. It was lovingly blaring away as Randall lay in bed just coherently mumbling along with the words.

On the next site down, the sun broke over the other large pool which had really seen better days. The brown ring around it was like a permanent stain and even though it was in this condition the residents still used it, never cleaned. It hadn't killed anyone, yet — a bonus really, given this downtrodden park was designated for the lower end of the food chain. Clean water was now a scarce commodity via global warming and profiteering. Still, one does ponder, why swim at all? Jarece the park dyke wasn't perturbed. She lived in the only house near the pool not totally ravaged by time or neglect and was out for her daily dawn skinny dip. She was now lying listlessly face down on her sun lounge, zircon earrings flashing in the early morning glare. The view, if anyone bothered to look, was similar to two hippo carcasses slowly decomposing lying on top a purple and white plastic retro piece of furniture. Gravity really is a bitch and seriously wasn't being kind to Jarece's razor-strap breasts, which were now piercing through the large holes underneath.

Everywhere you looked the caravan park was a mix of degrading old collapsing smallish homes, shacks, ramshackle windowless huts, rusty tin sheds, ratty threadbare tents, and, at the lower end of the scale, tallish grey trees with ropes slung between with a tarpaulin for coverage. The gardens were completely ignored and hadn't seen maintenance for years. The elderly man, Doug, who used to lovingly attend these had died two years ago and was buried in his latest creation, a pristine red-rose garden which absolutely flourished, full of colour, a testament to the nutrients of decomposing human remains and Mother Nature's sense of humour and irony. Everything else between these shelters was overgrown, weeds and grasses of all shapes and varieties spread out, looking like wild feral vipers, now on a relentless march to enthusiastically reclaim it all. The park was a brilliant mix of baby shit browns, scurvy, the black plague, rust and a biological chemical weapon gone bizarrely crazy. Yet life existed, no, flourished here, in one form or another. As the sun rose, the other local wildlife stirred noisily. A mixture of elderly and other residents of the caravan park or "Living Dead Zombies" started opening the lids to their nightly coffins. They rattled around, tucked their wrinkled skin and obese bodies into any old tatty clothing that would hang from their various shaped forms. Their morning caffeine and mouldy toast was beckoning. Outside his shattered filthy bedroom window Randall could hear the others. They were methodically working their way through their daily routine of walking around the park. Most hunted for food, others for water; some were speaking with and checking in on their neighbours. Others were picking over the pathetic belongings of those who were now dead. These were the ones lucky enough to have been removed recently from this incestuous gene pool, not the actual pool, that was last week. The mess and smell had now faded, plus the colours had blended into the background.

The local druggies were now coming out of their ratty threadbare tents, wet, soaked, red eyed, still doped up to the eyeballs from last night's jamboree. Exhausted by their drug-fuelled sex orgies, they began looking for their next big hit. They started chasing and harassing the morning fitness joggers from the local gated estate who were stupid enough to venture this far south, unarmed. So, situation normal really. Like the many, various cramped, disintegrating hovels at the edge of the large, overcrowded sprawling walled city, these parks were also filled now with ramshackle bits and pieces cobbled together into things called homes. Most were constructed from virtually any material lucky enough to be used to make weather-proof accommodation. At least this park was one of the better ones; it was full of actual dilapidated dwellings or structures that passed for homes. Plus no one here had suffered from any major disease or a brutal death, yet! At least here there was a sense of comradeship in this domain and fiefdom. People were returning to the behaviour of looking out for each other, another surprise of humanity. They mainly did this specifically for self-preservation, companionship, cleanish water, self-defence and the sharing of the communal food sources (mainly vermin). The further you moved away from the city the worse these sanctuaries became.

Randall had always thought on days like this how fortunate he had been to find this one after his departure from the pristine privileged world he'd once known. It could've been worse, a lot worse. In the local stationary traffic jam, horns were blaring, people were on their way to their pointless brainwashed jobs. That's if you were lucky enough to have a job, let alone a car given fuel prices nowadays. This was now all a part of privileged lives in the New Global World Order, "Go

Rothschild... thanks for this... you prick!" Someone had to wear the blame for society being like walking zombies and sheep, so why not stick with the most commonly adopted conspiracy theory. Damn shame no one had the intelligence or lived long enough to prove it was actually correct.

'Another day in fucking paradise', Randall thought just coherently, laying still for the next major seizure to kick start his day. 'Give me one day of peace for Christ sake, just fucking one'. It was then the seizure hit. "Fuckkkkk!" he screamed and thrashed. No one noticed, this was the routine, this was just another day in the making. Randall jerkily sat up on the side of his bed; he was quite wonky, hazy, fed up and extremely weary. He began to come out of his cannabis and spiced soaked rum-induced sleep from the night before. 'Another day, I'm still alive', he thought, "Yee fucking har!" he sighed, spastically doing the cattle tick sign of the cross. "Spectacles, testicles, watch and wallet". His uncle taught him that growing up, trying to teach him to believe in religion and faith, what a joke. Next thought, 'What a waste of time, that's three precious bloody seconds of my life I'll never get back. GOD, what fucking GOD, the world and the

Universe revolves around everyone else's anus, doesn't it?' He knowingly shook his head.

As he lay there Randall's flashbacks began anew. Today's society was all about what can you get out of it, plus, how can you push your own agenda. His daily reminiscing was always fun, sarcastically and utterly pointless, but fun. He started thinking about how it all began, again. How did he get to this new shitty low point in his life? His recent depression was fuelling these self-destructive thoughts. It had been a while since he had his last recounting session. His thoughts started to congeal and he began to remember. Society had degraded to the point that no one cared about anyone anymore, literally. Fights broke out everywhere for no sane reason. Road rage now extended to suburban life and crime rates rose as a result. The gap between rich and poor was now vast and the poor were beginning to gather in gangs, plotting a coup at every corner. The last big financial market crash had virtually wiped out everyone who was not unscrupulous enough to avoid being made bankrupt. Superannuation accounts were a thing of the past and people were now forced into government controlled pensions. Crippling debt was everywhere and overwhelming people.

All this was due to 'The System', a Government-imposed computerised gargantuan; it ran everything. Big brother had morphed into the love child of Godzilla and a genetically-modified Kraken and it had eyes and tentacles everywhere. An encrypted informational database that controlled the world's information was used to control the masses. Randall was regretting ever having helped; he was one of the creators who oversaw it. Your entire life was on it, nothing was sacred. Today was a cashless society, computerised real estate was huge money and 'The System' controlled everything. Those who had learned to work 'The System' thrived. They lived in the city, others bribed their way there, most however were born into this privilege. The cities were now large securely gated, fully-armed medieval urban walled castles. This was where the wealthy lived in their ivory and crystal towers. The securely protected server warehouses were in there too. If you could find a way into them and hack 'The System', for a skilled computer thief there was a fortune to be made on the black market selling modified identities. Living to brag about doing it or making a profitable living was something else entirely; those who tried were exterminated.

Everywhere else apart from the cities were mostly abandoned and overgrown and nature was reclaiming large portions of the once occupied run down estates. This was the underbelly of life that no one spoke about. This was where the lower socioeconomic classes lived and were left to rot. There were other prestigious gated estates, but they had now become rarer and were slowly decomposing. These estates were on the decline as jobs became more and more computerised as unemployment rose sharply. When the natural resources ran out and over population grew out of control, the inevitable happened. Humans began turning on each other to survive and crime became rampant. Large areas of housing seemed to be unoccupied for years as the death rate, poverty and disease rose. You lived where you could find a place to rest your head. Or live in a place like those here, if you were fortunate enough to find one. Black market guns were carried by nearly everyone. That's if you could afford one, if you couldn't, you stole it, along with the ammo.

Others used whatever weapons they could find as personal deterrents, pipes, wood, hammers and garden implements. For those born of incest their physical appearance was enough. People took offence at the slightest remark or gesture, political correctness was a thing of the past, no time for that bullshit now. Personal rage just became the norm and murders became a way of life, one less mouth to feed. The almighty dollar and rife consumerism had seen to this gruesome adopted attitude and the rising death rates.

WHOA BE ME...

It was these soul destructive thoughts that rattled through Randall's brain each morning lately as he was still and brooding. 'Really, Fucking Really? We would have been better off never having come out of those caves. Why did we ever allow uncontrolled breeding for that matter, human overpopulation was now rife, globally. We'd literally stuffed up our planet for profit'. The effects of this had impacted his life. This was just the natural thought progression he had every so often, no, fucking daily. He was sick and tired of this daily wallowing, it was sucking him dry emotionally and he was drained. Global warming had screwed everyone over. "We never saw it coming" was the standard one liner excuse people complained about. No, we were so selfish about money and we were too busy lining our own pockets to care or notice. The Northern Hemisphere was now in the grips of a new Ice Age, that was due to global warming and a shift in polar zones. Everyone was now moving south to warmer climes. The entire populations of China and India were on the march. If you weren't one of the major races of Chinese or Indian descent, or an inbred part thereof, and wealthy, you were treated like a major case of syphilis or just a pure inconvenience. These races were now the dominant controlling force as they had outbred everyone.

Survival today was all about huge recycled debt, sweat shops and extremely low minimum wages. People had multiple jobs just to survive, if they could get one. There were stricter government controls and curfews, food and water were rationed. You were either part of a definitive privileged social class or you weren't. If you weren't, you were in a word — Screwed. Life was literally a game of that ridiculous survival reality show, "Insert Suburb or Town Here". At least at this end of the socioeconomic

23

system, if you couldn't buy food, you would hunt or fish for whatever could be found. Around here people were slowly receding back to the hunter-gatherer glory days. Tribes were beginning to be formed as a matter of loyalty and safety. Mainly because employment was a luxury and survival of any kind now meant life.

Randall always started with this daily morning ritual, he was fed up with it. Now was the moment he had to take control and change his life. This could not continue, it was devouring his soul. To keep his sanity he had to have a ritual, no matter how trivial. It kept him focused and it kept him sane, even if it was bloody pointless. The small rectangular bedroom was a little blurry and slightly spinning. The paint was peeling away and no longer the original off white colour. It was more a sickly yellow and blood-soaked grey due to the weather and its previous owners. There was a hand axe still buried in the front door as Randall was too lazy to remove it, "Adds to the charm. Part of its alarm system. Don't fuck with me", Randall used to say to others. 'Oh, fucking vertigo, go away', was the next actual coherent thought going through his brain. Smells from his internal surroundings, the dead snake, and toilet blocks, assailed his senses. He nearly threw up. He swallowed back the reflux bile. 'Time to get moving', he mused?

Given Randall's health had started to decline over the last eight years due to a rare neurological condition with no cure, he was lucky to be alive. 'Lucky me' along with 'Oh fuck' were his initial reactions when he was told. Now this daily routine was situation normal, or a solution, your pick really. It was the norm now to just be able to survive the long nights of insomnia. Plus, there was the morning daily dose of one or more mind-controlling pharmaceuticals. Once, less than a decade ago, he had everything. Randall was on top of the world —Numero UNO — number one itchy bum. He began to reminisce and once he started these thoughts it was like a runaway bullet train. He remembered he had the big exclusive house, in a prestigious gated suburb, the red sports BMW (it went faster) with personalised number plates, and of course, the big black Merc SUV. He had the perfect combination of computer programming and finance career as a freelancer, shooting him into the executive stratosphere and high-flyer status. Computers still hadn't taken over his job, he was good at what he did, he was fortunate. Not like the others he knew who fell from grace. He had the perfect family, a supposedly happy marriage ('to that fucking gold digging Ex-bitch'). Then there were the children, a dog, a cat and those shitty fucking annoying birds his partner had to have. Mind you, he was the one designated to clean up their shit. He'd have rather that they were fucking crab bait. Oh yes, and let's not forget all those fake friends. He knew the ones. They would stand around on his coattails bathing in his glory and prominence, waiting to take advantage of any benefit they could milk out of him. They always expected to be invited to the next latest free weekly dining event to further one's status up the social ladder.

At this same time, Randall had been diagnosed with a rare medical condition. The odds were 1:14 million ever diagnosed. Even though the global population was only Thirty Billion, that was still shitty odds. His medical bills were expensive, the worse he became the more it cost. That was when his life imploded, literally. His poor health issues became his own personal Atom bomb, Hiroshima, Nagasaki, the ICBM that went through his life and this was now the aftermath. Randall lay still on the bed rocking his head. "STOP!" he screamed out. He was going through a daily clockwork religious ritual. Realisation and recognition that he'd lost everything had become the norm, it had all been taken away. You always needed something to keep yourself sane, this was the only way that made sense to him of what went wrong. His life had changed enormously. He started thinking again, "Argh!" he screamed out. He had lost everything, from his perfectly-crafted first world dynasty. From the walking, consumer-laden, materialistic, driven, wet, slobbering vagina he'd married, no great loss there, to everything else he had accumulated.

Randall was flat out taking care of himself now and his condition had worsened after he'd been fleeced by everyone of everything and left for dead, now a social outcast. The fall from grace he'd experienced was immense, he was lucky to be alive and he knew it. Others, friends whom he'd seen this happen to weren't as tough mentally, he kept telling himself that. Some had committed suicide, he was just a stubborn son of a bitch and proud of it. The fuck-you world attitude he'd adopted had gotten him this far. The crap he'd lived through and was continuing to live through was daunting. The big house was gone, so were the beach front apartments, the career dissolved, the cars were sold, the dog died ('Lucky Fucking Dog'), the fish were ceremoniously flushed down the toilet, the bowls went in the bin for landfill. The one thing he didn't miss were those birds and all their shit, so much fucking shit, everywhere you looked, the carpet, the floor, the walls, the water bowls, even in his shoes next to the indoor bespoke cage, "My bloody Italian black leather shoes", he'd always said. Friends vanished like smoke over water. No wonder he felt so alone, a lifetime building this work of art. His own personal empire was, GONE. That part of his life was over.

Randall was now singing aloud in time with the beat from the boom box, his throat was now hoarse and dry. 'Time to get moving, one... two... three... move', he was psyching himself up. Time now to start again. His so-called best friend and neighbour, Darren Levi, was a wine-soaked gun-toting psychopath with a slightly slanted viewpoint about life. Especially focused about who should survive in this world and who shouldn't. The last subject Randall broached with him was religion, ever! At least he was on his good side. Darren had taken an instant protective liking to Randall after he'd saved him from a randy two metre goanna. It was this goanna that thought Darren was its mate on heat one night and was preparing to impale him on its double-pronged penis. The barbs along its length looked extremely uninviting and would've inflicted unwanted pain. It had been attracted to Darren because he hadn't showered for a month and he'd just eaten some of the local scrub turkey. So, being on Darren's good side was the best place to be, especially when he'd been drinking and was locked and loaded. There was absolutely no doubt he was capable and extremely lethal.

At least Randall had a bed, a roof, running brown water and power due to some solar panels he'd pinched recently and installed himself. It didn't matter the doors and windows wouldn't lock, maybe someone would do him a favour one night, come in and slit his throat. Given the disaster that was his previous life, all the bullshit endured, experienced, his failing health and shitty accommodation, there was a silver lining. There was one thing that was completely out of place here in his own little parasitic-ridden hovel. After he completed this crappy daily ritual, Randall sat up and smiled to himself and voiced softly, "I'm free, I'm still alive. Time for a change, get moving and grow a set of balls Randall you need this". It was time to get off the mouldy mattress, out of his small bedroom, have a brown shower and into better clothes next to the only working urinal he had installed. Today was going to be a little different from the norm. Today was the day he would start to take back his life. He would make a difference and hopefully in the process help his newly-found friends. "Payback's gonna be a bitch people. Watch this space!" he gurgled to himself in the freezing cold shower as he set his mind and future plan into motion. He stepped out the shower and braced himself. There was only one problem. Randall now had to wake Darren without getting his fucking head shot off. Or at least stop being fatally mistaken for one of the local druggies or even that bloody goanna. "This'll be fun", he thought out loud as he dressed. He felt more refreshed and began to plan his approach through his rum-soaked haze, grabbing a wine cork he'd found earlier that week and nonchalantly shoving it into his pocket.

WAKING THE DEAD...?

The next few hours of the dull overcast morning passed fairly uneventfully. Breakfast was a mix of black coffee, burnt toast and some form of salted meat his neighbour Darren had provided him. Randall grabbed the jerky meat out of the makeshift pantry, opened the yellowing Tupperware container and sniffed it. "Ok... fine, edible? Yep", he burbled. There was no point harbouring useless thoughts wondering about where this meat came from. Food and water resources were now found from wherever you could locate or get access to them. If it didn't kill you, great, no need to worry about it, there were other more deadly things that could do a better job, people mostly. Randall took a look at his breakfast before he sat down and sighed at the sight, "Brown, black, beats starving".

At least no gun shots rang out today and no bloated dead bodies floating face down in the pool. Randall cracked his neck and thought about this, 'Woohoo, another welcome bonus to add to this gloomy atmosphere'. At least none of the druggies wandered into the house today looking for their hallucinatory cats that had gone missing. That was Enoria from a few tents down to the left two weeks ago. She arrived in her nighty, breasts bouncing free, it didn't matter she didn't own a cat. This was just one of those commonplace things that mainly happened after the drug-fuelled sex orgies took place. On this particular night Enoria had been the main event, the yelling seemed to go on eternally all night. He shook his head and mumbled, "Brrrr", as a cold shiver raced up and down his spine and his hairs stood on end. Through his filthy kitchen window, Randall could see one of his neighbours, Neville no friends. He was screwing around banging and hammering boards back into place on his roof trying to re-weather proof it. There was an inappropriate yell every so often of, "Fuck, fuck, fuck", as he swung in time with the hammer. "This'll be good", Randall said into his coffee. The previous night's torrential downpour hadn't been kind to Neville. This action was going to be undoubtedly pointless. Neville was an utterly useless scrawny human being and even worse handyman, everything he touched he broke. Last time he fixed the roof he fell through it, a sight to behold, he had been pissed off because some prick had stolen his last three solar panels. Randall smiled wickedly to himself. It was during this one particular incident

Neville tore off his left pinky on a jagged, rusted, steel beam that was part of the roof. Pretty funny for an ex-military engineer.

Call it good fortune or karma but the local crow got fed that day before appearing on the menu of that night's alcoholic binge. This event had earned Neville the nickname "Pinky". He took great offence to this and yelled at anyone who stirred him up calling him by his newly-anointed nickname. "That's not my fucking name you arse wipe, it's Neville!" This was the standard comeback or any other profanity he could think of, as he stamped his feet in a tantrum-like fashion. Neville knew everything about nothing. A specific pigeonholed type. The type who had an inflexible broom shoved so far up his arse he couldn't bend over to tie his shoes if he had any. Plus, the attitude, that bloody narcissistic attitude. It was surprising Neville wasn't already dead considering his foul mouth and the expressly poor way he treated everyone. The world owed him everything and he tried to impose his will onto everyone. He was the self-appointed ruler of this open-aired fiefdom. This was funny because he was diligently ignored by all who considered him to be the local court jester, as they all had their own problems, eccentricities and special needs to deal with. Plus, to add insult to injury, and, purely because it was just hilarious fun, people would salute him sarcastically, then flip him the bird as they went about their day. It was daily sport to piss him off so that most relished doing it, the reactions were — in a word — priceless. Who needed a credit card when you could get that kind of a response for bloody free?

The caravan park was full to the brim of unique 'Special' characters. Speaking of which, Randall could also see another resident carrying out a not-so-unusual activity. Neville's partner, Vicki, was on her dilapidated, front porch and had started screaming and screeching at Jarece for skinny dipping again. He lowered and shook his head at his kitchen table, desperately trying to keep his black brew down, not blurt it out his nose, as he knew what came next. It did, it always did, like clockwork. As he watched he lifted his right hand and counted with his fingers in practiced unison, one, two and three..., then, in preparation, put his hand up cupped to his ear. Out came the eruption. He sarcastically mouthed the words verbatim, in silence to himself as this comical exchange of words happened in his own private open-aired theatre. Vicki blurted forth, "You're nothing but a slut and you're a whore. White trailer trash, put some bloody clothes on!" Her OCD and mental health issues had obviously shifted into high gear again. This was subsequently met by Jarece without even batting an eyelid. She never moved, "Go fuck yourself, oh that's right, you got no power, no power, no vibrator, lucky fucking vibrator. Maybe Pinky can do it after he finishes throwing up!" Randall then counted again with his fingers for the final act as he drank, one... two... three... Vicki slammed the front door shut after storming off the porch.

Well, it was slightly better, but less comical than the tirade that had occurred last week. Vicki had befriended the local scrub turkey and was holding perfectly well-formed conversations with it in her front yard. It didn't seem to matter that she voiced back the answers to herself on behalf of the bird within these conversations. Everyone knew she was as mad as a cut snake and just as dangerous. Especially if she had you cornered. No, the tirade occurred because Darren was running low on fresh salted jerky and he'd trapped the scrawny thing to restock his supplies. After recounting this event, Randall slowly looked down with a quizzical expression at his jerky as he murmured, "Oh... I hope not?" then shrugged. Remembering the entertainment that followed was like recalling a scene out of a horror movie franchise. He grinned stupidly as he began recalling it. Vicki, one morning dressed in her nighty, had decided that enough was enough and screamed that Darren was a cannibal and how dare he kill and prepare "Gertrude", her cousin, for food. "You're a beast, you're a fucking sick bastard and how dare you kill my cousin. I grew up with her you know, Fucking Murderer!" This was the initial screeching outburst, what followed next was Vicki's brain snapped. She grabbed the nearest knife she could see. It was located in the garden, determined to finish off this cannibalistic neighbour, she then ran at him lunging across the space between their places in seconds. That's when Darren's pure instinct kicked in.

Darren was dressed in his ceremonial ratty frayed shorts, thongs and blue singlet. He raised the pump action shotgun to be perfectly timed with Vicki's vengeful arrival, over the low unkempt garden to stop dead centre of her forehead. It was like watching a comedy movie in super slow motion, the sheer look of horror on her face was entertaining to watch. Even better was the yellow fluid that ran down hers leg as she dropped the knife without flinching. The reverberating call of, "Piss off you psychopathic bitch", was then followed by, "Pinky! If you don't come and get your pussy, I'LL BLOW HER GOD DAMN FUCKING HEAD OFF!" Hence, the necessary scramble for Neville, who ran at a forty-five degree angle like a possessed devil from the right hand side of the house to the other side of his home. He tripped over his own feet then rebounded to retrieve his beloved partner and thus this fuelled the feud that continues till today. More and more like the post-Apocalyptic version of the Hatfield's and the McCoy's.

It was roughly just before seven in the morning when Poonta Jafari stuck his head and body through Randall's open front door. He'd tried to open the screen door quietly, unfortunately the aluminium door came off its rusted hinge into his right hand. It did so with such a cacophony that Randall jumped. He almost spilled his remaining coffee down the front of his jeans. "Morning honey, I'm home, jar miss me?" Poonta sang as he barged his way through the opening. He squeezed his way through the doorway like an elephant doesn't squeeze through a keyhole. Instead of using plenty of KY gel, he was like a sweaty pig on heat, just having had sex with the local butcher. He dry humped the door frame as he edged his way inside. Poonta had been out early trying desperately to lift more weights. Randall had frequently been helping and encouraging him, he even joined him occasionally. "What's for breakfast, sweethart?! Jar see shits 'n' giggles going at it again. Fark, them parents shoulda stopped adding to genie pool before thay had thim bitches". He grabbed some toast and went to fill up a mug with the recently brewed sludge.

Randall didn't move, Poonta was twice his size, you never scared Poonta, the outcome usually meant you got hurt. "You'd gonna speak with Darren bout what wes spoke about last time Hun?". Poonta glugged this out through his coffee in a particular inaudible tone as he sat down. Randall really liked Poonta, he was an uneducated, intelligent, gay, muscular framed black man. He was a bigger build than Randall, taller too, six foot ten. He cut an imposing figure ducking through a doorway or walking next to his friends. It's not like he stood out or anything, he was like the combination of a silver-backed gorilla and a giraffe at a midget convention. He was a walking human grizzly bear and just as deadly when aggravated. Poonta could hold his own, his hands were like ten pin bowling balls attached to axe handles. This made Randall feel safe and good about himself that he'd befriended this lumbering giant, his own personal wrecking ball. Poonta had a heart of gold. If you needed help, if you were fortunate enough to be respected, Poonta was there. He had connections everywhere. Piss Poonta off, disrespect him and you were rarely seen again. "Yes friend, I haven't forgotten, I made you a promise didn't I?" Randall laughed, snorted and said "Early morning is always fun to watch isn't it Mate? Damn we've got some oddities here, beats Tele any day, hey. Yeah look, about that, I just need to wake him up after last night, live through it and get him to stay sober".

"Better you then me baby", munched Poonta. "I'll get Vinchi, ok? Me like livin, better yous wake him, he likes you. Jew see what he done to that possum, Hahahaha, mother fuckers craz-zzy. Meet up later say round ten'ish sweethart, at the creek, usual clearing, bring the crew, ok's?" He then drained the coffee mug, "Gonna gumbo, bye, soon hey Hun". He heaved himself out of the chair which creaked, breathing a sigh of relief, "Didn't crush it Taday" he giggled. He laid his huge right hand on Randall's shoulder, patted it twice as he made for the door. He then turned sideways and breathed in squeezing out into the dull day. Randall began to think about Vinchi Chen, poor Vinchi, Poonta could just pick him up like a football and did so last republic day celebration. It was while he was reminiscing, he saw through his front door, Poonta lean forward, bend over and lift up the screen door in one hand. He watched him stand up with a quizzical look of utter confusion, screw up his face as he looked at the broken hinge, the wheels were spinning. He turned away, the screen door still in his right hand and absently flung the door over the dirt pathway into the overgrown wet lantana as he walked off.

Randall sat still, eyes open wide, sober now after the vision he'd just witnessed. "Come on man, let's get this over with, you only live once", Randall said out loud as he stood to clean up breakfast, the early morning drama over. The rest of the day was yet to start and it beckoned zealously, he could then hear the boom box screaming out another favourite tune from his youth. He started singing this time and danced the weird epileptic

40

strut he'd perfected in his small kitchen. He felt happier than he had been in a long while. If you looked strange or unpredictable you were left alone, he preferred it that way. You could pick and choose. You could surround yourself with friends of your choosing, real genuine friends. He turned on the recycled grey water and started cleaning up.

Randall had always been a fastidiously neat person in his previous life, right up to the point of being OCD about it. His mates used to chide him over it. His standard response when they said this was, "At least I can survive if I need to, I'm not a spoon-fed male who's only contribution to a household is the size of his bank balance and his fucking penis". Living here, the more you cleaned and moved the dirt, the more it accumulated. Chandie had told him that once after he moved in. "The more the dirt and dust that builds up, the less you're a target for theft, best to just keep it at bay, sweep it into a corner and throw it out as required. It doesn't get any higher after five years", she was a wealth of trivial shit like that. Chandie Quinn lived a couple of houses down and around near the only working lamp post in the park. She was another wonderful friend, sensibly dressed, always aloof, warm

41

and chatty with a wonderfully wicked sense of humour. Surprisingly not at all what he expected, charming, built and dangerous, all in one package. He'd never be the one to cross her, ever, her skills were legendary if you believed the rumours. One mischievous night Chandie had been the one to paint the lamp bulb near the pool red. The objective was to fuck with Vicki's mental state. Vicki then blamed Jarece, thinking she was drumming up a secondary income and told the whole park about it —Family Feud part two. Vicki had subsequently lost it until she badgered and nagged Neville into climbing a ladder to change it, mainly because it attracted the wrong sort of individuals to our little sanctuary. That's when Neville fell, broke his leg and started going grey and bald, another story for another time.

Chandie was older, sure, loved life, but was now a refreshing insertion into Randall's life. Randall and Chandie flirted occasionally, purely good fun and some nights they'd become great companions. Vinchi was now overly jealous. He'd seen her first. He was a skinny Asian man with a huge charismatic presence. He'd boasted one drunken-fuelled night he was the best thief around and could get into anywhere and at anyone. People disputed these claims until a federal security force came looking for a wanted Triad member for a major theft after a political assassination had gone horribly wrong. They'd torn the place apart, but no one dobbed him in and as payback deliveries of fresh bottled water started appearing afterwards. Not that much, but in a world devoid of this scarce commodity not one person took him for a liar after that. In the meantime, while lying low, Vinchi had been eyeing Chandie off for six months before Randall got here. The only problem was that Vinchi was two foot six, exactly two foot six, a genetic deformity. High enough to sniff her pussy, but not high enough to rest his head in her breasts, let alone look into her beautiful round eyes. Vinchi confided once to Randall that he got an erection every time she walked past his rusty shed. So, Randall never let this priceless piece of information slide, too good an opportunity to stir the pot and push Vinchi's buttons. Every time Chandie walked by, regardless of where they were chatting, Randall would raise his right arm, fist clenched to simulate Vinchi's erection. It was their standing joke, purely all done in jest. The reward was a punch to his balls, or what Vinchi thought was Randall's balls. Randall only recently found out Vinchi was one of Poonta's best mates. He'd made some really nice friends since his catalytic life change and all for the better it seemed. He'd decided at that point he needed a recruit, and Chandie fitted the bill nicely. 'I'll collect her on the way to Darren's', he thought, his plan coming together.

Randall grabbed the reddish brown mugs, the puce plates and cutlery off the glass topped timber table and walked to the sink. 'Funny what's important to us during different stages in our lives', he mulled over. Leaving the house he tried to shut the purple stained front door, closing it as far as it could go. It never shut properly, probably because of the axe, but maybe not. Randall set off for Chandie's place. His internal clock told him it was only about 8:00am, a talent he'd developed since his medical condition started, and it was coming in handy more than once. He started humming to the boom box, he was a bit surprised, Viktor should've woken up by now and collected it, but scanning the Park he couldn't see him. Viktor Belenko was an odd one, keeping mainly to himself, he engaged with people but there was something not quite right about him. Randall couldn't put his finger on it, something was definitely strange, sinister even. 'He's probably still asleep somewhere', Randall thought.

Randall wound his way through the blackened smelly puddles of water that stank like yesterday's un-emptied sewerage and passed the overgrown, dying, yellow, reddish Lantana archway. Wandering over to Chandie's he passed the high grass that sprouted as fast as sugar cane does and slipped into her side yard. As he did the smell of freshly cooked bread assaulted him from all angles. It had been years since he had tasted freshly cooked bread and she was out the back recovering it from her fire pit. She was readying herself for breakfast. "Had a feeling you'd come over this morning", she teased. "What's on the agenda today, honey?" She was wearing close-fitting dark navy jeans and black boots. Her top was reminiscent to that of a Caribbean pirate with all the flares and frills. 'Mmmm', he thought. "I need some help darl, purely a survival mission", Randall blurted out. She stood up, turned around and dug back, "I know you're special Hun, but don't we all need some special help?" "Can't do it without you", he encouraged, winking and running his fingers through his hair unconsciously. She brushed his hair ruffling his combing effort, "You Hungry?" She walked past, grabbed a plate, lard and knife, poking him in the stomach playfully. "No, thanks, I've eaten. Poonta was over for breakfast after this morning's entertainment", he paused. "I've a proposition for you". "Really, aren't we stepping over Vinchi's imagined property boundary lines here? Suppose I could live dangerously if I was tempted", she teased and flashed her long eyelashes as she laid her breakfast out, sat down and gestured for Randall to sit.

Randall and Chandie both sat in her old worn out cane papasan chairs, which was as uncomfortable for Randall as having a colonoscopy. No matter how you shifted and moved your arse, back and neck, it just bloody hurt. Besides that, he had trouble working out where the colour of the canvas started and where the wildlife excrement and secretions began. The little wooden deck had seen better days, but at least the termites were happy, the colony had expanded recently and were headed towards the next shack belonging to Alisha at a ferocious rate. "I need your assistance to wake Sir Galahad, he's passed out dead again after last night's fireworks display. Plus I'd like to live through doing it", the quaver in his voice showed. "Poonta's called a meeting, he reckons he can help me out. I need Darren's special skills, sober preferably. Poonta hinted last week he'd made the connection I need to reverse my current situation. Get back my life so to speak", he sounded hesitant. "You sure Hun, I like you being here, I'd hate to see you leave, so will the others, you've really been a treasure to all, you've been happier lately, you really think this is the answer?", the smile she gave could've melted gold. "Worth a shot at least, plus if I handle this right I can improve and pay back things here tenfold, pay it forward I mean. I owe people here a lot. Plus the fewer of us that are involved the less chance of getting caught". He raised his hand and crossed his fingers. "Ok, count me in, I like living dangerously", she said as she stood up and grabbed her diamanté mirrored compact. "Housework can wait".

Chandie walked off swinging her hips, turning back she saw Randall's eyes glued to her denim-encased cheeks and ordered back, "Come on, eyes up here, let's go". They started off for Darren's place like two black panthers stalking their prey, crawling through the undergrowth, prowling behind the section of tents, knowing full well any hiccup or slightest wrong move would disturb 'The Beast'. 'The Beast', that was the understatement. Darren prior to his incarceration, release and final epic downward journey to here, in a previous life was responsible for intelligence collection, covert operations and counterterrorism. Not many people knew, and those who did in his close circle of friends didn't betray his confidence. Upon his release or dramatic escape, that area was a little bit hazy and grey having left his country of birth, he wound up here to "Disappear" due to a certain 'Black' screw up. That's where the information evaporated, not much more was known about this pudgy, alcoholic adopted big-game hunter and park protector. The standing park motto was 'Don't piss him off!' so people didn't, except Neville and of course, in turn, Vicki.

Randall and Chandie crept into Darren's overgrown back yard, past the barbed wire, stealthily approaching it weaving their way to the dilapidated back porch, now looking like two slithering, slick pythons. They were ready for the kill. The plan was relatively simple — don't get shot. The execution on the other hand was going to have to be more elaborate. The smell that hit them was similar to a truck that had been carrying a cargo of live beef, which had slammed into a roadhouse outback concrete wall and left to rot in the full desert sun for a month. Overtime, this had been gently seasoned with a whiff of gunpowder, oil and animal faeces. Chandie gagged as she went around to the left side of the small porch, Randall veered off to the right. The porch at one time had wooden railings all the way around with rotting stairs in the middle leading into the back yard. Now all the side wooden railings were missing, eaten away completely by termites.

Having made it to the other side of the back porch, Chandie gingerly and quietly stood up next to Darren and peered around the corner of the weatherboarded house. There was absolutely no noise being made and Darren looked as though he'd departed this world as there was very little colour in his cheeks. He was drooling out of the left side of his mouth and there was no real noticeable breathing or chest rising and falling given the large coat he was wearing. He smelled like a brewery. He was close enough to her side that she could reach out with her compact. Inch by inch she moved her hand closer to his open mouth, diamanté compact mirror in hand, opened to catch any hint of breath to check he was still alive. She stopped just short of his fully-blown ratty white beard and moustache as the mirror fogged up, then gently withdrew it, giving a thumbs up to Randall. Looking directly at him she mouthed the words silently, "Not dead". Randall had to this point in time investigated the pump action shotgun and noticed the opened cartridge chamber. He ever so carefully, like a spinal surgeon removing a single human decaying spinal nerve, placed the cork he'd collected into it to stop the firing pin engaging. Darren hadn't even moved, 'Phew'. At that moment they both noticed the remains of a dozen empty wine bottles, life drained from them as dry as the Sahara Desert.

'Fuck me', Randall's mind jumped, 'No wonder he's not coherent, good for us too'. Having thought the situation was defused, Randall placed his right foot on the wooden back porch and leaned forward, it creaked loudly. The next movements and five minutes of scuffling were all a blur. Darren reacted with lighting reflexes. He lifted the pump action shotgun with his right arm, just as Randall, using both hands, pushed it sideways, before shoving his right shoulder into Darren's, forcing him back into his seat. Chandie just screamed, a real bloody help. At least the gun didn't go off. "It's me Daz, it's Randall". He then yelled in Hebrew, "Shalom Chaver, shalom chaver" or "Hello Friend, hello friend" It took a five minute wrestling match, a lost clenched shotgun along with several bruised ribs, multiple karate kicks and punches landed and deflected plus an extremely lucky punch to lay Darren out. The two friends hit the ground with a wet squelchy thud, eventually, lying still in the high grass, flat out, bruised, bloody split bottom lips, laughing. Darren spat out a mouthful of dark red blood into the grass, "I didn't know you spoke Hebrew", Darren said completely coherently and fluently. "Fuck, my jaw hurts, I think you loosened a tooth, Jesus, you can hit too, found a new talent hey mate?" "I can't" said Randall breathlessly, "That's all the Hebrew I know, I took a punt. As for the punch, pure luck, I'm sorry, survival instincts just kicked in, didn't want to be the next possum. You looked like you were dead". "Nah, not yet. I need a drink, you?"

Darren thumped Randall's chest, gesturing to the porch. "No, thanks, we're meeting up with Poonta later this morning — remember, I need you sober", Darren looked at him blankly, "Oh shit, that today?" Darren sat up, his stomach growled, he stood and placed a hand out to help Randall. They were both soaked with dew from the long grass. All the while Chandie was chuckling loudly sitting on the easy chair. The dual reaction in unison as they both turned toward her was hilarious. "BITCH!" She poked out her pink tongue. "I need a coffee mate, major headache now, come on, in we go, you too sexy", as Darren walked off, straight up the back porch and into his house, "Come on you two, hop it!" Randall stared like a rabbit in the headlights at Chandie, a touch bewildered and a tad sore. His bottom lip hurt. He blinked, instantly realising Darren had actually been playing 'Possum' with them, he'd known they were there all along, scary thought. Randall dusted himself off and then started forward in search of another coffee. As he followed Chandie into the house, he didn't even look sideways, but loudly yelled out sarcastically as he crossed the porch, "Morning Vicki, lovely day".

CHAPTER TWO

THE INITIAL PLAN...

Walking into Darren's place was similar to crossing over the event horizon. You felt the air around you actually crackle, tingle and your hair stood on end. Through this imaginary airlock, the darkness of this local black hole swallowed your soul and left you gasping for fresh oxygen. That was until your eyes refocused and your lungs adjusted themselves over time. The first thing you noticed before anything else was the smell. It tore your brain out of your skull as it smashed it against the blue mould-covered plastered wall, or what was left of it. It then shoved a nail gun up your nose and pulled the trigger, locking itself into semi-automatic mode. The odour was a cross between rat flesh rolled in sweaty underpants, fried in sweet smelling marijuana. Once you got past that odorous adventure, there was the clutter, everywhere. From parts of engines, broken furniture, circuit boards, cabling, electronics of every sort, multiple tools of various shapes and functions, clothing everywhere, shelves full of books, a solar panel (Neville's) and a wonky pedestal fan. Then there was the biggest gun safe known to man, with an LED alarm that appeared out of the gloom like Darth Vader's bathroom. Randall had never seen anything like this, it looked like it could arm a small government-funded militia. It seemed to be bolted to the floor as well as the walls. It had three cross-beams padlocked over the front. Darren had been a Doomsday Prep-per for years, he rarely talked about his previous life. It looked as though he was readying for the Apocalypse just around the corner, nailed it.

The main attraction in the room was the large flat TV screen, it was across from the easy chair whose twin was located out on the back deck falling apart. There were wine bottles strewn around the floor, along with an extra two-seater lounge that had seen better days. It was torn to shreds from what looked like possum claw marks and smothered in excrement, with a brightly-patterned floral sheet draped over it. The couch had been purchased from a World War Two surplus reject shop, prior to the arson-suspected fire. It was never proven that it was Darren, but he did however hold a grudge against the owner for overcharging him. Your eyes would move panning around the room, finally spotting the pedestal antique bronze ashtray full to the brim of deceased doobie's. "Brewbie's all round?" Darren voiced with enthusiasm over his shoulder as he stalked into the kitchen, kicking aside an unidentifiable pile of what looked like old dirty clothes. "Yep". "Yes please Hun" was the chorus line in agreement. "Make yourselves at home my friends, Mi Casa Su Casa", Darren charmingly espoused in a terrible fake accent gesturing like a drunken Italian godfather. "I give up, sit where...?" said Randall, "... My GPS doesn't work in the Bermuda Triangle". Darren tilted his head around and glared at Randall with a look that if it had had a physical impact would've flayed him alive.

Chandie smacked Randall in the shoulder playfully, pointed to the twin seater, then flicked his left cheek as she moved him sideways to shift the various books that had been flung onto it. As she started moving the books and floral sheet the awkward silence that followed was broken by a bloodcurdling shrill scream that pierced the early morning and was heard by everyone as it reverberated around the caravan park, like a Greek Fury. It was at that point Viktor woke with a start, sat bolt upright from under a huge pile of torn newspapers, grass cuttings, empty bottles and corroboree scraps that was centrally located not far from the main fire pit, BBQ and his precious boom box. He looked like a balding, weary meerkat, a Hitler-faced sentry wearing a banana skin hat whose bloodshot eyes would've betrayed him to the wrath of the clan for being pissed, having passed out while on duty. His left hand worked its way around and down to feel his arse, it was achingly sore and he looked downwards at himself, he was soaked. He'd pissed himself. He lifted his hand back up and sniffed it, flinched back, rolled his eyes to the back of his head and passed out backwards — again. Meanwhile, Chandie turned and jumped into Randall's flailing arms. "Snake!" she screeched as Randall struggled to keep his balance, reminiscent of a live vaudeville theatre act gone horribly wrong.

"Oh for fuck sake, I wondered where that bastard went?" said Darren sarcastically as he stepped forward around the kitchen bench with a machete he'd picked up. The machete had materialised from nowhere. He wedged his way between the lounge and his friends, raising the machete and cleaving off the snake's head in one fluid motion. Darren wrenched the handle, pulling it out of the seat. Using the blade, he flicked the head out the back door. He then lifted the body up by the tail, it looked about five foot long and grinned, "Brekkie, anyone?" Randall forced back his refluxed bile. "No...Thanks" he gurgled, keeping it down by sheer will power. Chandie glared at Darren, still in Randall's arms, eyeballing him like a serial killer. "Are you FUCKING KIDDING ME!" as her feet found solid ground. Darren grinned, blew her a kiss and threw the snake's body into the sink, "One for later", as he embedded the machete back into the wooden countertop and returned to finish brewing the coffee. They sat in the lounge, chatted inanely about the weather, neighbours, Chinese whispers and rumours circulating as they drank the wicked thick black brew. Now it was time to get down to the business at hand. "So what's Poonta up to?" Darren asked as he puffed on a newly-rolled doobie. Randall leaned forward excitedly "He reckons he can get access to an old networked computer connected to "The System", a relic missed". Randall raised his hands as he spoke for emphasis, gesturing inverted comma's in the air. "He's got a snitch that's found this old dig of sorts, no details, yet. He can be paid off apparently, or traded with, to get us access and keep his tongue or lose it. Get me in, get me out. If he has and it's operational I can isolate the program I wrote, upload a counterfeit stealth Trojan that'll alter my entire profile and 'voila' I get my life back, dosh, the lot and fucking more. The outcome is, I disappear."

Randall meanwhile held up the crimson red hermetically-sealed credit card container. "Oh, that's pretty, what is it?" Chandie admired plucking it out of Randall's fingers and rolled it over in her hands. She studied it quizzically from every angle before passing it gently back to him, patting his wrist as she did. Randall explained trying not to leave out relevant details, "It's what most of the upper classes use to enhance their social status, four different colours that designate the top social standing tiers or specialised pecking order in today's society-driven structures or 'World Monarch'. It gives you access to control one's life, open hypothetical opportunistic doors on your whole life from your finances to obtaining all the niceties and comforts one could afford, to basic human dignities that used to be taken for granted, such as medical access for one. It is used to buy medications, materialistic items, necessities others can't afford, plus exchange electronic cash for organically grown food, purified water and shelter. The purchase of actual homes granted you access to the most securely cordoned off guarded city facilities. It was all dependant on your security level and social commitment to the government. The higher the access the better. Unlike the lower classes relegated to breed outside the cities, hypnotised like sheep that needed to work, produce, struggle and now scrounge, thieve, kill and murder just to survive and eventually decline".

As these details were being recounted by Randall, Darren had quietly risen, wandered off creeping into his bedroom, pushing the snake's tail fully into the sink as he passed by, "I'm listening!" He boomed back. Chandie listened intently, watching him go, turned back murmuring, "So what's that got to do with Poonta?" and now utterly puzzled as she stared at Randall. "Poonta's so called 'Contact' can get me access to upload a Trojan, via an overlooked node. A falsified, fake-coded version of my Think Tank controlled profile, if my access still exists? If he does, I can speed up my return financially, hugely, radically in fact". Now he was looking down at his feet, "Then work a black market purchase, a sea passage for an isolated, smaller, less secure city, across the ocean. There I wouldn't be noticed or grilled about my previous involvement or past. Safe, maybe start again, live out what's left in relative peace, get the medical access I need to stop me getting worse and Vishnu willing, room for friends I can bring out of this biological chemical swill. We'd then be protected in my own reinvented Universe, Back to Paradise". He looked up at Chandie and smiled awkwardly.

"Alright smarty how come I've never seen one? I've worked in and around the city. I struggled until my life went to shit, thought I was doing okay as an accountant, until the debt did me over after making poor decisions. I punched all my money into the government line of credit and the pension fund until the last crash decimated it and we all had to start again. Like most, I lost everything. I've a different life here now at the lower end of society. Looking back, you tended to just put your head down and blankly work your way through life. I had the crappy car, small garish house, debt, the norm, the daily clockwork orange". Chandie seemed to be really straining to understand. Darren's voice was low and deep as he walked back into the kitchen "Because, sexy, you've been controlled, groomed and lied to since you were born. You've been cannon fodder and a slave to the upper echelon, providing them everything they've needed, working to maintain the sustainable system that serves their supply chains, purposes, profit and lifestyle. You've been living a life that's based on a lie in one of the hugest worldwide fucking con jobs ever, like the rest of all those fucking sheep out there. The so-called cashless society, high taxes, extended lines of credit, government pension, ever rising debt and cost of living was meant to control the masses, not help you. You're lucky, your fortune's about to change. By losing your life and coming here we can teach you to wake up, you need to step up or be left behind to rot in your own filth".

Darren was gesturing to Randall and himself throughout this whole speech. "Your eloquence, performance and behaviour was a tad over the top, Darren", Randall admonished as he angrily threw a magazine at him just as he finished his 'wake up and smell the bullshit' speech, hitting him in his right shoulder. "Never one for subtlety were you"? It gained Darren's attention, "Habit, hey that was my best Penthouse." He spat. "Apologies M'Lady, 'Twas a tad overzealous", Darren said, looking sheepishly. Randall lowered his voice, using his right upturned palm, he lifted Chandie's chin and eyeballed her. "In a nutshell, without the shitty shovel or sledgehammer, ok?" he glared upwardly at Darren. Looking back calmly and quietly stated, "You're about to learn I'm not who I seem sweets".

Chandie's thoughts were now spinning out of control like a horror movie, except with less wasted exorcism, eerie music or blood. "There was no crash Chandie", Randall said slowly allowing the words to sink in. "It was all siphoned off, an illusion, Trillions, absolute Trillions redirected to feed and maintain the selected upper echelon via misdirection, support the selected hierarchical cities' structures, the protected few elite percentile, to allow the overpopulation to balance itself out through extinction and reset the world". "That can't be right we would know, people would know, see, surely somewhere, someone would leak it out", Chandie's voice cracked, worried. Randall placed his hand reassuringly on her left shoulder. Her eyes began to redden, "How do you know this is right, you're one of us, you're here, you've seen how it is out there, day to day, it's probably all conjecture, guessing, rumours, you can't be right. That means everything I know and believed in from day one, was all fucking bullshit! We were told...." she trailed away into silence, stiffened and then sat back to set her resolve into stone.

Seeing this Randall continued, "In today's overpopulated, dying, resource depleted world, there are those who are methodically working behind the scenes to ensure the enslavement and control of the major lower classes, controlling what they think is the accepted "Norm". This stays commonplace, out of sight. People 'Work' to better 'The System', why: because it controls life. The cashless society and other bullshit was stealthily inserted into daily life over decades by government puppets to create a supreme superior exclusive upper class and keep everyone else in check and none the wiser. All by subversion, creating a pure and effective illusion. The major cities now house these 'Uppers'." "Darren, shut up." said Randall not missing a beat, without breaking eye contact with Chandie. "There are three ruling classes of wealth distribution and power, Black, Gold, Red and Green".

Randall began the brief explanation as he counted off from his left hand index finger with the right for emphasis, "The

Blacks are the top one percent, these are the ultimate power brokers or so called top Thirteen Families pulling all the strings. Gold's are the highest specifically handpicked and selected puppets or better known as The Committee Of Three Hundred. These are made up of the richest Politicians, Law Makers and Entrepreneurial Control. Then the Red's, they are The Think Tanks, The Implementers, groomed handpicked executives skilled at deception, lies, business espionage, profiteering, including Wars. If you think about it, this was Mission Control pushing all the right buttons to keep everything in check. The colour order gives you the amount of wealth, power, privilege, prestige, entitlement and most of all access to 'The System' to call the shots." He handed her a very old paper transcript illustration, "The System is built so it allows these classes to live above the laws that dictate to everyone else how to live, controlling what they do and to accept their lot in life. Invisible really, unless you know where to look". He hesitated, "And I'm planning to take some of it back".

BEWARE, LANDMINES AHEAD...

It was at this stage Randall stopped for breath, paused and fell silent. He could see Chandie and hesitated. The blood had drained from her face, her demeanor was one of utter disbelief. Similar to an unsuspecting tourist who had walked out into the unknown territory of the glass Zhangjiajie Grand Canyon Bridge in China. She appeared as if she was above the one thousand foot drop and had then frozen solid in the middle, right when the electric current filled glass got turned on to change it from opaque grey to completely clear. Petrified eyes wide open staring fearfully into the abyss. She was in fact staring straight at Randall, mortified. Gaining her composure, her brain switched on and gears locked, the wheels gripped and colour returned to her face. She howled out with utter precision, "Who are you then....fuck it...? My head's already set to explode, so beware!" Before Randall could answer, Darren jumped in answering from the comfort of his easy chair, lounging with his legs crossed. In a terrible fake Italian persona he started again, blurting out, "He's a Crimson sexy.... a Red..... a master manipulator, a professional liar and now...." He paused for effect. "He's The One... Icarus on the brick road, now one of us, wanting to kill the warlocks searching for a way back home baby".

Chandie was bemused, her head was ready to explode, it was like being an unwanted participant in a murder mystery and you were the victim having been led into the trap. She didn't know where to look and settled on the space between Darren's easy chair and the bronze ashtray which was currently overflowing, similar to her. It was awkward as both Randall and Chandie then responded to Darren in sync, "Are you quite finished with the sarcasm?" Chandie then added "So you two have obviously been talking for a while about this" as she gathered her composure, getting shittier as she went. "Left field question?" "You!" she accusingly pointed back towards Randall, "You said three? Who or what the fuck are Green?" As Darren raspingly cleared his throat, Chandie turned swiftly glaring at him, just as he flippantly tossed her a green hermetically-sealed credit card that landed like a 300 year old fragile, intact bone China teacup that she'd just caught from shattering on the floor. "Because sexy, we were their bodyguards. And apparently still,

FUCKING ARE!" Darren sarcastically retorted, his smile had completely disappeared.

"Look at it this way. At least this time you'll actually get paid for the suicide mission. If it fouls up you get the added bonus of double tapping the bullets into my skull. But if we do it right and survive, we'll all get to live in comfort and get to safety", Randall grinned as his tone was overly smug as he spoke. "We only worked out who each other was a month ago. You didn't even know me before I arrived here, you came from the Israeli compound". "Don't fucking remind me". Darren was quite apathetic as he puffed out a perfect triple ring of smoke, similar in shape to an old metal slinky, that only an experienced doobie wielder could achieve from years of practice. He reclined, mumbling just loud enough, "It'll be worse than a fucking double tap". Randall touched Chandie's left hand hesitantly, "I don't know if this will even work, but I can't miss the opportunity to find out. We have a small skilled group here and if we can pull this off, we all go to Eden". Randall then turned his attention outside, listening intently to the low humming. The birds and sounds of the caravan park had gotten louder, rising in volume slowly over the course of the morning as they'd been speaking. There had been another light shower and the day had turned into a light grey blue hue again.

Randall had recognised the very low humming sound, after acknowledging it with a brief inconsequential nod to himself, turned back to the others. The shower had drowned out any noise from Darren's should anyone have been close enough to overhear the conversation. Darren's place after a previous 'VickiGate' incident had been rigged up. It was ringed in a rusty barbed wire perimeter, lovingly decorated with bare copper wires carrying 240 volts to detract or fry anyone stupid enough to enter unwarranted. The humming was the electricity working its way through the copper wires like blood through your arteries, reacting to the light rain that hissed and crackled as it struck it. Darren had heard these two friends now sitting here, at his pleasure today, arriving from a mile away and switched off the humming, pop-fizzing current to play 'Possum'. It wasn't until they went inside for coffee he'd casually switched it back on again. The security it provided was also helped by the fact that Darren had hammered corrugated signs into several places around the boundaries stating, 'Anyone Caught Trespassing Will Be Shot — AND EATEN!'

Needless to say, no one from the caravan park violated this protocol — 'EVER'. There was one incident at this caravan park that no one dared speak of, even today. A uniformed Federal Officer entered the park a while back searching for something or someone, but never really interrogated anyone and for some sick personal reason began stalking Darren back and forth and had been for weeks. Why was not specifically known or common knowledge. The only thing people remember was that one day he was still here and then one night there was a major electrical blackout that took out the surrounding suburb. Over the next few days the power was restored, and Darren held a very hospitable raucous BBQ which everybody attended. He had provided what he said were rare wagyu steaks imported from a mate overseas who owed him a favour, with rare Japanese beers to match. An animated, randy, alcoholic-fuelled night was had by all. There was loud music, cocaine, sex orgies and most people had passed out in the early morning light. Bizarrely they never saw this Federal Officer ever again. Randall hadn't arrived here yet, to this day he thanked the Gods he hadn't. "Right, enough fairy tales for now, don't we need to be somewhere soon, Icarus?", Darren voiced, his sarcasm punctuating the pungent stale air as he rose and shifted with supreme purpose towards the gun safe.

Darren began the ritual of unlocking the three padlocked straps that held the doors securely in place. It was only then Chandie noticed Darren had changed clothes. Obviously having done so when he'd gone into his bedroom. He was now dressed in a red and dark green stripped polo shirt with black jeans and worn steel capped boots. She and Randall stood up and followed him at a safe respectable distance, now both looking a little stunned as to why he was doing this. He eased the six steel, quarter inch thick, triple concertinaed doors open from the middle. The experience was similar to a head first descent into one of the hellish heavily armoured military camps of Vietnam. The smell of fresh grease, gunpowder, Agent Orange and well-oiled steel was only overpowered by the sight that stood before them once the six doors were fully opened. The cabinet was a good four feet deep. Yes, Darren was a Doomsday Prep-per, they knew that, it was common knowledge. This scale of the collection that stood before them, took it to a whole new level, several notches entirely above, insane psychopathic professional military assassin meets the personal militia of Satan himself. Armageddon and Judgement Day all rolled into one lethal concise package.

Randall could only smile as he thought to himself 'Fuck, I knew I liked this guy'. Darren began selecting specific items that he'd predetermined were required for today's reconnaissance mission, for the personal discussion on a lonely deserted creek riverbank with a government snitch. 'Discussion', not an initial debrief! As he started handing out the armaments he met their eyes and verbalised as if preparing to calm them down just enough. "Preparation is the key to the perfect place to be ambushed, better off being the biggest Alpha Dog in a fight than the Dead Dog. The bigger more powerful stick you carry, the harder you hit back if ambushed and never, ever, walk into a surprise unarmed".

Darren started with Chandie first, handing her one large military boot strapped with a 12-inch serrated Bowie knife. She began strapping it to the outside of her lower left leg above her boots. Next was a black leather ammo belt with six individual cartridge cases clipped into place with a double holster for the twin Hi Powered Glock 17's, light, fast and incredibly deadly. The vision of an apocalyptic female post nuclear survivor, confident, at ease, intelligent, just plain deadly. Upon watching her check the weapons, load each chamber and click the safetys into place prior to holstering them, Randall stared wide-eyed as though he had just found the newly formed version of the word 'Respect'. Darren looked at Randall and grinned evilly. He descended into the depths again. As he came out adding, "You wanted to be point", passing him a similar Bowie knife setup and an Ammo belt with five cartridge cases and holster that held dual chrome Desert Eagles. Fifty serious calibres that came with 325 grain explosive head bullet points that reached up to 1,550 foot per second, providing enormous impact and serious accuracy.

Randall pulled each one out of the holster in turn, checked the sights, loaded the barrel, locked the safety, re-holstered, rubbed his fingers, they felt a little oily. "Um, yeah sorry about that, just cleaned them", uttered Darren. Lastly, Darren dived back into this death vault once again. He resurfaced, stood vertical and finally clamped everything onto his body. Two military boot-strapped Bowie knives on both legs and his personal favourite. An automatic self-feeding ammo backpack, attached to an A-XM556 Micro-gun, a small yet compact, extremely lightweight, motorised Gatling gun that fires 5.56 NATO ammo like it's going out of style. He then passed out three jet-black body length, specialised bulletproof military cloaks with sleeves. All three of them put them on, zipped up, locked the hoodies into place, now resembling three of the four horsemen of the Apocalypse. Darren securely locked up the gun safe and armed it once more. He smiled, which then disappeared and his persona changed to stone as if looking at Medusa. He was now literally the vision of a deadly personified Yuletide Terminator. He spoke calmly. "Okay, Ready? Let's go have a civil 'Discussion' with this friendly above-board government snitch, shall we". The sarcasm wasn't lost on the others.

MEET THE MOLE ...

The three friends walked out of Darren's home in single file, across the porch, down the back stairs and out through the long wet grass, a column of nightmarish black hooded wraiths.

Confidently, methodically, making their way through the thick, swirling, dissipating mist as the humidity made the wetness of the grass and ground evaporate as an eerie curtain of steam. They were all completely aware of the solitary figure peering out from behind the dilapidated yellowing cream blind next door. Vicki was peering out from her kitchen window under the confident impression she couldn't be seen. If these wraiths bothered to look around, they would've seen on her face that her mind was racing, trying to work out what the cloaks were concealing. The mental wheels were definitely turning inside, a real shame considering the hamster was actually dead. It wasn't until they'd walked right past parallel to the kitchen window, that Darren the designated rear guard, flipped her the bird with his right hand and never even flinched or glanced sideways as he kept moving forwards. Vampires disappearing into the cloudy mist.

Water beaded right off their night black cloaks as the three figures cut a purposefully stealthy path. They made their way across the grass, around the humming barbed wire where Darren indicated and off into the thick scrub that bordered the creek. If this was going to go south at least they could fight back and inflict some real damage. Trudging along, it was starting to get muggy, but the humidity was tolerable. They wound their way through the long undergrowth onto a barely-used walking track. Poonta and Randall had blazed this one day to create a new way to a clearing they'd found by pure accident. Chandie broke the silence, she was playing around with the Bowie knife, hacking and parrying with the bushes when she scared the shit out of a single small brown bird she'd only just missed, who then screeched alarmingly as it darted away, its left leg still intact. Both Randall and Darren had reacted in alarmist fashion, their weapons drawn ready to start blasting, they were now all on edge, as if the tension wasn't already fucking high enough. "Sorry, sor... so, awesome collection you've got at home, when did you start?" She spoke charmingly as if nothing had occurred.

"Seriously!" Randall spewed venomous sarcasm back to Chandie. Darren ignored him and without missing a beat he stated, in a bad British spy impersonation, "Roughly... my dear.... I had most of it shipped via the various black market trade routes over a period of ten months. I couldn't raise too much suspicion given my background, plus a failed 'BLACK' hit, prompted my vanishing act". This emphasised Black statement was specifically designed for Randall's benefit. "So, you are a failure?" Randall copped a rock in the back of the hoodie for that comment. Continuing on Darren elaborated briefly, "I'm not taking chances, I like being alive, end of story. So Christ only knows why I'm now assisting a RED!" "Money, chum, Mate, friend and mainly because I'm so honest and convincing. Plus if this isn't bullshit we're about to encounter a better life". Randall laid on the condescending charm as thickly as possible, not looking back. "No, that's not it", Darren flung another rock — 'Yes, direct hit' and pumped his fist to his hip in celebration. Randall, turned around, "Will you stop that!" Chandie stepped between them and let out a giggle, "Now, now boys, don't we have somewhere to be? Come on, move on", waving her right hand forward egging them both onwards. Randall huffed, turned and started walking, shitty and silent. Darren just smiled smugly to himself as he looked down at his boots, mulling, 'You're the only RED I've seen I think I can trust'.

When they arrived at the clearing they noticed it wasn't anything seriously special. The total area was a thirty by twenty metre oval, abutting the overflowing creek. It had once been a local picnic area. Water had risen, so underneath the tables was soggy and muddy. But it was slowly receding, only the foul stench remained. It was completely overgrown with lush green weeds and flowers of all colours of the rainbow. There was a myriad of weed-like varieties, high grass and this stinking, thorny reddish green lantana, relentlessly covering it all. Everything was still wet and humid, a perfect duplicate of the Biosphere Wetlands Reserve near Ho Chi Minh City. Darren was making this physical assessment, 'Not much free space to run and gun should things go astray, it's a rat trap'. The whole area appeared as if Mother Nature was trying to hide it all away, purposefully. It looked like a teenager's unkempt bedroom, a time warp and a bloody disgrace, just more noxious weed. There were two old broken and chipped concrete mouldy tables still standing. Their tops were painted a cringingly lime green colour, so common to earlier eras as being 'All the rage', but now peeling off into non-existence. The tables had two cracked plank concrete benches on either side of them, room enough to seat sixteen people at a pinch and a dog-hitching post. Above the tables someone at one time had erected a makeshift roof of quarter inch rusted steel plate, which had been built in four large pieces on rotting termite ridden, unstable grey timber posts. The area had been swallowed up by the thickly growing greenish red lantana, creating a bird watchers' hide.

The tables were roughly fifteen metres from what was supposed to be the edge of the creek at low tide, however it wasn't low tide. Panning out across the creek, Darren had determined the width from them to the top of the other side was roughly forty metres. It had a steep inclined bank covered in the same foliage with large trees scattered along its length. It rose upwards at roughly thirty degrees. 'Higher ground, perfect for a fucking ambush. What the hell was Poonta thinking'! The three comrades took up selected spots behind the picnic tables and lantana, wary of their surroundings. Darren had provided them a security debrief, always the professional, looking for the exits and escape routes, potential hazards as he was a survivalist to the core. The tension began to rise.

It didn't take long as there was loud rustling coming from the east, in the direction of the bay. The day was getting drier, the sun heating objects to their natural state. The evaporation and humidity was steadily increasing, the sweat and every smell assaulted the senses. Through the stench of rotting trees and creek vegetation there was a hint of a sea breeze lightly entering this glorious Death Valley. The saltiness in the air was unmistakable. Darren was beginning to think that this secluded wetland arena where Poonta had chosen to meet their doom was done for a reason, it did still feel a tad constrictive. The tall grasses to their right parted as if a tectonic plate had just shifted violently and plants were being ripped from the ground with such force that Zeus himself had unleashed hell on earth. Poonta was hacking his way through, with two five foot machetes, carving a path so angrily his whole demeanour was one of uncontrollable devastation. This vision reflected one of utter power, a force not to be reckoned with — ever, except if you had a death wish. A six foot ten shirtless black man of glistening sweaty solid muscle, his six pack abs each had six packs. His arms weren't axe handles anymore, they swayed like huge palm trees in a hurricane tearing up anything in their path. Making his way out of the grasses he'd destroyed, he walked another few metres forward and paused. Poonta buried both machetes into the ground, tip first, by his legs, within reach should they be needed, then reached around behind, grabbed a small towel and began wiping himself down. He was an imposing sight to behold with those black guns and not the firearm kind. Chandie just grinned, raised her eyebrows taking in the eye candy, there was absolutely no compensation happening in those desert-coloured jungle fatigues.

From behind him emerged his protected quarry. Compared to Poonta she was of average height for an Indian woman. She was a slim wiry build with long black hair and really not dressed or physically at home here in the wild. The white, now bloodied, grass stained, dirt-smeared blouse and torn red skirt was a dead give away. At least she wore flat shoes whose colour and odour were now a combination of mud, grass and animal faeces. She would have looked more at home at the local accountant's office or crystal tower as one of those personal assistants, whose job it was to deny access to her boss and to give you the shits in the process. This initial impression of uselessness would be overturned the moment she spoke. Randall, Chandie and Darren watched these two start making their way through the green reddish lantana and overgrown recreation area. They slowly closed the distance between them. Poonta looked right at home, the enormous blades swinging like deadly scythes as he strode forward. They could now see he was also wearing a twin holster belt. His hips bulged like he had some sort of genetic deformity, instead he was wearing the highest, biggest-bore velocity production handguns on the planet, two XVR 460 Magnums with ammo to match.

This mystery woman was the total opposite, she was awkward, unbalanced and clumsy, she'd tripped over her own feet twice. When they finally arrived facing the trio, Poonta began reassembling and readjusting himself. Lastly he put on his desert coloured jungle fatigue shirt. This other person gathered what little composure she had left, straightened herself up and reached into her top pocket to put on tortoiseshell broad rimmed glasses, then ran her fingers through her hair to make herself look presentable. As if this entire act of self-grooming would restore her self-image and confidence somehow? It didn't. Poonta finally readjusted one of the belts from around his waist onto his chest and clamped the two steel scythes to his broad back. "Mornnun, how ya traking? Jar made it fine eyes sees. Dis lass here's Ishita, shes me source eyes told ya about. Came a diffrent root so wes not seen. Sorry if eyes scared ya. Needed to bee careful". Poonta used his hands as he spoke to accentuate and support his grasp of the English language. Ishita was now looking around like a caged ferret and completely out of her comfort zone.

Randall didn't speak, he simply gestured for them to sit down around the first concrete table facing the creek. Poonta and Ishita sat with their backs to the creek. Randall and Chandie sat opposite with Darren standing close by on point as designated sentry. "Ishita... Hello... Down to business... So just the facts... Ok... Nothing else... Our names are unimportant... So I hear you have some information for us? Our ominous friend here tells me that you can get us access to The System'? You've found a relic, a node, a dig that seems to have been missed, overlooked, abandoned? One with absolute direct access feeding into the main servers? Before you answer that... Firstly, who are you? Who do you work for? And why are you placing you're head in the guillotine to help total strangers?"

Ishita unloaded. Talking in a soft, highly intelligent, well spoken, extremely well educated, but rushed tone, "I like a man who doesn't waste time. You're quite obviously the Alpha, so I won't vacillate. My position is one of very low stature, I'm a gopher, a facilitator, a menial slave if you will. Invisible but privileged to the information from the highest level meetings and decisions made. I'm never seen, heard or acknowledged, usually a ghost, with no recognition, ever. The people I'm indentured to don't even know I'm alive. I'm used specifically for my coding efficiency in intellectual artificial intelligence, nano technology and high level security database encryption along with other informational coding. A master of manipulation and lies within the cloud. I worked alongside others of my family who were also specifically handpicked to assist and hide information pertaining to the Merovingian family within 'The System'. I was known as a RED. So, why am I here? Concisely, my brother obtained information that he thought was profitable and tried to use it, when he involved a few friends. They were found out and trapped as a result. They then slaughtered everyone in my family and our immediate friends who were involved. Obliterating four generations back and then replacing them all, three hundred human beings, men, women, children and babies. Your ominous friend here got me out!" She paused, out of breath.

Randall was brutal, and his cold and response reflected monotone searing frostbite. "So, we all have problems. Answer the questions, who knows you're here? Where's the node? How do we get to it? What's the security? Does it work and what do you want out of this?" Enunciating each word clearly and concisely, poison dripping off every syllable. As he did so he drew one Desert Eagle out of its holster, screwed on the silencer, placed it on the table facing her, finger on the trigger. No one flinched, you could hear a pin drop. He looked her straight in the eyes, his brows lowered and his lips disappeared into a cruel thin line.

Darren meanwhile had been scanning the whole area, completely on edge pacing like his feet were on hot coals and he was sweating balls to match. His internal senses were literally screaming at him, something was very, very wrong here. Something didn't smell right. His instincts had ripped out his guts and were smashing them continuously against a jagged concrete wall laced with double-edged razor blades. Yes, he was out of practice and out of shape, once he had a finely-tuned body along with the reaction time, now just the senses remained. These finely-tuned senses were on fire and they were going to keep them alive. He was looking for and working out every conceivable escape route. Calculating the steps, seconds and pathways to every way out of here. The one thought that kept going through the back of his mind was, 'Where's Vinchi'? It was then he started scanning the tree line across and up the opposite creek bank, while listening to the conversation Randall was controlling. He had no idea Randall was so resourceful. That was the exact moment he saw something move.

Looking at the weapon, then up at Randall, Ishita's response was one of sheer terror mixed with anger, she looked up at Poonta then back to Randall, "Firstly, I want to live. The deal was, I help you screw these pricks over! Then, I go with you! You're my ticket out alive, protected!" Then more slowly. "It's still active, I've tested it, just before everything went sideways a week ago and it fucking works! Here's the archive blueprints, relevant, the way in!" She slid them across the table. Chandie reached out, grabbed the rolled up blueprints, opened her cloak and without looking, inserted them into an interior pocket and zipped it closed. "There's zero security, no cameras, no motion detectors, no bio scans, no physical security force. It's in an underground bunker no one remembers. My brother found it, but never disclosed the location or told anyone about it. He only wanted money that was his motivation. He played that with some intelligence, at least. So, unless we were followed through that incestuous cess pool getting here, which I doubt, no one knows we're here. I'm trying at all costs to avoid getting 'FUCKING' killed, remember!"

CHAPTER THREE

REMEMBER THAT INSTINCT...

Chandie was watching Ishita as she spoke directly to Randall. Their eyes were locked unmoving, both set in stone. She was desperately trying to convince Randall she needed a way out and was prepared to take any step to get there anyway she could. Her whole family was gone, her friends were gone too and this was her last bastion or card to play. Serious enough to get out alive while fucking over the people that were out to get you. Ishita really had absolutely nothing to lose. 'A gorgeous, Indian, female version of Randall', Chandie thought making the connections. She was a RED too, she'd just given away her final trump cards to Randall in one complete and utter leap of faith, another RED trusting another RED manipulator. That took guts. The small group of comrades gathered here wasn't that far from the caravan park when you thought about it. The only reason Chandie had this random thought was because she could make out very light music in the background from Viktor's boom box. She snapped herself back into the moment.

It was at that very point Chandie flinched back. She was reacting to the red spot in the middle of Ishita's forehead. Ishita's mouth stopped speaking as her blood and brain matter exploded, splattering all over Chandie and Randall. Everything had just gone to shit. The next sequence was an eruption of simultaneous fluid movements by all concerned. Lives were now at stake. Poonta jumped panther like backwards over the concrete seat he was sitting on, away from Ishita's slumped body. Without flinching, he took a strategic step forwards, detaching the two huge metal scythes as he went. With two perfectly timed arcs he cut through the rotting posts holding the steel roof erect, rolling backwards and away after the last blow. Randall and Chandie instantly lurched away from the concrete seat as the steel roof tilted, then crashed into place. It slammed against and over the concrete seat and table, burying itself edge first into the ground, providing perfect temporary cover, bulletproof. The two back posts split and cracked violently as the huge weight's centre of balance shifted. The roof came to rest just as Chandie and Randall began repositioning themselves either side behind it. They scrambled under the table ends, dual Glocks and Eagles drawn.

They then peered out from behind the steel barricade as Poonta landed dead centre behind them. It'd taken him two strides to get up and over this steel monolithic barricade.

It was Darren who fired first. Standing a little off to one side of Randall, his motorised Gatling gun whirred to life like an unearthly steel demon. It spewed forth a hellish steel rain of deadly bullets as if possessed by Satan himself. Whatever had delivered that deadly blow from the tree line wasn't walking away alive. The arc he produced spreading out down the opposite creek bank was so slaughterous, small shrubs were being torn from their roots. At over three thousand rounds a minute, everything exploded as it was hit. Randall, Chandie and Poonta thought they could see movement in the centre of the tree line two thirds of the way up. Six deadly weapons discharged an accurate lethal volley into this space at equally-spaced intervals, high, low and centred. This is also the instant when the entire tree line detonated. Across the opposite creek bank and down its length at various zig-zagging intervals, the torsos of larger trees exploded in a horizontal shower of splinters and wooden spikes as these giants came crashing to the ground, crushing anything they hit. This nightmarish barrage of fire and brimstone lasted maybe a minute, if that, but felt a lot longer. Very soon the entire area was reduced to blackened vegetation, dirt, trees and foliage.

Darren screamed, "Stooop!" and everyone held fire, ceased the barrage and watched. They all took a deep breath, nothing moved. The silence that followed swallowed everything. It was only punctuated by a small sound of moving brushes higher up the opposite creek bank. Everyone was about to raise their weapons again and release another barrage, until they recognised the voice that bellowed, "DON'T FUCKING SHOOT. IT'S VINCHI!" He was moving to the most central point of the opposite bank, working his way through the carnage of scarred earth and slaughtered flora. They could only just make him out, scrambling about in what appeared to be a snipers ghillie suit. The image was similar to a long-haired teddy bear scuttling through the forest undergrowth. They watched and waited for a response still tense and on edge. Vinchi's words cut through the fetid air like a massive weight lifting off their shoulders, "We got them!" There was an ominous pause "Or what's left of them!"

By the time they reached Vinchi he had already rifled through the clothing of the bloody mutilated bodies. The two corpses were virtually unrecognisable with entrails exposed, limbs severed, crushed torsos and a face only their dentist could identify. Vinchi had extracted the only clue, a source of possible identification, two Green hermetically-sealed cards, along with the Finish-made 7.62 Tkiv 85 sniper rifles. He held them up so they could all could see, blood splatter and all. Randall turned immediately to face Darren and everyone followed suit. With Darren right in the crossfire, he took a step back, holding up both hands, palms forward, "Whoa! Whoa! Whoa! I don't know these two", pointing at the bloody corpses. "Remember I'm on your side". Vinchi piped up, "Hang on, slow down, Darren's right. These two were professionals and knew exactly where Poonta was going and that he wasn't alone". "Okay, I'm open minded. Please explain?" Chandie stuttered like an ancient red headed politician. "Darren", said Vinchi "I gather you know what these are?" Throwing a couple of mini black tablets on a chain at him, screens cracked, completely inoperable. Darren caught them both in mid-flight, rolled them over and inspected them thoroughly before he spoke. "Slick... High Tech... Accurate... They're randomised personalised GPS trackers based on RFID implaaaants? Poonta, your snitch was carrying her own personal electronic bug. I'll guarantee if we check her hands there'll be an implant. They were tracking you chief. You would have had no idea mate."

"Meaning?" was all Randall could bark out a tad confused. Darren responded "One of three reasons. One, she had absolutely no idea she was being tracked and it hasn't been imbedded into her body and it's on her clothing somewhere. So she's a dupe, mule, patsy or just plain unfortunately born with no real street smarts. So they haven't been able to pin point us yet. Two, she's a willing co-conspirator that's set you all up with whoever's tracking her, straight to you and that's these two poor unfortunates." He pointed to the bodies." "If we're lucky, they haven't had time to report their location, identify their final quarry, or provide any information back to a support team as yet and they were a solo act at this stage." "Three?" quizzed Randall now feeling as though the weight of the world had resettled on his shoulders. "Or three. We've Predator drones and satellites over our heads, we've all been instantly identified, our location has been pinpointed to within two metres, the reinforced designated backups are already being dispatched as we speak and we're all in fucking danger... To summarise we are now the walking dead no matter what we decide to do." Poonta broke in, low and menacing, "An how do wes know what wes is, alives or dead's meat." That's when Chandie standing on a fallen tree, which placed her head high facing Poonta, put a hand on his shoulder and said trying to hold back the vision from making her throw up, "We'll search the body, Hun".

It took less than five minutes for the group to make their way back to the picnic area where Ishita lay. Her body had been crushed by the weight of the steel roof that had crashed into place. They all assisted in straining to heave the roof off her body and over onto the ground. Poonta didn't hesitate, he was the one who'd been duped. He grabbed her bloody crushed body by the scruff of her blouse and top of her shirt. Then peeled her off the concrete table and seat, dumping her unceremoniously onto the wet, muddy, soggy ground. It looked like a group of vultures picking over the dead carcass of its unfortunate prey. Everyone took turns, getting their hands bloodier and bloodier as they checked every part on her body and clothes. Chandie finally yelled, "Here's something, I think." She used her Bowie knife to split open the lower seam of Ishita's skirt and pull out a red flashing RFID chip. She looked up at Randall and Darren to get the double nod before smashing it to pieces on the concrete table under the butt of the Bowie knife.

Chandie then looked for answers in Darren's face about what happens now? "That's a One", he breathed out slowly. She turned to Poonta, put a hand on his hip and tried to say as supportively as possible, "No harm done Hun, it's not your fault, okay?". Vinchi looked upwards at Randall and asked the question that was on everyone's mind, "So what do we do now?" Randall began to speak as slowly and as calmly as he could to ally their fears, "We regroup back at Darren's. We dissect and debrief what just fucking happened here and make a decision on what we plan to do now. We do it together, unanimously, it affects all our lives now, without question". He turned to Vinchi who was still holding the green cards, "I'll take care of those, Vinchi" then held out his right hand. Vinchi complied. Randall placed them in his back jeans pocket, composed himself and started walking back the way they'd come from Darren's place. "Come on, this is something that can't be decided sober" he chided.

EVIL NEVER SLEEPS...

Santos Nerezza was the absolute head of security, he had been in charge for three decades, highly trained and respected, ex-Black Ops. His handpicked militia was supposed to be the very best in the business, all loyal mercenaries, no mistakes, ever. At this level there was no room for errors, no excuses, none. The job just got done, period. No one ever, ever screwed up to the point that it put the family in danger. In this business, at this end of the food chain, you were expendable. He had devoted years of his life offering unquestioned loyal service to this family. He oversaw every order, every death, every success, every manipulation and every piece of the puzzle to the point of utterly obsessive micro-management. No one ever gave the 'Head' bad news and this was one of the worst pieces of fucking news he ever had to deliver. So he wasn't going alone, his next in command, his protégé, the one who he trusted had let him down, it was he who'd fucked up. He was going with him.

Both of them rode the mirrored elevator up from the 'War Room' in their luxurious Brioni Vanquish single breasted black suits, black shirts, black leather shoes and Armani blood-red silk ties, a perk of the job. In these positions reporting to these people, one needed to at least look the part of the confident, professional, modern day assassin. Stepping out of the elevator they entered a narrow hallway roughly eight feet wide. The floor was highly polished black and white Italian marble that echoed underfoot. The walls were made of the finest mahogany rose wood panelling with insets to hold beautiful Renaissance oil paintings from all the masters on one side and the exquisitely-gilded frames of the previous appointed ancestral 'Heads' on the other. The art dated back hundreds of years, all in pristine and mint condition. The parquetry ceiling that held the twelfth century chandeliers was amazing, it certainly gave you the feeling of being distinctly inadequate, as you made your way to the formal briefing room. The lighting in here was gloomy, as if entering the tunnel of death. The chandeliers gave off a dim light designed specifically to stand your hair on end while making your throat dry. A door at the end of the hallway contained a panic room specifically designed to keep the 'Head' safe in a time of crisis, such as now when something had gone horribly awry.

Santos and his underling stopped at the beautifully-crafted mahogany door lifting the Ouroboros brass knocker at the centre of the door, rapping it twice. As they both stood back, the video motion cameras that lined this hallway shifted with them. The automatic door then clicked, and slowly swung open. Peering into the gloom the room from the hallway was a strain on their eyes. The large room beyond wasn't fully lit. Stepping through the doorway they could see across the expansive room towards a massive oak desk where bankers' lamps emanated a soft glow. The room was twenty metres long and ten metres across, impressive was an understatement. The desk was covered in documents inside red folders. They lay on top of the huge touch screen built into it. The very dim glow it emitted highlighted the high leather dark green banker's chair that faced away from them, its occupant seated facing the warm marble fire place. Both walked four paces into the room and stopped, a sign of respect and protocol. The door slowly closed behind them and clicked into place. "Forward", the baritone tone was menacing, full of distain. Protocol resumed. Both men veered apart by two metres as they walked another ten paces and stopped, taking care to watch were they were walking. The lighting was seriously messing with their eyes. More protocol, if you addressed the 'Head' you would be viewed in your own personal space, uninterrupted or influenced by anyone who was near you. Body language was everything to communication in this room. They stood in silence, at attention, hearing their own heartbeats, it sounded like the room had just breathed in. "Santos. Report!" The monosyllabic booming tone sounded like Satan was in the room with them, with a voice it seemed that could tear flesh from your bones.

The chair swung around, the solitary outlined figure didn't stand, it simply waved a hand over the touch screen emanating from the desk. "Ishita escaped our original net. The subject has now been eliminated. No loose ends." Santos could feel his whole body tremble, thirty years of reports and now he was genuinely scared. "Really?" The voice resonated like judgement and execution had already been decided and all that was left was the final act itself. Santos swallowed. "The two guards", the booming continued, "Off grid, reason?" Santos cleared his throat trying to stop it constricting and swallowed again to lubricate it. "They ignored orders, protocol, I'm processing..." He was cut off mid-sentence by a fist that slammed the table. The voice boomed louder, slower, full of malignancy, "Not you! Aguilera, you nephew, enlighten me, you were in charge, were you not." Santos physically reeled in his mind, it almost snapped, 'Nephew? What The Fuck." He looked sideways at this man who he'd been grooming, training, mentoring. 'Holy shit, I'm dead'.

Aguilera was slow to speak, "The target was neutralised, the last remaining sibling. Blood line has been wiped out. Example has been set." "Not the question I posed, that's a result! Explain?" the voice echoed. Aguilera cleared his throat before responding. 'Uhhuh, so not just me, good', Santos smiled internally, silent. "The operatives choose to go radio silent, completely off protocol, the reason is, unknown. Kill was confirmed by GPS tracker then it all went dead. Location currently is unverified. Last known location was Hockalugie

Bay". The voice was silent, it waited, the pause was excruciating. The 'Head' enquired intensely, "You were in control, totally?" "Yes". Aguilera appeared a little confused. "So you've obviously recovered the blueprint, Nephew?" The venom reappeared. "B.b.blueprint?" there was utter surprise, confusion and shock in that stuttered response "Blueprint, she had a set, to what?" Now the voice took on the life and projection of a pyroclastic cloud, "They were blueprints that belonged to the Family. WHERE ARE THEY?" Aguilera quivered, "We don't know. We can't even find the operatives, they went off grid before we could pinpoint their exact GPS location". He sounded like a scared child now. "Right, so utter failure. Thank you. That makes my decision easier", the voice took on a tone of judgement and closure. There was an audible click in the room, sounding like one of those old-fashioned light switches.

Aguilera started screaming, "Uncle. No. Please I can set this right!" Smokey white gas began to hiss, Santos looked left towards Aguilera as the lights started to rise in their level of brightness. Aguilera was clearly contained inside a glass cage, smoke rising from his ankles, swirling all the way up his body.

This glass square coffin went all the way to the ceiling from the floor. Santos could now very clearly see small vents in the floor under and around Aguilera's feet. The gas rapidly filled the container and began to take effect immediately. He began to bang on the glass walls which were obviously built to withstand a rocket launcher and hermetically sealed to stop any leakage. VX is an extremely toxic synthetic chemical gas compound developed for military use. Aguilera's facial skin began to bubble and fill with fluids, some burst in sick red, yellowing green puss, his eyeballs swelled up and erupted, blood drained out of his nose, mouth and ears. He was violently coughing up all sorts of fluids and colours, as he did so large lacerations were appearing on his face and hands. The worse he became the more violently he spasmed, releasing chunks of flesh off his body. As his body was melting off his bones in such a violent and excruciating painful way, the 'Head' began to smile, quite cruelly. His body slumped to the floor obviously dead, the whole glass coffin began to gracefully slide downwards. Once it was completely swallowed up by the floor, a panel slid into place to replace the area where Aguilera had once existed.

"General, walk forward" the voice showed zero emotion. Santos walked very slowly forward until he was about ten feet from the large mahogany desk and stopped. "Your orders are very simple, recover the blueprint and eliminate any threat." The poison dripping off these words was extremely evident, 'Don't fail'. Santos looked directly now into the eyes of the most evil man he'd ever witnessed, only to be greeted by the following words. "He was family, you're not. Think of what'll happen to you if you fail me. Get to work. I want daily updates, dismissed." Santos just nodded, body completely stiff now, he turned with head bowed and walked back out the way he'd come. The door closed behind him as he left the room of death. He stopped and reorganised his thoughts, he'd physically shit himself. Gathering his composure in front of the video surveillance cameras he walked confidently to the elevator and pressed the button to the 'War Room' and waited. The elevator arrived, he strode upright and forward into it looking composed. The doors closed as he spun around facing them. He was definitely not composed. He definitely wouldn't fail, the 'Merovingian' made it very clear, his life depended on it.

As he rode the elevator down, faeces ran down his inside left trouser seam, sweat beaded on his brow and his brain began processing what had just occurred. His thoughts ran rampant, 'Never seen that glass cage before. The gas was a new toy. So there's another team with security clearance to that room even I don't know about. Builders' maybe? I don't know them. If I don't, they are probably dead, secrets never leave that room. Moving on'. The elevator stopped, he gained his composure and steeled his facade. Santos made an uninterrupted beeline for the bathroom and shower. Once redressed in a similar navy suit, except for the light grey tie, he walked over straight towards his newly-promoted first-in-command who stood to meet the boss. As this gaunt man swivelled and stood out of his chair to face him, he didn't speak, he just looked to one side at the elevator and back, raising a single right eyebrow. Santos returned the favour, closed his eyes and slowly shook his head from side to side in the universal sign for no. As he opened his eyes he stated, "We're going hunting Colonel, congratulations, pick your team and report to the black room, two minutes". "Yes sir", was the formal reply. There was no need for salutes, you either knew who was in charge or you didn't belong here. If someone here was further up the food chain than you, it meant one of two things. Either they'd killed more humans then you, physically. Or it just wasn't worth thinking about what they'd done to be promoted. Put simply, follow orders or die.

Santos entered the black room, there were fourteen entities seated at the debriefing chairs, eagerly waiting to hear what mission their commander had handpicked for them. The skill set in this room was enviable. They were all ex-Black Ops, Mossad, KGB, SAS, Navy Seals, Green Berets, Marines, Airborne Rangers and strangely Vatican Guards. Each had a specialised knack for eliminating a threat, extracting information and leaving no trace back to the source. Santos began his speech, "We're going hunting people, the previous target has been eliminated, but the threat has not. We've been charged to recover a relic that was stolen from our leader, a blueprint. Recovery is at all costs, a clean slate operation, delete any and all loose ends, after interrogation and data extraction. Individual reconnaissance missions, reports every two hours, active live imbedded tracers. Starting point is the last known locale, Hockalugie Bay. On point people, the last two disappeared, don't let it be you. Gear up and report to Colonel Tagion before departure, ETD one hour. Dismissed" Santos nodded to the group and exited.

As Santos walked out of the black room he went straight to the armaments quarter master. He requested the highly loyal, mute subordinate to make sure he used specific tracers on this team. RFID explosive head chips were to be implemented, in the chest, there was going to be no lone wolves on this mission. His next stop was predictable, mission control, the trackers' Chief of Control, another underling. No one was going off grid on his watch, even if he had to detonate the tracers himself. The black carpeted floor to the 'War Room' was immaculate, no sound emanated off it. He approached the Chief quietly and purposefully, this was one aspect he was going to micro manage if necessary. The Chief was a large muscular woman, ex-KGB, Pricilla's whole persona was one of a stone golem. She never smiled and her charges followed their orders to the letter. Her command was legendary, it didn't matter the two trackers weren't to blame for the two who went off grid. The trackers lost them, they should've initiated shadow ops protocol before they went dark. It was unforgivable. It earned them a double tap to the back of their heads. She loved her Beretta, small, slick, loud. It made the point.

The two who were promoted that day were made to clean up their predecessors, point made. You fuck up, you fail me and you're next. Santos barked orders quickly and concisely, "I want this mission's tracers linked to my personal tablet!" "Yes Sir" she responded immediately, it was clear she understood. Santos moved off, 'Rottzilla' turned to her underlings and issued these orders. He smiled as he turned away. This was his pet nickname for her inside his head, never to her face, he had more respect for her than to do that outloud. Priscilla reminded him of the genetic crossbreeding that would have occurred if a Rottweiler and Godzilla had an offspring. The touch of lipstick and makeup she used made him grin. The one point she was good at was efficiency, five years of devoted service and not one error. Santos respected efficiency and Pricilla hadn't failed him, yet.

Santos ascended and walked into his glass office, he could oversee everything from up here, mission control at dead centre, the debrief or black room at back right, quarter master or armaments area was front right, the pre-mission assembly point at left front and lastly the docking bay or transport area. The hexagon of death was one perfectly crafted to assemble an elite death squad. He'd lost count of the number of operations launched from here over the decades. This one was a little different though. Failure on any scale and you would be deleted, erased or replaced. Fail now and your retirement would be a permanent one at the hands of a man he knew wasn't human. The 'Merovingian' was just that, unfeeling, unearthly. He flicked a switch, his glass sanctuary went black as he needed to think without distraction.

The hour passed by like Santos had walked through a worm hole, blink and you'd miss it. He heard the troops in the pre-assembly area and flicked the switch again. As the electric current turned on, the glass cleared. His right palm flashed across the desk touch screen. At a glance he could see the all clear green indicator from the quarter master, all RFID's were inserted, another flick bought up all fourteen green lights, operatives' profiles. He touched the microphone symbol, his voice boomed through the pre-assembly area, "Listen up, I want that blueprint back in one piece, at any cost. There will be no lone wolves off grid out there. There are no individual agendas here and this is just to make sure you remember that...." he paused for effect and then he flicked the switch on his desk. One of the operatives' chests exploded. What was left of them rained out over the group, blood, brains and vital organs. He grinned to himself, 'The Bakers Dozen, perfect'. His voice echoed, holding extreme authority, "You're employed to get results. NOW GET ME THOSE FUCKING BLUEPRINTS!" His office went black.

SO WHAT'S NEXT...

Trudging back to Darren's house the mood was sombre, everyone was mulling over the morning's previous disaster. They were all hot, sweaty and the stink of the receding creek waters flooded their nostrils. After the fire fight and all that blood and bodily fluid, the stink of the undergrowth was a pleasant reprieve. In comparison, human bodies, having been torn apart, have a rustic sweet tinge that makes you want to vomit, similar to burning a fly with fire and literally snorting its ashes. They'd regrouped earlier. Poonta had approached Randall with Vinchi just before they were about to leave, Poonta mumbled something about it all being his fault and that they were going to erase the evidence from leading back to them.

The companions now sat in Darren's lounge room on whatever piece of furniture they claimed as comfortable given their physical aches and pains. Apart from Chandie, she'd taken up residence at Darren's dining table or what was left of it. She'd cleared the mess with one sweep of her arm and found a rag to wipe up the liquid, then spread out the blueprints and associated documents to study them. She was now trying to decipher them over a very large glass of white wine. Every so often she'd look up at the sink and cringe, that bloody snake was still in there, headless. Darren and Randall had slumped into a comfortable position after de-cloaking. Once settled, Darren then started handing out bottles of his home-made grappa, his own personal version of alcoholic rocket fuel. What they didn't drink, he could store for later and use it in the generator. All three appeared like a trio of dishevelled, sullen militia, drinking to memories of fallen comrades from a battle they'd just lost, plotting revenge. It didn't take too long before Poonta and Vinchi joined the others looking a little worse for wear. It was roughly an hour since they had left the picnic area. There were no words exchanged as the two of them joined in with the fluid medication. They explained to their accomplices that they thought it best to take what remained of the two operatives and sink these into the creek, piling rocks on top, out of sight, out of mind. It was now time to dissect what their next steps were, if any.

"Well, that was fun", Darren bubbled into his glass as he tried to find his mouth, flailing his arms around. "What next, we paint a red and white bullseye on my roof?" "Snot my falt, me conticts says Ishita waz straight ups, nose strings. Hadz all Randall needs, ticked all boxes. Eyes no idea she's waz traked. You wait'll eyes see him necks. Hez got a lots to sweat balls about. Feed him hez nuts I will. No ones Fux with my mates!" Poonta thumped his chest, he was pissed and now showing all his teeth as he growled. He was turning a darker shade of black under his indigenous pigmentation. He was seething. Poonta was the blackest, native man Randall had ever seen. If there was a blackout and no moon, he'd light up the room just by smiling his usual toothy grin, as he had perfect teeth. All carnivores did, someone was going to pay dearly and Randall was glad it wasn't him. "No one's blaming you mate, least of all me. You used your contacts and they didn't screen her properly. There was no way you could've known, don't beat yourself up over it. Concentrate on what we've got to do next".

Randall was really trying to put his friend's mind at ease, he was being sincere and it wasn't Poonta's fault. He turned his attention towards Darren and furrowed his brow, "Darren? You've been turning those bloody broken tablets over looking like you're searching for the lost city of El Dorado, what gives?" "Not sure, something's stuck in my craw. These look familiar. I'm just guessing here, but these could mean we've a smidge more than a One here". His voice cracked a little as he looked up at Randall. "Meaning?" he replied as he raised his voice slightly so all could take this in. "They may not have been able to pinpoint us out as entities, physically, you know, like sonar picks up other ships in the area. But, they definitely would've been able to track the RFID Ishita was carrying. Plus, I think maybe these tablets would have been sending back to mission control, the two operatives' general GPS location, before they... umm, blew up!"

This is when Vinchi chimed in, "So, roughly what you're saying is, THEY KNOW WHERE WE FUCKING LIVE?" He gestured wildly with his arms outstretched. He hadn't removed his ghillie suit and was impersonating an angry, vicious teddy bear about to attack.

"No. Well not exactly.... Could be that they may only know the basic area. If we're lucky just the Bay, which, when you look at it, is good. The Bay is still quite a large place to search as they would just need to send a professional clean-up squad to neutralise any threat from clues they'd find on the operatives or their quarry. Which wasn't us... So no immediate threat, yet". Vinchi lost it. "Oh fucking wonderful so, we're going to be 'Neutralised' by a bunch of, FUCKING CORPORATE JANITORS! Great, just fucking great. Poonta your contact's got a lot to fucking answer for". Flippantly, Darren calmly retorted "No... Maybe I didn't make myself clear, I said 'IF we're lucky'. But if we're not it'll be a suicide death squad". "Enough boys, calm down, reset it a bit. We need to cover all angles, not tear each other to pieces. No one here is to blame, for anything, OK". Chandie's voice was as soothing as medicinal honey, it spread out over everything making it soft, sweet and palatable. "Think logically. They were tracking Ishita right, not us. Poonta and Vinchi disposed of the two operatives, so nothing links them back to us, correct? If they get here and can't find them, there's nothing leading back to us. Poonta, honey.... You and Vinchi disposed of Ishita's body didn't you?" There was a long pause. Poonta caught Chandie's eyes dead on, making solid eye contact, his eyes as wide as dinner plates, "Umm, No.... Wes didn't have time. Wes finish the others and all of a sudden wes needad to splitz, cause heard somz really loud noises coming owws direction downs the crik". That particular statement from Poonta killed the mood in the room right there. It went deathly silent, if no one was worried before they certainly were now.

Randall unexpectedly exploded, "Enough, it's not Poonta's fault! I trust Poonta. So stop this bullshit. He was trying to help me, I asked him to. So if you're going to blame anyone, direct it at me, take me head on, if you dare? No? Okay, then let's start looking at this logically shall we?" Randall got up out of the lounge chair walked over to the bar stool so that he could sit and face everyone. "Firstly we don't know who these bogey men are that we eliminated, let alone IF they are now being followed, or even being led to us. Secondly, we don't know IF they've even located us, let alone pinpointed the Bay", he pointed to Darren, "Be honest you're guessing." Darren shrugged and then nodded in agreement, his body language confirming what Randall was saying. "Poonta and Vinchi did it right, it's better to have them back here alive than not at all. Besides, surely even a 'Death Squad' would take time to assemble even if those operatives were being tracked and things went south. We can always go back to the picnic area, reconnoitre and dispose of Ishita's body. Or we can simply take a leap of faith and check out the blueprints to see if they are even authentic and decide as a group where we need to go next. But, even that needs a well-formulated plan. We could all decide that it's too dangerous to even attempt to access 'The System' and stay here and life goes on as normal. Personally, after listening to Ishita, I've forgotten how ruthless these cunts can be, sorry Chandie, I'd prefer my friends not put in further danger, maybe I've been over zealous and self-centred. I like being here, its home, its safe. There's no manipulation, lies, deceit or hidden agendas. I couldn't ask for better friends and if it means staying, then I'm all for it."

Darren piped up, puzzled and angry, "So you mean you'd give up everything you've been planning to get your old life back? Plus all these bloody subtle enquiries, the deceitful manipulation of all of us to help you, let alone the danger you've put Poonta through, arranging this... The promises you made to me, let alone Chandie and Vinchi. The self-promotion and chest pounding of how you could get us all out of this stinking FUCKING cess pool, to Paradise, to Eden? What, where is that by the way? Don't even fucking think about lying to me RED, you know better than that, remember who you're talking to? You've set all this up, we've all agreed to back you to the hilt as we've all got our reasons too. You'd walk away, just like that? For some self-righteous, self-centred belief that you don't want us hurt and we'd all be fucking safe now! ARE YOU FUCKING INSANE!"

"What would you have me do?" expressed Randall. "There's no evidence that anyone's coming here. We don't even know IF the blueprints are authentic. So, I'm supposed to put everyone that I trust here, in further danger and lunge headfirst into some plan we haven't even formulated yet based on a bunch of IF's?" Randall couldn't contain himself. "We don't even know if any plan we come up with will work, it's all...." he trailed off, fumbling to finish his own thoughts. "A leap of faith...?" Darren concluded the sentence, his arms raised in disgust.

Vinchi interrupted the awkward moment. "Look at it this way. We have the blueprints. Why don't we study these and work out where these lead us? Everyone has input and we agree on a plan, plus assess our own parts to play should we proceed. We cannot worry about what IFs. As for me, regardless, I'm in completely. I'd rather spend my time getting to Paradise, Eden or wherever and die trying, than to live one more day in this piss hole." Poonta stood up, walked over and grabbed Randall by the shoulder with his hand. It felt like a very heavy small car had just parked there, slowly crushing his bones and tendons. "You an eyes is friends. I used me conticts cause I wantz outta this shit hole. Ishita convinced me too, shes wooden shut up. But more zen anythin eyes trust yous. You come ups wes plan, Poonta execute it. Me in sweethart." He lifted his right hand, cupped it and tapped Randall on the side of his head as a sign of affection. Chandie watched all of this unfold from her perch at the table over the open blueprints and documents. When the time was right, she slammed her hand down on the table grabbing everyone's attention, "I know what these blueprints are for, anyone interested?" They all gathered around Darren's table glaring at the blueprints and listened intently to what Chandie had to say.

Over the next few hours they exchanged deadly serious and jovial banter. A few heated arguments blew out but were settled in an adult-like fashion. The wine and grappa reduced to a flow of smaller, more cognitive amounts as Vinchi and Darren sheepishly nursed their swollen black eyes. The conclusion they reached was, should they follow this madness of Randall's through to its ultimate result, it would have to be unanimous. They would all stand by each other shoulder to shoulder. As evening started to settle the conversation turned to dinner as Darren's stomach growled, he blurted out of left field, "This is going to be a long night, so why don't I start the fire, we've got dinner." He pointed towards the sink and the snake bulging above the top. Chandie was the first to answer, looking up hazily, "Why not, this wine's stripped my tongue of any taste or feeling." She paused, "I can't feel my left cheek". She looked a little distracted, poking it.

There was a loud clap of thunder which sounded as if it cracked right overhead. They all jumped. "Looks overcast out there again, we're supposed to be in for another huge downpour tonight", Vinchi seemed a little rattled, lost in thought elsewhere. It started bucketing down, the rain began slowly and soon built up to such a torrent the noise was deafening. "Well, there's our answer to our first conundrum", Randall said with authority, "We're not going out in this shit to move another body, this has settled in, we'll discuss it later with clearer heads." All five then pitched in without a word to organise dinner as more wine flowed. The whole affair was completed in a quick and efficient manner, in silence. Once cleared away, they all sat down around the dining table again and conversation turned to one of serious concentrated overtones. Darren's place looked like a temporary World War Two bunker, they moved some of the clutter so they could walk around the dining table. Chandie spread all the documents out, separating them into blueprints (structural, electrical, security, air, water and sewage), then the briefing notes jotted out in Ishita's hand writing.

Chandi began the conversation, "Let's look it this logically. We now know what the blueprints are for. It's an old media communications station or what was a news broadcasting building. The actual structure is halfway up and built into the Barraiya range. Maybe a kilometre, if that, away from the city. Electrical, communication, water and sewerage conduits snake out from the city and connect to it underground. It was converted into a huge server or database farm. Think of it as rows and rows of computers over two decades ago when information was being stored to the cloud. This was before its supposed decommission." "Plus", interjected Darren, adding to Chandie's explanation, "According to these plans and notes, it's a seven-storey facility with two being above ground. The back of the facility is built into a sheer forty-foot cliff face right behind it with guard towers and gantries that run along the whole back roof of the building." Chandie scrunched up her face at Darren as if he'd take her last piece of chocolate, jumped back in controlling the discussion. "Yes. When the conversion to a server farm took place, they added the substation around its exterior, increasing the land space to just over two acres. This added a dedicated electricity connection specifically for the extra power to be drawn at peak times for the servers and the cloud. That would explain the security fencing and razor wire further inside the tall outer concrete perimeter walls". She paused again gathering her thoughts, "Curious? The single road leading to it snakes its way up through the thick scrub at a thirty to thirty eight degree incline, so frontal access is open to the elements."

While all this was going on Randall had picked up some of Ishita's hand scrawled notes and had been analysing them, the footnotes in particular. "According to her notes the steel gates are on automatic hydraulics, due to their size and locked by massive sliding bolts. This road allows access for supply or maintenance trucks as the road entering leads right through the middle to a loading dock. There's also a garrison or barracks on the second floor above ground level. It used to hold a security force of up to twenty personnel. She determined that her main access in appears to be via the unused, empty water and sewerage pipes from outside of the facility that lead under it. It's too dangerous to abseil down the range or take a direct route in the front. Her notes also showed that the node was four levels below ground, here and here". Randall pointed to the separate blueprints, one was water and sewage and the other structural plans. Vinchi moved his way closer towards him and was straight to the point with Randall. "So. Are there notes on security and how do we get in?" Randall's whole demeanour changed, "There's not a lot more here Vinchi, I was hoping to get more direct information out of her. Maybe even bring her along, she would've made a good guide."

Randall could see Darren and Poonta had started to wain as the alcohol seeped into their heads. Even Vinchi appeared drained. "Look, how about you all sit back and chill out a bit, there's no real rush here. I presume we can all crash here tonight, Daz?" he quizzed. Darren didn't even look up, as he moved off to his easy chair. He raised a hand above his head and gave the Monarchical wave, "Yeah all good, crash wherever guys". He took another pull at his home-made grappa. Randall acknowledged this as he addressed the group, "Great ok. Why don't you all unwind, chill out and hit the sack. I'll pour over these blueprints a bit and try and make some sense of it all. Poonta I might have some questions for you in the morning". After issuing that statement they all looked around to pick out a place for the night and curled up with what alcohol and blankets Darren could muster and chatted. Chandie grabbed a couple of dining chairs, indicated for Randall to sit, held a handful of his long hair and said softly, "If you going to do this all night I'll try and help ok?" Randall weary and still hazy sat down slowly, turned toward her, looked up at her charmingly and said, "I'll need all the help I can get, thanks Sweets".

CHAPTER FOUR

HARD DAY'S NIGHT...

It was still raining steadily when Vinchi found Randall. He was sitting out on Darren's back porch in the easy chair, simply staring into the clouds, watching the sky. It was still very early and a little before dawn when he joined him. "How'd you pull up? My heads still throbbing", he murmured at Randall. "Hang on, have you been up all night?" "No mate I haven't, I covered up Chandie with a blanket about 2:00am and came out here to get a power nap, to recharge and think. I may have a plan given the small amount of data we have. But I still really don't want to proceed as I could be putting us all in real danger." Randall was bleary-eyed and still had a brain full of fog. Vinchi raised an arm and placed his hand on the easy chair just above Randall's shoulder, "Randall, hang on mate, all kidding aside, hey. None of us would be here if we didn't believe. We're all prepared to help, we're all friends, plus we all want out of here, whether it's through you or not. You're just the present conduit, we've all got an agenda. If you've got a plan, why not share it with us, we're all adults here, we can all make own choices". "That's the problem Vinchi, you're my friends, friends don't place other people's lives at risk, not anymore, not here", he whispered staring back out at the rain clouds. "Well, no one's going anywhere today, this weather is set in well and truly", Vinchi observed as he patted Randall's shoulder. The floorboards creaked behind them, "What's all the conspiracy about you two?" It was Chandie yawning quietly, hair all messed up, blanket draped over her shoulders, bleary-eyed, she moved out onto the porch with them. "Randall has some options we need to converse about. We need to spend the day planning. I'll go wake the others", Vinchi stated as he tried to move inside, as steady as a midget being thrown at a prize wheel.

"So you've an option Hun, I didn't think there was anything further we could extract from those papers?" Chandie seemed a little befuddled, but still ruffled his hair. "It's one option. I still think its suicide, there are too many blanks and anomalies really", Randall said in hushed tones. "Better one than none Hun, come on inside, I'll start the coffee", she cupped his arm by the elbow and began lifting him up to steer him inside. "That's it, steady". They were halfway through the door when

Randall's seizure hit "Fuckkkkk!" he screamed out as he went down like a bag of bricks. "So much for waking the others quietly", Vinchi murmured, he'd almost reached Poonta who sat bolt upright, eyes wide. Darren came running out of the toilet still retrieving his shorts up to his hips, "Fuck me, you scared the shit outta me, fucken literally, what gives!" Chandie spat back, "Give him a break, it's not his fault, you all know Randall's "Special". Let's have breakfast and listen to what he has to say, ok!" By this time Poonta had raised himself up from next to the lounge and lumbered over to the dining table. They all mumbled in agreement and the morning ritual of a slow breakfast began.

The debrief of Randall's plan was soon underway once the blueprints, notes and maps were all strategically placed back onto the table. Randall cleared his throat to try to be heard over the rain. "Ok, let me make this perfectly clear from word go, this 'Plan' IS NOT set in stone. So, if anyone's has a better idea, interject, ok?" Randall then ploughed into his explanation determined to be as exact as possible with his wording. "Right, now we know where the old communication station is, it's roughly 100 kilometres away from here. No one has a car so unless we're going to steal one, bringing us unwanted attention, we need an alternate mode of transport. So, that means with the station on the range, the easiest, least predictable way to get there is to go by the river. It winds to within about ten clicks, by then we can go on foot". "Whoa, whoa, whoa back up. River, what about transport?"

The look on Darren's face was one of curiosity, with his palms raised up in question. "Easy mate, think. There's three canoes right here in the park, all in relatively good condition and we can carry all the gear we need. One in the corroboree area, plus Viktor will part with his willingly and the other one is behind...." Darren cut him off, "Neville's, oh I love this already, count me in, go on". Randall retook control, "Uh huh Ok...so this is all going to be rough. We're gonna have to wing it a bit and adapt along the way. In a nutshell, along the route, this is where we split into three groups. Vinchi goes in via the water and sewage pipes large enough for him, here". Randall began using the blueprints and documents as 3D tactile examples. "All the way under the perimeter to here, two levels underground to the water treatment and cooling area. The pipes can be burned open by Thermite flexible putty. From here you can get access to the generator controls for the loading dock". Vinchi glared at Randall blurting out, "Glad I'm not fucking claustrophobic, there's no fluids or shit going through here right?" "No mate according to these notes, it's how Ishita got in and out, but you need to go further because you need to get us in. They've been disconnected, I think. Since none of us are vertically challenged, we need you".

Randall rubbed Vinchi's head in a circular fashion, turned back to continue as Vinchi pushed his hand away annoyingly. "Next. Since we don't know anything about security at all, Darren and I are going up to here", pointing to the topographical map of the range above and to the back right of the station. "Alpha Dogs, if there are any 'Forces', sniper rifles." He paused, Darren gave a thumbs up. "We will eliminate the top level visible threat at all towers and upper level gantry. We then abseil down to the back roof, clearing out any 'Further Threats' to get to the loading dock". "We fucken what now?" Darren jumped in. "No one said, nothing about free falling down a sheer fucking drop. You're...", as he pointed to himself with a wave of both hands up and down his body, "Wanting to drop this Adonis over the edge of that fucking abyss? You're first, I want something soft to land on". Randall's face was a sight to behold, it looked like someone had stolen his lunch. "I can get the climbing equipment.

Proceeding on, Poonta, according to Ishita's earlier mud maps, we need you to scale the middle sentry tower. This will give you the opportunity to fire a zip line over the electrical sub-station so you can get access to the control hub. Break in, that's where your sparky skills come into play. Try and breathe some electrical life back into these facilities arteries for Vinchi, then while inside switch open the front gate controls and make your way down to the loading dock, here". Before Randall finished this last sentence Chandie moved in like a starving seagull, butted her way in front of him, bent over, viewing the blueprints right in front of him, "So what am I doing?" she eagerly wanted to know, looking back up at him. "Oh that's easy, you'll be waiting right here", said Randall and grinned sarcastically pointing at a clearing on the map well away from the station. Her whole body language and face changed from an angelic creature, to one of blood dripping succubus almost instantaneously. Randall felt his throat tighten and he regained his composure. "Right, poor joke, point taken. No, seriously, you have the most important job of all. You are the bait in our trap". A floor board creaked ominously under Randall's foot.

"Bait? I'm bait! Am I the only one who doesn't understand here or is this just another joke?" Chandie yelled while glaring around clearly unimpressed. Randall tried to pacify her as best he could. "This is extremely crucial Chandie and we can't send Poonta out in a skirt now, can we? You play the role of lost, pathetic, voluptuous, but deadly black widow, in need of assistance, pure sex appeal. If there is a security force, you're the distraction for the two front towers, so that Darren and I can blow their heads off. Once you get to the loading dock first, you're the broom, eliminate anything that moves that's not us and wait for Poonta, we'll get there shortly after." Randall breathed in, then with another long exhalation, he began pointing back to the documents. "From here at the loading dock which is the central hub to everything, Darren and Poonta hold the line against possible reinforcements. You and I make our way to Vinchi and then down to level four to the node. I breach 'The System' using my access and weave my magic, hopefully without detection and

129

do what we need to. We then get the hell out. All of us, Stage One Complete!"

Randall went quiet, he searched the faces of his friends for the slightest detection of hesitancy or objection. Dead silence descended on the room. After a brief intermission, Randall queried, "Thoughts? That's it, that's all I've got. A lot of what IFs and no real answers. This could all go south at any time." "That was better than I could get outta that frigging mess. Yes, I'm in full agreement, done". Darren dived in first adding, "I'm sure I've got all the gear, too." Poonta looked at Randall and gave a confident thumbs up. "All in sweethart." Attention shifted to Chandie who added, "Bait? Seriously, yeah, yeah, okay" and put her arm around Randall, "I'm joking, I'm in Hun, I'm sexy-y-y", she flashed her eyelashes. This was followed very audibly and grumpily by, "So, and I get to crawl through shit". Vinchi was and looked dejected.

The day unfolded at a steady pace. Darren spent most of the time cataloguing his Vault of Death. Meanwhile, Chandie spent her time searching and pilfering from the caravan park. She'd pinched numerous duffle bags, backpacks, tarpaulins and rope, being careful not to draw attention to herself. She thought at one stage she saw Viktor protecting his precious boom box. Poonta and Randall collected the canoes while it was pouring with rain, figuring common sense would keep prying eyes and everyone else inside. Having strategically placed these canoes out the back of Darren's in the long grass, they covered them up with tarpaulins. Ropes were firmly attached to the front of the canoes to drag them to a different, deeper part of the creek. Neville's canoe was in his back yard, in pristine condition, he never used it. Part of their clothesline was attached, along with Vicki's red, lace sheer, large underwear. These "delicates" somehow wound up displayed on top of the purple and white plastic retro piece of furniture near the pool. Vinchi scuttled about unseen, liberating unguarded food and bottled water. By the end of the day, this long and exhaustive stockpiling had concluded and it was late afternoon leading into evening. The rain hadn't abated all day, it was windy, wet and just plain depressing. Everyone was soaked, miserable and tired, they all reappeared in Darren's back room and collapsed. Darren handed out towels given they all needed to 'de-zombify'. It was agreed that not much else could be achieved

131

that day and it was time to shower and regroup. A wash-up, clean clothes, alcohol and food were now definitely in order.

The evening progressed well into night, the storm had turned once again into a torrential downpour. Usually this area would've been too far south for the monsoon rain, but given the seasons and weather were subject to weird patterns now, every biometric activity in the Northern Hemisphere had moved south. Ignoring all of this activity as standard, and, after a belly full of food, lots of laughter and shit-stirring Darren opened with, "Brilliant Plan, Icarus, ever think about dropping back to a Green at any time over your career? I certainly could've used you in Israel". "No, not really. I was too wrapped up in manipulating the truth, it got to the point fact and fiction started to blur. I'm kinda glad events went sideways in a strange way. I wouldn't have such true friends now". Randall sounded a bit reminiscent. "Wes loves you too sweethart", Poonta dribbled out obviously pissed. "Thanks mate, ditto, I still really don't like this, it doesn't sit right. We could still just walk away and stay here as is. Sacrificially destroy the access cards etcetera and go on with our lives. It could be suicidal for any of us, these arseholes don't play nice". Randall was being as genuine as he could when Vinchi chirped out just coherently, "We all want out. The plan seems solid and we're all willing and skilled participants. As I said before, you're just the present conduit, who better to go out with in a blaze of glory? This is our best, if not only REAL shot. I for one am with you all the way". "We all are Hun, we'll go out fighting", announced Chandie as she stood raising her full shot glass, arm outstretched. "Salute", they all raised their glasses.

It was right at that moment thunder cracked overhead, it sounded like a hydrogen bomb went off. The lights went black and the generator kicked into emergency lighting, Darren spat "Aww...Fuck, early night, hey?" They all ignored him and went back to drinking, if they were leaving tomorrow it was going to be a while before they did this again.

EXIT STAGE LEFT...

This had been a serious storm, it hadn't let up all night. In conjunction with record king tides sweeping inland, the creek simply hadn't coped, again. The cyclone, a category three, had changed course overnight, the eye had gone back out to sea prior to being north of Hockalugie Bay, gathering and gaining strength as it went. This was going to get a whole lot worse before it got better. This time when the banks broke, the water, filth and stench had risen to such an extent that all three canoes out back were washed up against the barbed wire fence. Water had flowed right through Darren's backyard and was just underneath the floorboards. Thankfully, during the course of the night Darren had switched off the generator cutting power to everything, including the safe. The entire park was flooded. Poonta was an early riser, seemed fair since he was the first one to pass out last night. It was approximately 7:00am, not that you could really tell from the sky, which was still drowning everything it touched. Poonta had been overly pissed last night and tried to give Vinchi a huge pash, expressing how much of a best mate he'd been since arriving at the park. He'd settled for an affectionate vice-like bear hug and had passed out with Vinchi still locked in his arms on the twin lounge. Vinchi looked like a macadamia nut being cracked in a vice after someone had lost interest and walked away. Poonta disconnected himself from Vinchi who was snoring his heart out. He'd walked onto the porch to check out the day that lay ahead.

134

The water had turned into a black, brown greenish primordial soup. It was as if the earth itself had partied all night long in a really bad nightclub, shit its pants and hurled up the contents of its stomach against the toilet block wall and then gone back for more. There was a mix of floating debris, everything from rotting vegetation, road kill, dirty nappies and all sorts of colourful filth and garbage floating around. The item that caught Poonta's eye causing him the most distress was the set of familiar looking entrails he'd buried the day before, spread up against the torso of the gumtree in Darren's backyard. In his haste he walked back inside to wake the others.

Viktor was up and about and had been since about four. He'd forgotten to turn off the alarm on his boom box and it had woken him up. By the time he'd found it and turned it off he was fully awake, so it was pointless going back to bed. The ritual of self-grooming had taken a bit longer this morning. His nerves were completely frayed. He was on edge, overly anxious and any little noise jolted his senses, the tic above his right eye was doing the Parkinsons' jive. This really had not been the day to decide to shave his head completely bald and get rid of the threadbare comb over and mini moustache. The toilet paper blotting his head wasn't a good look and his spindly skeletal frame made him look anorexic. But his motto was, you do the best with what you've got, not everyone could be a sex symbol like him. The clothes he put on were warm, he'd need that today with all this rain, besides he was going to get wet again soon, so no real need to be eye candy for the ladies. He'd had an extremely stressful time the day before. The park had started to overflow with stragglers, strangers of all various shapes, sizes and smells. The population had literally doubled overnight. They'd just moved in. They were camped out everywhere, under trees and in his yard. Plus he'd offered some refuge in his small ramshackle 'home' that he was now stepping over to get breakfast. They smelled, Jesus Christ they stank. A rich bastard wouldn't put up with this shit, he'd have just bought a bigger house, locked the doors and let the dogs loose to chase these pricks away. All these people were just overwhelming for his enochlophobia, he hated crowds as they made him violent. He knew why they'd come here, but that wasn't his fucking problem. He was going to the only one he knew could sort this out for him. He was going to the designated park protector, 'Darren'.

By the time Viktor arrived onto Darren's back porch, he looked like a drowned rat and that was a compliment. He'd fallen over twice in the 'park swamp' and come up a dead ringer for some swamp creature. At least that had gotten rid of the toilet paper clinging to his scalp. His cardigan had stretched and was smothered in grass and weeds. That wasn't the best part. He went everywhere with his precious bloody boom box. He'd placed it into a large waterproof zip lock bag to bring with him to calm his nerves. Each time he fell into the swamp, there was this raised arm holding it out of the water, keeping it safe while the rest of him went under. He knocked on the door frame carrying his own theme music, this was not the sight Chandie wanted to hear or see upon waking. She poked Darren awake and told him he had a visitor then rolled over. Surviving on very little sleep, Darren walked slowly hunched over towards Viktor, a dark forbidding look imbuing his whole persona.

'This'd better be fucking good', was the first and only thought travelling through Darren's head as he passed the kitchen bench, casually collecting the machete as he went. He stared straight at Viktor eyeball to bloodshot eyeball, "Turn. That. Fucking. Thing. Off!" he growled. 'Click' went the boom box, silence. "What?" was the next cognitive verbacious word to be expelled. "There are people everywhere", Viktor explained. "No fucking shit?", Darren groaned, raising the machete blade to his shoulder. "No, you don't understand, there are literally people everywhere, hundreds of 'em", Viktor embellished spreading his arms. "They're in my house." Darren knew this wasn't going to go away anytime soon, he turned around and started walking away. "Come in Viktor, you want a coffee?" "No, I want you to get rid of these people, they're everywhere. They just started squatting, everywhere". Viktor was presently groaning. Darren was waving his hands at Viktor, minus the machete. It was too late to talk quietly as this ruckus had woken everyone. They were now resurfacing and making their way to the kitchen to watch this comedy duo. By this time Viktor planted himself at the dining table and Darren was sitting at the end, head buried in his hands. "From the beginning please, Viktor. Just stick to the facts, only the facts, I'm really not in the mood today!"

The stage was set. Viktor's internal drama queen and body language took over, possessed, "Ok, look, people have moved into the park, they're camped out everywhere, literally. I hate crowds, you know I hate fucking crowds, you know how I get around crowds. The only fact I've been able to grasp and congeal together is that there was some kind of violent, holocaust type event in 'three separate parks' around here. Some guys turned up, military maybe, armed to the teeth, started asking questions and then all fucking hell broke loose. People were getting killed everywhere, randomly at first, then whole groups were getting fucken mowed down. Why? Don't know, I don't fucking care! They're. In. My. House! I just want them gone, you can do that right now, please?" The others were just standing around watching in silence, no one spoke, it was safer. "So some random dudes have just been going around asking questions and killing people? Did you hear what they were asking about?" Darren was trying to be very specific. "No, I told you, I don't know and I don't fucking care. I just want them out of my house. I don't fucken know. One guy said they were looking for 'Shit'. I mean come on, who looks for shit and then goes around blasting people away because they can't find shit?" Everyone in the room went white, except for Poonta. He just looked like everyone else, frozen in place, scare shitless.

In one fluid movement, Darren stood up, moved around to Viktor, completely composed. Putting his hand on Viktor's right shoulder he announced, "Yeah, sure, look... no problem Viktor. Tell you what I'll come and sort it out later, I'm just busy at the moment. But I'll get there later, ok? If it doesn't work out you can stay here for a bit, deal?" "Cool, awesome, I knew I could count on you Darren, thanks", Viktor was up now moving towards the back door as Darren was reinforcing, "No problem, I'll get there as soon as I can, I'll meet you at your place. Just go back and do the best you can until then, okay?" he said as he walked Viktor out of the house and off the back porch into the flood waters. He watched him walk off, turning on his boom box, to calm his nerves and disappear around his neighbour's hut. As he crossed the threshold of the doorway, Darren scanned his audience and stated what everyone was thinking, "We need to get outta here today, now". "Agreed", Randall chimed in, "They're here already. It's only a matter of time before they find us, seems like our decision has been made for us".

Everyone had designated jobs to do. Less than an hour had passed when all the equipment and provisions were stacked at the back door ready to be loaded into the canoes. The rain made it hard work, but at least it stopped just as they were about to leave. By the time they were outfitted in the gear they had used at the creek, the mood had changed. Instead of fear and anxiety each of them had taken on a steadfast resolve. They had a plan, it was going to work and they were going to get the hell outta here. After dragging the canoes through waist-deep water to the actual creek, each of them were grateful that Vinchi had accidentally come across three pairs of fishing waders. Prior to leaving the park, Darren had made damn sure he'd emptied the vault of everything he thought they'd need. What was left behind could stay, he wasn't planning on coming back. He and Poonta were the last to get into the canoes, they loaded the fuel and three small boat motors, the tarpaulins were lashed down, this was going to be a helleva long trip. It wasn't long before they were upstream and out of sight and earshot of the caravan park.

As they travelled, the day finally provided some relief from the hasty emergency exit. The rain had abated and made it tolerable. The humidity rose and sweat replaced the wet, a fair exchange. Conversation was at an absolute minimum, each of them were focused on making progress as far away as possible from the park. It was going to be a long haul before they set up camp. The panorama of the creek had now widened. The environment spawned an incredible amount of life. Both sides on each bank had an abundance of flora and fauna making it an essential breeding ground. Amazing really, considering humans had done their best to destroy the rest of the planet. Occasionally Chandie would trail her hand in the water by the side of the canoe, leaving a small ripple as they went. Simply being able to touch nature in its purest form gave her a warm optimistic feeling that everything would turn out as they'd planned. Then upon trailing her fingers again she felt a touch like sandpaper. She'd inadvertently touched a bull shark's back, ending that blissful action temporarily as she flinched away. The water here was cleaner and smelt fresher. Mother Nature was doing her best to flush away the man-made rubbish, filth, stench and infestation

142

being dumped into her environment. Being able to enjoy nature, taking in her grand majesty is an indulgent experience, better suited to another time, when you're not running for your life. Nature has a way of saying, "Look at me, aren't I pretty? Relax, enjoy, kick back". Then once you do, it hits you in the back of the head with a cast-iron frying pan.

Chandie was soon blissfully thinking, 'My feet are wet'. She looked down and realised the canoe had sprung a leak and was taking on water at an alarming rate. "Oh shit, oh shit, OH SHIT! We're fucking sinking here!" She screamed urgently looked around for something with which to bail. Poonta was in front of her, so the weight of the canoe including the cargo was dragging them down faster. Everyone has stopped rowing and the two other canoes were making their way over to help. Both Poonta and Chandie were bailing furiously. "There's fucking sharks in this creek!" was all they could get out of Chandie who was hysterical. They tried to calm both her and Poonta. Poonta wasn't a fan of water. To begin with, he was waving his hands up and down like a small flightless bird as if this very action would shoo the water out of the canoe. By the time the other canoes were lashed side by side to the other to help, he'd composed himself and was bailing like a madman. As they bailed, Darren and Randall steered them towards the left bank in an attempt to ground the canoe and fix this disaster. "Randall, thems snakes in here wes us. Theyz in the water. Eyes hate snakes".

Poonta was literally beside himself. This amazed Randall, he was utterly lost for words. This hulk of a man, this perfect human male specimen had been reduced to a blubbering, scared gay piece of kelp. "All good mate, don't stress, you know what happens when you get stressed. Calm down, breathe in, breathe out, repeat. It'll be fine just focus on bailing". This just happened to be the widest point of the river and fresh water fish could be seen jumping in abundance. Vinchi as resourceful as ever had selectively ignored all of this kerfuffle and started laying drift lines out the back of Randall's canoe. He quickly caught six fish as they headed for the bank, 'dinner' he thought. This chaotic mess moved towards the bank, trying not to drown in the process or lose any of the gear under water. Chandie's voice broke the mayhem, "YOU'RE FISHING! ARE YOU FUCKING SHITTING ME!" she screamed at Vinchi. She was furiously bailing, arms flailing and hyperventilating, "WHEN I GET MY HANDS ON YOU I'LL JAM THOSE FISH HOOKS UP YOUR ARSE AND USE YOU FOR BAIT!"

They finally arrived at the left bank, all of them hauled the canoes up, grounding them, including the gear and then stopped to take a breath. That's when Chandie lurched over some of the equipment they'd place on the bank, lunging straight for Vinchi's throat. "You selfish little maggot. We could've drowned!" Her face was bright red as she screeched. Randall intercepted her, both arms around her waist, pushing her backwards and steadying her with all his strength trying to calm her as her hands tried to grab Vinchi. "Chandie, Chandie, it's all ok, please calm down." "You fucking calm down, I'm going to throttle the life outta this little shit. He was FUCKING FISHING! Poonta and I could've drowned". "Yeah, I know, but you didn't", that sarcasm earned Randall a fury of slaps on his arms, shoulder and head. Randall had had enough. Darren and Poonta weren't acting this bad they'd just gone about repairing the canoe, quietly. Randall swept Chandie's feet out from under her, landing her square on her backside, full force. "ENOUGH!" he yelled, pointing his index finger at her. "ZIP IT! You're ok, you're safe, shitty but safe. Now shut the fuck up, pleeease". Chandie sat still fuming, hands in the mud. Randall would keep. She stared at Vinchi, like a bloodthirsty cannibal eyes off its prey. "Sorry", said Vinchi as sincerely as he could muster to Chandie.

It took a good hour to repair the canoe to a point that Darren was happy with it so it was waterproof. Vinchi steered clear of Chandie, no point poking the tiger, he admired a woman with moxie. They eventually started off again heading upstream, time was precious and bickering wasn't going to help, that part Randall had hammered into these two adversaries. Parts of the river were now becoming overgrown. There was a long section that serpentined for at least a kilometre. Of the trees that lined it, most grew out of the side banks at a weird angle, their tops completely intertwined, forming a dense canopy. Strangler figs were a noxious weed that grew everywhere, wrapping themselves around the trees, feeding upon them. Their foliage virtually blocked out the sun. The greenery, flowers and colour were breathtaking, it was like being in a peaceful Amazonian rainforest. After the last hour's tirade it was a welcome change, humid and wet, not seething or pissed off.

By the end of the first day everyone was exhausted, having taken turns at the paddles pushing forward determinedly. A couple of hours before dusk they'd found a place to beach safely, checked over their gear and set up camp. The weather had eased, it was now dry and the temperature was mildly pleasant. The glow of the fire beckoned. Poonta and Vinchi had found dry kindling and set out the dining area. The smell of fresh fish cooking was intoxicating, it beat the smell of the caravan park on a good day hands down. Chandie and Randall erected the temporary accommodation ensuring everything would be secure, dry and bug free, while Darren set up the makeshift perimeter alarm system. All were now drawn in by their noses, hungry. "Smells fucking great" Darren said, "Compliments to the chef". "*Bon appetit*", espoused Poonta, as he dramatically and theatrically waved everyone to their individual rock seats. "Bloody decent sized fish, what did you use for bait?" Randall queried Vinchi as he hoed into one. "Vicki's red lace panties. It was either the colour or the smell that attracted them", joked

Vinchi, with all the sarcasm he could muster. Chandie nearly choked. Raucous laughter bellowed out and broke the dusk, releasing the tensions of the day. "So how far do you think we travelled?" Chandie queried as she munched on her fish, jerky and chugged some wine. "I reckon we made good time and distance given the weather. Somewhere between fifteen to maybe twenty kilometres. If we can keep this pace we'll arrive in maybe about four, five days?" Darren noted, looking thoughtfully, poking a stick into the fire scattering the hot embers.

Poonta spoke after a brief interval, "Do yous think thez found us, or nose where wes is?" "I highly doubt it mate, they seem to have been preoccupied with the other surrounding parks. From what I presume from Viktor's dramatic foray back there no one has any idea why they started attacking everyone and no one has any idea it's actually us they're looking for", Randall replied, trying to convince himself more than the others. Vinchi offered his opinion, "If they did, they'd be right on our tails so I guess we've got a reprieve for now. Though it won't be long before someone makes a connection as to why we're missing. The bonus, if you'd call it that, is how long, where and why?" He took a bite of his fish. "Bit over zealous in their approach, don't you think? Wouldn't the police think it's odd and start making enquiries?" Chandie seemed a little confused as she tried to formulate this question. "Not specifically, when made to look like a gang-land style shooting or lone gunmen, no common sense will trigger. Remember, it's all about procedure, motive and opportunity, plus laws that govern society. We are outside those boundaries now, as they don't know what they're really seeking. No upper level alarms will sound off. That's all conspiracy nutcase shit, not worth looking into, someone will get paid to look the other way. It'll take weeks of tail-chasing before they even start getting close".

Darren seemed pretty damn sure. Chandie reminded herself he'd been an expert in counter intelligence. "So, for now we have a plan and forge onward, no deviation, no interaction with anyone attached to the 'The System' or otherwise, if it can be helped. Avoid the public, where possible. Stick together and keep focused. We'll get through stage one and hope nothing goes pear-shaped any further than it already has". Randall was now shuffling his shoe around in the dirt. He wasn't sounding too convincing, but his friends either missed or overlooked that. They needed to believe there was a reason they'd all come together, because now they were on the road headed for the land of their dreams. Any thoughts about the warlocks even being remotely real hadn't even entered their minds. Up until recently, they were blindly unaware of the global chess game being played with people, let alone players higher up the food chain. Not until Randall had started pulling this all together and the pieces were now all moving. What had he started? It was going to be the deadliest game they'd ever played. Their lives were literally on the betting table at a major casino and this particular 'House', had never lost a game.

NO LONE WOLVES...

There are times when you walk into a room and you physically quiver and tremble, your spine is electrified, your heart races, your mind has a feeling that something is dreadfully wrong. It's like the air around you gives off a shivery icy chill. Walking through it has the viscosity of Antarctic molasses. At this very moment in the Hexagon of Death, that was exactly the consistency of the atmosphere that resounded through it. The mood, attitude and functioning within this arena reflected one of supernatural efficiency. It was as if the entire, cognitive, collective hive of underlings were fully aware that their lives depended on perfection. It did. This along with any errors, no matter how minuscule would mean individual lives would be forfeited, they were right.

The glass to Santos's office was jet black, the door was closed. There was a white, eerie, thin, vaporous smoke seeping from underneath the black sliding office door. It was ever so slowly creeping out, before cascading down the metal staircase. Everyone in the Hexagon knew this was a homeopathic vapour. It was used in "that office" when stress levels were past the point of no return, it was supposed to calm the occupant. This was also the warning signal that someone was going to be exiled or deleted and that meant a lot of messy bodily fluid to be cleaned up by the promo-tee. 'Rottzilla' was making her way up the metal stairs in total silence. Her underlings knew this wasn't a reassuring sign, no one ever climbed those stairs. Some smiled internally, others were shaking in fear. In the time the longest serving agent had been there, tracer number nine, those stairs only ever had one set of shoes scuff "their soles" over the unforgiving surface. If you were retired it was usually done here, on the operations floor, an example to all. Promotions here were usually quick, efficient and mostly sudden, never relished. She had been summoned by the Angel of Death himself.

Santos was sitting forward in his high black leather chair breathing in deeply, eyes closed, arms outstretched. The vapours usually made him think more clearly. The lighting and temperature in the office had been reduced to that of a morgue. Even the artificial plants strategically placed around the office were starting to form a film of condensation, adding to the gloomy atmosphere. The four vents high up that ran the length of the back wall oozed out this white ominous vapour. Gravity was drawing it down, slowly encasing the office's occupant and everything it touched. It flowed out over the large touch screen surface on the cherry oak desk and onto the floor. Santos was now darkly glaring at the twelve green operatives' profiles still active, utterly incensed and fuming at the one deep blood red LED he'd terminated. He thought he'd made himself clear. No one eats, breathes, moves, shits or acts without first getting his approval. Obviously the message hadn't been effectively delivered. He was going to enjoy this part, it'd been too long. Time for a "hands on" approach, lead by example. There was a knock at his office door, he touched the desk screen, the door then slid open and 'Rottzilla' entered the room, her body language reflecting her position, power and ultimate control. She'd been summoned to report, her underlings had screwed up, the buck stopped with her. She stood rigid, at attention, steadfast a few steps inside the door, readying herself should the Court Marshal not convene in her favour. "Where's Taigon", was the deep guttural growl that came out of Santos's mouth. She stared blankly at this Jurassic Armani Beast who now had stood up and moved from behind his desk to tower over her. "He's in the Black Room, just arrived back", 'Rottzilla' barked still at attention. "Tracer number?" Santos was cold, succinct and chilling. "Nine", was the only answer. "Follow me", came the order as he walked past her out of his office and down the staircase. You could hear the whole room breath in.

"Azrael" never surfaced when a mission was in progress, there was only ever one precedent that 'tracer nine' remembered and he was the sole survivor. That was seven years ago, he swallowed trying to cleanse his dry throat. As Santos walked down the metal stairs, the echo was deafening. It throbbed along with every heart beat in the operations room. 'Rottzilla' followed him closely as he made his way onto the gantry where the tracers sat, overviewing their technology and screens in front of them. Not one of them flinched or turned to watch. Each one was concentrating on doing their job, tracking the field operatives. As Santos walked onto the metal gantry, it too echoed, he took seven paces, then stopped, 'Rottzilla' stood two paces behind him at attention. Santos's voice detonated the silence, "What part of, NO LONE WOLVES, does anyone NOT understand?" No one spoke, no one turned around from their screens. No one moved. "Obviously, I was not understood. If someone tracked goes 'off grid' without approval, you scum are supposed to intervene and report it. If I need to take action, then, WHY THE FUCK, do I need you?" He turned around to 'Rottzilla' who opened the right side of her full length black leather trench coat. Drawing out the twenty-eight gauge pump action shotgun he turned and walked forward along the metal gantry, the echo was horrifying. He stopped directly behind tracer nine. In one fluid movement he emptied two cartridges, one into the back of his head, the other through his heart. Without flinching he handed the shotgun back to 'Rottzilla' and barked the orders. "Clean this up. No more errors". Santos stalked off in the direction of the Briefing Room, hunting Taigon out. 'Rottzilla' didn't even hesitate, she'd escaped retirement. The shotgun clicked to life once more, tracers eight and ten were soon smeared all over their consoles. Promotions were about to take place.

Moving towards the Briefing Room, Santos's demeanour darkened, his pace then quickened. The reincarnation of 'Azrael' glided purposefully across the floor to his final destination, vengeance seething from every pore. The door to the room slid open as the biometric scanner identified the entity approaching. Colonel Taigon met Santos halfway across the room as he was the recipient of, "YOU HAND PICKED THOSE PRICKS, EXPLAIN!" Santos pointed in the direction of Hockalugie Bay. "Three off grid!" He raised a hand and fingers indicating his outrage. "One more and I'll be using your internal fluids to paint by numbers! I don't need lower official forces sticking their noses in where they don't belong or learning about our operation. We are supposed to be above this, UN-FUCKING-SEEN FOR CENTURIES, NOT ON MY WATCH! One more and I'll be handing what's left of you over to him". Taigon swallowed, "It won't happen again". "NO SHIT, Sherlock. I told you what happened to Aguilera. Did you think I was fucking joking? So where are we information wise? Do we know what the blueprints were for? Or where they are? Do we know who Ishita was involved with? We know she wasn't working alone", Santos was demanding answers.

Colonel Taigon was now physically shaking as he responded, "Not yet, but we do know who handed her the blueprints. Operatives have been sent to extract that information and delete the source. We're interrogating all possible leads in Hockalugie Bay and have two solid leads. A clean-up crew has been sent in to smooth over the 'Fuck Up'. It's highly probable there's another RED here, the lead has to be one hundred percent confirmed. "A RED? WHO? What level? Santos was now intrigued. His curiosity had been peaked. "Level 7". Taigon was being careful and concise, no room for errors here, he'd heard the promotions take place and wasn't eager to join the demo-tees. "Fuck me. That's one step off GOLD. We're talking a relative, a protector of the Committee of 300. A member of the round fucking table here". This clearly rattled a solitary bar of Santos's cage. Colonel Taigon had never seen him like this, ever. He tried to be helpful and add, "Sssir, look the only piece of information we obtained was, that they're possibly of Jordanian descent, but that, too, is very sketchy. No name yet". "Oh fucking brilliant, Abdullah II of Jordan. We're talking the Second most powerful Olympian in "Fucking" command under the British Monarchy. Death follows him so closely, his feet are permanently wet. Get me a name, now!" The single thought going through Santos's mind was, 'I'm not looking forward to today's fucking debrief'. Santos dismissed Colonel Taigon. He needed him alive. Always keep your enemies close until they we're expendable. He made his way back up to his office and sat down in his leather chair. This was not a conversation to which he was looking forward. Best to deliver this news remotely, thinking back to the panic room. He skimmed his hand over the biometric scanner on the desk, a large 70-inch flat screen monitor, the length of the desk, rose out of the depths at its front. It flashed alive with a Life-Size image of the 'Merovingian' with surround sound echoing every dark syllable. "Report Santos", the voice growled. "No major news yet. Quarry is dead, clean up crews are active. Leads to blueprints being followed to conclusions. We may have an issue though. There's a possible "Knight" involved now, Round Table. Nothing further", Santos was pulling together all his energy for this particular facade so as not to crack. "What family?" the reply was ever reaching, or at least the tone was. "Jordanian, not confirmed yet". Santos was now genuinely scared internally. "Hmmm... Tread carefully, dangerous water. Get a name, soon!"

The 'Merovingian' was not happy, that much was evident. So, why the slip in monosyllabic description? Was it on purpose? Did it mean danger for the family directly or would this have the 'Butterfly Effect'. Either way it wasn't good. If this went to shit there'd be nowhere to hide. His hand flashed across the screen again, he was trying to see if there was a pattern developing. Six profiles were randomly scattered, three methodically working in and around Hockalugie Bay, three seemed to be off in LaLaLand, not really where he expected they would be searching. It was possible they'd click, so no more master blasting at this stage of the game. He could always send reinforcements as the mission unfolded. Four were heading in a seemingly north-west direction on separate paths, but there was an obvious common bee-line being determined here. Typical, the ones on point always came from the same backgrounds, worlds apart, all ex's, Black Ops, Mossad, KGB and Vatican Guard. The Vatican Guard didn't surprise him as his pedigree was impressive, direct lineage and service dating all the way back to the original Swiss Guard established in 1506 under Pope Julius II. These pricks were just devious, manipulative, aggressive, intelligent people and he was obviously onto something. When this was over Santos made a mental note to delete this one, they were also usually ambitious and he didn't need that dividing the ranks.

Santos summoned Taigon via video conference in the Black Room. The monitor hummed to life. Taigon materialised. "Sir?" was the question resonating in the speakers. Santos turned down the sound. "The tracers are heading north-west, find out why? Get back to me. We may need reinforcements sent. If that's the case I want them issued immediately, armed to the teeth. Use an entire brigade if necessary, clean the map and wipe away any interference, zero trace, understood?" Santos's booming overtones were not lost, the monitor slowly sank into the desk. Taigon grasped the point, 'Don't fuck up again'. He wouldn't. His whole attitude was one of fix-it-now-mode. He moved to the control console in the 'Black Room' and reconnected his remote access to the four operatives out in the field, all initially on solo mode to glean what each had detected and obtained. He'd activated the body cams, splitting the monitor onto four screens and then each earpiece. He muted the ones he didn't need and began the perpetual debrief so as not to delay proceedings. Randomly in no particular order he started with the KGB operative, "Bortnik, report, designated target and information". "Colonel, information extracted from a dove regarding potential suspicious fugitives headed inland, no destination, fled upriver, no further data. Dove deleted. To be advised", grunted Bortnik in a thick northern Russian accent. Taigon hated Russians, rude, obnoxious, vodka-swilling pigs. His hand flashed over the touch screen and a quarter of the screen disappeared. Next was the Mossad. Taigon never deviated from his chosen monologue,

"Mizrah, report, designated target and information". "Quarry, Ishita, her contact was identified, source physically interrogated, dissected and deleted. Blueprint to possible server farm inside city walls, investigating, request backup". Taigon responded, "Granted, full score initiated. Drop Zone will be ten clicks south-west of current location, three hours, confirmed, report when connected". This meant trouble, potential breaches of 'The System' weren't always detected. Half the screen blacked out and the last two filled the remaining space.

Taigon opened communications with the ex-Black Ops. He sighed briefly prior to flicking the audio switch, he hated all the operatives, put simply, wasn't a fan, they were all pond scum to him, but this particular operative was the worst. "Cletus, report, designated target and information". "Yes Sir, Colonel Sir. We found a state of the art gun safe, empty. No identifying serial numbers or marks. Locals were extremely uncooperative so not much to go on. Clean slate on those interrogated. Possible movement upriver by canoe. Identities unknown at this stage", was the long-winded response. "Continue on, report in at 0800 tomorrow". Taigon switched off the channel as quickly as he could. He wasn't going to talk to him before then. One to go as Taigon continued on unabated, this was getting monotonous. Solitary and face to face now with his Swiss Guard operative, the epitome of shear and utter efficiency, at last he opened with, "Moretti, report, designated target and information". Then he waited for the response. The answer was not the one he was expecting at all. He demanded Moretti repeat himself three times for clarification, then a fourth just to make sure his hearing wasn't failing. Colonel Taigon who never lost his composure in front of an operative, went white. Moretti had to ask him if he was unwell. Taigon disconnected the communication without notice. Moretti could wait, he'd continue on mission.

If Moretti was right they were up against an adversary that knew all their moves and their secrets. The legends and myths of these adversaries and their lineage was undeniably, lethal. Generations ago this lineage had taken out the entire De Medici family and fortune. They'd been completely obliterated as if they had never existed and this was three levels above the 'Merovingian Family' in the successional line of thirteen. This was no fucking RED! This had nothing to do with the Jordanians, no Knight, or Round Table. This was a direct descendant of 'SATAN' himself with all the bells, whistles, knowledge and power to match. They needed more intelligence and fast. This was a game of chess they couldn't afford to lose, it would be a bloodbath, 'THEIRS'. He'd never met the old man upstairs, this information needed to get there fast. Santos was the direct link now. If this information was right it would change everything. He was now running at full tilt, out ofthe Black Room, across the metal gantry and up those metal stairs. He needed to get to Santos immediately, protocol could fucking wait.

CHAPTER FIVE

NEVER LOOK BACK...

Randall opened his eyes blearily, it was early morning and he couldn't see anyone else awake, the sun wasn't up and it was close to dawn. Darren hadn't even set himself up as a sentry, given the temporary alarm system he'd constructed. Everyone was exhausted given the previous day's events. That was fair because the rest of this journey was going to test everyone's skill to their absolute limit. Some might not survive, that was a hard fact. The dawn wasn't even peering out over the horizon as he started checking their gear, all seemed intact. He then sat down on a dead tree overlooking the camp and its occupants. He sighed and looked regretful, he didn't like this feeling, honestly all he really wanted was to get his old life back. But deep down he knew that wouldn't be happening any time soon, or easily. Choices needed to be made, he'd have to choose, he didn't want to, but pawns were always utilised and sacrificed for the ultimate goal. Having moved the pieces, the chess game was too far advanced and the results hadn't been his intended plan. His 'real' friends were now in danger. That was about the change, time to get his act together.

Opening a waterproof satchel Randall noted all four cards were still there, he resealed it and glanced out over his rag-tag group of miscreant comrades and smiled. Getting his confidence back was good, it was now time to get into his groove. Time to take the chains off the beast and kill off all emotional reactions and react purely on instinct, at least for now. Relaxation could come later once the objective had been eliminated and he'd finally reached Eden. Having been trained well, beyond the point of breaking, they'd remoulded his alter ego which he'd kept hidden from the world. His ex had no fucking idea what his real role was, a stupid, fatal mistake. That one'd be a freebie. Snapping back into the zone, no time to waste, there were bigger predators to exterminate at this point. They'd had it their way uninterrupted for too long. They would regret this awakening, ripples would resound globally like a Neptunian tsunami. They would remember this and would have no choice but to leave him alone. Over the centuries they'd been feared. Not long ago, in present times, there were still whispers, rumours and myths. The elite used to look over their shoulders and hide in their corridors of power, afraid to wake the evil. Only he knew the source was real. Now wasn't time for second-guessing his abilities, he was good at what he did. Time to drag the depths of Hades, dig deep into that fetid rotting earth and let the 'Ghost' resurface.

That's when Randall realised someone was behind him, looking over his shoulder. Chandie looked half asleep stepping over the tree to join him. She yawned as she said, "You ok Hun? You look somewhat preoccupied. A penny for your thoughts?" "Hmmmhh", Randall hummed, lifting his eyebrows, he shook his head slowly as he said more alertly, "I'd rather have my freedom, but, all's good, just planning, better to be prepared, Alpha Dog Shit", as he stared at Darren then back to her. "We've got some hard times ahead and some interesting choices to make. We all need to be on the top of our game now, some more than others. These arseholes play hard ball and for keeps. Everyone needs to pull together, now". He was fidgeting with his 12-inch Bowie knife, sharpening it then cleaning his fingernails with it. She ran her fingers through his hair, "Point taken, we're all in agreement here". Her other hand swept out over the camp at the sleeping grizzlies. "We'll be ready when the time comes Hun. Teething issues only. I wasn't really going to kill Vinchi, I just wanted to see how'd he react. We need to know how far we can push each other's buttons, could be useful in a dead end and we need a way out. You, however, still surprise me every time".

Randall responded in kind, as he put his hand on her knee, "You know that makes some weird sense. But we're not all getting out unscathed, this will get very rough, possibly permanent". "News flash hero, we all know that we might all wind up roadkill. So, what's in the bag?" Her eyes flashed as she spoke, trying to unbalance him. "Your Christmas present. I'm keeping it hidden as a surprise, so no strip searches, nosey". He cheekily beamed back, then added, "Seriously, it's the way out for all of us". He gestured across the camp, adding an evil smile she'd never seen before, as his whole demeanour changed. She didn't know this 'Randall' as he said in a low guttural growl, "It's about time I left a parting gift to some admirers they'll never, EVER, FORGET!" It was then Chandie's throat went dry as she tried to swallow.

Randall placed his hand on her knee again. This particular 'Randall' demeanour seemed to have settled unnervingly in place, "Enough, time to move, we need to be outta here before dawn, let's wake the others for breakfast". They both shuffled downhill to the makeshift camp, Chandie following Randall as he circumvented the alarm system with ease, hardly even looking. She knew Darren had set one up. But she watched Randall and did as he did, as she didn't even know it was there, hidden, 'Impressive Instincts', she thought, 'Wonder if Darren knows this RED is as skilled as him, if not more?" Randall had Chandie wake the others so as not to make unnecessary noises, he started up the fire again. He had breakfast and coffee made just as they all lumbered into the fire-pit area. Not much was mentioned about the previous day, Darren saw to that with, "Well, I assume Icarus that we plough on through the day, *status quo* and push as far as possible until nightfall?" "Best way, we've got no idea what or who have arrived, could be anything given Vinchi's assessment. I'm not betting our lives on it though. My dominant instincts say we're already being, HUNTED".

All sat in silence as Alpha and Beta chatted, there was a clearly-defined respect in place now. They all brought certain skills to the table, but Randall and Darren were clearly in charge. There was a knowledge and mastery being utilised here on another plain of existence, engaging well together, levels above the average Jane and John Doe's. Randall had the topographical map out so the others could see. He then indicted fluidly, "I really want to push to get here by tonight, but failing that, here", pointing a little further back. "I want us to be able to physically respond if we're caught off guard, lethally". "Fuck, who taught you to read maps? If this map is up to date these are perfect vantage points, natural cover, river depth and viewpoints", Darren trailed off, thinking. Randall stopped him before he could connect any dots, "Ok, time to move, Darren, you're the GREEN. Stealth, efficiency, protection mode. As we're getting the canoes prepped, erase the camp site, zero trace, nothing. You know better than us what needs doing. These hunters won't be regulars, deception, illusion, misdirection and perfection mate". Darren rose and disappeared quietly, he'd retrieve the alarm system first. Randall turned his attention to the others, satisfied his guard dog was on point, "Ok, friends, let's arm up and disappear".

It was then Randall went down in a screaming heap, straight into the dirt, face first. His friends were all there in a flash, steadying him, cleaning him off and giving him water. They were all genuinely concerned, as this was a severe seizure. Even Darren had come hurtling out of the scrub to see what had gone down. It took a good five minutes for Randall to re-humanise. He was genuinely appreciative, but there was a mission to get underway. Not one to rest on his laurels, he began assisting everyone to load the canoes. Chandie approached Randall once this was all completed. She took him aside from the others and said as reassuringly and as angrily as she could, "Stop pushing so hard, you don't need to prove you're bigger, stronger or can out do everyone here. Leadership needs the head, stability is what's required here, now. You're not ten foot tall and bulletproof Hun, we need you alive, and you are point. If this all goes fucking south, we're all possibly dead if you don't start taking more care".

Randall shrugged and shot back savagely, "I'm not asking anyone to do what I'm not willing to do myself!" Chandie fired right back at him furiously, "Whoopy, William Wallace we don't need a martyr here. How do we know if we lose you along the way that we can continue on to get what we need done?" That's when Randall secretly handed her the pouch he had out earlier when she disturbed him before dawn and whispered, "Because you're going to keep this safe until we get there, it has a biometrical seal imprinted onto me and only I can open it. Besides it's got your Christmas present in it and I want to be there to hand it to you personally". He winked cheekily at her, but she wasn't overly impressed. Then he added, "It's called trust, Chandie, I have absolutely no intention of letting anyone here down, I'll be there to open it, you'll see to that, I have faith in you". Extremely rare words for a RED, Chandie made a permanent mental note of this statement. Soon all five began arming themselves to the teeth. This was when Vinchi discovered Darren's grenade launcher under the tarpaulin and called dibs. By the time of their departure before dawn, to the trained eye, you would never have known they'd been there.

The trip upriver was arduous and physically demanding, positions were swapped for the subsequent battery recharges and power naps. Everyone put in superhuman efforts. Randall's plan would work and this is now what drove them. Eden beckoned and the thought of a harmonious existence and safety was the motivator. Thoughts of living a permanent existence in the park zoo no longer enticed them. The issue more importantly now, was that according to both Randall and Darren, they were being 'HUNTED'. The thought of dying prematurely overrode any feeling of whinging about exhaustion or aches and pains. The mission now was to stay alive and get the bloody hell out of this cesspool, unscathed if possible. 'Get it done' was now the internal motto. The rain had given them a night's grace, but it turned ugly around two in the afternoon.

Distance made so far had been to the first point Randall had indicated on the map. However, the cyclone had veered back towards land overnight and brought a monsoonal squall with it. The river was rough and was now getting dangerous, the current was being pushed back upstream from huge monsoonal king tides. It didn't help that massive amounts of water deluged downstream from the range and eddies were forming everywhere. Mother Nature was now angry and doing her best to kill them.

They had been looking for a place to land that wasn't awkward, but as Murphy's Law would have it, there wasn't a perfect spot of any description to be seen. The swell was getting worse, options were quickly becoming limited. There was one spot further down where a tree had been torn out of the bank and was precariously overhanging a section of the river, like a low-lying limbo pole. Water rose and crashed around it and there was vegetation askew in the water and growing out of the bank around it. It wasn't safe, but the river wasn't either. This was the only option, so they began to start towards it.

As they grew closer, the canoes were being tossed around like toys in the ocean by Poseidon himself. If they weren't careful they were going to lose the equipment or a whole canoe. It was a disaster in the making. Poonta was first in. He used his whole bulk and muscle to stand upright, and, grab the horizontal tree's torso that straddled across the river at this point. That stabilised the canoe as Darren used the paddle to keep it from twisting around. This would be the guiding bridge or wedge into the river bank, so to steer the others onto land. The bobbing up and down with such ferocity like this would've given anyone motion sickness. Vinchi was next with Chandie. Their aim was a fraction off but not overly poor. It was a harder landing, nose first up the bank, not exactly the way they would've wanted. They eventually pulled the canoe out of the water, high enough away from the river to go back and help. Randall lined himself up. He had the lightest load being by himself. The water now was unforgiving, one mistake would be horrendous, especially since Randall's canoe had all the water and food, plus the fuel, for the three small motors. His canoe bounced, jerked and oscillated a full three sixty degrees in a huge eddie that had just formed underneath the canoe. That's when utter disaster and good fortune struck simultaneously.

Randall had another major seizure and fell backwards unconscious out of his seat onto the floor of the canoe, just as the swell dipped and then rose suddenly in the river level here. The eddie spun him viciously around and the cyclonic wind barrelled down through this small neck of the river. The whole event took place in extra slow motion, time slowing down to such an extent that everyone was caught off balance and couldn't react quickly enough. Mother Nature gave them an enormous bitch slap.

Randall's canoe was pitched forward by the tidal surge and eddie at such a pace, the back end of his canoe slammed into the tree base to which Poonta was attached. Having only missed him by inches, his canoe was flung clockwise around, nose-first onto the bank, flipped and wound up facing the river, safe. Vinchi and Chandie grabbed the bow rope, at the front of Darren's canoe, wrapped it around their forearms for grip and braced. Darren was still in shock, unable to move. They pushed and solidly dug their feet into the bank and heaved as hard as they could to stop Darren and the gear being swept away. The rest happened as a direct result of the impact. Stuck in place with all their strength being expended to keep one companion of this alliance safe, the inevitable occurred. The sound was deafening, the tree torso split in a sickly unforgettable ear-splitting crack. It sounded as if lightening had struck and exploded in the earth next to them. All they could do was watch in undiluted muted horror as Poonta screamed and was torn away from the bank, still attached to the rest of the tree as it crashed away under the water to be sweep away with the current.

There was absolutely nothing they could do, they were still attached to Darren's canoe. If they lost their balance they would be in the river with him. The flow jerked the canoe savagely and snapped them both back into reality. Poonta was gone. This was inconceivable, Poonta was GONE! Darren could still be saved. The rain hammered down, the weather was seriously getting uncontrollable. The cyclonic wind was throwing objects everywhere, both Chandie and Vinchi were being hit by all sorts of vegetation, the rain was stinging their faces and eyes. Eventually they were able to get the canoe out of the river to safety along with Darren, who, by now, was also in an utter state of shock. Adrenaline kicked in, all three whirled in haste, this way and that. In separate directions they each organised to tie things down, retrieve items and make sure that they were all safe. After lashing down the final tarpaulin for a temporary shelter, all three huddled inside with the unconscious Randall. Their little troop had lost their hardiest, strongest deity. GOD, what hope did they have if this could happen to Poonta?

It was a long night, the wind howled and buffered their makeshift shelter and the rain battered down, soaking everything.

At least they were alive and hoping to live through the night. Huddled together under the tarpaulin the tension rose even though no one spoke. This was a matter of praying to live through the night, survive and move on. The onslaught was unrelenting, these were anxious times. At one point Vinchi lost part of the tarpaulin that had come astray, but scrambled to retain it and lash it back into place. A piece of timber had ripped through the tarp, slashing his left palm and he was bleeding profusely. By the time he'd lashed it down and settled he'd lost quite a bit of blood. Darren, ever resourceful, had an ex-military suture field kit. "Need to be prepared on a trip like this", was all he said as he patched up Vinchi's right hand. By the time the wind and rain had settled down to a lull it was once again simply heavily overcast. Morning had arrived and the river level had lowered slightly. The area surrounding the canoe was one of mayhem and destruction, it was a miracle that the canoes had survived. As the others started dosing off Randall came too, not knowing where he was. "Oh shit my head. What happened? Where am I?" Randall seemed acutely disorientated. "You had a bloody seizure and passed out, Poonta's dead", was cried out by an extremely distressed Chandie. Randall sat up as quickly as he could and looked around this area of the river, specifically where the fallen tree had been. It resonated with accurate clarity that the tree was missing and the only piece left was its base. He glanced around swiftly, and noticed the canoes were okay.

Vinchi had stitches in his hand and everyone looked severely drained and emotional. Randall was slightly rattled by what he thought he'd heard that looked like it came out of Chandie mouth. "What? What do you mean Poonta's dead? What the hell happened? I don't remember a fucking thing?" Randall was genuinely both confused and disorientated. Darren spoke as he was the only one who had composed himself to the point that he could utter coherently as he enunciated, "Briefly, Mate, you passed out in the canoe, the weather, wind and river threw you onto the bank after hitting the fallen tree. The tree cracked with Poonta still on it, fell into the river and he was swept away with the torrent". "Holy shit. So have you found him yet?" Randall was desperately grasping at reality. "Well, no. But the way that tree hit him and pulled him under, I don't think even he could've survived that". Darren sat back clearly thinking about Randall's positivity after he'd made an assumption no one had thought a necessity to find out an answer. "I could be wrong, but wouldn't it be logical to actually try to find him before pronouncing him dead? I mean I'd like that you would look for me if this was me? He might have survived at least for a little while". Randall was still very groggy as he only just mumbled this out. "We're going looking for him, once I regain my faculties. NO Debates!" was the next order that passed his lips.

NO-ONE LEFT BEHIND...

There was no dissuading Randall once his mind was set, his whole attitude was one of sheer ruthlessness and bloody-minded efficiency. Chandie had noticed this persona settling on him since this journey began and the way Randall conducted himself now seemed other worldly to her. He took organisation and micro management to a whole new level, letting Chandie and the others know in no uncertain terms no one else was going to be placed in danger unnecessarily while he was conscious or breathing. He didn't blame Darren, this was evident, but this was now his watch and he was undoubtedly in command. He would conduct himself

179

in such a manner that allowed for input and ideas from others, even left field if necessary and then adjust accordingly, but at the end of the day his decision was final. He had regained his senses and was functioning coherently, then came yet another seizure. They were coming thick and fast now and getting much worse. He made the suggestion that everyone else sleep until eleven. This was not a debate, no one argued, Randall kept first watch.

The decision was made that from now on, the further they progressed sentries would take watch from dusk to dawn. If they were being hunted and had lost Poonta, everyone was to pull their weight and share the duties. While the others slept, Randall scanned the banks and the distances in either direction with one of the Finnish made 7.62 Tkiv 85 sniper rifles' they'd acquired. By the time he went to wake the others, they seemed to be stirring anyway, eager to begin searching and at least keep moving. Given the way they were feeling, each of them needed a positive approach to the mission now. The task of searching for Poonta filled the gap inside. Not only was it rational, but it provided a sense of hope, it meant that should they not find their cherished gargantuan friend, they were still moving in the right direction. It also suggested they wouldn't focus as much on being the prey for more insidious executioners now prowling the landscape.

Vinchi joined Randall. He was handed the sniper rifle and told to keep watch as he fished. They would need to ensure that they weren't being followed, at least by what could be seen. Fish would be an additional bonus. Plus, the latter was done to alleviate any guilt Vinchi felt at not being able to assist Poonta while in the midst of saving Darren. The orders were simple, three canoes, three positions. One close to each bank and Randall's directly down the middle. Scan the banks for any unusual disturbances, call out regarding anything strange or a sign of their friend, but keep moving. The river through the next long section wasn't very wide and this gave their small alliance much-needed boosts of encouragement. The pace they set was slow and methodical, the most minute detail would not be missed and concentration would be at an absolute premium. Twice, Chandie yelled out and they stopped and searched, she was certain she had seen something of interest and a possible clue. These both turned out to be dead ends, each time Randall would provide the much required buoyancy needed to lift her spirits. He encouraged them just enough to ensure nothing would dampen their enthusiasm. By late evening, they pulled the boats ashore as light spasmodic rain settled in again. The mood was a little more sombre. Everyone pitched in and camp was struck, meals were prepared and they ate rations in their tents, as silence filled the air. Chandie and Vinchi soon mulled around the gear looking busy checking this and that, then retired to their tents for an early night.

Darren had sought Randall out after the meal. He'd scaled a small tree and was sitting in the 'Y' of the trunk, sniper rifle adapted and fitted with the night vision scope Darren had retrofitted, his black cloak and hoodie in place. "You got a minute?" was the quiet composed query up into the tree. "Yeah, of course, come on up, no need to yell, it's a perfect view from up here", Randall seemed flat but composed. "Not bad. Jesus, you can see in every direction up here. You're a real piece of fucking work, you know that?" Darren accused Randall quietly. "Huh. What, what's your bitch, what did I fucking do?" Darren had climbed up to the horizontal branch jutting out next to the 'Y' Randall had perched himself. "I've spent a long time in and around the trenches, I thought I was seasoned, I smell something off, you're acting less and less out of character, if I can pick it up, how long before you think those two are going to take to work it out?" Darren was pointing in the direction of the camp. "What do you think you smell?" Randall lowered the sniper rifle to his hip. "Don't get me wrong, I'm on your side..." Darren didn't even get to finish that sentence.

Randall fell backwards out of the tree as if he'd been hit with a giant's baseball bat hitting a home run. Darren launched himself out of the tree as he felt and heard the next muffled shot strike the tree where he had just been. Randall wasn't moving at the base of the tree, 'Silencer. Fuck no, no, no, not here, not now, he's MY ticket out', Darren thought as he realised he was unarmed. 'Shit, fucking idiot'. There was nothing he could do for Randall here, unarmed. For all he knew, the way Randall was hit and fell, it was an instant kill shot. 'Guns, now, move!' Was the next thing ticking over in his head as his whole body accelerated low towards camp. As he moved he was pissed off, Darren knew he was better, much better than this. Unarmed and thinking, 'You fuckwit', he'd let his guard down. Not again, he needed to survive, he needed to disappear again. From now on he would be armed to the teeth even while asleep. If necessary, he'd booby-trap his own body. These wraiths were well above efficient, he hadn't even picked up the scent that they were this close. They usually worked in pairs. The timing was right, he had to get them all out of here tonight, they weren't going to die here in the mud, filth and rain. 'Fucking rain, again, really, now?' Darren thought. Hurtling through the scrub he knew he wasn't far from his makeshift tent and he was in top gear now. He then tried to stop when he reached it. As he hit the brakes way too late, he realised all the rain had turned the dirt into a muddy slush and he slid past his entrance. Throwing himself onto the ground, he dug in with his fingers grabbing handfuls of earth and roots to stop. The heavens then opened up and a small part of the earth exploded next to his right hand. 'Christ he's fast, he's moving', Darren scrambled into his sanctuary. No time to think, he was in one end and out the other in the blink of an eye, scurrying low across the ground and into the surrounding bushes, dual Glock 17's still in their holster. Thank fuck he'd packed that second pair. There had been no time for warm and fuzzy warnings or group hugs. As Darren was ransacking his gear and on his way out in one fluid

184

continuous movement, he screamed the words to Vinchi and Chandie, 'SNIPERS...RUN!''.

Vinchi had been under the tarpaulin with Chandie chatting softly trying to console her about Poonta when this almighty calamity shook their moment of serenity. Seconds later two silent projectiles sliced through the tarpaulin. One had zipped in past Vinchi's head and out the other side, like a small brief meteorite. They furiously scattered items to collect their arsenal and took off in separate directions. They were now huddling behind some bushes and tall grasses. Chandie could feel a strange wet, warm trickle down the middle of her back. She ignored it, no time to worry now, 'Be fucked if I'm dying here'. She searched the darkness, her eyes focused, scanning desperately for the monster hunting them. Each of them figured their best option was to move and turn the tables on their pursuers. Working their way silently through the mud, slush and razor-like grasses was painful, however, the instinct to stay alive provided the stealth, strength and fluidity to move in such a way it appeared like they were part of the wind and rain. Darren had worked his way downstream, looking over at the opposite bank and thought he saw a muzzle flash towards where the camp was, he was hoping they'd heard him and gotten out. He found a spot to cross the river, narrow, shallower now dammed up with vegetation. He hunched over as low as he could without drawing attention to himself, working his way through this shaggy wet mess to the other side. Glocks in both hands. The 12-inch Bowie knife was still strapped to his leg, this prick was going to regret he ever messed with an ex-Kidon Senior Officer. He would take him alive, only just, and where possible 'interrogate this cunt, excruciatingly and slowly'. He would physically peel off one layer of flesh at time, like an onion, causing as much pain while leaving his captive alive, practice always made perfect. He smiled evilly. Every instinct flowed to the surface in vivid rich colour, even the smells of inflicted, malicious torture flashed back. It had been way too long since he'd worked with his elite group of expert assassins under the Caesarea, he was going to enjoy this.

Vinchi was pinned down behind a stout, stumpy dead tree just big enough to conceal his small frame. Each time he put out a hand or his shoulders moved, a single deadly shot zipped out and split the earth near him. There was no solid cover close in any direction, he was now trying to control his breathing. Calming himself, waiting until a pause presented itself. His training took over, focused, intense centralised meditation gripped him. He hadn't made his way all the way up the ladder from deadly, manipulative, successful assassin (one fuck up, he grinned) to that of Slipper Rank or Deputy Mountain Master by losing his focus. In his career he'd eliminated every threat, removed landmines, slit throats, he'd even reinvented himself as people went missing, toughening himself mentally and physically until he was ousted by a coup. He caressed the throwing knives around his waist feeling their keen edge, internal patience would see an opportunity appear. When it did, that would be the last mistake this prick would ever get. Vinchi was physically quick and by the time he'd finished with them he'd have fish bait for this adventure and the next. He'd hunched on his knees and waited — eyes closed — the instant he needed would come. Chandie couldn't see Vinchi now, he'd disappeared into the low bush and behind some tree as she scurried off in the other direction. She gathered her thoughts, remembering how earlier he'd been caring and sensitive. Moving on, she saw that the scrub and bushes next to her were so thickly intertwined it made perfect cover. If this assassin was using a night-vision scope she had it covered, thermal imaging was another story. Jerking her mind back to reality and ditching any further procrastination she made for the area she spotted. By the time she got there across that small gap, three insanely quiet hollow-pointed bullets fractured the silence. Their recognisable zipping sound, unmistakable now in the darkness. They cracked into the scrub near her, one missed her right ankle by millimetres, she never saw it, but felt the breeze.

Dual Glocks were out and loaded. Chandie's brothers had all been in the armed forces, special ops, reconnaissance and infiltration. All highly decorated and over protective of little sis growing up. Boyfriends never stood a chance as none were ever good enough or strong enough to meet their standards of interrogation of what a protector should be. 'Protector my arse', she could hold her own and set out to prove that she was better than all her brothers, so they'd leave her to choose. By the time she was twenty two, she could outrun, outgun them all and was an expert in Krav Maga, a brutal and lethal martial art. There is no spiritual journey, no harmony to be achieved in Krav Maga, kill or be killed was the mantra, no mercy… ever. Protection gave way to respect and love for their little sis. A shame they weren't here now, all killed in the line of duty. Chandie was trawling her way along the ground to the left of the camp, she crossed the river and inched her way downstream to this 'Arse wipe'. She would make them proud, she could take care of herself. When she cornered this adversary he'd be that riddled with holes he wouldn't be able to crawl away. That's when she would really unleash, she'd obliterate and snap every single bone in their body physically. She needed the exercise, toning and therapy. Mercy? What fucking mercy, she was the deadliest fucking accountant in this part of the jungle. This unlucky cunt was going to find out how a ledger was balanced, real soon.

The silence along this part of the riverbank was like being on the surface of Jupiter's moon Titan, cold, wet, eerie and its intensity was building. The rain hadn't stopped, only easing off to that of a solid spring shower. It was dark and the weather seriously wasn't helping. The sniper was refocusing his attention on Vinchi, he'd lost sight of both Darren and Chandie. Instinct kicked in like a mule getting a colonoscopy, he would have to move very soon or be caught between the two that separated left and right of the camp. If he stayed in position any longer Bortnik would be cornered and there would be no room for variables. His mission was a clean slate protocol. He was next to and wore what was left of the operative that had exploded back at the Hexagon of Death. He was ex-KGB. The absolute best Russian training could fund. He was an expert in hand-to-hand close-quarter combat, a sniper and communications expert. He was recruited late in his career to the service of 'The Family' and was out to prove a point. He deserved to be Colonel Taigons mongrel-in-charge of training new recruits. He would be relentless, if they broke they weren't good enough, those around him were already too soft, amateurs, fucking Hipsters. Santos needed a force he could rely on at all times, not just for Pussy-Whipping missions. This was a waste of his time and skills. He was recalculating which one he would pursue first as he couldn't get to the fucking midget. Bortnik was up from his crouching position, kneeling and in mid strategic thought. That's when he heard the branch snap behind him and two 12-inch Bowie knives entered each ear cutting that last thought off permanently.

Darren and Chandie knew they were closing in on their adversary and were almost on top of them when they saw something launch out of the bushes and into the river. Three seconds later the river erupted upwards, detonated, parts of Human flesh rained down everywhere. Chandie's Glock 17 was out, raised in the approximate direction of where she thought this entity had taken flight from. Her arms were locked in the recoil position ready to fire, that's when an ear landed on her left hand which held her loaded Glock. Instinctively surprised, she fired a shot.

Chandie was in shock and a little rattled as it fell to the ground, but composed herself just enough to steady and aim. That's when she counterintuitively looked to the left a fraction off to where she had unloaded her weapon. Focusing intently in that direction, she saw a huge white toothy grin split the jungle night. Every emotion, every tightly-coiled steel spring inside her body discharged, her whole persona of deadly female black widow went out the window. "POONTA!" she screamed and catapulted herself at him, re-holstering her weapons as she went. She jumped straight up into his arms and coiled her arms and legs around the front of him like an anaconda that hadn't eaten for a month and was about to crush the life out of its next victim. He flinched in pain and grunted as she did so, but nonetheless wrapped his huge arms around her and squeezed, head down, exceptionally glad to see her. Darren was breaking his way through the undergrowth, racing forward as he heard Chandie yell. He quickened pace and came to a halt beside them, Chandie still clinging onto Poonta with absolutely no intention of letting go. Eventually, Darren peeled her off as he could see Poonta was in serious physical pain and not exactly one hundred percent.

Slowly, steadily, they made their way over the river. Vinchi met them on the bank as they crossed, Chandie and Darren each held an arm assisting Poonta forward. Vinchi took a machete off Poonta, turned and hacked a wider path back to camp. When they arrived they gingerly placed Poonta on a log as the rain had stopped. There was no use getting their sleeping quarters wet just at the moment. They needed to check if their cherished large friend was alright. They were all busy fussing over Poonta, asking a myriad of questions which he was desperately trying to answer as his head began to spin. It was like the Spanish Inquisition, unrelenting and mostly unnecessary. It was a good ten minutes before, right in the middle of all this jubilation Darren burst forth with, "HOLY FUCK, RANDALL!" He raced away with no explanation. Right in the middle of Poonta's stuttered responses, Darren headed directly towards the tree Randall had been perched in. The others ran after him. Poonta stood up, held his chest and lumbered behind them into the scrub and to the high tree not very far away.

Vinchi and Chandie reached the tree to find Darren sifting about as if searching for vanished crop circles. The look on his face was one of sheer perplexed confusion, he was literally lost for words. When Poonta arrived all he could hear was Chandie saying, "What the hell are you talking about, stop mumbling". "He was here, he was right fucking here where I left him?" Darren was pointing at the ground around the tree as if he'd lost his wallet and if he kept looking for it, it would miraculously reappear. "That prick had shot him in the head, he'd fallen out of the tree, and ..." again Darren didn't finish his sentence, this was becoming a habit. The ground beneath him was fading away into the distance. Poonta had Darren by the scruff of his shirt and had lifted him a clear three feet off the ground. He had thumped him against the trunk of the tree. Poonta opened his mouth and growled, "Explain, wats yous means shot in the head? Wats yous means wes yous left him?" Darren had his hands on Poonta's trying earnestly to remove them so he could breathe. "We were just talking when that bastard opened fire. Randall looked like he been shot in the head the way he fell out. He was like a rag doll that fell to earth. I couldn't do anything because I wasn't armed, I had to go back and get my second pair of Glocks just to stay alive. Seriously, he wasn't moving when I left him. I really thought he'd been shot in the head. Poonta, Mate, I'm on your side, I need... want Randall back, too. It's not like anyone could've picked him up and carried him off. I mean look his sniper rifle..."

Darren trailed off again. This was becoming a really bad habit. "The sniper rifle's gone too?" Darren indicated pointing to the ground. Poonta eased his grip on Darren and lowered him slowly, grunting in pain as he bent forward. Darren put a hand on Poonta's shoulder, straightened himself, coughed and stuttered, "Mate, I want him back too. I need him here too, but he's not here. We've looked around to see if there's any sign of a struggle,

194

there is none". Chandie now spoke clearly and succinctly, "Darren, there's also no blood on the ground, explain that?" "I can't, if I could I would... Can't we just take some time to search the area a bit just in case we can find something?" Vinchi spoke up, "Not now, it's way too dark, we've just been in a fire-fight. All our nerves are rattled to breaking point, plus Poonta's not well. I suggest we regroup back at camp, reassess our immediate needs, which should be to check Poonta out, set a sentry up and get some sleep. We can resume in the morning at dawn. Well?" "I think that's sensible, come on, let's go", answered Chandie who didn't even wait for an answer, she was off. She put her arm through Poonta's and led him away, leaving Vinchi and Darren to trail behind them. Arriving back at camp not a lot was said. Each went about their respective duties and Chandie shuffled Poonta in with her. Darren and Vinchi clumsily set up the alarm system and Vinchi eventually crawled into to his tent, Darren taking first watch, this was going to be a long night.

THE BRICK ROAD...

Darren was the first one awake, he looked slightly unkempt as he surfaced from under the tarpaulin. He noticed Vinchi was readying the breakfast area as his watch was finishing. He was making coffee and had already started cooking fish caught the day before. Darren approached him and murmured indicating with his hands, "I'll be back shortly. I'm going to investigate the area where Randall fell in more detail". "You want company?" Vinchi offered genuinely. "No mate, you look after the others, they need encouragement, you're in the best position to do that, not me", Darren seemed genuinely drained as Vinchi watched him walk off. He reached the tree site which wasn't that far away from camp, then searched the base thoroughly and wandered off looking for signs of a struggle, anything that could explain this sudden, disturbing, vanishing act. By the time Darren had got back to camp breakfast was well underway. Chandie looked up at his arrival. He had the look of someone whose best friend had never said goodbye and was shattered.

Chandie walked over to greet him and hand him a coffee. "Nothing, zip, nada. Absolutely no clue where's he's gone?

196

You're right, there's no blood anywhere, but there's also no sign of a struggle. Everything's been cleaned over, that's bloody obvious, it's been reset. To a layman, it's like Randall never existed". He breathed all of this out quietly as Chandie held his arm, guiding him back to camp as he continued. "It doesn't make sense, something's just not right". Vinchi handed Darren a plate of thick fish mornay mixed with a side of root vegetables. By this time Darren had noticed all the canoes had been packed, repaired and made ready for travel. Poonta was sitting shirtless. He'd been patched up with bandages from the field kit by Vinchi, including a bespoke back brace, he was not in good condition, the Silverback was broken.

"What now?" Vinchi asked generally after breakfast was over. "We continue on, we make our way to our ground zero", Chandie chimed in confidently and steadfastly. "Whats bout Randy?" Poonta exhaled with a grunt as he moved to stand up. "If we can't find where to search next, we need a goal, Chandie's right", Darren agreed putting his hand on Chandie shoulder. Chandie touched his hand thankfully as she lifted her coffee mug to finish the brew. "Randall will make his way there if he's able to. I for one believe him", she said reassuringly, mainly for herself. "What makes you so damn sure he's not been captured, being tortured, let alone alive? After what we just went through, there's no way of knowing he's capable of even getting there in one piece", Vinchi was pointing off into the bushes and behind him downstream. "Because he made me a promise he would!" Chandie's voice was guttural as she stood up to full height towering right over Vinchi, trying to intimidate him. Vinchi didn't even flinch, he looked up at Chandie menacingly holding his ground. "Meerkat versus giraffe... The fight of the century, let's get ready to rummmble!" Darren sarcastically broke the ice by mimicking the voice of that famous ring announcer perfectly as he moved towards Chandie. "Stay outta this Darren", Vinchi snarled, pointing a finger. Staring up at Chandie he didn't miss a beat, "No, seriously what makes you so damn sure he hasn't gone off by himself to access this fucking computer-type techie thingy to work his geeky voodoey magic stuff and then split? We can't do what he was talking about. I know I can't, can you princess?" Not Vinchi's brightest moment, one of them would recount at a later date.

Chandie exploded, "Why you little yellow turd! Randall's resourceful. I have full confidence he won't let us down, he'll get back to us, he trusted me to..." The Black Widow was back. Stopping herself midsentence, she relaunched viciously, "I'm gonna fucking turn you into liquified mucus you shitty little wonton!" She then lunged at Vinchi. Poonta intercepted her just in time, putting himself right in the middle. In one physically painful, aqueous ballet movement, he lurched forward and as gracefully as he could, circumstances prevailing, lifting Chandie off her feet into the air. He placed her unceremoniously onto his right shoulder, arms and legs thrashing. Poonta took five enormous steps away from Vinchi for his safety and turned around, Chandie still in place. "Enough!" Now it was his turn to flare up. "I believes Chandie", he bellowed as he cradled Chandie's bottom so she couldn't fall. "Shes right, Randy promise me hes getting me outs too. Enough bulls shit. Wes gotta works together. Fighten betweens us ain't helpin. Ifs Randy says hes bees there, hes bees there. You not touch Chandie, you try goes through me, I bust your nog".

Poonta glared heatedly at Vinchi. Chandie had her head in her hands on Poonta's back and had stopped thrashing around. "Alright, alright, calm down, calm down Poont, I was just making a point, I over stepped, I apologise", Vinchi whispered trying his utmost to calm the situation and smooth things over. Then quietly, "Look seriously, logically, how do we know he'll be there waiting for us?" By this time Chandie had tapped on Poonta's back to let her down, the signal she wasn't going to squish Vinchi, Poonta complied. "Because he promised he would", Chandie repeated herself. Before this could start all over again Darren chimed in, cutting off Vinchi's retort, "Randall's always been there for us, we can't start second guessing now. We don't know what's going on here, that's a given. The decision's made, we move onto ground zero. We just need to take a leap of faith". On that note, agreement had been reached by all to forge ahead. There was nothing they could do about Randall's disappearance and there was now a clear objective he'd laid out before them. Gathering their composure, they shoved the canoes into the river and began their journey anew, genuinely missing their wizard, the architect of this whole odyssey. They were so busy concentrating on the journey ahead, they never noticed a Meerkat-like figure hunched over in the tall grasses, armed to the teeth, glaring after them as they disappeared around the bend.

The mood in the darkened panic room was one of unfettered anger, there had never been an incident in recorded history like this before. Never ever had there been a direct threat against 'The Family' in all of their proud genealogy. No 'Head' of the Merovingians ever had to deal with a 'Chimera'. These entities were touted as myths, legends, illusions of the mind, or simply deadly shadows that lurked in the darkness. Unfortunately, the current 'Merovingian Head' knew better, the Chimera were phantasms, the real life ghouls that actually went bump in the middle of the night. They never sought ultimate power or control themselves, this sovereignty merely used strings as a guiding force to enlighten the Council if one sought to create a monopoly up above the rest. Enlighten was a delicate turn of phrase, timid even. The truth was more terrifying as the De Medici Family found out the hard way. The Chimera's patience and vengeance could outlast everyone.

The meteoric rise of the House of De Medici began in Florence in the thirteenth century as they began to control all commerce, trade routes and banking. Through these conduits, they amassed enormous wealth and huge political power, increasing their social status through clandestine means, by circumventing protocols of the Council unable to keep them in check. At their collective height, the Family's support of the arts and humanities was made famous by becoming patrons of both Leonardo da Vinci and Galileo Galilei, evolving Florence into the cradle of the Renaissance. Soon the De Medici Family seemed to be uncontainable. The Chimera viewed what was occurring as a personal affront to the balance between the families and took action. The use of subtle shadow-manipulation, lies, deceit, persuasion and active encouragement took three agonising centuries. The De Medici Family members were so interlaced in a complexity of parochialism, that they dangerously began clinging to successes of the past, not embracing any form of forward progress. Decisions that imploded both family and fortune, were finally leading to the last De Medici Grand Duke dying without an heir, eliminating the Dynasty with him and the destruction of a magnificent legacy, including bloodlines. By consensual agreement, powers and fortune passed into the long European reign of the Hapsburg-Lorraine Family. The hard lessons learned by all the Families was never to upset the Chimeras, and never overstep your authority. Chimeras were the keepers of true balance, no matter how long it took, they kept the leaders of the New World Order in close check.

This certainly was not the additional news The Merovingian expected to hear when Santos debriefed him earlier. Santos had delivered this information in person, this news was critical it reached 'The Head" immediately. Protocol was rarely if ever broken, as his General usually communicated via com link. Only under extenuating circumstances did he ever physically speak with Santos directly. The information had come from a Vatican Swiss Guard in his employment. Over the decades of service, Santos had been solely responsible, piecing together and connecting the extremely bizarre, rare left-field answers first. It was exceptional that one operative held all the information. The missions, operations, whatever you labelled them, were all built and managed this way. This was an operative to watch. Santos was getting sloppy as this situation should have already been contained. Succession planning may just be in order soon. The pressing concern here was that if the information and documentation that had been released into the wild contained clues that could lead back to 'The Family' and a 'Chimera' could link it back to him from the shadows, it would be devastating, perhaps fatal. The Merovingian's bloodlines dated back to the fifth century where this illustrious dynasty ruled over a territory largely corresponding to ancient Gaul, as well as the Roman provinces of Raetia, Germania Superior and the southern part of Germania. As families go, certain ancestors tried their turn to have individual ambitions, increase their standings, wealth and status. The Merovingian were no different, which culminated in the Chimera's manipulating and subsequent removal of, the Merovingian kings, with the coronation of Charlemagne, the Holy Roman Emperor in the year 800AD. Merovingian wives were manipulated, as they were gifted to the Charlemagnes and Carolingians to guarantee the continuation of the Dynasty at a more acceptable level of control, thus escaping obliteration completely.

It had taken centuries to regain ground lost given that today there were family lines in both Europe and Britain such as the Plantard, Luxembourg, Montpezat and Montesquiou who were of Merovingian linage and each had been jockeying for control until now. If the Chimera knew of the modern-day agenda that the Merovingians were planning they would cease to exist, permanently just like the De Medici. This all had to stay silent. If the other families knew a Chimera had surfaced and the Merovingian bloodlines were a possible target, they'd be able to smell blood in the water. It made no sense to provide them any possible advantage. Maybe he could handle this in house and redirect pain elsewhere? His hand flashed across the surface of his desk and it flared to life, a wide large screen monitor rose up and locked in place. A moment later he was conversing directly with Santos. This time there was no single word threats, he needed to be clearly understood. "Santos, issue a second unit to assist the Mossad. I want that server farm locked down to eliminate all threats. Send another one to back up the ex-Vatican Guard, if he's uncovered what he said we need to take precautions, now!"

"Immediately Sir, consider it done. Formal report will be at two as requested", Santos channelled back in sync. The screen went black, the Merovingian opened up a second line of communication. He wasn't leaving anything to chance, time to start moving some higher-level chess pieces of his own. The encrypted communique opened to the world's most influential single sovereign state. 'The Head' was calling in a favour that was owed.

Under the lower levels of this sprawling estate Santos wasn't leaving anything to chance. He and Taigon were busily examining every angle of the information Moretti had only recently disclosed knowing he was hot on the trail. A Chimera. Both men had acknowledged that this information would shake the very foundations of 'The Family' and each had formally agreed to put their differences aside, at least for now. This not only affected 'The Merovingian' bloodline, power and wealth, it would also shake the elite tree much higher up the hierarchy if this were to get out. Unfortunately, that meant they would be expendable pawns should this all go to shit. It was best to form a precarious alliance to survive should 'The Family' and its branches not. There was no information of one working alone, at least none they could find. Information was sketchy at best regarding these myths and legends. Pieces of information extended all the way back to ancient Sumerian cultures in southern Iraq, governed by all-powerful entities around 4000BC. Their far-reaching influence continued and resounded throughout history. There was some mythology about these ghostly entities assisting in both the rise and fall of civilisations through the regions of Mongolia, Greece, Persia, Syria, Phoenicia, Egypt, Babylon, Rome, and across into India.

Seriously these were all summations, nothing had ever been thoroughly documented. What existed was either lost through the annals of time or now in private collections, fabrics would surface at times. But most tended to dismiss these shadow activities as they echoed through history as folklore and more dismissively as 'The Bogeyman' tales to scare people. There was more than enough reason now to be nervous. The way the Merovingian reacted to this news engaged both Santos and Taigons fear-glands. Mainly because both of them had no idea how an operation was run from the other side. Nor what assets would be engaged to neutralise their forces and efforts. How do you combat something that isn't supposed to exist? Sheer brute force and numbers might solve most conflicts, specifically if you're dealing with blood and bone. But if you were trying to kill a phantom, bullets, knives and conventional weapons would be like trying to kill smoke. It was now time for self-preservation as someone had kicked the vipers' nest, and, if SATAN had sent his messengers of death both Santos and Taigon weren't going to die or fall on their swords. They'd seen enough death to last them the rest of their lives and both were quite prepared to make a deal with the devil should an opportunity arise. But for now, they had a mission to run and pawns to set in motion. Orders were issued and a contingent of two fully-armed units of forty operatives were now on their way.

CHAPTER SIX

DESTINATION UNKNOWN...

Emotions of relief, regret and searing pain flooded him instantaneously as Randall winced and tried to open his eyes. The only feeling that came even remotely close to what he was experiencing now was one wild night out on a drunken bender. This particular memory resounded in fuzzy recollection. That particular night, he was awarded a bronze placard for an adrenaline alcohol-fuelled evening out and the official record still stood. More importantly there was proof. The rest was a blur, involving not a lot of clothes, friends, loud music, a police car, sirens, more alcohol, some handcuffs and a huge white stuffed rabbit with large ears and pink paws named: 'Tiberius'. He smiled to himself then hit his internal reset button. Big mistake, the other emotions took charge again and flooded back, overwhelming him. His head pounded as he had another major seizure and crashed back against the floor.

The seizures were getting worse, that plus Randall wasn't really sure where he was, but his surroundings were different. Looking through the haze, he could make out that he was in the back of some kind of All-Terrain Vehicle outfitted for serious off-roading. The vehicle was bouncing along the track it was creating so the ride was not one of luxury, a real kidney puncher. The one circumstance that was very evident was that he had been strapped down flat to stop him moving around. Returning to the pain in his head, he began having flashbacks. He recalled that he'd been talking with Darren in the tree when he was sure he saw something move across the creek. He remembered instinctively turning his head to the right after what he thought was a muzzle flash. Thank Christ he'd been wearing Darren's bulletproof cloak and hoodie as the sniper's bullet had hit him in the back of the head sending him hurtling out of the tree backwards. That's when it all went dark, from there to here was black, nothing, he'd lost approximately at best guess, maybe a whole day.

Assessing the situation, Randall was still in the clothes he'd been wearing. Strangely, he hadn't been stripped of his clothes or boots. He could actually see his weapons and cloak packed into a black payload net overhead, attached to the roof of the armour-covered ATV. Looking from side to side, there were a lot of strange-looking weapons and other equipment in more netting that lined the back cargo area roof space. There were black leather seats to either side of where he lay in the middle of the floor. In fact, the whole interior was black, everything, the designer definitely was not Van Gough.

Every so often Randall could hear the driver breathing and inhale sharply as they hit what felt like every hole, divot, meteor crater and dead tree along the way. He at least knew the driver was female, that much was evident after she exhaled, "Shit!", when the reinforced frame hit a huge bush, crushing it as the massive wheels lurched forward over it, gears and revs spinning. It was night outside but he couldn't make out much more, clarity of focus was not exactly a strong skill at this moment. He could feel every part of his body and it felt like it'd been through a wood chipper. His thoughts wandered, 'Must've hit every branch on the way down. God I hurt'. They then screeched onto what felt like road base so they'd obviously left off-road and were somewhere closer to civilisation. 'I'm alive for a reason, why? Where are we headed? Should I speak? No, let's see where we're headed first', fairly sound reasoning for someone in his condition. Randall figured he'd find out soon given that there was now tarmac under the wheels. About an hour or so later the huge ATV pulled over. Life was about to get very interesting.

Randall heard the driver get out of the ATV and move to the back of the vehicle. The armoured-back double hatch opened and the figure stood looking in at the captive quarry. "You're conscious, I heard you wince and groan with every little bump, princess. If I get you out do you think you can stand?" the female voice said, after a long pause. "I won't ask a second time. I'll just eject you and let you find out for yourself if you like? Oh, yes and please don't think about trying to overpower me. That bracelet on your wrist isn't a trinket from Cartier's. It carries twenty five watts or fifty thousand volts so your balls will shrink to the size of raisins before you hit the ground. Are we clear?" The voice sounded as if she was having one of those days. At this point Randall was just happy he could get out of the restraints, and frankly, if the figure behind the voice had wanted him dead already, they wouldn't be having this conversation. "Yes, I think I'm okay, my head's killing me though, you'll get no trouble from me". The figure leaned forward and flicked a switch. Randall could feel the floor he was lying on move. In one relatively fluid hydraulic motion, it slid out of the back doors and raised him up to a standing position, aligning his feet with the ground. It was at this point he had another seizure and thanked God he was restrained.

After returning to the land of the living, he realised he was looking into the eyes of someone he thought he knew. She had flaming copper hair, average height, muscular build and fairly nondescript features. Yet he somehow had the feeling they'd met before, he just couldn't place her. The clothing she wore seemed similar to full tactical assault gear worn by Black Ops or Special Forces. The weapon she carried was unlike anything Randall had ever seen before, it looked almost alien. Wherever she was going she was completely prepared for whatever awaited there. "We need to stop and get fuel, that's why we're here, plus I need to rest, it'll be a good place to recharge the batteries, we're not all human you know", was the statement made. Randall couldn't work out if she was trying to make light of the mood or if she was serious. He must've had an expression on his face that made him seem simple or physically stressed somehow as she added, "Name's Simmie Cruz. Yes, we've met. Let's get inside safe and we'll talk, ok? You're pretty banged up, you'll be a little unsteady for a while, but you'll be fine in a day or so. You were bloody lucky you had that cloak, very special gear. C'mon, one, two, three", she said as she unlashed the restraints helping Randall find his feet. 'Let's get you inside and I'll organise a meal, we'll talk then".

Randall was in absolutely no position to argue as he thought his head was now going to explode. He placed his left arm around her shoulder as she walked him inside the deserted fuel station. Randall noticed there were no front doors. The sliding glass doors had been smashed a while ago, along with all the looting. She then sat him down in what you could only guess was a previous staff room. After handcuffing him to the table, she looked him in the eyes, patted his shoulder and said with what sounded like genuine remorse, "Now, no running off ya hear, I'm just off to stock up some provisions and then I'll be back, play nice and we'll get along just fine". Randall had already decided he wasn't going anywhere, there was more happening here than what appeared on the surface and he for one was going to find out if it was to be to his advantage or demise. Upon Simmie's return

Randall was full of questions but remained as restrained as he possibly could without giving away any body language.

Simmie unlocked the handcuffs and by now Randall had been able to take in his surroundings. They were sitting out the back in a small room with a basic table and two chairs. There were two-way windows out here, you could see into the store section and a cashier's station. It was obvious that the old structure hadn't been deserted very long as the power and lights still worked, however the shelves, fridges and displays were almost completely ransacked. Simmie started, "We've got a bit of time so I may as well get you up to speed". She was passing out snacks plus bottled water and casually sat back with a hand on her hip, the activation switch for the bracelet was there. "Can't have you passing out on me again, now can I? Feeling ok? Yes, good. So, you were hit by a sniper's bullet, the cloak absorbed the entire impact. Beautiful secret material that one, razor thin polymer, composite technology, stops anything from knives, to grenades. A little antiquated now compared to my outfit, stage five generation". She rubbed her hand up and down her flat stomach in a seductive acrimonious fashion. Then took a slow alluring sip of

215

her bottled water like she was mimicking a blowjob. "More adaptable, flexible, shock resistant, but yours is effective nonetheless. Can only imagine what your head feels like, though. Must be like trying to concentrate on theoretical equations inside a cement mixer, near impossible. Anywho, your friend has got you involved with a nasty little organisation, The Merovingians, they're getting too big for their britches, again. Time for extinction, this time round, methinks. Orders not official yet. Can't wait for that one. We'll go into that later but that's who the sniper was from, a Russian, a nasty little arsehole". Randall hadn't spoken, he simply leaned forward chewing on his snack and drinking his water as he was now totally absorbed and concentrating on this woman he swore he knew. Simmie took this as a sign to continue, all very matter-of-fact, rattling this information off as if she'd told him this totally boring story several times before.

Simmie took a deep breath, like it was such a huge effort to do so and then launched into, "For starters, your friends are alive, maybe a little banged up, rattled and scared, but alive. They took care of Bortnik before I had a chance to. Plus I wanted to watch to see how efficient they were and what I was up against. Good crew that lot, very hardy, even if they are sloppy, noisy and leave a trail a blind, deaf-mute could follow". Simmie was constantly assessing both the storefront and Randall's reactions at the same time with her peripheral vision as she scanned around trying to nonchalantly carry on the conversation. She was sitting inside the open door to the staff room with a clear view straight into the store. Her hand was caressing the silver alien weapon attached to her left thigh, blue lights flickering. There was a audible hum being emitted from it, similar to the way a large thermonuclear reactor hums away just before the plutonium core explodes. "Your head's lucky to be in one piece and it's probably spinning at the moment. Unfortunately I can't fix that, it'll take time, I am however about to make things worse, because if I could do this on my own I would. If it was up to me I would've let you be, obliviously dysfunctional, unaware and unattended. But I've been given orders to reactivate you, because if left unchecked you're one dangerous son-of-a-bitch. Plus, I don't feel like cleaning up the trail of bodies you'd leave behind in your wake should you actually snap back to 'Normal', thinking that

217

you'd been left to rot. I hate domestic chores. Couldn't really have another historical 9/11 or US / North Korean War from another bored unattended motherfucker.

From the looks of it, Randall, you'd already started pissing off the wrong family and maybe exposed our existence. So, hence the apparent kidnap scenario you think is occurring. Suuurprise!" Randall's brain reeled, listening to this hint of sarcasm, mixed with a lackadaisical laissez faire attitude to this whole event that was unfolding. 'Reactivate, what the hell was she on about? Reactivate to what, who, how. Fucken what?' His mind felt like it was caught in free fall. It was exactly like skydiving out of a perfectly good aeroplane. All was going insanely well, perfect weather, clean jump, beautiful scenery, naked blonde co-diver with nicely shaped breasts. Only to find out that you had no parachute and the secondary chute as you opened it was where you previously repacked your clean underwear, the co-diver had vanished and the only thought vividly screaming at you is, 'I'm screwed'. The look must have been quite apparent on Randall's face as Simmie passed him a chewy caramel chocolate bar. "Sugar, you'll need it! Ok try and stay calm and I'll explain. It's all true so don't bother with any useless debates, I'm exhausted, pissed off and not in the mood. Think PMS on steroids, never ever mess with it, there's enough blood going on", was the only response to Randall's apparent dilemma. His stress levels were now rising at an alarming rate.

Keeping her voice low and sweetly melodic so as not to alarm Randall any further, Simmie began with the same calm tones. Randall felt like this was more trouble than it was worth as Simmie opened with, "Rigghht. Sounds like I'm going to need to provide a history lesson so I'll be brief. Ooooh fuck, this'll be fun." she said looking down at her feet then eyeballing Randall with, "Look, I don't like this shit any more than you, but I'm under orders. I hate orders, certainly not the kind you don't get fries with. So, you've probably heard all these conspiracy theories or a version of them. They're real, your part of them, you're quite high up, get over it, moving on. You and I used to work together two decades ago, so yes, I know you. We're extremely high-level mercenaries, genetically created with very specific skills. Genes, stem cells, genetically modified DNA, brain, bone, muscle cells cloned from multiple humans, a genetic selected bio-goo, split and recombined, all juiced together in a blender and grown in an artificial womb to create AB Reece-negative rare bloodlines. The perfect killing machines with exceptional intelligence. First World Chimeras. Front line assassins, were used, when and where required, to realign world balance to keep the families in check over the millennia. We're the phantoms in the shadows that go bump in the night". Simmie smiled at him cheekily. "We work for the Ancients, the Anunnaki. Supposedly a powerful group of deities from mythological traditions of the ancient Sumerians, Akkadians, Assyrians and Babylonians.

Mesopotamians believed they were the physical embodiment of the Gods, their knowledge was imparted to build and create civilisations. Mankind's genetics and DNA were messed with to suit their needs of control. They're the ones who created this New World Order", she trailed off, because it was at that point they both realised someone was standing in the doorway. They'd been in the store, gathered food, had walked right up to the doorway leading into the staff room and were listening to all of the explanation Simmie had detailed so far. Without flinching, showing zero emotion or breaking eye contact with Randall, she casually lifted the silver weapon and blew three wine glass size holes right through them, crutch, heart and head. Blood and organs went everywhere. She actually looked a little bored doing this as the body collapsed to the floor and she re-clipped the weapon back into place. Without missing a beat, she stared at Randall saying, "Sonic Railgun, powerful, no ammo, sweet hey, where was I? Oh yeah. When you volunteered to be a martyr and your brain became scrambled you lost all sense of your original purpose, genealogy and then dropped off grid. I've also noticed you're having seizures and convulsions. The only fact I can assume from that is your brain has had some traumatic upheaval and your newly-imbedded persona is conflicting with who you really were, are, and well, the result is a massive electrical short circuit. That part you're gonna have to deal with, as I'm no medic, you're stuck with it. But at least I can give you some background as to why the flashbacks accompany them". By this time Randall's mouth was hanging open and he was staring wide-eyed at her in utter disbelief.

"I, what?" Was the only utterance that came out. Randall's brain was screaming at him. He was staring from the dead body to

Simmie and back again. He did this a couple of times before his brain reconnected and he let loose with, "I'm a Chimera, an Assassin? Why don't I recall any of this crap? If any of this is remotely true how come I don't know and how do I know I can even trust you?" He was having a moment of déjà vu, realising he was literally starting to sound like Chandie and the conversation they'd had recently, that was scary, it sent a chill up and down his spine. "O...K... take it slow", Simmie lent forward and shuffled her seat next to Randall. "Let's start with some trust". She took out what appeared to be a remote and tapped it against the bracelet, which unlocked. She palmed the device, placed her hand on his arm and stroked it as if she'd known him intimately for years.

"Look I need your help", Simmie confided. "I need your skills and most importantly the reactivation comes with an out clause I negotiated for you. We were once a team, that's over, I now need to organise the decline of The Merovingians and you need to disappear, for good. Yes, we're genetic hybrids grown for a purpose. But look at it this way. You got to live. Organs, limbs, blood and humans are grown and cloned for body parts nowadays for the elite. You, on the other hand, were designed and utilised as a tool to bring peace to an otherwise unstable world regardless of its design. You're not just another assassin, your intelligence helped build and configure the 'The System'. You volunteered to blend in secretly to design it and did such a good job as a RED no one knows what you hid or configured some parts of 'The System' to do. The aim is for you to handover those blueprints, instructions and framework, then the payment for that is your freedom. Simply provide the coding framework back under the control of the Ancients so they can rebalance the powers of control throughout the world".

Randall had tried to keep his composure all the way through this faux-circus routine, which was now sliding way out into left field, packed lunch in hand. His initial reaction was, 'What a load of fucking shit', until his mind began racing away in the background, gnawing like a carnivore feasts on carcass bones. Suspicions began surfacing that he'd heard all of this before, but he wasn't sure where. Deluded or not, Simmie was being up front with everything, it was clear she was capable and not prepared to stuff around wasting time that could be productively used elsewhere. He decided to continue to harbour his cautious nature for now and go with the flow. If it was true she needed him, she would make a compelling asset and ally. He needed to pace. He thought best when he moved about. Standing up, he walked behind the chair and started a circuit of the staff room. Simmie leaned back into the chair and just watched him as he began his own justifications with her. "The RED part I get, that was a huge part of my life, high level finance and coding the infrastructure for 'The System', overviewing the main active and subsequent cold backup sites, storage, firewalls and encryption networks. You're right, I've coded numerous untraceable back doors to force my way inside unnoticed should my life go to shit and I needed an escape clause. Which apparently I now seem to have two, Ishita's and yours. I've still got the access cards".

Randall now waved a hand at Simmie. She nodded back silently. "But talk of Ancients, Families and cloned assassins is all a bit fuzzy, I don't have any recollection of any of that, Simmie. I don't see volunteering as something I'd do? However, should this all be real and I'm not delusional, the bottom line is this. If you're above board, and I'm not saying you're not, then I want out, to be left alone, to disappear, alive and breathing. Grant me that and I'll assist. Christ only knows why, but I feel I can trust you and I've never had that gut instinct before. Call it Faith Enough to Leap", Randall was being as brutally honest as he could. He was seriously at the point of no return now. If he was going down, why not follow someone from his past who knew him well and someone he thought he could intrinsically and instinctively trust. Simmie rose out of the chair smoothly and walked straight up to Randall. She put her arms around him and rested her head tenderly on his shoulder and hugged him intensely. "I knew you were still in there somewhere, that was our 'mission phrasing' you just used. I promise all is well and I'll provide more information as we go". She turned her head slightly and gave him an alluring kiss on the left cheek. She leant forward, tightened her hug and whispered seductively into his ear, "It'll be nice to have you back. I'm sorry", she said. "What for?" Randall asked curiously hugging her back thinking, 'This is nice'. That's when Simmie unbeknown to Randall slipped out a device, now in her left hand, up to the back of his head and jammed it onto the base of his skull. She gently whispered, "For this, my love". Randall's head felt the voltage rip through his whole nervous system. His brain was on fire. He was consciously aware of all the visions, photos, images, documents and information strobing away, thousands of them. It was as if he was downloading the entire Internet, all of it. Then everything went black, again…

IT WASN'T ME…

This was becoming a habit… Randall opened his eyes and once again his head felt like someone had been using it to knock down a skyscraper. He could physically hear his heart beating inside his head, "Fuck me!" was all that came out initially. "What the hell was that for?" he protested loudly, while looking directly at Simmie. "Just a reset. I needed to unlock the information disk imbedded in your brain so that you could once again access it. It was locked down when you went out undercover. It hasn't been active for well over two decades, you'll feel a little disorientated. I need you functioning back at full capacity". She sounded genuinely upset. "What was that last incoherent whisper I heard before I blacked out, oh, fuck my head hurts", Randall admitted, holding the back of his head. "Nothing, it was nothing. I was just saying sorry that this needed to be done. I knew it wasn't going to be pretty and ahhhh, would hurt. Can't do much about that, princess. Moving on". She seemed sincerely apologetic. "All good, just tell me what you did and what happens now", Randall mumbled, as he reached absently for the bottle of water in the middle console of the ATV. "Whoa, whoa, whoa, how the fuck did I get dressed into these clothes and the ATV?"

Randall accused pointing feverishly with both hands down at the new black outfit he was wearing and then at the road blurring beneath them. "We needed to make up time to meet up with your friends. I dressed you into something more appropriate like me and we..." She never finished that sentence. Randall exploded, "You stripped me? You're telling me you actually stripped me? Then redressed me and got me into the ATV?" Randall was sounding a little more than furious. "Well, yeah it's not like I haven't ever done this to you before". She didn't finish that sentence either. Randall erupted and his face went red, "WHAT! You couldn't just wait until I came to and debrief as we went. No, you had to strip me NAKED, dress me and put me into the ATV to save time! And NOW you're telling me you've done this BEFORE?" Simmie retaliated gently with, "Oh calm down, it's not like you've got anything I haven't seen before. You've just put on a little more padding, besides, be grateful. Everything still works". She shot him a wild, cheeky smile, winked and licked her lips, giving him a little poke while hurtling around the winding road. "We're headed towards the old media communications station your friends need access to, at least to begin with. We'll meet them on site. I've sent those Merovingian wombats off to another active city server warehouse, by the time we're done they'll have no idea what hit them", she grinned masterfully.

There was pause in the conversation as Randall glared at Simmie. "The disk in your head", Simmie espoused breaking the awkward pause, concentrating on the road ahead, "Is standard issue. All Chimeras have one. Think of it as being able to access every piece of data ever recorded just by concentrating on it, it's integrated with your neural network. The data can be uploaded and downloaded wirelessly as required. Saved my... and your arse... more than once". Randall still hadn't smiled, he was waiting for the rest, so he muttered, "And?" "Alright, alright, next steps. The gear you're wearing is the same as mine, adaptable, bulletproof fifth-generation polymer, extremely flexible. The hood's retractable and comes with standard clear-responsive electronic HUD. Waterproof from top to toe, with built-in weapons' kits and storage. The Sonic Railgun in the door is yours. They're now based off the deadly modifications you created years ago when you were bored, plus a few minor tweaks you left behind on some schematics. Its three weapons in one, short, medium and sniper range, with blasts designed and adapted off the reactor settings, including sonic bombshells. Like I said when you get bored you're bloody lethal. No wonder they wanted you back rather than causing fucking havoc. So, since you showed more intelligence than any prior Chimera, the Ancients decided they needed to imbed failsafes into 'The System' and what better way than to get one of their own to do their dirty work for them".

Simmie nonchalantly took a drink out of the bottle from the centre console to wet her throat, one hand on the wheel as they rounded the bend. What happened next was that she hit a boulder in the middle of the road which had fallen down from the

Barraiya range. The ATV seesawed sideways until Simmie wrenched the vehicle back onto four wheels after doing a three-sixty and came to a shuddering halt. The bottle somehow landed back from its mid-air flight into Randall's lap and spilled everywhere, thank God his clothing was now waterproof. "Shit! Didn't see that one. Let's pull over. I need a break and you can get some target practice in while I recount your promised history lesson". She found an open abandoned picnic area off to the side of the road and stopped. They both exited the vehicle. Randall grabbed the weapon out of the door, as did Simmie, and sat down on the picnic table. Simmie placed some food and bottled water on the table. Randall started rolling the alien weapon over in his hands inspecting every aspect of it. Simmie watched him do this and started rattling off what sounded like a mocking speech she'd done many, many times before.

"The Ancients have been around since 4000BC maybe earlier", Simmie began. "They've been controlling everything ever since. They assisted in the rise and fall of civilisations across the Millennia. This all began throughout Mongolia, Greece, Persia, Syria, Phoenicia, Egypt, Babylon and Rome, right up to the present day. Never really coming into the limelight, but controlling all the power, content enough to pull the strings, just enough, allowing a select few families to think they were running the whole show. If any of these bloodlines tried to get the upper hand they were either disseminated, dismantled, amended or eliminated to maintain balance. That's where we come in. Since the Ancients have been messing around with DNA genetic modification and cloning for eons, we were born out of necessity. The disks were inserted to provide a sense of autonomy, loyalty and trust. We have a genealogical history of being superior beings, living twice as long as a 'normal human'.

You're now defective so who knows." Simmie continued, "but we were born and took on the persona of ghostly apparitions, mythology and legends that bring death, destruction and extinction. No one knows about the Ancients, there's rumours circulating that the Chimera are them. Little do they know? Anyway, we used to work mainly through lies, manipulation, subterfuge and assassinations. Which is why these families sometimes tried to vary and increase their level of control and power by changing names, mixing bloodlines and aligning with others. The Ancients would get wind these families were retrying to rebalance power in their favour and simply send us out to rebalance the books, yet again. The De Medici Family was a prime example of the Ancients' patience, resolve and excruciating extinction over time, three whole centuries of very public floggings. Others were a lot quicker, only days really, trust me, this was just an example as a testament to the fact that 'One' the Ancients will outlive you, and 'Two' that they never forget".

Simmie stopped as if she'd been cut off mid-thought. She started to get frustrated with Randall as he was just fooling around with the weapon. She watched him acting like a teenager trying to work out which end of the condom you fire into, same expression on his face, stretching it this way, then that, then juvenilely blowing it up like a balloon. "Oh shit, just stop" She snatched the weapon out of his hands and worked him into position like she was rearranging a manikin. "This is the sight, the trigger, the safety, the sniper extension and the sonic bombshell. So point it away from me when you're playing around, ok?" Randall let loose with a sonic bombshell across the road and levelled a huge tree, smashing its base to splinters. The tree crashed sideways, crushing an old bus stop shelter as it thundered its way to the ground. After the dust and leaves started to settle, he turned to Simmie with a huge satisfied grin. "Like I said, a dangerous child, when bored. Where was I?" She waved her left hand like she was shooing him away and pointed down the roadway, hoping he wasn't going to blow them up next. "Right, so. Next. That's when these families decided they should bring about, the construction of "The System" by subversion, and manipulation of power, and keep it unknown to the Ancients. Which is where, fast forward to 2035AD, when you were at the height of your activation, having been on an extremely successful team of Chimeras, as we always worked in pairs. You volunteered to use your skills to become a RED to build access into this gargantuan, Total Information Technology System, and, allow access from outside influences undetected by the families. Your disk was shut down, your mind was remoulded. That's when I lost you, after ten years. For twenty fucking years…", she paused in quiet solemn reflection.

These last few statements were lost on Randall when he found the Sonic Whip mode. He was aiming at a tree behind them when a seizure kicked in while he was lining up his flora victim using mid-range settings. He went down quite savagely and awkwardly, almost knocking Simmie over. On the way down backwards, and, to the left, he accidentally flicked on another setting. With an almighty sudden crack from the Railgun he'd sliced three large trees next to each other at a forty five degree angle. These then subsequently began to topple directly towards them. Simmie reacted quickly, seizing Randall, and hauling him out of the way, as two of the three trees smashed the picnic table into oblivion. They dusted themselves off and checked each other over for any sign of damage. Simmie then burst out into a fit of laughter. "Christ, you're unpredictable, aren't you? Quite spontaneous seizures aren't they? How the hell did you survive in one piece for this long?" They gathered themselves, sat back against one of these deceased giant toothpicks, laughed and shook off the dirt. "At least I'm not boring, makes for interesting daily living", Randall blurted out laughing. "Oh, you were never boring, I'll grant you that. These episodes just make you more exotic, unpredictable and an enigma. You never really know what you're going to get at any time. Drink?" she offered, "Your bottles been crushed, see", she laughed, spraying Randall with water as she pointed at the bottle poking out from under the nearest piece of foliage. "Ta, don't mind if I do", Randall smirked, as he mockingly pushed her shoulder. He took a chug then handed it back to Simmie, who slowly took a sip. "Ok. So where was I? Yeah, well, you were imbedded into the Astor Family to eventually become lead programmer. These arseholes have been around forever". Simmie took another sip of water and steadied herself again.

"The current Astors are direct descendants of the Astorga family from southern Italy before the sixteen hundreds and both are descendants of Astarte or the Semiramis from Babylonian times. Some think they're connected somewhere along the line to the era of Osiris, Isis and Horus in Egypt". Simmie looked over at Randall who seemed absolutely fascinated. He could see her expressions and encouraged her, "Come on Simmie don't stop, this is giving me some perspective. I've a gnawing feeling I've missed out on a lot and that I've been living with blinkers on for years. Keep going, please". Simmie looked down and grinned. It was nice to think she had her 'friend' back again. "Right so, they have testicles, sorry tentacles, everywhere, throughout history. They seesawed up and down, being pulled back into balance by the Ancients, until the last four hundred years when it all began to bloom again. Starting with the occult and witchcraft, which was practised everywhere throughout southwest Germany, the Astors grew in stature as leaders of these cults, but the restrictions being imposed by the Roman Catholic Church in Europe and the science orders, made the social ladders difficult to penetrate. All mainly due to an inbreeding of the aristocratic stock being totally self-absorbed, and not allowing the new kids on the block to play. So they turned their attention to the New World of the Americas. This is where they established themselves as high level aristocrats, syphoning huge amounts of money overseas. With their involvement, they began investing their efforts of manipulation into the creation of the Freemasons.

There was speculation that members included Governor DeWitt Clinton, General John A. Armstrong and Benjamin Franklin, who took up the position as one of the founding fathers of the United States. So, as their control of the Americas grew, highly secured in power, wealth and stature, with the elite, and governing heads, their tentacles spread back to England. Returning as well, renowned Aristocrats, Philanthropists and business leaders were forging trade and communications with the colonies and the Queen bestowed titles of nobility on them. This is when the Freemasons extended and flourished in England, also creating the well-known but extremely secretive 'Hell Fire Club' and the rumoured inclusions of enigmas such as the aforementioned Benjamin Franklin, Sir Francis Dashwood and John Wilkes (Lord Mayor of London). This latest connection gave them direct access as Post-Master Generals allowing them to spy on all communications at the highest levels including Royalty, trade and politics. Doors closed previously to them began to open and their wealth increased alarmingly. In America they began to expand into the fur trade, and the opium narcotics trades, thereby using their contacts in the other various families to extend their attention into banking and finance throughout the world. This is when the idea of 'The System' was born. When the subterfuge, manipulation and control of the masses extended from banking to personal information, the concept of the New World

Order, under a single group of power brokers, became hugely appealing.

If the masses would embrace this with complete and utter interconnectivity like mindless drones in all aspects of their lives, then with this amount of power no one would be able to keep them in check. 'The System' would be an isolated living, uncontrollable entity in the so-called cloud, you designed multiple cold sites, backups and encrypted restrictions. Ishita and her brother created the artificial nano intelligence and neural network which is allowing 'The System' to think autonomously and make decisions based on a learning, thinking, evolving, artificial, life form. That's why you were implanted, not only to build and manipulate 'The System', but also to plant access tunnels, importation routes to upload and download failsafes and even landmines. Basically, the necessity to be able to hobble this gargantuan A.I. in favour of the Ancients. Plus, if ultimately required, the complete and final destruction sequences to take down 'The System' from within, back to the Stone Age, literally. With everything interconnected, nothing would be safe and every infrastructure would implode and be wiped clean. The families would need to start again from square one, and endure the loss of four thousand years of work, wealth, control and power. However, if it came to that, the entire Chimera force would be deployed on an extinction mission and generations of families would be erased." Simmie stopped, took a deep breath and a long drink of water. Randall had holstered the weapon by now and was totally engrossed, taking it all in.

Randall was concentrating so hard, when she stopped he had another seizure, but this time it was hugely different. Along with the excruciating pain, trembling, spasms and the standard "Ohhh fucckkkk!" from Randall, his brain's neural network connected with the implanted disk in his head. A massive information download occurred in parallel with the seizure. Not only was Randall having to deal with his standard daily shit, here was another completely unexpected scenario. Images, documents, confidential files, video footage all flashed live, it was all being uploaded wirelessly from the Ancients' Network, completely separate from 'The System'. There was no way all this amount of data could be installed on the disk, it was simply a conduit funnelling the data into a brutal, cognitive reality. Everything

Simmie had been talking about was being shown in full vivid colour. Randall was screaming and thrashing around, he'd never experienced a situation anything quite like this. The Universe was peeling away his sense of reality, one layer at a time, and tearing the flesh off his bones. At least, that's what it felt like. Simmie had a hold of Randall, she cradled him in her strong arms as firmly as she could, saying, "It's ok, Randall its ok. Come on babe, just let it wash over, don't fight it, come on, just let go, let it take control and it'll be all over soon, I promise". Her voice was shaking by now as Randall wasn't stopping, in fact he was getting a lot worse and now foaming at the mouth. "Let it go!" she screamed at him. "Randy, come back to me, please". Simmie was pleading now, almost on the verge of tears, when Randall went limp in her arms. He'd settled down and began breathing slowly and strongly. Simmie breathed a sigh of relief and held him to her tighter.

Randall slowly regained consciousness. As he opened his eyes, he realised that his head was in Simmie's lap. He was looking straight up at her face, her eyes were closed, but he could see she'd been crying. She was stroking his hair, trying to comfort him. He slowly lifted his hand upwards and stroked her cheek gently, whispering, "Nice to see someone cares about an attention seeker, been a long while since that's occurred". Randall smiled up at her as she laughed out a small stuttering cry, "Oh, thank Christ you're still here, don't fucking scare me like that". Simmie leaned in and hugged him as she blurted out, "Enough history lessons. I'll answer anything you need to know, but not yet. I'll explain the disk and its functions as we go, you're going to need to learn how to control it properly. Time we found a place to make an early evening meal, come on princess, let's make a move, no time to lounge about, we're on a mission, remember". She began to help Randall back to his feet and they moved off towards the ATV. "We'll find a place off-road and out of sight. We'll camp out, let you recharge your batteries and then attempt to catch up with your friends tomorrow at the media communications station".

CAN'T STOP NOW...

Back with Randall's rag-tag group, it'd been a long hard day's trek from where they left the canoes. By now, Darren had organised and encouraged the troop to a point that even though they seemed dysfunctional, they could react to any unpredictable situation. Tensions were so frayed that yesterday when Poonta saw a glint flashing in the long grass, he didn't hesitate, he opened fire twice with both XVR 460 Magnums. Chandie followed suit with her Glocks and Vinchi unleashed four deadly throwing blades. The coke bottle had been thoroughly killed, it never had the chance to protest its innocence. After that blunder, the rest of the day progressed relatively well. Without further incident, they made up lost time. They doggedly tried to prove to themselves that even though Randall wasn't with them, they could make this mission work. That evening, over dinner, Chandie had convinced them that Randall would get there and wouldn't break his promise.

Poonta broke up another fight with Chandie and Vinchi about accessing 'The System', but in the end it was Darren who made them see sense. He clearly positioned himself on Chandie's side, firmly stating that the only way they'd get this to work was if Randall could access the 'The System'. He went on to say that he couldn't confirm whether Randall was alive or dead, but from the way the area was left 'disguised' from where Randall disappeared, it was highly likely that he was alive and he'd find a way to meet them. It was also a given that Randall would be relying on them all to get to the target prepared and waiting for him, and, if not, they'd deal with that when the moment arose. A white lie, but it seemed to have done the trick. They'd broken camp early the following morning, each encouraging the other that tomorrow or the next day they would reach their goal, which was the media communications station up Barraiya range. Randall would be there to meet them, hopefully.

By midday they'd made their way up one third of the range. It was time to recharge, stretch sore muscles and eat to top up their energy. From the vantage spot they chose, looking down they could see parts of the winding road that led up to the station and random spots of bare patches across the heavily-treed range where undergrowth was exposed. Being this far away from the city, the distance provided a sense of perspective. Chandie was taking in the view to the right which was one of concrete and steel. A large fully-walled city rocketed skywards, a refuge of the elite, the wealthy, the Chinese and Indian plague that had outbred

243

every other race, all mixed with a smattering of Caucasian entrepreneurial arsewipe's. Anaemic colours of grey, rust, glass and brown — harbouring two million people — all surrounded by high verdigris green black walls, completely intended to keep out the scum. Around the edges sprawling out in every direction, as far as you could see, was the lower food chain.

Thousands of trees had originally been cleared to create lower multi-dwelling living, gated communities, caravan parks and now disused residential spaces. Sixteen million at last estimate and counting, a drop in the bucket of the thirty billion infecting this world. In the distance, multiple crematoriums ran twenty four seven and plumes of smoke constantly filled the air, the joys of overpopulation. There were large random green areas where Mother Nature had had enough and was trying to reclaim it all back. The humans who lived there were either too lazy or busy attempting to survive to do anything about it. Looking out to the left was Hockalugie Bay, beautiful, deep blue, and peaceful. Shame there were so many extinct species of marine creatures now, most fished into extinction, to feed the masses, and others killed off by huge desalination plants. Still there had to be a somewhere better than here! Randall obviously knew where that was and given the look on everyone's face, Chandie was hoping he was right.

Vinchi was off in the bushes taking a well-deserved leak. While everyone else had removed their packs, and began to share out the rations, he'd scrounged around the scrub and found some smooth leaves before moving off to find a nice secluded place to unload. Finding a well-positioned rock formation to perform his precarious squat-over, he began to take in his harmonious surroundings. Gently humming, to himself he starting psyching himself up with an awkward version of his favourite song. It's moments like these you tend to hope won't be pungent, noisy and at the very least uneventful. Unfortunately, that wasn't to be on this occasion. All was going well and Vinchi was in the final phase of redressing when a darkly-clothed figure walked right past him. Vinchi didn't move. Thank God he was smaller than the bush covering the rocky-like grotto, so he hadn't been seen. Whoever it was was heavily armed, he'd seen that much. They were dressed in all black in what appeared to be military spec, including boots. He was pissed as he hadn't heard them, he was better than that. This was going to be a hard one to explain to the others should they get out of this alive, especially if this turned out to be one of the hunters. Vinchi feverishly looked and listened to see if the figure was alone. Nothing. Seemed like a solo mission, at least for now. They were still a distance from the others because Vinchi was a little self conscious. Fish usually made him constipated and he wasn't going to allow Chandie the satisfaction of hearing him groan in pain. Something else for the bitch to complain about, his illusion of her as a good shag was slowly becoming a de-boner. The partner proposition scenario had started to slowly dissolve, not completely, but dissolve, nonetheless.

Snapping his thoughts back to reality, Vinchi began hunting the hunter. He took his time stealthily winding his way behind this wraith, using his height and size to his advantage. There were a few times the figure stopped, looked and listened to his environment. Vinchi took a mental note, professional training this one, not great, but it was focused. They were edging higher and closer to the group and Vinchi knew he'd have to intervene soon. Whoever this was, they figured out higher ground was the better vantage point to pick off a target with the Finnish sniper rifle they were carrying. Vinchi had calculated that they'd worked their way up behind the group by the time the wraith stopped. From this point, you could clearly see the small unwooded, but overgrown area in which the three friends were gathered. Poonta and Darren had already started munching away sitting on a large log. Chandie was the only one who seemed genuinely concerned about where Vinchi was. She could clearly be seen looking everywhere for him, anxiously pacing around the perimeter of the clearing, then turning to say something to the other two.

Time was definitely running out. Vinchi could see the sniper detaching the rifle off his back and the ammo cartridge off his belt. His mind raced through his options in haste, he'd need to be quick whatever he was going to do. He scanned the environment furiously and as the sniper began screwing the silencer into place, Vinchi launched into action. Foolishly, the sniper had positioned himself forward between two medium-sized trees now at his back. Yes, he had a clear view of his prey, but his own position was one that left him exposed, at least from behind. The torso of the second tree had split into two and the second half had grown into kind of a natural archway. 'There', Vinchi thought as the idea struck him and he launched into top gear.

Completely absorbed in concentration while aiming at his quarry, it would take the sniper three quick successive hits, all closely grouped together, to dispatch these pests and he would take biological trophies to claim his reward. He had Chandie's head lined up in his crosshairs and was just about to squeeze the trigger. The first of three lethal shots. That's when he found out fatally that the mythical 'Drop Bear' does exist. In one fluid movement Vinchi had raced up the torso of the arched tree, stopping only for a split second to realise that his left hand had landed in a huge mass of possum shit, but not enough that it stopped his momentum. Catapulting himself off the tree arch, this deadly mythical creature sprang to life, wrenching out his razor-sharp kyoketsu-shoge double-edged blade. He landed square in the middle of the sniper's shoulder blades, shoving possum shit into his mouth, then he pulled his head backwards, and, with surgical precision, slit open his throat. As they both crashed to the ground, blood spewed out everywhere and Vinchi rolled out of the way.

The trio heard the commotion off up the ridge and everyone sprang into action. Poonta and Darren took up positions behind two separate fallen logs. Chandie dashed off into the scrub behind a tree. All had their weapons out in a flash, searching everywhere for the next onslaught. Nothing happened. There was dead silence apart from the daily scrub noises and the wind. It was sparsely overcast which made shadows appear where objects shouldn't be, so no one was game to waste ammunition, unless it was absolutely necessary. The tension broke when Vinchi called out, "Don't shoot! It's Vinchi!". The bushes parted and out came their dwarf friend walking towards them, scared, bloody, and scratched up, carrying a sniper rifle. As they gathered together around their gear it was Darren who spoke first, "We're being followed, aren't we?" "I'm not entirely sure how many. This is the only one I've come across that I had to neutralise. I didn't really have a lot of time to check out or survey the rest of the area. Could be a solo as far as I know". Vinchi moved around a little stiffly. Chandie tried to at least sound sympathetic, "Are you ok? How did you know we were being followed?" She moved towards Vinchi who shifted closer to Poonta. Chandie stopped,

249

hint taken, she'd try to talk to him later about this. "I was behind a bush when I saw him go past. I was lucky not to been seen. Followed him all the way up the hill, and, as he was going to pick you lot off, I struck. Effectively I might add!" he added gruffly, as he began brushing himself off. This was all obviously added for effect. Just because he was small didn't mean he couldn't take care of business. Chandie, by this time, had rifled through one of the backpacks and pulled out the medikit, "Please let me have a look, those scratches look nasty Vinchi", "No, I'm ok", he said, "I would rather go back out and check the perimeter". He was now sounding more like a petulant child.

"Do as Chandie says", Darren growled. "Plenty of time to be a hero later. Poonta and I will do a quick search. We'll be back soon. NO DEBATE! Come on Poont, let's go", he indicated the opposite side of the clearing and Poonta moved off in that direction. Darren grabbed his weapon and moved off. Vinchi looked sheepishly at Chandie as she waved him over to a log saying as sweetly as she could, "Come on, you big baby, let me look at that gash. I promise I won't hurt you, I'm sorry about before. I don't like fighting with you. I do like you, you know, even if you think I don't" Vinchi moved as he was told, "I... It's all good. I like you too. I just get embarrassed. I try too hard I suppose. I know you're not interested in me that way". He seemed upset. Chandie put her arms around him and gave him a big hug as he sat on top of the log, "Oh Vinchi, I might not like you that way, but you do mean a great deal to me. You're my friend, a bloody good mate. I'd do anything for you and you for me, that's completely understood, you ditz. Now let me look at those scratches, you silly little prick". Darren and Poonta did a thorough search of the surrounding area. It took them a good thirty minutes to be absolutely sure that at this moment in time they were not being followed... yet. Having settled, reorganised and satisfied themselves that they were safe from harm currently, the march up the range began anew.

It was close to evening when the Death Squad found the body of the operative which Vinchi had dispatched. One of the original Hexagon of Death team came across it while tracking and following a very specific trail. The cry went up over the encrypted headset and the other two operatives in the area were informed along with their self-appointed leader. "So, they're in one piece?"

Cletus responded. "Yes, all except for having their throat slit", was the answer. "How close are you other two to me?" Cletus queried. "One hundred metres". "One Hundred and Fifty Metres", came the responses. "Meet up and we'll move onto the zone together. Is that clear", ordered Cletus. "Yes", came the corresponding echo. Cletus's voice went cold and menacing as he thought to himself, 'Time to usurp my authority here, I'm better than these arseholes'. "Check the body over of anything that's missing and inform me. You'll need to cut out the chest RFID chipset. We can't have us being traced back to our source, understood!" He snarled into the com piece. Cletus stopped and waited while he was sending a highly encrypted communique back to Santos. The message that was sent was, 'Operative down. Throat slit. Failed deactivation. Extra in GPS attendance. Bungled tracking. Prey now aware of presence. Three close together. Pursuit in progress'.

The other two operatives arrived next to Cletus, just as a loud detonation took place, followed very quickly by what seemed like a louder second one. "What the hell was that?" One operative said to Cletus, a sense of fear and horror all over his

252

face. "Preventative measures from Home, I assume. What did you think was placed in our chests when we left, simple GPS trackers? Fucking wake up. If we pull this off maybe we'll live to get them removed. I gather the dead one failed or delayed. Be glad you weren't the ones to find them". Cletus lifted his mini tablet and the black screen flared back to life, again. He read the encrypted report and replaced the tablet stating, "We've been ordered to catch up as quickly as possible. The quarry now knows someone's following, given that prize idiot gave himself away and paid the price. Problem is they've made it a lot fucking harder for us as they've taken away our prime advantage. That and the fact Home added to the noise factor. Ok, standard procedure, half a click apart, forward in a pincer move up the range. I'll take the middle, move out". "Who appointed you fucking lord, judge and jury, we don't answer to you. We're individual trackers!" One of the operatives voiced angrily.

Cletus was already pissed that the advantage of surprise had been taken away from them, he didn't need this arsehole messing with his leadership as well. "How fast can you run?" he said looking, at the other operative. "Why?" was the answer.

Cletus hadn't even waited for the operative to answer. He already raised his handgun and blew a hole through the defiant operative's head and started running in the opposite direction up the range. Behind him, two more explosions took place. 'How can I soar like an eagle when I'm surrounded by fucking turkeys', Cletus justified to himself as he soon slowed to a walk. 'More gratis and reward for me', he thought, as he stopped and took out his tablet. It flared to life as he began to type, 'Dangerous prey, landmines. Two down. In hot pursuit'. He was not going to be held back by idiots. If Home knew he was still active and operational, he'd survive, if necessary backup would be provided. He need just ask, there was more cannon fodder where those dickheads came from. He waited. As there was no detonation in his chest, he composed himself and set off up the range. Once he could assess the situation properly he'd calculate when and how much backup he needed. For all he knew he was tracking only one person.

Randall's little troop stopped in their tracks as two loud explosions rocked the air on the range. Each looked at the other with the same hurried fearful expression of 'We're being followed'. Darren yelled at the group to expedite their way forward, "Fuck, we need to get moving and find higher ground. Let's move!" All shifted up a gear, finding their second wind. If their pursuers were that close now they'd need to find a place to stand their ground. They hadn't gone more than a hundred metres up the range when the next two explosions sounded, stopping them in their tracks again, dead still. "What the fuck is going on here?" Vinchi questioned, "Why would they be setting off explosives, down range?" Poonta jumped in immediately as he lumbered ahead past Vinchi, "Eyes don'ts knows bout yous. But I ain'ts hanging round to finds out. Darren's right, we moves, now". All of them knew something was definitely wrong here. They regained their previous momentum and were off up the range as fast as they could, given the weight in their backpacks. Soon evening began to close in around the range. They were now only about three quarters of the way to their designated target. The scrub was getting way too thick to forge on. The trees and undergrowth caused the light to turn an eerie, inky black. Chandie started to hyperventilate as Darren ordered, "OK. That's it. We make our stand here. Poonta, you and Chandie take cover behind those fallen trees, the rocky part of the range to the right will give you natural protection on one side. Vinchi and I will assess how many and we'll be back". "How do you propose we see anything in this light sunshine, there's no stars let alone any moon tonight?" Vinchi protested waving his arms around. Darren was already burrowing his way through one of his packs, "Stop whinging at least it's not raining. We use these, one for each", he began handing them out, "Their high-res slimline night visors. Very high tech, the Mossad use them. I... Um borrowed them... Yeah well, so, they're just like wearing sunnies on the beach, high tech HUD, thermal and night mode switching". "Cool", Chandie said as she caught hers.

"Hey, so how are Poonta and I supposed to know you two from the hunters?" Chandie queried, as she started adjusting her set to her head. "Vinchi, catch", Darren said as he threw a pen light lanyard to him. "We'll each be carrying one of these. He flashed them on the ground in front of Chandie. There blue lights, they cast a black oval shadow with a light grey aura so they won't blind your eyes like a flashlight. You see anything else in your sights, shoot to kill and ask questions of the corpse. Ok, off you two, move, we'll handle the front lines". Poonta and Chandie grabbed the gear and shuffled their way up the range, where the dead trees were. Darren watched them go He turned to Vinchi as he was adjusting his sidearms and fitting his visor saying encouragingly, "Ok Vinch, two hundred metres apart down the outside, nice and slow. Stay low and no heroics. Use your training, if you can take them out do so, zero survivors and don't let them through to Chandie and Poonta, got it?" "A hundred each I get more then you, you Mozzie you", Vinchi wagered. "You're on my Triangular little buddy, just make sure they don't get through, deal?" Darren bet back. "Deal", Vinchi said. "Right. Let's go. See you on the other side", Darren patted Vinchi on the shoulder as he disappeared into the woods.

It was hard work for Cletus slogging up this range, he was hot and sweaty and the bush stank. The terrain was painfully uneven and it was killing his heel spurs. The rain previously had given the scrub a dank, musty rotting stench and this really wasn't his style. At least his gear was waterproof and state of the art. Urban settings and assassinations in the concrete jungle were more his style. At least then you could go out for a stiff belt afterwards he thought. Cletus stopped and pulled out his GPS briefly to check the terrain scanner. Thirty six fucken degree incline, no wonder he was puffing, but now there were these shitty little buzzing insects to deal with. He'd already decided that once this was over, and, this RFID chip was out, he was going to drown himself in as much overproof 'Jack' as his body would allow. That and a dead bovine-like animal, barbecued on a really hot grill, horns and all. He was pleased that Home-base hadn't flicked his switch. It would have been extremely plain that if this was the quarry they were after they'd know by now they were being hunted. Home-base could have just deleted him, too. But since there were a lot of unknown variables he was spared. He knew the chief was unforgiving and a psychopathic prick, killing anyone instantly, any simple error was just not tolerated. Cletus liked his work. Where else could you continue to kill and savagely interrogate people once you were discharged from any of the forces. Nowhere, that's where. That's why, when he was approached whilst on mission to butcher people for a handsome income for a privately-run organisation, he'd jumped at the chance.

It's why Cletus set up his own Missing In Action scenario, so what if six of his own company got annihilated or butchered, he was out and would be better compensated for his specific skill set. Plus the added bonus was that you got to keep trophies from this occupation. Everything from Dictator's teeth to peasants eyeball's, "Ahh the perks", he thought aloud. He started off again, certain that the informant he ruthlessly tortured gave up the right information. It was when she was begging for her life he knew he was on the right track. It didn't matter he'd peeled her skin off her back and arms in small strips like a banana with his Ontario Apache TAC-1 knife, a personal favourite. The real truth came when he started wedging the steel razor spikes under her finger nails, that did the trick. Always take your time his mentor had once advised him, make them suffer, give them some hope you'd keep them alive. He never did, these were the confinements of his profession and current role. It was good clean sadistic fun, a part-time hobby really. It was interesting to see how much punishment the human body could actually endure. He rattled the zircon earrings over a couple of times as he pocketed his mini tablet. These would be an interesting addition to his collection. Zipping up the cargo pouch on his trousers, he grinned and began moving

uphill, through what he thought was a clearer path. By luck he'd

make the top by morning and maybe catch up to his current prey.

He was going to get promoted for this. He could smell and even

feel it.

CHAPTER SEVEN

RUN RABBIT, RUN...

Darren was making his way steadily downhill between the foliage. His previous training kicked into gear, pure second nature, the sound he made seemed to blend in with the evening chorus of insects and nocturnal wildlife. He was aware of the space between them and so far Vinchi was keeping up with him. They hadn't heard or seen anything, the paths they were taking would've been chosen by any professional hunting them. They were less dense so as to keep noise to a minimum, but would also allow the hunter speed and access for physical close-quarter combat, should it be needed. They'd stopped once when they heard an unusual noise in the bushes, the tension relaxed as a satisfied randy brush scrub turkey appeared. Moving forward further down the slope, Darren thought he saw a glow towards the middle point between him and Vinchi. It was dead centre, surprisingly slowly-moving through the undergrowth, less unabated by scrub, this was unusual, sloppy. He enclosed his hand around the pen light and toggled a switch at the base.

Vinchi halted when he felt the pen light vibrate. He lifted it with his left hand and looked at it through his visor. These were seriously good pieces of kit Darren had provided him. The side of the pen held a small rectangular screen that showed grey letters visible in night mode, 'Danger'. Every muscle tensed, Vinchi huddled up to a tree and began scanning the area around him. 'Time to be cautious', he thought. Darren had obviously spotted something. Vinchi composed himself, pulled out his kyoketsu-shoge and opened the razor claws in his specialised metal glove on his left hand. He entered the meditative baleful mind set of the 'Killzone'. Now readied for anything, he moved off, blending stealthily into the noises of the bush. Darren didn't second-guess, his training and experience reminding him doing that would be fatal. What he'd seen was a low-level tablet light, no doubt. It had disappeared now and nothing showed up in night mode. From his crouched position, he stared in the general direction from which it had emanated from. He switched to thermal imaging mode and 'voila', there was definitely a person moving steadily uphill and roughly sixty metres away. Options were running out Front, middle and side rattled around when Darren decided to let them pass and come up from behind. Before working his way over diagonally and quietly through the scrub, he sent a quick message to Vinchi, 'Thermal'. That was all he could do. He hoped Vinchi received it and acted accordingly.

Cletus was angry now, he hated this pursuit. It was in an environment he loathed. God he abhorred nature, give him a bar at a five star establishment any day. That was the other perk he was keen about this job, unlimited access to business expenses. The higher up the food chain the better, or so he'd heard. If he could just get to the top of this wretched range he could settle in for the night and get some sleep. Then tomorrow assess where and how many quarry he faced. This was a predetermined requirement before he re-established contact with Home-base. He'd have to make bloody sure that this was the target that they were seeking. He certainly wasn't going to waste Santos's time on random people, he'd just wind up stone dead. Given the shit that had gone down recently, he figured whoever they'd been following were well ahead by now. He'd need to wait until he reached the top of the range to determine which way, as it was too dark to track properly tonight. He moved up roughly another hundred meters and halted. He was knackered. 'Fuck it, let's find somewhere to bunker down, tomorrow's another day', he thought, utterly exhausted.

There was nothing around but the bloody scrub and irritating insects. Unfortunately, that was the exact moment Vinchi tripped over a vine and went face down into the undergrowth, only twenty metres away from Cletus. Cletus recoiled like a cobra. Down to one knee, unsheathing his twin Beretta PX4 Storms, he unleashed six successive shots. Vinchi screamed as a bullet ripped across the outer side of his right foot, piercing his military boot. He scrambled behind a pile of rocks determined not to die tonight, cursing the fact he had fucked up, big-time. "Fuck you, you little motherfucker! You're mine now you little shit!" Cletus sprayed forth another round of six bullets. This last barrage hit Vinchi twice in the right shoulder as he was readjusting his position, ramming him backwards into the earth. 'Jesus Christ, I'm hit', Vinchi acknowledged as the breath was knocked out of him. Hitting the dirt, he instinctively rolled away and slithered over behind a tree. He came to a halt and propped himself up against the rough bark. He wasn't dead just yet, the vest he wore had absorbed the majority of the impact. His body would really feel this for days to come should he live through this encounter. Darren watched in horror from a distance. Springing into action, he closed the expanse rapidly as the Glocks he carried split the night air. A rain of bullets hammered into Cletus, starting at his feet, and rapidly moved in an upwards arc across his body, thumping him backwards physically with every strike, twenty bullets in total.

Cletus's body moved like a rag doll in a cyclone being hit by random flying debris. The black polycarbonate, cross-meshed armoured fatigues halted all but three lead vipers that struck pure flesh. Cletus dived over the log behind him in a desperate attempt to save his hide and landed in some very long grass. Landing heavily he moved like a man possessed. There were two of them and he'd been struck. 'Fuck, fuck fuck, move your arse, Cletus', was the notion racing through his scrambled skull. These dick-swallowers were going pay for catching him off guard. He ejected two normal cartridges and rapidly loaded two special payloads of explosive heads. Should he die tonight he'd take at least one of these motherfuckers to pieces with him. Leaning against the log, it was now or never, Cletus couldn't let whoever this was get the drop on him around the log. Pulling his hood into place, he stood up, rock-steady and with absolute precision lined up Darren's chest dead-centre. The pain that opened up Cletus's chest from one side to the other was excruciating. In one massive monumental swing Poonta had two-handedly almost cleaved Cletus in two, detaching most of his top torso from the rest of his body. His left forearm and hand that held the weapon dropped to the ground without being able to release its deadly volley. The look on Cletus's face was one of sheer pain and confusion, and it was all over virtually instantaneously. Poonta ducked for cover but nothing happened, there was no way he could have known he'd shattered the RFID chipset.

An unearthly silence settled over the scene. Even the native nightlife had the common sense to stay quiet. The whole area seemed to grow darker and blacker as clouds rolled overhead, an eerie chilly wind began to blow just to make matters more uncomfortable tension wise. Nerves were already frayed and partially snapped. No one knew if there were any more of these mysterious Black Armoured-clad predators of death going to jump out of the bushes. Darren stared as hard as he could in Poonta's direction as he dived away, he too had hit the dirt waiting for the explosion and body parts to start raining men. He relaxed when he saw the darkness ignite with that all-too-familiar huge white toothy grin. Making his way over, he watched Poonta rise slowly off the ground, Godzilla and the devil's five foot scythe. 'Imposing', Darren thought. "Man, I am so glad to see you, you ok?" Darren spat out as quickly as he could walking forward, "So much for following orders". "Yous welcum Darren, wheres Vinchi, he ok?" Poonta looked around genuinely concerned about his best mate. "He's hit, not far from here, come on we'll go get him", Darren halted and waved him onwards as he turned towards where he thought Vinchi had wound up. They both arrived at the tree Vinchi was propped up against within seconds of each other. "You alive, friend? What'd I say about bloody heroics?", Darren jibbed as he knelt to attend Vinchi's wounds.

Vinchi, as Alpha male as he could, whined mockingly, "I'm fine nurse, really, it's just my foot, plus my shoulder, I'll survi...ive... Oh shit! And what about you, Rambo? You give me orders, but you? Hey look I'm Dirty Harry. I'm ten foot tall and bulletproof... Fucking shit, you arsehole! That's my God-damn foot you're trying to wrench off there". "Poor baby, it's just a flesh wound, it'll need stitching and cauterising, other than that you seem ok, let's get you back to Chandie. Poont, can you carry him?" Darren gestured towards him. "Quarter fucking what?" Vinchi said shocked. "You're bleeding you dick, we need to stop it. Chandie's got the medikits and the mini flamethrowers in the backpack", Darren nonchalantly mumbled, while slowly standing up, "Poont, can you elevate our friend uphill please?" "Flamethrower... I'm not a fucken chicken!" Vinchi went white as Poonta began raising his friend up and slung him over his shoulder. "And I'm not a sack of potatoes either for Christ sake!" "Just shut up, ok. Be grateful you're still alive. Besides we're not that low on rations yet", Darren chided as they set off uphill towards Chandie.

Poonta lumbered on with Vinchi as gently as he could. "Eyes glad yous ok Vinchi. I was worried sweethart, yous me best man". "Me too Poont, me too. Let's just get my foot seen too, it's fucking killing me", Vinchi grunted and moaned, the walking jarring everything as they went. It felt like his shoulder had been dislocated from the shots to the vest, 'Way more than nine grain ammo used there', he was thinking as Poonta heaved him over the other shoulder while steadying himself. In the amount of time it took to regain ground and reconnect with Chandie, Vinchi had passed out from pain. He came too just as Darren began cauterising the wound, "Holy Fucken!" the scream echoed, as he thankfully passed out again with intense nerve pain. "He'll be fine", Darren explained to Chandie, rocking her shoulder. The decision was made to break camp for the night. Darren wasn't going to push too far, given the way Vinchi was. They'd already had a really close call and because of the incident earlier with Poonta, he wasn't risking any other lives today. Tomorrow would be another day, they'd deal with anything that came their way. That plus they were still on schedule, luck willing. Cross fingers, Randall would be there waiting for them.

The smell of camp cooking was so intense Vinchi woke up, his entire attitude oozed 'steer clear grumpy dwarf'. Snow White would've been proud of her most recognisable entourage member. He pushed aside his pain, it'd been forever since he'd smelled anything that good. His olfactory sense was in overdrive, he had to regain consciousness, there was no way he was missing out on this particular meal. Foot throbbing like a bass drum, he shoved his way up, leaning against one of the back packs for stability. He could hear the others chuckling and laughing so something was obviously funny. It was a nice change to hear that considering everything they'd been through to get to this point. A decent meal would go down a treat, whomever the chef was he'd congratulate them afterwards. The smell itself was overpowering, a combination of what he thought was satay pork belly and wok Asian stir fry vegetables. That and the distinct aroma of oyster chicken with just a hint of lime. Chandie saw him heave himself up, excused herself and moved over from the camp fire to see if he was ok. "How you feeling now, Hun?" She said with genuine concern. "Yeah, ok I guess, given my foot hurts like hell and my right shoulder feels like it has been bashed in by a silverback gorilla. I'm a tough little shit, you ain't getting rid of me that easy, my dear. Long as downstairs still works I've got hope to live for", he grinned as he tried to lighten the mood between them. "I'm sorry about before. I was a prick, forgive me?" he returned, with remorse in his voice. "Already forgotten, Hun. You hungry? Poonta been cooking up a storm", she placed a hand on his good shoulder, as she stared down at him from her kneeling position. "Damn you bet, that smells insane, I didn't know Poont could cook". Vinchi was clearly impressed and bewildered. "Yeah, apparently he grew up cooking with his Aunt as a way to spend time with her. She treated him more normally than any of the other siblings or relies did. I'll pop over and get you some, don't move I'll bring you a drink back too. You'll need all your energy to begin healing. Once we get to the top we're counting on you to get us in, remember?"

Chandie rubbed her open hand over his left cheek. "Back soon". Vinchi watched her go. She even looked good from the rear, he thought. That and she was a genuinely nice person, a rarity in today's times. He was really lucky to consider her a friend. He could hear Darren and Poonta talking, but was just unable to make out the words, his head was still hazy. Chandie was on her way back, plate full of food in one hand and a canteen of drink in the other. "Damn that smells so delicious. Poonta's a genius to be able to pull off a meal like this out here. What is it?" uttered Vinchi, just prior to hoeing into it, as Chandie handed him the plate and utensils. "Let's see... It's... um... reconstituted smoked rat, dried snake eyeballs, possum testicles and local wild herbs and flowers". The look on Vinchi face was priceless as was the first, second and third gag reflex. Chandie couldn't contain herself any longer. She lost all sensibility and seriousness. "I'm kidding, Vinch, I'm just joking, Hun... No, Darren packed some military rations before we left. Poont just did the best he could with them and local wild herbs. But word of warning, I would drink in between bites, it's a little spicy".

Chandi sat down and settled herself on one of the backpacks to watch him eat. Given the fright he'd given them, she wanted to ensure he was going to be strong enough to carry through his side of the mission. This next part was completely dependent on Vinchi getting them 'inside'. Even if the others were able to take care of any other threats, it would be pointless if they couldn't get inside the media communications station. The rest of the evening progressed rather well considering the day they'd had. Both Darren and Poonta checked in on Vinchi, chatted and planned out the tactics Vinchi would have to undertake. Darren even tried to work out an alternative approach to compensate for Vinchi's bullet wound, but Vinchi wouldn't have anything to do with it. He was stubbornly determined that he would carry out Randall's plan as stated at their original debrief, verbatim. He assured Darren he'd see it through, no matter what. 'Grumpy' was made of tough stuff and he wouldn't let down the only friends he had now. They were counting on him to see this through. Night rolled on and eventually everyone sorted themselves out for sleep. Chandie found a couple of blankets and settled in beside Vinchi to ensure he saw the night out without further incident. Soon after, their snoring blended into the surrounding bush sounds and became part of the night's melody.

Leaning over his console screen staring at the original batch dispatched, seven inactive LED's blinked back at him. Santos was seething. There were six crimson red and one amber LED. He had no idea why one had gone offline 'amber' and no matter how many times he pressed the detonate icon it wouldn't go 'RED'. The last thing he needed now was malfunctioning equipment and off grid operatives at this point. Those he could easily replace, malfunctioning equipment was another story all together. This just made his mood worse and if anyone would have interrupted him at this point he would've just simply strangled them. He was getting a taste for the hands-on approach again, leading by example, survival of the fittest and all that shit. The fact that these icons were grouped together annoyed him, something just didn't seem quite right. Taigon's chest coms vibrated and he tapped his earpiece. He knew that custom vibrate and gathered Santos was in a foul mood. What followed next confirmed his theory. "We've seven obsolete operatives now. I thought you said these arseholes were supposed to be good, best of the best, you said. Have you been monitoring point?" Santos barked into the microphone.

Not giving Taigon time to answer, he said, "Well if you had been, you would have noticed that six in-operatives are all well within an area not all that very far apart. Wouldn't common sense tell you that seems kind of suspicious? I'm not exactly impressed. 'I'M' bringing this to 'Your' attention". Taigon knew he needed to tread very carefully here, one false slip and it'd be his head on the guillotine. "Yes, I know, it's unusual to say the least. That's why I've redirected thirty ground troops back to that area. Moretti is almost on site. Once he's there I've asked for a full report and advised him to wait for reinforcements. The others are still on their way to the server farm inside the city were Mizrah is waiting. That'll give him twenty to get the job done, more than enough. So, either way, we're covered. Plus, if both turn out to be a dead end, we can reassess after they report in. Sir", he added the last part for emphasis. 'Feed the bear's ego and I might just stay alive long enough to see this through', Taigon thought trying to stay one step ahead. The earpiece went dead Taigon hit it just to make sure it was off, "Fucking arsehole. Like I'm not on top of things, what a dick". That's when he flashed the touch screen in front of him to life and at a flick of the wrist redirected twenty operatives towards Moretti and sent other communications out ensuring all was now in place. No need to let Azrael know, he had enough on his plate. The urge for coffee kicked in, this was going to be a long operation. If Moretti was right and he always was, it was about to get a whole lot worse. Had this operative really uncovered one Chimera they were going to need a shit-load more than thirty expendable bodies. Last known interaction with 'One' that had been cornered a decade ago had netted close to seventy dead in one encounter. Should there be two, since they always, always, worked in pairs, he was going to need to check the number of body bags they had in the inventory. That, including working out a plan to establish contact safely so he could extract his hide in one piece.

Screw Santos, now was not the time for loyalty, if push came to shove, it was all about self-preservation. In the humidity-controlled glass office, Santos was now accessing specific systems for information, this operation was not going to go to shit on his watch. He'd been warned by the 'Head' there were no options or excuses for failure here. Fail here and he was a dead man. Time had come, it always did playing these games at this level, for all those at the lower levels, to access your extraction options. Had one, let alone two Chimera surfaced, it had to be for a very specific reason. He had a gut feeling the 'Head' had bitten off more than he could chew and had overstepped designated boundary lines in the sand intended to maintain the balance of power. Before he made any concrete decision, he would find out exactly what and how far The Merovingian had pissed off the powers that be. It may well be that loyalties needed to be realigned, given he had no ties, now was the time to jump ship if the operation went horribly wrong. Self-preservation wasn't cowardice, it was survival of the slickest to make a deal. Knowing that, Santos went about ensuring whatever the outcome, he would extract himself out of the faeces they had inadvertently found themselves wallowing in.

PREPARATION IS KEY...

Darren had already done his security rounds after being last on watch. With everything seemingly fine now, he'd made his way back to the centre of camp and started preparing breakfast. He began to unconsciously assess their rag-tag little group. Everyone was slowly beginning to rise. Poonta was stiff and his chest was aching like crazy, he wasn't exactly the Greek Adonis Darren had come to know and admire. A tree across the chest would've killed any average man, but Poonta wasn't average, and hence, full of surprises. The key to Poonta was to never ever underestimate this man, there was a lot more deeper down that made him tick. He was exceptionally intelligent and very street savvy. Chandie looked as though she'd spent the night at an orgy, all bent over, walking uncomfortably and her hair was a matted bird's nest. She, too was an inspiration, handling everything that had been thrown her way so far with the ease and grace of a professional assassin. She'd definitely come a long way in his eyes, he'd have been glad to have had her on missions years ago, but that was another life. They were okay now hoping to get the hell out of this one and with any luck, all of them could disappear.

That's where Randall came in. Randall, an enigma wrapped up in a mystery, with a past that was completely unknown. There was something Darren just couldn't just put his finger on and it gnawed at him savagely. Randall was unlike any operatives he'd encountered before. Professionally trained, certainly, and more highly than him, yes, but he seemed to be holding back, why? There were also body language indicators that unsettled him too, unusual little signals that no normal person ever gave away. He shrugged this off, he'd already decided to have an in-depth conversation with him if they both survived this adventure. No real benefit mulling it over now, there was real planning and work ahead if they were to stick to the plan and pull it off. That left

Vinchi, a tough son-of-a-bitch who was determined to show that initial impressions of him were always wrong. He set out to prove at any cost he could do anything anyone else could do and he'd never ask anyone else to do something he could himself. They were hugely reliant on him now. Time he went over to check if Vinchi was ok, they'd need to make a move once they reached the top of the range and Vinchi would be on his own for a small time until they met up again inside. It was critical to assess that he was capable of carrying out his part of the mission.

As Chandie and Poonta settled down to eat, Darren made his way over to Vinchi, meal and drink as a peace offering for the chat ahead. "So, how's our resident hero going, reckon you're up to it today?" Darren queried, handing Vinchi breakfast. "Yeah, sleep did me the world of good. Foot's painful, but I've had a lot worse. You can cut the crap, Mozzie, I know why you're here and, yes, I'll be fine, I can do what we all need to happen. So no, you're not talking me out of it", Vinchi announced as he stared while wolfing down the food. "All good, just checking. You say you're fine so I'm not going to argue with you", Darren offered accepting Vinchi's retort. "We're relying on you to make it inside safely, Vinch. Last thing I personally want is you getting stuck along the way, fair?" There was honest concern in Darren voice. Vinchi picked up on it adding, "It's all good, friend, I'll make it. One way or another, I'll get the job done". "Good, ok. Enough then, finish up and then let's get ourselves organised. I want to get started soon. It's gonna be a big day my friend, you need to be in tip-top shape, champ". Darren started moving towards the others as his last sentence trailed off. Soon afterwards, camp was struck and they were on their way up the range in single file. The mood was good and everyone seemed keen and psyched up. They were finally getting closer to their specific goal. This mission was about to get very interesting very soon, and given what had already occurred, none of them were under any illusion that this was going to be easy. Each was going over in their minds that now was the time to lift their contribution and go hard or go home. It was everyone's 'A Game' now or friends would die. The pace quickened, and, with the attitude set, determination would get them there on time and ready for anything. They needed to all be in place by tomorrow. Nothing was openly mentioned, but all of them secretly hoped Randall would make an appearance. The last thing they needed now was to adapt the plan without their key player.

Given the travelling Randall and Simmie had done this morning, they'd actually made good time. There were no eventful incidents, no surprises or hidden assassins and no sign of surveillance satellites or drones. Simmie advised Randall that given the time they'd made up, they would be hiking the last small distance on foot. The ATV would be left in an advantageous spot to allow them all to make their escape. In the meantime, as they drove up the range Simmie started with history lesson number two. "The disk", she said, beginning slowly and methodically, "is implanted deep in the neural network path that's responsible for recall, concentration and memory retrieval. By concentrating on a specific topic, the disk assesses the data required and uploads the information accordingly. The key really is to be as accurate and concise with your thoughts about what you want to retrieve. Verbatim takes on a whole new meaning here. Initial training reinforced the use of key words so that the upload didn't overwhelm your brain intake. That's bad. The beauty of the wireless system is that nothing was retained on the disk and your brain is allowed to fluctuate normally, memory-wise. So, the old adage of 'use it or lose it' is a phrase that means so much more with this technology than you realise". "Sounds straight forward enough. Be careful, or fry your brain", Randall repeated, trying to sound like he knew what Simmie was teaching him. "Ok, so now it's your turn. Start easy, hold onto the Sonic Railgun and concentrate on it. Think about the design and how the specs are supposed to work in a combat situation. Try and use bullet points, in here", she tapped her left temple, while keeping her eyes on the road ahead. "Right, seems simple enough, don't overthink it. Let's give it a crack, shall we. Ok Randall, concentrate mate", he said out aloud to himself, as he held the Sonic Railgun in both hands. Simmie could see him really trying and encouraged, "Don't force it, just try and let it flow through you like a wave rolling onto the beach".

Randall did as he was told, he had no idea what to expect and the last consequence he wanted was to wind up hanging out the ATV window like a dog going for a drive, dribbling a mess all down the door. 'Not a good look if you're trying to impress Simmie', he thought, encouraging himself. 'Ok, here we go.

Sonic Railgun, safety, trigger, short, mid, long range, sonic bombshell, Holy Shit!' were the thoughts bouncing through Randall's head. The download he experienced was simply amazing. The smoothness of the data, the fluidity, images, video sequencing and memory retention was unlike anything he'd ever experienced. This was one hell of a piece of technology and to think it was all accessible in his head. "WOW, oh my God. This is intense. This is seriously amazing, the clarity is just breath-taking". Simmie could hear from this that Randall was impressed. "You're doing well, keep going, don't let it overwhelm you. When you think you've got enough stop concentrating", was the advice she gave him. "This works for everything I can think of?" Randall spat out excitedly, like a fat kid in candy store, looking for the next huge sugar rush.

"Easy cowboy, you're a greenhorn again. Take it slow and it will all come back to you. Just don't rush it and it'll happen. Like I said, it's saved my arse more than once", Simmie admitted, trying to settle Randall down to some sense of reality. "Yeah, well, it's a nice arse", Randall came out with. Simmie looked at him cheekily, taking her concentration off the road briefly, and then sniping back, "Just keep it all in perspective, Fabio". Simmie changed the subject, "All going well, we should be hitting ground zero by nightfall, so not much time's been lost. Just keep practising before we get there". She patted his knee and punched the accelerator. The engine roared and the ATV's G-Force slammed them back into their custom-designed leather-contoured seats. Simmie shifted gears like she was possessed, now determined to reach their target before the time the next satellite was due overhead, given what the dash indicators were presently telling her.

Moretti was getting bored waiting around. Not only was it unproductive, it was a complete waste of time. But orders were orders, and, if you wanted to increase your stature in 'The Family' you definitely followed orders. He'd seen others die for less and he simply wasn't prepared to be another statistic. So Moretti waited for reinforcements. Taigon had advised him he was in charge. The Colonel had redirected six of the original death squad in his direction and then another twenty. This meant they'd arrive together. A good-sized company, he could achieve a lot with that many operatives. As long as they followed orders he wouldn't have an issue. If he played the game right, he'd move outta the field and into Operations. This had been his goal all along, whether here or with another Family didn't matter. He'd gotten as far as he could in Rome, in the Vatican Swiss Guard, now was the next phase of his sheer ambition. Unbeknown to Santos, he'd already disabled the RFID chipset in his chest and redirected the signal back through the mini tablet he carried. This way, he could carry on knowing Santos wasn't able to detonate his chest. These pricks would learn the hard way that he was a cut above the rest of their cannon-fodder. He'd been privy to the highest secrets, including guarding the conclave in Rome. This bullshit was easy given his level of intelligence and what he'd seen take place security-wise within those sacred walls, unbeknown to the faithful. So, time to make plans for his entourage's arrival. According to his source and the information he'd extracted from a contact of Ishita's, as well as two of his reliable street 'snitches', they were up against a fiend whose presence hadn't surfaced worldwide in over a decade. Or at least that's what they'd been led to believe.

Even the Swiss Guard knew, and, the Vatican archive had these entities recorded, well back to Biblical times. Myths, legends, rumours, all accounting for the rise and fall of every major civilisation and dynasty on earth. His intuition and internal alarms were at deaf-con one and screaming at him. Death and destruction surrounded these beings, no one walked away unscathed. If the information was right, he'd definitely need a lot more men, or body bags more like it, plus any plans would need to be carried out with pin-point precision and zero errors. From the information obtained and analysis thereof, Moretti came to the conclusion that the only worthwhile target of interest for miles around was a recently-abandoned media communication station. This didn't make sense, there were more important high value targets that could do more damage and Mizrah and his crew were off to secure one of those inside the city. The only conclusion he could come to was there was more going on here than just surveillance. There had to be a huge amount of misdirection, deception and well-constructed illusions in place already. He sent for more information via a mini tablet about this particular abandoned media station. There had to be something he was missing. In any case he'd decided that would be the target on which they'd concentrate.

There was only one way for Moretti to find out and that would be to sacrifice some pawns to see what the King and Queen of Chimeras had planned. They always worked in pairs, every footnote, every rarely documented entry, every rumour embedded into folklore, every encounter tabled across the Millennia stated this. So let's kick the vipers' nest and see what we're dealing with. Serious strategy and tactics were required here, because, if a pair 'HAD' surfaced, it would be a bloodbath. Moretti wasn't prepared to go swimming anytime soon, he hadn't climbed this far up the food chain to see it lost because of one Family's selfish self-centred lunacy. If push really came to shove, and, the balance of control shifted as dramatically as he suspected it would, he'd position himself to take advantage of any situation, even if it meant abruptly jumping ship. However, that wasn't an option just yet, so he began formulating a strategy to see how many Chimeras they were dealing with, who was involved, and helping, then act he'd accordingly. This would have to be winged a bit and adaptation would be the key. He settled back and waited for the data to be uploaded…

TWO, THREE, GO...

The undergrowth and foliage was being torn to shreds. Darren and Poonta were using the devil's blades to carve a way forward through grass, flowers and vines in their path. They decimated a perfect trail for others to follow right behind them. Vinchi was still nursing his foot while Chandie acted as the rear guard. Lara Croft would've been proud, the sweaty dark maroon sports tee she wore set off her figure beautifully, shiny Glocks holstered and all, lethal, sexy archaeologist, all pointing in the right direction. Considering they all wore fully loaded backpacks, their progress was impressive. The sweat was pouring off everyone, the thick, intense scrub around them gave off a pungent foul-rotting odour. If anyone had lit a match the whole place would have gone up like a tinderbox, rapidly. In one way it was a good outcome as the cyclone had gone back out to sea and the rain had dried up. Birds, bats and wildlife scattered everywhere out of their way. By the time they reached the top of the range, they could see the media

288

communication station in the distance. Provided all went to plan, execution would be two hours away, max. They could clearly make out all the objectives Randall had planned out over a week ago and were high enough to see the whole area. No one said anything about the obvious absence of their leader, given the circumstances, Darren had zero intention of raising it. As they'd risen for breakfast just after four thirty, around dawn, the sun now indicated it was still only really about six o'clock. Gathering together, they set down their gear.

Darren began mapping out the day's objectives. "Right people, this is where it gets real". He was speaking generally to everyone as he rummaged through a sack after specific items. "These are our communications friends, mini mics fully-charged, ready to rock, selected to one frequency, they should outlast the mission, all going to plan. Right. As you can see on the map we seconded from Ishita, we're here. This is where we split up with Vinchi. Your time to shine mate, all good?", Darren sounded quite anxious but sincere. "You bet, I'll be in and have her opening her skirts before you can say free drinks". Vinchi tried to put as much confidence forward as he could, his foot was giving him real grief, but he wasn't going to let on. The frown on Chandie's face conveyed her disgust, but she countered it with, "You better be around to buy me a drink after all of this, you little prick. You owe me that at least", and, with that she gave him a big bear hug that Vinchi gladly accepted. "Ok, ok. Frivolity over with", Darren continued using his index finger and the map to verify landmarks, "Vinch, you make your way along the ridge to that point over there, to the left of the station. That's where Ishita used a maintenance hatch to get inside the sewer pipe and made her way into the cooling room two levels down underground. You'll need to go further because the next room's the hydraulics area for the front gates. That's where you're going cut through with the Thermite. Don't fuck around. That stuff burns like lava, so get back a safe distance and wait until it cools. For Christ sake, don't look at it, you'll burn out your eyes. By that time, Poonta should have breathed life back into the old girl's electrics. Once you're off, we'll all need to move on so it's all systems go. You sure you're ok, mate?" "If I'm not, you'll hear me I promise. Like you said, no heroics, fair? Besides you lot are counting on me, right, I'm not letting you down and I ain't planning on dying in a sewer pipe. Be a fucking shitty way to go".

Vinchi was now making light of the fact, as his foot was utter agony. He collected and organised all the gear he'd need. Upon leaving, he shook hands with Darren, gave Chandie a seductive smile and Poonta lifted him off the ground, like a teddy bear, and gave him a huge bear hug, "Yous bees safe ok sweethart. Me sees yous on the other side, Kay?" He then settled him softly on the ground and gave him a single-finger salute. "All good Poont, see you all inside, I'm off!" Vinchi gathered himself and walked off through the bush and didn't look back. Glancing back meant you weren't coming back and Vinchi had every intention of living through this. He believed in Randall and he was going to see 'Eden' no matter what. "What now?" Chandie looked at Darren, trying to recall Randall's plan. "We all move on to here, over there". He pointed to a valley where the range split. "You and Poonta set off downhill to the base of the station. Poonta takes out the two front guard towers 'IF' they're guarded and scales the wall there, zip lines across over the electricity grid inside, as the generator controls are in this part of the building.

"Got it, nose problems", Poonta grinned "Easy, was best electrics guy in Havna, coulds breeve life inta anyfing". Chandie looked a little bewildered again, "And I'm bait out the front gates looking like a damsel in distress right?", "Bit hard for Poonta or I to look sexy, we don't have the legs or equipment for it", Darren quipped back, indicating her breasts. "I don't know about that, looked in a mirror lately, beefcakes?" she said back with as much sarcasm as she could muster. "Funny, haha, come on sexy, you too big man, no time to waste, let's get to our objectives. Vinchi will need us there on time and on schedule. Let's move", Darren picked up his gear and walked off in the lead. A few footsteps later, he yelled back, "We'll work out the gear when we get to out next check point".

Simmie pulled into what appeared to be an old rusted-out hay shack. It looked as if it'd been here forever the way it was only just standing up. The timber frame was grey, full of termites and resembled dried-out kindling, it was so brittle. The corrugated iron roof had seen better days with major rust holes that wouldn't keep out bird spit. Randall fondly remembered Jeremy, a mate who overflowed with trivial crap that no one would use in everyday life, but what he did remember from those times was the Edible-nest swiftlet. It was a small bird ten centimetres long, weighing twelve grams, whose only defence was spitting acid at predators. Come to think of it, the whole structure looked as if a bird of that weight would definitely knock it over. Randall looked quizzically at Simmie, as if to say 'why here' and she responded, "Out of sight of the spy satellites. There's a number up there, we don't want to give away our element of surprise. Do we my dear?" "Uh... Ah no. How the hell do you know we're even being spied on?" Randall queried with a dumb look on his face. "Call it woman's intuition", she flicked back at him, "That, plus the tracker". She tapped the ATV console, then her head, "Plus, a little added assistance. All good, once you get used to it, you'll be able to tap into it too. It's all about timing, dearest". So what was your grand scheme for when your lot get here? I need to work out if I need to change it." Simmie rattled off very matter of factly, as if she was simply organising an evening dinner for friends, food check, venue check, time check, numbers check, weapons check, ammunition and body bags check. Randall gave her the complete run down, he didn't leave any details out. He figured instinctively that he could trust Simmie like no one else he knew.

There was something else going on here too, Randall couldn't quite put his finger on it, probably nothing so he dismissed it. Once he'd recounted the whole plan, Simmie responded. "Pretty good for an out-of-commission, amnesia-ridden assassin, newly-activated. One minor flaw, though. We can fix that, we might lose one or two, but given the force headed our way, that's not bad odds. Besides, I need to move you through this bloody cakewalk, so I can achieve my ultimate goal". Randall felt insulted, "I thought that was bloody good considering that's all the information we had to work with. Moreover, what the hell do you mean 'cakewalk' and about losing one or two?" Simmie cut him off by raising a fingertip to his lips. "It's all good dear, just needs a bit more finesse. Remember, you've been away from this game for two decades. I've had a little more practice at this than you. We used to be good at this, but you don't remember... yet. It'll come to you all in good time, start trying to connect with the disk about me", she winked at him, making Randall feel very unsettled, "It'll help with the long-term memories, too". "So, what changes are we talking about and how many?" Randall was past being insulted, he was now deadly serious. Simmie acknowledged him and tried to explain as rapidly as she could, "Ok, well for starters, we'll arm everyone with my arsenal, deadlier and more effective. Sonic weapons take no ammo, they're reactor-driven, use the environment and can change to automatic mode instantaneously, plus crank out thousands more hits per minute than conventional weaponry. Which by the way we'll be up against. We've got one, two, three, in total. Bugger, I thought I'd got more. Secondly, we'll need hand weapons. I'm sure I've got enough 'Greasers'. Yep, yes, I do, six in holsters. Nasty pieces these, latest production models too, direct from the Ancients' vault. I, um... kind of borrowed them. You know, act first and ask for forgiveness later".

Randall raised his eyebrow. "Don't look at me that way I've learnt from the best". Simmie poked his chest, while blaming him. "They're nasty, spitting an acid genetic compound that turns human flesh into a gooey mush. It reacts quickly, too. I mean it's wonderfully lethal, really sinister. Bit of a marvel really. One hit consumes a whole person, clothes and all in roughly three seconds. Conventional armour is useless, bulletproof or otherwise. One hit from these mothers and you're fucked. I'll be cleaning you up off the floor with a sponge. Human bodies are real cesspools. Like I said, I borrowed them, so we need to get them back before they're missed. I really, really, really don't have permission. So I could wind up a fugitive if the big boys find out, which they won't. 'Cause one, you're not going to rat on me, and two, we'll get every last one back, ok, yes, great, good, moving on". As she started regaining her breath, Randall interjected, "Ok, all points taken in. My thanks for some added assistance", he remonstrated, as he tapped his head disk. "I think you're already in deep shit". "Oh fuck, I forgot yours was an access-level above mine. Hey shit, that was quick, how'd you…?" she pouted. That's as far as she got. Randall put his finger up to her lips. "Quick learner, maybe you should remember that. I'm not sure about you, I'm just guessing at the moment. Moving on. So who and what are you planning to change. Let's get that sorted first, shall we".

Back at the Media station Vinchi had reached his ground zero. This was the access hatch that their snitch Ishita had advised was the way she entered into the facility. He reached it without too much interference, given his skill and size. The surrounding vegetation didn't pose too much of a delay along this part of the range. He scrambled over and around rocks and between fallen trees, all of various shapes and sizes. The colour palette was an interesting scale of browns, greens, yellow-black and reds. Some flowering areas were as if hammered artists were sobering up and projectile vomited everywhere, the stench matched the colour, so he moved on quickly. The undergrowth scratched him and he was beginning to detest the call of Nature mantra that tree huggers had. But he made it to where he needed to be without too much trouble, reaching it in one piece, only face-planting once. He was just glad no one was around to witness his stupidity. His foot was throbbing beyond the point of caring, his friends were relying on him. Given that reality, he was determined he wasn't going to fail. A lot of faith was riding on this information from the 'late' Ishita, and Vinchi wasn't real sure about accessing through this uninviting sewer pipe.

As Vinchi levered his way up and onto the huge pipe, he thought of Poonta. Poonta had gone to an awful lot of trouble, skilfully using resources and networks he'd developed since growing up on the streets to find this contact for Randall. He trusted Poonta's judgement, it had seen him out of many, many scraps and if he hesitated now that would be as if he didn't trust his best friend. There was no way he'd start second guessing his mate, if Poonta trusted this source and information he would, too, so now was the time to set to work. The hatchway was roughly a hundred metres away from where the pipe went into the side of the range, it's bedrock up at a slight angle. 'Drainage angle' he bemused, 'Let's hope I don't come sliding out with all the shit'. It was a metallic maintenance hatch that was large enough for him, he just needed to turn the locking wheel, lever the opening and make his way inside. He adjusted his backpack and placed his legs either side of the pipe and set to work turning the wheel. After grunting, straining, pushing and pulling for a few good minutes, Vinchi started to get a horrifying feeling that the hatch had rusted shut. He looked around anxiously and began taking in where he was sitting, knowing he was running out of time and behind schedule if he couldn't find a way to open it. The hatch wasn't rusted shut, if he'd looked harder, initially, he would have noticed it'd been welded shut. "Fuck me, you piece of shit", was

298

all that came out, "No, no, no, not now, I don't need this crap, shit, shit, shit!".

Examining the welding, Vinchi breathed a sigh of relief. The rusting and blackened discolouration provided the clue that this had been done fairly recently, as the elements and natural corrosion had already really started to affect it. Gut feel told him that no one expected this particular media station would be used again and it really was decommissioned. 'A good sign', he thought. He began digging through his backpack and sorting out what he needed. Night visor, yes: wading trunks, yes: ear coms, yes: plus he examined the Thermite Putty. 'Good man, Darren', he thought, as he noticed the amount. Darren had packed twice as much, probably more than needed, overkill really, but it also meant that Darren had thought Vinchi might screw up or get the first package wet. He set to work, this meant he didn't have to stop and figure out another plan or waste precious time. He wrapped the Thermite around the circumference of the pipe either side of the hatch, given they wouldn't be needing to come back again. Why not just cut this entire bloody section of pipe out? Once cooled, he could just simply crawl into the pipe with ease without worrying if the hatch could be closed behind him. Finishing off the putty, Vinchi added the detonators and jumped down, getting as far back within range as he could, and, pressed the handheld wireless switch as he turned away from it.

Crack, sizzle and pop. Both sets of thermite started ripping through the pipe. Vinchi looked away, closing his eyes. Darren had warned him not to stare at the flare. 'Holy shit, that's hot', he thought, referring to the radiating heat he could feel on his back being generated from the thermite flame. The light and sound it was emitting was insane. He'd never heard anything like it before. It sounded as if the gates of hell had opened and magma was bubbling to the surface, exploding as it went. He looked at the ground, once in front of his boots, and, the light that was being emitted was intense, so he closed his eyes again. He heard it before he turned. The thermite began to splutter out and then, 'Bang, Clang, Bang', the whole hatch-section of pipe crashed to the ground. 'Brilliant, plenty of room' He noticed the section between the two ends were wide enough to get him and his back pack inside, 'Yes it's dry, yeah'. He rummaged through the back pack again and started to get geared up while he waited for the steel to cool. Night visor, wading trunks, head lamp, gloves, more thermite then, "Hey, Whoa what's this?" he whispered to himself. "Oh, you're one smart cookie, Darren", Vinchi praised as he rolled over the very small head-strapped breather and oxygen tank in the palm of his hands. Small spaces, especially a sewer pipe, would not only carry fetid, putrid air, but such an enclosed space could be toxic. Surprisingly, no one had thought of this when they initially developed the plan, 'Brilliant, just brilliant', he thought, as he strapped it into place. By the time the steel had cooled, Vinchi was fully geared up and looked like he'd survived the bombs and was a nuclear holocaust survivor, exploring the wastelands, hazmat suit, goggles and all. He was pleasantly surprised that the decommissioning team had been thorough, they'd even flushed out the sewer pipe. The end point would be a lot drier than he expected. Settling himself into the entry of the pipe, he psyched himself up, turned on the head lamp and then disappeared into the inky black, like Darth Vader's satanic offspring.

Pushing their way forward, Darren, Chandie and Poonta had made good time since leaving Vinchi. Darren informed them along the way that by the time they reached their designated check points, Vinchi would already be inside and working on getting them in, too. Attitudes were tempered with a lot of anxiety, it didn't help when Chandie fell and took some skin off her shin, Darren had called her a baby, to stop whining and wasting their time. He sincerely apologised to her after his feet found solid ground, again. Poonta had raised him up by a single hand to smell the minty fresh pine leaves in the lower canopy they were passing beneath. Regaining his composure a short time later, he stopped at another check point, indicating on the map that this was where they parted company. He would make his way up to the cliff face that enclosed the back of the facility and pick off any security, sniper-fashion if required. He also espoused that that was where he'd hoped to meet up with Randal. No one spoke, so Darren did, "Look, we keep to the schedule and hope for the best.

If Randall doesn't show once inside, we can try and use the cards he gave you, Chandie, and figure something out as we go", explained Darren. "What are you talking about?" she shot back, trying to look all innocent. "Don't give that 'I'm innocent' crap, my dear. I saw Randall hand them to you prior to him going missing. I don't miss much, remember. Besides it's not a big deal. It just means we can at least have a crack at it ourselves, should the need come to pass", Darren sounded serious now. "I'm sure you're prepared for your part in all of this?" he quipped. Chandie reinforced that she knew she was to act as bait at the front gates, pointing to the trees on the map contours where she would emerge. "Yes, Hun, I know my role, I'm the sex trap and distraction while you lot take out any interference encountered". She waved her hands around through the air as dramatically as she could. This was done with emphasis so Darren was placated. Poonta then agreed he'd split off from Chandie to get a clean shot at the two front towers. He then also acknowledged that while Darren abseiled down the cliff face to clean up the top level gantries he'd raise himself up to assist him via the grappling hook. Darren saluted the two of them as he set off further up the range, "Keep to the schedule and remember timing is critical. See you soon". They watched him as he walked off, disappearing into the scrub. "Ok Hun", she said looking up at Poonta, "Let's go", she hummed sweetly as she started off with Poonta in tow.

CHAPTER EIGHT

ROCK THE SYSTEM...

Rarren had reached the spot of the range he was aiming for with time to spare and began settling himself into a perfect camouflaged sniper's spot. He started unloading the gear he'd need for this part of the mission. It reminded him of home, in Israel, on the local runs and gun ops. Adrenaline had already started pumping and his blood pressure was rising. His senses began ramping up and his nerves were on fire. The mix of granite rocks, boulders and foliage around here would give him amazing cover, providing the deception and protection he needed. Not only could he see every aspect of the media communication station towers and gantry from up here, but once finished he could make his way quickly to abseil down the cliff face to the top back gantry. He could see quite clearly from this distance and what he saw made his heart sink. There were clearly sentries of some description posted across the roofline, so it wasn't deserted after all. 'Oh well, time to test out the old skills'. Darren began thinking as he assessed where he would locate himself in his craggy nest. He'd started unpacking the sniper rifle when he heard a twig snap behind him. 'Oh shit', he thought. Turning as quickly and as effectively as he could, with no time, but to adapt, he unholstered an Eagle, pulled up his hoodie and spun around. He was ready to unleash when the hooded masked figure stepped, spun him around and held him in a strong embrace, disarming him as he buckled to his knees. He was being held close enough that he couldn't release his Bowie knife for close quarters combat. Whoever this was, they were good. Darren was mentally going through his options when the hooded wraith spoke. "Stop Darren, it's me, it's Randall!" "Really, prove it", was the direct response to this ridiculous outburst. "For Christ sake, you dick, it's me. Get serious, where's Chandie and Poonta?" the entity blurted out, as they struggled a bit further and he squeezed Darren's throat. "If you don't stop squirming, I'll squeeze and you'll pass out. You know we can't afford one down, you lazy shit. Have you been drinking again? Besides, I need you to help pinch the new solar panel Neville's acquired recently before we leave, you just volunteered to distract him".

"Oh hey, shit it is you", Darren exuded with genuine utter shock in his voice. He let his body relax. "Its fine, I'm fine, I'm all good, let go, please", Darren begged, "My knees are killing me, I'm not a priest, little boy". Randall let go slowly so as not to start this farce all over again. Darren spun around on his haunches, leant over to grab his Eagle, as Randall dropped his hoodie and lowered his slimline combat oxygen mask so Darren could recognise him. "You're alive?" Darren pointed out the obvious as he stood up. "No shit, Sherlock", Randall fired back. "How? Last time I saw you, you'd been belted out of the tree in which you were perched. Could've sworn you were dead, with a head shot. Didn't get time to check, we were under fire. Where the hell did you go?" was the confused speech Darren blurted out, as he poked his chest. "Whoa, cool gear. Where the hell have you been? Chandie's been making everyone's life a living hell since you went missing". "I took a leap of faith, my friend, and found something I'd lost a long time ago. I'll explain later. But, what about you, couldn't you at least have come looking for me, couldn't care less, right?" Randall lightly admonished. "Nice to see you spent time looking for me?". He raised an open palm

306

cutting him off. "It's ok, champ, it's a long story, one we don't have time to go into at the moment, okay. Later, I promise, keep the faith friend. In the meantime, I have a present for you to savour. Pack up that archaic piece of crap".

Randall pointed to the sniper's rifle that was lying on the ground. Darren raised an eyebrow, but knelt to pack away the rifle. Once he was finished, Randall unclipped a Sonic Railgun and handed it to him warning, "Be careful, she bites. I'll give you a quick rundown and then we can get started". "Cool, very alien, hums like, ah... Abducted, were we? Anal probe and all that?" Darren joked, his mind melting away with sarcasm. Randall was a little abrupt as he brought Darren's attention back to reality, "Almost, I'm still trying to work that one all out. But why don't we go over the Railgun quickly so you don't kill yourself and me in the process? We have business to attend to, right? We'll catch up as we go". Three quick minutes later, the look on Darren's face was like a kid who'd been told he'd won an entire candy factory. His previous weapons training kicked in as he flicked in and out of the different modes, testing the scope and taking in everything that Randall elaborated on. "Cool", Darren said, excitedly. Putting his hand on Randall's shoulder, he said in a low voice, "I'm glad you're back, mate, the others will be too. Shall we get to work. We've got some cleaning up to do down there to keep the others safe. Come on, pick out a nest and I'll show you".

Chandie had watched Poonta move off and vanish into the thick bush to locate and take up his position. Timing was going to be hugely important here and Poonta's timings would all depend on how well she did her role. She forged her way across the uneven ground, soon she'd gear up and take on the role of 'damsel in distress', combined with local porn star. Making an approximation, Chandie halted and began organising herself. In this role, she would be slightly more vulnerable and be enormously dependent on the guys to keep her safe. She took a deep breath and dressed. By the time she was finished, she had torn her maroon top into a low-slung version, removed her bra and cut her jeans to became ratty-ended short shorts. The rest of her gear was packed into the backpack arranged ready for access once she was inside. She clipped her Glocks onto the back of her hips and covered these up with a wild floral half-skirt, opened at the front. She tossed her hair as she thought, 'Pure sex appeal'. Or at least she hoped it would be, as she clipped her ear coms into place, thinking, 'This really needs to work'. Failing any kind of seduction, she needed to ensure she could fight back. That's when she heard right behind her right ear, "What, no makeup?" If she could've jumped out of her skin she would, she didn't even hear whoever this was sneak up on her. Spinning around, she tried to pull out her Glock as she readied herself for the onslaught. It was all a blur and happened so fast she had no chance of getting off a shot, let alone dealing a defensive blow.

Before she realised it Chandie had her feet knocked out from underneath her and she was on her stomach, one arm pinned across her back and something pushing into the base of her skull. "I'm a friend of Randall's, honey. Our beau's alive, so stop squirming. I have no intention of hurting you. In fact, I promised our boy I'd play nice. I wanted to see for myself what I was up against". Chandie struggled a bit more, testing the grip and limits that held her, while trying to be seen as an act of aggression. "Utt tut tut, girlfriend. Take it easy honey. If I wanted you dead, you wouldn't have even known I was here. I'm here to help you lot stay alive. Like I said, Randy beau's alive. So play nice, calm down and I might just let you eye him off again. We're running out of time, too, so choose wisely. The last complication I need is female emotional baggage slowing me down and I've been doing this shit for decades, with a higher kill rate than him". Chandie stopped struggling, still face down, "Ok, so who the hell are you? You can let go now. If you're really here to help, let me get to my feet". She went still as she felt the other lifting off her back.

Rolling over slowly onto her back, Chandie took in her adversary, looking her over, assessing the entire package. 'Mmmm, copper hair, striking green eyes, slender face, muscular frame, good sized breasts, thin legs and high hips', this woman was the whole package, including weaponry that wasn't mainstream. "How do you know Randall and that he's alive?" Chandie's wasn't going to give her an inch, she would make her work for it. "Because I kidnapped him and nursed him back to health when you lot left him for dead. I'm a very old acquaintance, so I know him 'very well'. Name's Simmie, I gather you're Candy?" Simmie held out a hand to help her up. Chandie disregarded Simmie's hand, getting herself up, "That's Chandie, now back off me, so we can have a proper, civilised conversation", Chandie spat back. She was having none of this one up-woman-ship shit, as they both found a piece of the forest to sit back against. Propped against a log and a rock, the Alphas faced off. 'This'll be interesting', Chandie thought as she started with, "So Randall's ok? He's not hurt? Who are you? And why are you here?" Simmie repositioned herself so her body language wasn't overly threatening, but still exuded she was in control. "Randy's fine, he just took a knock to the head. Baby's had a headache for a few days while we re-bonded. I've kept him safe, Candy. He's been doing a little soul-searching lately, but our boy's back and ok. I'm a very good long-life partner, Randy's known me for years and trusts me. Name's Simmie. I decided my boy needed help to get him back on track and I needed his expertise, shall we say, so we...", Simmie paused for effect, "connected again". "If you think that's an explanation by any fucking standard, try again. Plus stop the mind games or I'll slam you into next week. So are you that ex-bitch of his? Because, if you are..." Chandie was interrupted as Simmie spoke over her. "Look, we can get all lovey-dovey later. Right now, all you need to know is to be grateful I'm on your side, Randy's alive and well. I simply need a favour from him and in return I've made a lifetime deal with him. So, God no, I'm not his ex. If I ever go out of my way to find that bitch, which I might still do yet as a freebie, I'll snuff her fucking lights out for what she did. I've been around in the background for a long, long time, Randy just got a little lost a while back and didn't return home. So I simply figured I needed to reintroduce myself, jog a few brain cells, who knows what'll rise up out of it?"

"Right, so the plan is to distract the guards in the towers. I'm assuming from the get up?". Simmie was being a little condescending, "Tell you what, I'll go find your other huge silver-backed gorilla and we'll provide cover support between the two of us, while you play loosie-goosie, shall I?" "Look we don't have time to waste on this shit, if you're here to help fine, just don't get in the way, or fuck it up. If you're here to assist Randall, then help don't piss about thinking you're calling the shots. He needs all the support his friends can deal out and one more th..." Chandie was cut off again, as Simmie spoke, "It's fine, Candy, I'm not here to cause trouble. I have my own agenda, ok. I help you, you help me, simple. Depending on the outcome means

312

whether you're rid of me. Besides, with two powerful women like us, they can't miss, right?" Simmie sounded now like she wanted a truce. Chandie wasn't fully convinced, however, they could mess around all day like this and get nowhere. "Fine, ok. We need to get moving if Randall's here. Vinchi's probably already inside by now, so we need to move. You go find Poonta. He's a nice guy, so be gentle", she explained, trying to guide the conversation along to its conclusion. "Alright, point taken. I'll be kind. But here add this to your arsenal. Consider it a favour from Randy. Just point and click at the target, be careful as self-inflicted wounds are fatal. See you soon, girlfriend". Simmie rounded out her statement by handing Chandie the Greaser...

Scanning the gantries and towers, Randall could see five sentries, four in the towers and one walking the perimeter. "Odd, I thought this was a decommissioned media station", he queried of Darren. "Me too, obviously there's more going on here than we realise, my friend", Darren murmured back, "Appears Ishita didn't cover all bases. Let's hope the others aren't running into interference as well. Anyway, you ready to rock the system?" Darren invited settling into place and lining up his new-found toy.

"Yes, no, hang on, not just yet. One more question before we start this Darren. How are Chandie and Vinchi handling the loss of Poonta? What about Vinchi? Poonta was his best mate so he must be gutted. Come to think of it, I haven't stopped to consider it until just now, I'm not real sure how I feel about losing a good mate", Randall poured out, as he sat down heavily against a rocky overhang entombed by a strangler fig. "He's alive Randall, maybe not one hundred percent, but he's alive and functioning. That tree would've killed you or me. No, don't ask, even I don't know how he survived, but he and Chandie are down there", Darren pointed to the front of the media station. "We're waiting for them to start the distraction, before we unleash fire on the upper levels. Vinchi's already on his way inside". "Well that's a good start. I'm relieved to hear that the big man's A-okay, that was one hell of a hit he took. Um... yeah well, given that I didn't know he was still alive, I kind of sent Chandie some support", Randall confessed in a low voice. "Say what now? Who? I hope it's someone we can trust".

Darren put his Railgun butt on the ground, leaned it against his left hip and stared at Randall. Given the look, Randall tried his best to justify what happened, "I... ran into a blast from my past, an old friend of mine. We used to work together years ago. She was the one who dragged me away to ensure I lived through that encounter after I passed out". Darren's mouth dropped as he came back with, "SHE... Oww, Chandie will be pissed. Fuck, you're in deeeeep shit, my friend. You do know Chandie, if given the opportunity, would be all over you like white on rice", Darren jibbed and shoved Randall's shoulder. He took one look at Randall and read all he needed with his body language. "Holy shit, you two?" Darren pointed down to the roadway and back to Randall, "Fuck, I'm slow. I thought I was all over the caravan park nocturnal activities. Missed that one. So what about the new one on the scene?" was the next jib. Reading Randall's body language again, Darren chided, "Oh, you're a fucking dead man, better you then me friend! You've got major female problems. You are sooo screwed", Darren sniggered softly, desperately trying not to laugh out loud and give away their position. That was the exact moment when the right front sentry tower exploded in a shower of bricks, mortar and tiles. It was as if someone had used the Mother Of All Bombs. Not only was the whole left top sentry floor gone, the entire roof was missing, too, and so was half the tower. "Christ", Darren jumped as did Randall. "I assume that's your support team?" Darren pointed in the direction of falling debris. "Oh this is going to be priceless. Come on mate, I think we're needed before they can get a signal out". Darren lined up the communications tower array and let fly a series of automatic sonic long range blasts, "Shit, this is a brilliant weapon". Randall by this time had taken out the two back tower sentries and the top level gantry figure. Three fluid, accurate shots, head, heart, and the last one slightly difficult as the guard was halfway diving for cover when the second front tower erupted. Bricks and tiles ruptured his way, just as he was about to seek cover, making him drastically change direction. He came straight into Randall's sights, allowing his brains to be smeared all over the concrete gantry. "Ok Darren, let's make a move. We need to get down there and fast. That was not as quiet as I would have liked. I'm going to kill Simmie. This was supposed to be infiltration by stealth, not hello, we're fucking here, look at what we did".

Randall had already holstered the Sonic Railgun onto his hip and was bolting for the abseil point. Darren collected his thoughts, hurriedly packed the equipment into his back pack and rocketed off after Randall. By the time he'd reached the section of range they had to bolt into, Randall had already set up his line and started on Darren's. All Darren could hear was, "Wait until I get my hands on her, she's screwed everything up. I'm going to nail her to the wall". Darren couldn't help himself, "So that's her name, Simmie, nice. If you're going to nail her, don't let Chandie find out, could be a rather awkward situation". The laughter and sniggering was not helping. "Shut up, you're not exactly helping the situation. Hook up! I need to get inside and moving, time is not on our side now", Randall spat, absolutely fuming. Darren swore he could see Randall's blood raging and the adrenaline racing through his system. Everything had just become deadly serious all of a sudden. They launched off together, two black glider possums hurtling towards the top level gantry into the complete unknown. It was at this point Darren only just realised he had ear coms in place and started calling for Poonta or Chandie to ask them what the fuck was going on?

Vinchi heard the explosions from two levels down and wondered what the hell had gone wrong. No point getting stressed at this stage, he told himself, he had a job to do. There was really no point getting distracted until you could do something about it. He'd had enough trouble getting inside already. His bandaged foot had got stuck in a drain offshoot and he'd been delayed getting to the generator room. Surviving that and in distressing agony, he'd pushed onwards setting the thermite putty to cut through into the generator room. That's when he wound up being slightly singed, right after he flicked the detonator switch. The combination of burning thermite and methane gas build up wasn't exactly what he expected. His whole head tingled now with having lost all the hair off his exposed body parts and his skin surface resembled deep fried, crispy chicken. That and the fact he now had no eyebrows. But he was okay, just tender, he'd deal with Poonta and the other's joking later. Tearing out the large hatch section prior to entry had saved him, allowing the gas built up inside the pipe to seep out just enough, an educational tutorial and trivial fact he'd never forget. So even though the explosions rattled him slightly, given what he'd been through, he would soldier on. He was out of the pipe and gearing up with the weaponry and kit he needed next. They'd be going out this way, he made up his mind to let Randall know that the pipe was large enough to accommodate them all, even Poonta, at a squeeze.

Vinchi was now fully armed with a pair of silenced Glocks and a compliment of razor-sharp throwing knives that crisscrossed his chest. He shouldered the backpack and started searching for the generator controls. It wasn't long before he located the operations panel. The thought that nagged him was that he had expected to have emerged into complete darkness, this was supposed to be a decommissioned media station. Maybe Poonta had been able to get the power started sooner than expected. But having experienced these gut reactions before, he unholstered a companion, just in case. That's when he activated his ear coms and tried to contact Darren. Problem was all he got back was an enormous amount of static. Undeterred, the best course of action was usually the one option that was blatantly obvious. Pull the switch to the front gates. Everything seemed to be in order so why not just do it, he could then make his way upstairs to meet the others at the loading dock. That's when a voice behind him bellowed, "Shéi tā mā de nǐ shì zhūrú?" He froze, recognising a female Chinese accent and he did the best he could returning the accent, "Maintenance, you lot called for a sparky remember?" He didn't turn around, holding his hand gun downwards in the centre of his body. The voice responded with, "Zhuǎnguò shēn lái gěi wǒ kàn nǐ de bàozhǐ". Vinchi moved in accordance with the deception, "Papers, yes of course. They're in my pocket hang on. Here they are". As smoothly and as gracefully as he could without arousing suspicion, he whirled around and let fly with weapons in both hands steadily and accurately giving off three silenced volleys, right into her forehead. "I'll give you fucking midget", he spat as she slumped to the floor. 'Great, we've got company', was the rapid thought as he hit the gate switch. "Let's get this party started", he mumbled out loud as he left the generator room in search of a way to get the loading dock open. "It's been too long, let's go have some fun" He loaded both chambers and marched down the corridor outfitted in an urban ghillie suit, Teddy Bear, predator elite.

Chandie had made her way out into the open and began walking along the tarmac road that led to the front gates. She readjusted her assets and made sure that she could reach her metal vipers and the new toy. As she got closer to the towers of the media communication station she commenced her Academy Award performance of local lost drunken whore in distress, seeking her white knight. She passed the densely-packed scrub and undergrowth where Poonta would've been in the trees near the road well within view of the towers. Knowing he now had backup gave her a feeling of reassurance, however there was going to be one hell of a showdown once this was over. Randall had some explaining to do, to all of them. But 'Simmie' would be right in her firing line! If she pissed her off again it wasn't going to be pretty and fucking how. But now was not the time or place for petty crap, there was an operation underway and everyone's lives were on the line. It was now early morning and the heat was rising off the bush, the stench of rain from the previous days assaulted every sense. It started playing havoc with her hay fever, 'Oh Christ, not now!' She was walking up the road leading directly to the front gates, her swaying mimicked a night out on the grog and one hell of a hangover. She casually veered towards the left tower, noting that both were actually occupied. 'Bugger, wasn't expecting that, put on a good show girl, give it everything', was the internal encouragement racing along with her heart beat. 'The boys will take care of the rest', she thought. The tower and the rest of the station was really in a state of disrepair, it had been neglected for years. No wonder it had been decommissioned. Still the thought racing through Chandie's head, was why in God's name was it occupied with guards now? It just didn't make sense, at least it didn't to her, there was more going on here than they were led to believe. Did Ishita set them up or were there other forces at work here?

Stopping just before the left tower, Chandi backed up far enough so that she could see the guard's face and look him in the eyes. Brushing her hands over her breasts, she straightened herself up to the point that her left breast was exposed, she called up to them, as slurred as she could without hamming it up totally, "Can you help a lady out, love?" The male guard thought Christmas had come early this year, he leaned over the safety railing and stared straight at her bare nipple, responding with, "You lost or something? This is private property". "Yeah, lovey, me car's outta gas and I had ta stop befar getting here. So hadda

322

walk to find a honey to help me. Can you help honey?" oozed Chandie, with all the charm, sexuality and wonky body language of a seductive feline on heat. "You're not supposed to be here, madam. You need to turn around and go", the guard said as slowly as he could, still ogling off her breast, as Chandie began playing with the other one, teasingly. "Awww, come on honey. I just need some gas and a jump. I'll make it worth ya while", she said blowing him a kiss and swirling her right index finger under her right nipple. The guard was touching his ear coms with his left hand and replied, "Look, I'm really sorry, I need to ask you to leave and go back the way you came". It was at that point Simmie had seen enough of all this bullshit and walked out of the bushes in all her glory and simply let fly with an overly excessive blast. Bit of an overkill really, but she'd made her point. The last thing the guard ever saw was the Sonic Blast rippling its way through the air and as a last comforting action stared straight back at this wonderfully formed, beautifully-sized set of breasts. The next moment bricks, roof, metal, concrete and mortar began raining down around Chandie, who was now running for her life.

Seconds later, the next tower exploded in the same fashion, dust debris and body parts flew everywhere. Poonta came racing out of the bushes to help Chandie away to safety, grabbing her right arm, moving her just as a mammoth chunk of brickwork shattered on the ground next to them. Gathering her composure and straightening herself up she turned on Simmie, "ARE YOU FUCKING SHITTING ME! Why the hell would you do that, we're trying to get in here 'Undetected!'". Unfazed, Simmie shot back, "Yes, I need to get inside now, not dry-hump my way in, Candy. There's other agendas going on here and I don't waste time, period. Oh look, the gates are opening, you coming, Barbie". Chandie saw red. Simmie had already begun walking off, but Chandie was going to tear her head off, enough was enough. She started after her determined to flatten this bitch out, when Poonta intervened by grabbing Chandie around her waist. He looked her straight in the eyes and uttered, "Not now sweethart, waits a bit. Nile help, but nots now. We needs to sees if Randall's here and if Vinchi ok. Later, settle, ok?" Chandie shook herself out of Poonta's grip, straightened herself up, settled her anger down, grabbed her back pack, readjusted her weapons and

324

patted Poonta on the hip. "I'm fine. This bitch can wait. Let's get inside and sort out this fucking catastrophe". Chandie moved in the direction of the front gates and Poonta lumbered behind her. He'd make sure she was safe, she was his friend. Randall's acquaintance had been very convincing, but she was still a way off to prove herself, yet.

ADAPT OR DIE....

Randall was detaching himself and suiting up just as Darren fumbled the last few feet and got the line so badly twisted he had to cut himself loose. He swung wildly in the air like an overweight piñata briefly before he was able to get out his Bowie knife. After all, they weren't going to be using the ropes or equipment again, or at least that's what Darren hoped. Thumping heavily onto the concrete gantry, he looked up at Randall whose face resembled Darren's younger sister when she was six and he'd been making sandwiches on orders from his grandmother. Instead of putting the meat and relish evenly on both, he'd kept all the meat for himself, putting all the relish on hers, he hated relish. The look was the same, 'Ahh, fond memories', he reminisced. "What? We're down in one piece aren't we?" Darren mused. "Stop dicking around will you. We need to get to the loading dock. God knows how many or who's inside at this point! Were you able to contact Chandie or Poonta yet?" Randall grunted this out, trying to ensure Darren knew this was no time to stuff around. "No, not yet too much static, not sure why, could be a jamming signal. Nothing seems to be working". He rolled the mini tablet over in his hands. "It's got power Randall, but it's just not working. Only ever seen this when a jammers in the area. I don't use shit gear, you should know that". "Simmie!" Randall spat, "She hasn't been totally up front with what's going on here". "Are they ever? Like, c'mon Randall. I mean have you ever known a female to be honest about anything?"

Darren started spruiking on as he was gearing up and organising his equipment, "Dishonest, manipulative, use sex as a weapon. I mean take away the makeup, the curves, the breasts, the supple skin and the well, you know", he was salivating by now as he gestured down at his groin. "Stay single, I say. No harm in self service. Saves all the fucking hassles and grief, I say.

Plus, you fork out less dosh". Randall just glared at him, "Have you quite finished? You're beginning to sound like Chandie or Simmie for that matter, on a bad day". Darren chuckled. "Oh testy, aren't we. We are stuffed like the Christmas goose aren't we! Well better you than me, I say. You can deal with all that Alpha female shit. Just be prepared for the bomb to go off sooner rather than later, mate, with those two". Randall didn't hang around for Darren to start up again. It was unbearable when he was sober, all that deep and meaningful crap, espoused with a side dish of emotions and feelings. Once they were out of trouble and this was all over, he was going to make bloody sure Darren was hungover for a month just to get some peace, quiet and relief. Walking away as fast as he could, he made his way around the back gantry looking for an entry way inside the opposite tower. Locating the door, he walked down stairs. No use looking back, he could hear Darren behind him. He just wasn't in the mood right now for any kind of lecture. Making his way down, he began having another seizure, stupidly he had also started thinking of the communication station and the combination of muscle spasms, the exuded expletives and the data download occurring in his head all at once was overwhelming. He grabbed for the railing and missed, hitting the concrete stairs hard. He bounced down about eight steps and came to an abrupt halt, sat and waited for his head to ease.

"Fuck me, they're getting worse mate", Randall groaned as Darren came up next to him to help steady his frame against the wall. "Christ, you're an attention seeker aren't you? You simply have to be the life of the party. Can't be content with just being the good quiet geek, you've gotta be the loud, obnoxious jock. You ok, Randy?" He looked up at Darren who had genuine concern written all over his face. "Yes, yes, I'm fine. I'm just dealing with a lot of shit at the moment", he spewed back at Darren, "God I hate this crap. Just once I'd like it to skip a day". They waited until Randall could stand and moved off again. Soon after they reached the bottom of the stairs and were confronted by a large fire door. Knowing Darren was directly behind him, Randall hit the switch and walked straight into the adjoining room. They'd both taken about five steps into the room when they realised this must've been a studio at one point with a temporary staff room attached to one side. There was old video equipment and recording consoles, a sound room, mixing board, dust everywhere and large black screens. Curiously, the lights were on. "Either someone forgot to turn the power off or this area of the station is still active", Randall whispered back over his shoulder as he kept moving forward, "Come on, follow me". They wound their way down some corridors and outside into the sunlight. The glare was bright and they needed to allow their eyes to adjust. Darren had no idea where they were, by now he was furiously searching trying to recognise any kind of landmark. Randall just kept moving, he obviously knew where he was going, so Darren raced along with him. They slipped through an area where the newly-constructed electricity grid had been erected. It was already humming away and there was what appeared to be a storage room. They hadn't run into a soul yet and being on edge didn't help the nerves any. Finally, they turned a corner, ran straight into the loading dock and arrived right at the same time as Poonta, Chandie and Simmie.

The ex-Vatican Guard Moretti, had been going over the plan in his head for about the tenth time when the first of the operatives started emerging out of the scrub. It was hot, everyone was perspiring and all were carrying small packs. For most of them, it had been a long hard slog, it was an hour since the last update from home base and Moretti was getting angrier by the minute. He'd lost good time because he had to wait surrounded by insects buzzing, plus the stench of the scrub, grass and rotting foliage didn't ease his condition. In fact it made his attitude a whole lot worse. As a result he'd already decided that some of these 'operatives' would be cannon fodder to test the limitations and strength of their adversary. Home base could always find more where those came from. He could, and did however, have a plan formulated for an assault on the media station. As the operatives started filing in there were two loud rumblings in the distance, his gut feeling was that they would be seeing action very soon. It reinforced that they could at least be on the right track. Once the full complement had arrived and started milling about, he stood up on a rotting log above the rest, looked down and bellowed the orders. "Alright, come together, move. We're about to assault an old abandoned media station. The quarry is believed to be inside. We are to eradicate everything with extreme prejudice, clean slate and retrieve blueprints". He split the company into four distinct groups, "Group one. You're the smallest, so abseil down the cliff and clear a path so that we know the top levels are secure. Groups two and three approach from the left and right flanks leaving two behind to clean up any escapees, blow through the walls and sweep inside making your way down level by level. Group four with me up the centre front gates, across the courtyard and into the loading docks. We'll then sweep through to the lower levels also. Like I said clean slate operation, nothing gets out alive. Once clear and the package is secure, we're to level the site. Right. Move out. Double time". The fully-armed contingent split into their various groups and marched off up the range.

Unexpectedly, according to Randell's plan, the five of them stopped abruptly in the centre of the loading dock not far from the ladder leading up to the rusted back platform. Each took turns looking and locking eyes with each other in recognition that all were still okay. No one spoke until Chandie broke the awkward silence, "So where the hell have you been?" she blurted out, while pointing and accusing Randall, "Picking up bloody hitchhikers from what I can see. Well?" Randall had the feeling no matter how he answered this loaded question it was going to blow up in his face. So very quietly, he responded hurtfully, and mustered all the body language he could to assist, "Healing, I'm still not a hundred percent. I was fortunate Simmie was on hand to extract me given the excitement and drama that unfolded for you. I heard it was intense. I'm pleased you're safe, though. You look, um, stunning!" Darren by this point was looking at his feet, thinking, 'Nice recovery, just don't overdo it, mate'. Chandie briefly softened, but added a sting for Simmie, "I do, don't I? Thank you! So where does Bambie come from?" "Yes you do". Randall flashed a sheepish smile, ignored the rest, then turned to Poonta to shake his hand, "Hey mate, I saw you take one hell of a hit, you ok?" Poonta nodded. Turning back to Chandie, he hardened slightly, "She's an old friend", adding emphasis to the word friend, "But for once I'm pleased she was there to help. I wouldn't be here otherwise. She's got some equipment we can use and I for one am glad to accept any offer from an ally".

Chandie was about to speak when the loading dock door groaned to life and started opening. "Looks like it's time to move, we'll catch up later, I promise. Come on", Randall encouraged moving towards the ladder. He could see Vinchi off to the side of the doorway in the shadows. "Damn straight we'll talk later", Chandie mumbled under her breath. Simmie straightened up and came out with, "We need to move people, the sooner the better", adjusting her head away from her ear piece. That was it. Chandie couldn't contain it any longer, "Look, I can deal with the fact that 'Rambetty' here almost killed me out there with falling debris and woke the whole world to our existence now. But when did we start taking orders from her?" Darren watched Randall stop, lower his head, then he took one step back and sideways towards Poonta, presumably for protection. Randall then raised his head slowly and turned to both Simmie and Chandie who were directly behind him and raised his hands up, palms out in a request that stopped their momentum. Not one to take a submissive role, Randall had had enough, "Let's get something straight, right here, right now", he started pointing at the ground for added emphasis, "You two are going to learn to play nicely together, at least in the interim. Once we're out of here in one piece, together, we'll have a conversation. But until then... Everyone has a job to do! Even you two roosters". He looked savagely at Darren and Poonta, then

333

back at the women. "Got It!" Simmie couldn't restrain herself, "Oh, he's so nice when he gets angry, don't you think? But seriously, Randy, we do need to make a move, we've got about an hour before they get here. So I need to set up a perimeter before then".

Randall's face said it all, the evil look he gave her was coupled with, "Christ Simmie, I was trying to do this without drawing attention. Right, you woke the beast, you can be damn sure there will be some renegotiations going on here, remember that. Plus, it's all flooding back thanks to you!" He tapped his head, "Do you really want to push the limits with me, given I now have full access?" It was Simmie's turn to look stunned. She figured it would take Randall a while to get over the shock and plenty of time before he could upload and use his long-lost abilities without stressing out, given his other uniqueness. She should never have underestimated her mentor. "No, not in the slightest babe", returned Simmie, after a lengthy pause. "But we really need to take advantage of the time allotted to us now. Poonta and I will man the rear guard starting at the lower level under the loading dock. That's where the main access points converge. You're going to need someone to cover your cute butt, may as well be us. So you four get moving, we'll catch up. Here take the rucksack, it's got the toys in it". Simmie handed him the bag and blew him a kiss. Looking Randall in the eyes she then finished with, "Once we're done here, you lot are all coming on a clean-up duty with me, then we'll negotiate your freedom with them dearest, deal?" "Deal", Randall agreed. "Ok, Darren, Chandie let's go" Randall started climbing the ladder to the dock, "Vinchi, lead the way, mate. We're running out of time and I still need some to work my magic".

Leaving Poonta in Simmie's capable hands, Randall followed closely behind Vinchi. Making their way down the internal fire stairwell, Randall spoke over his shoulder back to Chandie, "Still got my package sweet?" "Never left my side, unlike you", she said looking for somewhere to plunge the knife. "Look, I never planned any of this, and frankly I'm a little pissed you lot didn't bother to seek me out longer than you did. I mean what would've happened if I was really dead"? Randall defended himself just before he collapsed forward in pain taking Vinchi with him down a single flight of stairs. "Fuh, uh, uh uh, ouch", was the reverberation that came out as Randall bounced on the concrete stairs and kicked Vinchi in the sore foot. This was followed closely by, "Oww, ow, shit, shit, shit, my foot, fuck my shoulder", from Vinchi as they came to rest against the bottom wall. Chandie and Darren ran down as quickly as they could, assembling behind them trying to assist. "Oh, God no", Chandie yelled as Darren blurted out, "Here we go again", having wound up tangled together on the return platform facing the fire door.

Vinchi burst into laughter with a muffled, "You can take your groin out of my face anytime now". Randall, equally disturbed, replied, "I would if I could, stop laughing, you're vibrating". "You're sick, both of you. Just shut up and let's get this mess sorted. Darren, you grab there and I'll get Randall", Chandie pointed for Darren at Vinchi before she placed her hands around Randall's waist. "Bloody attention-seeking again, aren't we. I'm sure Bimbee loves pawing over you when you do this". Looking up at her with all the grace and innocence he could portray, Randall watched her awkwardly help pry the two of them apart. Randall voiced gently, "Nice to see you actually do care". She hit him playfully on the shoulder, but hard enough to reinforce that she wasn't mucking around. "It's fine, Chandie. I couldn't really remember a lot about Simmie until the last few days when we met and talked", Randall confessed, straightening himself up. Darren leaned over Vinchi, hauling him to his feet, "Well, we've lost the element of surprise all round guys, congratulations. If there's anyone down here apart from the force we encountered above, we're not exactly going to have an advantage here". "Maybe not, but we do have these". Randall held the black bag Simmie had passed him and unzipped it. He handed out some weapons, "Courtesy of Simmie, they're called Greasers. Point and shoot, internal ammo source, don't mind the humming, you get used to it". Everyone took one in turn and buckled the holsters in place. "So far so good", Randall murmured, as he composed himself, "At least we're on the right floor. Let's go through and see if there's anyone home".

Simmie approached Poonta as the quartet of friends disappeared from the loading bay. "Hello again. You ready to protect your friends?" Simmie began, "Let's get started, we don't have a lot of time but if we do this right, we can buy them time to get done what they need to do. You up for it?" She

337

unceremoniously dumped the black bag onto the concrete docking bay. "All of these are proximity charges, see that section of wall over there and the same on the other side? You set the charges in an arc pattern with the senses like this". She used a charcoal piece of rock to draw a rough sketch on the concrete. "I'll take care of the gates and the stairwells to the back two towers. We'll then meet up back at the loading dock. Got it champ?" Poonta looked at Simmie and gave a nod of acknowledgement, "Yes, eyes understand. See yous at the tops of the dock whens wes done". "Great champ, let's shimmy. Once this is done we'll make our way down to level one and dig into our positions to make life unbearable for this lot coming. Let's go", Simmie finished, updating Poonta, and she was gone, making her way to the front gates. Poonta picked up the second bag Simmie had sorted out for him, surprisingly it was lighter than he expected. He hadn't seen anything like these proximity mines before but they looked nasty, small echidnas covered in deadly spikes, he also noticed they rattled as Simmie moved them about. 'Balls bearings inside', he thought. Whoever was struck by these motherfuckers would be lucky to survive the amount of blood lost, especially if you were

338

next to them when they went off, there was quite a lot he had to plant.

Simmie apparently never did anything by half-measure. His kinda gal, go hard or go home and always have the upper hand. She might've rubbed Chandie up the wrong way, but he'd thought he'd seen an inner glimpse of the real Simmie if ever so briefly when they first confronted each other. He then starting to thank God she was on their side. He set to work laying out the pattern Simmie had indicated, flicking on the individual switches and setting loose his small but scary little packages of death. It'd taken nearly ten minutes but soon everything was in place on ground level and Simmie and Poonta met inside the loading bay. "Well done, champ", Simmie thanked him, lifting the velcro on her wrist while looking at the small low lit screen, "Everyone's active, you're a real pro. Here's a pressie for you". She handed him a Greaser, "It's a nasty piece so be careful, I don't want to scrape you up off the floor my dear". "Okays, Cool. Where we digs in. Eyes gather wes gonna be the fronts line? Blast anything thats move", he gushed, trying to keep his enthusiasm low-key. He hadn't really been trapped like a rat for a long time, not since way back when he was a youth in a gang. He was thirteen then and twice the size of anyone else his age, the designated muscle. He locked eyes with Simmie before moving and asked softly, "Wes are gonna get outta here, ain't wes?" Simmie placed a hand on Poonta's shoulder softly. "I'll make you a promise. Even if I don't, I'll make sure you're safe. These clowns are going to need you whether they realise it or not".

INTO THE DEPTHS....

Ensuring all was prepared and ready to proceed, Randall gathered his thoughts as the others steadied themselves. They were as composed as they would ever get. Randall leaned against the fire door and heaved his way through. Moving inside the first corridor, the automatic door closed silently behind them. It was as if they'd walked into a huge technological wonderland, there were thick glass partitions which cordoned off rooms and lined the corridors. They contained banks and banks and banks of computer servers. Each way you looked from where they were standing, left, right or straight ahead, one would swear you couldn't see the end of the corridors. The light was extremely low-level and played tricks on your eyes. They saw movement where there was none. It was as if this whole area was a living, breathing, clinical entity made up entirely of glass, wires, cables, electricity and LED bulbs. An artificial intelligence that was capable of killing you at a moment's notice. The colours of the clear reflective glass partitions and black servers went on forever, all blinking away with their blue, white, orange and red lights. The whole spectacle looked like Santa had upgraded the North Pole into the twenty second century and Christmas had been entirely computerised, including the reindeer.

The humming and the heat produced was amazing. The group's skin was being cooled by the extensive air conditioning throughout this level, however there was an underlying wave of heat and radiating warmth coming off the computer servers as they hummed away crunching petabyte after petabyte. "Where the fuck do we go?" Darren asked scanning the area. "There's no signage and as far as I can tell everything looks the bloody same". "Didn't we get some notes out of that mess of papers of Ishita's?" Chandie said with a slight tinge of confusion in her voice. "Yes, there was a mud map Chandie, you've still got my package I entrusted to you, haven't you?", Randall questioned moving closer to her now, his left hand on her hip, the other opened, palm up. "Um.. Yeah, yeah Hun. Hang on its right here", she answered back still taking in the concept that this floor had no real end in sight, in any direction. She lifted her maroon top and unstrapped the ziplock bag from around her waist. Randall's hand moved up a touch from her hip as he took the bag from her with his right hand, "Later, Romeo. Much later, keep focused Hun. We are not sure yet that we're the only ones down here", Chandie chided, but grinned at him all the same.

Darren looked over and just smiled, 'The gangs back', he reasoned to himself, "So where to Icarus? We might not be flying to the sun, but all my intuitive senses are on fire". He eyeballed Randall, giving off the look of 'Something doesn't feel right'. Randall unzipped the package, took out the folded map, zipped up the bag and handed it back to Chandie. "Keep it safe for now, ok sweet". He tried to sound heartfelt. Opening the map Randall studied it and closed his eyes, concentrating, "Jesus Fucking H. Christ", was the next loud expulsion he uttered as he was swamped by images, blueprints and a video construction feed of

342

the media station. He very nearly collapsed to his knees as Darren caught him halfway to the floor. "What in God's name was that? You ok?" Darren interjected as he had hold of Randall, "That was very different, wasn't a normal seizure mate?" "Recent firmware upgrade, unfortunately. More to add to the confessions later once we're out of here. Let's hope it doesn't kill me before then", Randall joked as he found his feet and stabilised. Chandie didn't find it at all funny. "I knew that bitch was trouble the first time I saw her. When I get my hands on her I'll..." She never finished as Randall grasped her hand in his while hunched over, "Its not Simmie fault, she was ordered to find me", Randall confessed. "Don't blame her, she fought to leave me out of this whole exercise. There's a lot more going on here in the background with some very major players. Confessions will occur later, I promise. I'll just be satisfied to get everyone out of here alive".

Darren and Chandie both stared at Randall quizzically, "Yeah, so its news to me too. I've been out of a very large loop for a very long time. But if we're smart we can use it to our advantage. Having said that, let's leave it for a later time when we're not being hunted, shall we?" Darren was the first to speak,

Sonic Railgun gun in hand. He turned to Chandie smugly and very matter of factly stated, "You good, I'm fine, later it is. I can handle being ignored, kept in the dark and lied to. You Chandie?"

"Yep, yeah I'm fine. We'll talk later", she said stingingly. Randall, having taken the not so subtle hints, started walking directly ahead about a hundred metres then turned left, as they all followed behind him. He stopped abruptly, head cocked to one side as if he was deep in thought, then started off again. Like obedient fledgling chickens imprinting on mother hen, they all moved again, watching where Randall veered in and out of computer banks as if this was second nature. They went right, left, right, left and wound up facing a huge bank of servers and what appeared to be the end corner of this enormous room. Way down the end there was a line of vending machines and what passed as a maintenance and staff room. Randall walked past the line of vending machines, stopping almost at the end. He then disappeared between the empty Mars bar and a weird looking banana machine, whose pulpy fruit had rotted to black. They stopped and waited for him to reappear. "Follow me", Randall urged them onwards as he once again walked down beside the banana vending machine. He then wrenched it forward, exposing a doorway and an entry behind it, and squeezed through before disappearing down into it. A hand came back out waving the others on to follow suit.

"Pull on the handle and close the vending machine", Randall indicated back to Darren, "Time to see where this actually leads". The hallway was dim but not entirely dark, there was just enough light to see to walk without tripping. There was an audible click and a whoosh of air inside the corridor as Darren shut the vending machine which acted as a stop gap. The corridor itself wasn't very long, probably thirty metres in total, there was dust everywhere and some scuffed marks on the floor. This corridor hadn't been used very often or in a very long time, yet somehow it seemed familiar to Randall. Eventually, the corridor opened at the end into what appeared to be a large rectangular room, lined with computers on every wall and off to the left was a large sturdy glass-enclosed room or bubble. This small glass bubble was built into the infrastructure of the computers, cabling, lights and wires, it had a sling seat and high back for the occupant and what looked like multiple consoles, keyboards and screens.

The door was open and beckoned the curiosity of all three to come and examine it. "I assume this is what we're looking for?" Chandie whispered to all. "Could be, the notion that's got me concerned is that someone's been using this before us". Darren couldn't hide his anxiety, he was clearly on edge. Randall tried to allay any fears, "You're both right". He tapped his head and pointed the Sonic Railgun towards the ceiling, letting loose with a small but effective shot. What was left of the blackened semicircular camera in the centre of the ceiling dangled there from a single singed wire, "Ishita's been the only one in here apart from her brother knowing about it. Among others. I figure we needed privacy before someone knows we're using it. There's only one set of tracks going in and out, same shoe size if you've taken notice: Ishita's".

Chandie was confused and voiced her concerns, "No, it never occurred to me to use my archaeology skills to determine my environment or previous history of this place. How the hell are you so certain all of a sudden? How did you know that video was there?" "Just trust me for once sweet, fair?" Randall walked over to what looked like a keyboard screen and flicked his hand across the surface. The entire room flared to life, they could hear old hard drives whirring, electricity hummed and pumped through the cabling like blood through arteries. The low-level lighting increased in intensity ever so slightly. There was all manner of clicking and popping sounds and the door to the glass room opened slightly wider. The sling seat lowered ominously and slid out on unseen rails inviting whomever was in the room to jump on for the ride of their life. "This my dear friends is what is known in geekology or those who built it as a node, a relic or more dangerously, an umbilical", Randall explained as he waved his hands around like a poorly practiced magician. "Umbilical? You're not telling me you physically hook up to that system are you?" Chandie latched onto his arm as she queried him, pulling him away from it towards her. "There is no way you're getting in that contraption. We'll just turn around and go back out the way we came in. We'll find somewhere else to go, shall we, that's safer?"

It was here Randall knew he would have to come clean. In the softest voice he could portray, trying to make Chandie see reason, "Its way too late for that now. We've already got the attention of some major scary players. These monsters don't take witnesses, Darren found Jarece's zircon earrings on that arsehole that was hunting you up the range. Poonta inadvertently contacted someone who couldn't keep their mouth shut and already had created suspicion about herself, given she was trying to cover up for her brother. They tracked her to the park, eventually, extracting information from now non-existent people, eg. Jarece, so God only knows who else was dead now. Simmie activated her plans at the highest levels to rattle the controlling regime and is now out on a blood mission and I've been reactivated back into active service for my previous employers. God only knows what purpose they want outta me yet. So, in a nutshell, my sweet. I'm screwed either way I choose to go. But we're either all already dead and don't know it yet or there's a way out for all of us and it's via me, manipulating 'The System'. Can I have my package now, please sweet. We don't have long?" Chandie hesitated, utterly confused. Darren, never at a loss for words, chimed in, putting his hands around Chandie's wrist, promising, "I kind of hate to admit it, but for once Randall's actually right, sexy. We've been through too much to get here. Yet, if anyone can pull off the impossible, it's this jerk right here. Make you a deal. You hand Icarus his toys to complete the job we came here to do and I'll bludgeon a full confession out of him later and let you watch. I'll even throw in a fat lip for good measure, just for you, sound good?"

Randall looked stunned, he hoped Darren was joking just to support him and talk Chandie around, so they stood a chance of getting out of here in one piece. "Okay, here give it to him", she said preparing to hand over the package Randall had entrusted to her earlier. She then pointed to Randall accusingly, "This isn't finished, you had better emerge from that death trap in one piece. You owe me that much and a full bloody explanation. 'Cause if you die in there without any kind of explanation, I'm coming in after you and I'm gonna kill you myself". Darren took the package off Chandie as gently as he could, "He'll be fine, maybe before I take a piece outta him. I'll get in line, huh?" He leaned forward, gave her a hug and whispered softly in Chandie's ear, "Be nice, he really likes you. This could actually kill him". Turning back, Darren confidently handed Randall the grey ziplock bag. "I gather we're trapped like rats in here until you emerge. How much time do you need so we know how many to kill?" He placed his other hand on Randall's left wrist, lowering his voice, "You better get this done, you owe us an explanation, my friend. Good luck".

"I won't know until I'm in 'The System', but if I were to make a guess let's shoot for at least an hour", Randall admitted, overlooking his poor choice of words. Randall looked Chandie and Darren both in the eyes. He stopped at Chandie's, lasting just that little bit longer, hoping she got the message. "Alright, let's get on with this shall we", Randall said rolling up his jacket sleeves to above his elbows. Chandie went the palest shade of white as he sat down on the sling seat. He activated the controls on the side of the seat and it slid him back inside the glass chamber, locking into place. The doors to the bubble drifted shut with a whoosh of air and a soft audible humming filled the room. Four touch screen keyboards lowered into position in front of him and slid back into place. Two robotic arms with evil-looking needles aligned themselves with his neck's internal carotid arteries. Chandie looked horrified as did Darren. Randall watched their faces for a moment longer and flicked a switch which tilted the sling seat backwards at a forty five degree angle and another which turned the glass bubble black. An eerie silence filled the small room. It was soon shattered by a familiar sound of 'Fuuucckk!' as Randall obviously had another seizure. Chandie moved instinctively towards the black sphere, Darren stopped her, "No, no, he's fine it's just another of his attacks. Have some confidence in him, he's knows what he's doing. I trust him, ok. Plus, he's doing this for all of us not just himself. Cut him some slack. Just because there's someone else on the scene with our crew now doesn't mean he's gonna flip-flop". Darren knew he was lying through his back teeth and prayed the Almighty wasn't listening. He had to keep Chandie focused now, so he started the checklist.

"Chandie", Darren enunciated in his worst English accent ever, "Let's go over our game plan. We're here in what appears to be a secret room and a dead-end corridor. Supposedly the only ones who'll know about this is the bad guys, right, maybe? But they've all got one agenda. To kill all of us. So I for one am not prepared to die today. Since we can't communicate with Poonta or Simmie or...." he trailed off. "Where the fuck is Vinchi?" He looked at Chandie worried, "Oh shit, I hope we're all ok. You stay here, protect Randall. Anything moves in this corridor that you don't recognise, kill it!" He took off down the corridor leading back to the vending machine. He went about two thirds of the way when a crack of light illuminated the doorway at the end. Vinchi appeared in the doorway draped in his ghillie suit. This always made Darren laugh inside. Whenever he saw this sight it reminded him of his great grandfather's old DVD collection and Hair Bear, the Afro-wearing leader of the 'Hair Bear Bunch', only shorter.

"Where in God's name have you been?" Darren scolded Vinchi, "I could cheerfully throttle you, we thought you'd been… Never mind, what going on?" Vinchi indicated to follow him outside. "I've backtracked our way here and planted some surprises should we have visitors. We'll hear them before we see them, we'll at least what's left of them. In addition I think I've found another exit outta here, should it be needed. I just need to check with Randall and Ishita's map. "He's a bit indisposed at the moment. Maybe we can chat on the run when he's finished if we have enough time. Although somehow I have a really bad feeling it's all about to go pear-shaped real soon. Say one word to Chandie to upset her and I'll kill you myself. Randall put himself in real danger for all of us so we need to support each other to get outta this one alive. GOT IT!" Darren emphasised every syllable to Vinchi, registering his facial expressions. At that point both Vinchi and Darren could hear and feel the vibrations occurring overhead. "I think we've got company", Darren said staring at the ceiling, "You prepared, mate. I think we need to get ready for the onslaught".

Simmie and Poonta had spent a good half hour prepping everything they could and Simmie tested the remote frequency to ensure all was working and active. They'd closed the loading dock door and started moving down to the lower levels, specifically level one, where they would make their stand and pick off the remaining ghouls hunting them. That's when they heard the first of two explosions go off on the side walls. Bracing themselves, Simmie patted Poonta's shoulder and motioned, "Come on we need to move, chief. Once we get to level one, we'll bunker down and hold the line, let's roll". As they made their way down the stairs, that's when they heard a series of five loud detonations, one after the other followed by excruciating screaming echoing out of Simmie wrist tech. She checked the video feeds she'd set in place. They were sticky little cameras that wirelessly fed back live wide-angle camera images at each of the death traps she and Poonta had set out to decimate any force stupid enough to follow them and take them out. "Well, that's a body count of sixteen so far. That's thinned out the herd a bit", she grinned up at Poonta. "Cheer up buddy, that still leaves plenty for us to eliminate. You're a natural at this kinda stuff, ever thought about taking it up full time?" She smiled again this time genuinely, she could use his skills here to get what she needed. "Time to plant some more surprises and then move into our nest and bunker down. You up for it, my man?" "Yous bet. Theses the most fun eyes had in ages. Wheres does we start?" Poonta grinned back evilly. He really was having fun and starting to enjoy Simmie's hidden talents. They moved off in separate directions planting more spiky echidnas and sticky cams. Finishing up, Simmie, satisfied they'd done enough at this stage, led the way downstairs to checkpoint B or 'The Killzone', as she so brazenly described it. Now to make time for Randall to complete his task and then they would find a way out of here, together.

Santos's minion, Moretti, had a gut instinct when they arrived at the media communications station, the 'atmosphere' seemed off. This was confirmed when the operatives descending onto the twin towers at the back level gantry encountered professional climbing gear and reported this back by a physical messenger. 'This is not going to go as planned', he thought. Their communications had been blocked the moment they arrived with no access to email, audio coms or anything attached online, including satellite. This meant whoever they were after in here was definitely a cut well above simple mindless drones, this would mean loss of life no matter how you sliced it. He was more determined than ever that it wouldn't be him and having total control he'd use his pawns up first to test the barriers they were up against. The biggest problem was they couldn't call for reinforcements so unless Home base worked out what was going on, they were on their own for now. Having observed Santos for a year now, he knew reinforcements weren't far off, he was no one's fool, Moretti was now banking on it. Given those thoughts, he ploughed ahead with Plan A, hoping to adapt quickly enough it went south.

The company forged its way into the breach only to encounter the deadliest onslaught Moretti had ever seen in any field operation. On one miscalculated underestimation of the quarry inside, he'd lost sixteen operatives in a single coordinated movement. They had been cut to shreds by ball bearings, nails and razor sharp scalpel blades. Those who weren't killed instantly bled to death soon after, no field kit would've saved them. The five distinct breeches looked like Jackson Pollock paintings, the exception being the only colour used here was 'red'. Making their way into the surrounding courtyard of the main structure, Moretti sent messengers to collect anyone left alive to regroup in the loading dock. Once his remaining force arrived — some injured, others just shell shocked — he took stock of what his options had dwindled down to. There were eleven operatives remaining and now he knew that the quarry they were up against was unpredictable, it became obvious that more stealth and caution was required. According to the data he'd uploaded to his wrist com prior to the communications blackout, he acknowledged that the servers were down four levels and the area was huge. The main way down was either by elevator or stairs. The latter seemed the best option as it would be a controlled environment and the way ahead could be cleared by grenades or small explosives. There were two fire stairwells available so splitting the remaining company into two, they set off downwards to the target. This time it would be kill or be killed, everyone had been given orders to go 'Hot'.

Back at the Hexagon of Death, Santos had gone on a psychopathic rampage and four technicians lay dead on the gantry floor, their blood pooling around his feet. He was literally yelling and growling at 'Rottzilla', "Get this fixed or you're next". He stormed off to find Taigon, he wasn't in the mood for failure and his next in command was going to either earn his recent promotion or start questioning whether his life insurance covered violent horrific endings. "What the fuck is going on here? Our systems are supposed to be un-hackable. We're the ones who do the hacking, not the other way around!" Santos had burst into the debriefing room to find Taigon hitting and kicking his console as if that would bring it back to life. "Well, if you don't know, how the hell do you expect me too, that's what we have technicians for! Or have you killed them all off? My entire communication to the outside world is dead, nothings working properly, it's as if we've been neutralised technologically and fed some kind of duplicated data with major constraints". Taigon's voice broke as he responded, clearly angry that the mission had gone awry. "My connection to the operatives has just gone blank, get your techs on board to fix this shit, or get others, now", Santos barked. "I'm already on it. We'll have a tech crew here in the next thirty minutes. They'll strip it down and rebuild where required. Satellite coms are out as well, orbit hasn't been affected, but no coms are active. I'm still trying to work out how that occurred as well. So get off my back unless you think by putting a bullet through it will correct it!" Taigon shouted back. "Fine, let's not lose our heads here. The less the old man knows the better. See how many field operatives can we arrange and contact to activate, given our limited resources problems at this point?"

Santos was thinking aloud and trying to get Taigon on board to help. Taigon stared at Santos thinking, then a light bulb moment struck and he replied, "Maybe thirty, quickly. But we'd need to use more archaic tech to activate them, well, pagers really. So if we want to send them out without RDIF's, which we can't activate, they could be in the field wherever within two hours". "Do it! We lost six operatives in the space of an hour on the Barraiya range. That's not a coincidence, that's suspicious. I've checked the local area map and there's an old decommissioned media communication station there that was the property of the Astor Family. I know it's like we'd be trespassing, but if we're wrong the old man can smooth the relationship over, 'Head to Head', make concessions and ask for forgiveness later. If we're right we could just be the first to neutralise a Chimera". Santos ordered this attempting to portray an aura of, 'We're still in control here'. Taigon raised an eyebrow at the last comment thinking silently, 'Don't bet on it', but actually said, "You never know if we don't try. I'll get onto it immediately. Once they're active and on site I'll provide a quick debrief, plus I'll extract out of the tech team what the fuck is going on here. Fair chief?" "Fine, get on it. I've got two hours before the next debrief with our 'Head', I'd like to give him something concrete soon". Santos walked off. Taigon could see from Santos's body language he was under a huge amount of stress. 'I'm in no hurry for that job', was the thought that fleeted by as he set about activating the next company of field operatives, followed closely by, 'God, I hope this works'.

CHAPTER NINE

EYE OF NEWT...

Back at the 'decommissioned' media station, Randall began settling back into place, at least the sling seat wasn't uncomfortable. He wouldn't want to spend anymore time in here than was absolutely necessary. He flashed his hands across the touch keypads and the multiple screens flashed to life on the surface of the bubble. The mini screens on each side on the internal apparatus showed minor system specs, fluctuations in processing, power, server activity, etc... Twelve screens in total to keep a track of, use in sync and process applications to simultaneously crack open an undetectable electronic hole without leaving a digital footprint. He found the card reader to the right and flicked the switch. The vacuum seal hissed open and a double tray slid out. He lifted the zip bag Chandie handed him and placed the RED and MIRROR FINISH Chimera hermetically-sealed cards into the tray. Pushing gently, the tray slid closed and he heard the vacuum hum away, then that recognisable click as the contents of the cases began accessing, 'The System'. He braved himself for the next painful step, as the needle penetrated his neck and began assessing his access levels, by checking his DNA and biological makeup. To comfort himself being unsettled, he started chanting his old favourite piece or at least what he could remember from that famous Scottish play by William Shakespeare. Since he couldn't remember it all he started accessing the 'Disk' by concentrating on what he'd built into 'The System' coupled with an upload from the ancients. That's when he had another seizure, screamed in pain and then wondered how his friends were progressing outside of this bubble. This was going to be an interesting ride, one he was not keen on staying in any longer than absolutely necessary.

The screens accessing the cards flashed to life, espousing audio in ancient Latin, 'Gratissimum Vilicus'. Randall's first reaction was, "Thank God for the upload", and began typing in Latin fluently, 'Hello Anartes, Overseer requires access to Kronos, DNA sample provided, Level -1 Bypass Initiated'. The next phrase to flash on screen translated to, 'Verifying....'. Randall breathed in slowly, feeling the needle in his neck slowly draw out his sample and then retract. He recalled that when 'The System' was implemented these nodes or relics became necessary to provided added security at the very highest levels to stop unwanted breaches. These nodes were extremely rare and usually once reprogramming was completed they were destroyed as standard practice, which was why he'd built numerous software back door entry points. He couldn't help wondering why this one had been overlooked until the recent disk upload showed that this whole facility belonged to the Astor Family. Knowing that they had hidden this one from the others and they were one family highest up the hierarchy he needed to move fast and once completed they would need to level it to unusable components. This particular node had biological testing coupled with Advanced Encryption Standard (AES-1024) the highest levels of military encryption algorithms using Twenty eight cycles of repetition for 1024-bit keys cycling at six hundred and sixty six petabytes a second. Anyone caught hacking 'The System' any other way other than a node was met with a brutal response.

Any external hack detected would see the equipment being used have a massive internal failure after a time, but would keep the hacker busy with cloned phoney information until a hit squad arrived, or drone strikes, whichever happened first.

Breaches were considered an act of treason and punishable by death, immediately. Having had access at the top level Randall ensured he built in secure undetectable access should he need it one day. He smiled as he recounted it would be like sneaking into a completely blackened sealed room with people inside and you were the only one with night vision goggles, then doing anything you wanted to them without being identified. That's when Anartes's black screen echoed to life with, 'DNA verificatur, Epifcopum verificatur, Level -1 bypass verificatur, Access est Kronos verificatur'. Randall relaxed and breathed a sigh of relief as he understood he'd been verified as the creator. 'I'm in, here we go', he thought as he started typing furiously, opening and closing applications in sync and modifying code. He located the autonomous coding packages on the Chimera Card and started the upload. This was going to take time, time he hoped his friends could buy for him. Once he duplicated the data to both cards, he'd pass the other to Simmie and keep the RED one, complete with Chimera codes. He had a bad feeling there was a double cross going here.

Simmie and Poonta had made their way down to level one, mining the stairways as they went. Then they prepared themselves to dig into the first of the gun and run checkpoints Simmie had already mapped out on her wrist coms. Bunkering down on either side of the long hallway, they heard the first set of explosions go off, quickly echoed by the sound of the second loud eruption. Poonta could see Simmie furiously accessing her wrist coms. She held up her right hand with all two digits. Poonta acknowledged that they'd erased another two, so some eighteen in total. 'Not bad for a morning's work', he thought recalling some of the self-preservation events he'd escaped from and the tallies racked up. That's when a hail of bullets started chipping away at the off-white painted concrete wall between them. Poonta tried to fire one of the Greasers Simmie had handed him, but found out it wouldn't operate for some reason. He raised his arms in a shrug and resorted back to unholstering his two XVR 460 Magnums and fired back. The booming that echoed in the close quarter hallway was followed by a 'Holy shit' from the other end. Simmie unholstered her Greaser and casually leant around the corner with her left hand and fired. Nothing happened. She fired, again

365

nothing happened. She looked at the weapon quizzically, fussed over it and verbalised, "Piece of shit... Next time Simmie pinch something that bloody works, fucking prototypes". Poonta heard her scold herself. He grinned wickedly to himself thinking, 'Even the most elite warriors are fallible'. He liked Simmie, she was a no nonsense gal, take no prisoners mentality and that copper hair made her very exotic.

Poonta watched in admiration as she re-holstered the Greaser, pulled out the Sonic Railgun and flicked a switch on the side. He heard the weapon hum to a loud audible high pitched squeal. They heard movement coming down the hallway and Simmie leaned out quickly and let loose with a single shot that hit the side of the hallway part way down and the whole hallway exploded in a barrage of concrete pieces, paint and body parts. It all went silent, there wasn't a response for what seemed like an Eternity, but was in fact only ten seconds. Simmie and Poonta both acted in sync, peering around the corner and saw that the whole hallway had been destroyed, the ceiling had caved in and the walls the blast hit had crumbled into blocks cutting off any access in or out this way. There was a lower left leg on their side of the rubble, Poonta saw this and gave a thumbs up to Simmie.

"Glads yous on my side gal", gushed Poonta. "I hates twos upset yous or bees your enemy". Simmie moved over towards Poonta past a small section of rubble and gave him a bear hug, throwing Poonta completely off guard. "Thanks, big beau, you're safe for now. Looks like I kinda screwed up with the new weapons. Sorry, I was hoping for more firepower", she explained as she snuggled her head into his massive chest. Poonta hugged her back, this was nice, she didn't smell like Vinchi. It was times like these he got confused batting for the other side. 'Maybe I could experiment with... no Poont, keep it nice, I like nice. Damn' , he thought, 'another friend'. Simmie stepped back and looked up at her newly-bonded friend, "Come on, my Man Mountain, next check point, we're not out of the woods just yet". She rubbed his chest and they moved off as swiftly as they could, planting small charges as they went. Once they were done here and out, Simmie had orders to level the place. That was one order she wouldn't fail in and maybe, just maybe, if she got the cloned card back to the Ancients they'd overlook her indiscretion with the Greasers.

Vinchi and Darren had now checked out the secondary route should it be needed back to level two and the sewer pipe exit out. They used the rest of the thermite to cut a much bigger hole for their fellow militia. As well they hadn't wasted any time dismantling a bank of servers that appeared deactivated, and, upon further inspection, realised that they weren't even connected. Strangely, there hadn't been anymore encounters with personnel. The barricade was now arranged in a scene directly out of Les Miserables to provide some defence against the impending good old Western gunfight. There would be one exception here: they had Simmie's new toys. Luckily, they decided to test them out. No matter what they did, they couldn't get them to work. Frustrated, Darren heaved his weapon down on top of one of the servers in absolute disgust, and it went off, a blue dot ricocheted down the corridor, hit a glass partition and melted a major hole the size of a person out of it. Picking up the now humming weapon, as if cradling a live baby cobra, Darren kept it pointed away from himself, "Christ All Fucking Mighty... Cool, well, this one works", he said turning to Vinchi, "Do that to yours and see what happens?". Vinchi soon complied hurling it at a part of the barricade making extremely sure that it was pointed away from him, then nothing. He did it again, and once more nothing happened. Being left handed he aimed it at the end of a corridor that opened onto this one and was looking down the sights when he noticed there was a small lever located underneath it. 'Must be a hidden safety', he mulled over.

Vinchi flicked the lever not expecting anything major to occur. That's when it all happened at once, a maintenance person, dressed in grey overalls ran out of the side corridor and down towards them at full speed, tools in hand, obviously having heard the commotion. She halted to a screeching abrupt stop, almost toppling over. She was utterly shocked to have encountered anyone at all down here, let alone two gun-toting black-clad military types. But that's when Vinchi instinctively flinched back, not really expecting to encounter anyone just yet, pulling the sensor pad trigger. The weapon fired its weird blue liquid paint ball, striking the target dead centre of her chest. She emitted a brief blood-curdling scream as both Darren and Vinchi watched in absolute horror as this person just disappeared and was consumed before them, including their clothes. In a matter of

369

seconds it'd turned into a red, yellow, white, orange tinged puss ball, a sticky gooey mess the size of a basketball. "Shit, Oh, I'm keeping this brute", Vinchi yelled looking at Darren and then back at the weapon, "Think of the damage we could do with these?". "Ok, Wild Bill, We're not in the Wild West now. But I agree, these will really provide an advantage here. Pick a spot, dig in, I'm going back to inform Chandie", Darren offered as he marched off behind the banana machine.

Chandie heard the vending machine open and knocked out two rounds from her Glock, both slamming into the back of it just inches from Darren as he entered. "Chandie, stop, it's Darren... Gees, sexy, I didn't even get a chance to scream out it was me. Stop shooting, I need to tell you something". He was making his way slowly towards her, hands held up in a sign of peace. Upon reaching her, he gave her the full rundown on how the new weapon worked and what to expect. "Any news from our boy in there?", Darren pointed to the bubble. "Not yet, but there's been a fair bit of screaming, so I gather he's had a number of seizures in there. I just hope he's able to get done what he needs to, for all our sakes! What was going on out there before?", she mused,

"Sounded like you two were buggerising around?". Darren grinned, "No, no we were just testing out the new toys. Unfortunately, we accidentally tried it out on a live target who wasn't supposed to be down here. It's a nasty piece of equipment so treat it with respect, or you too will end up as a gooey mess on the floor". Randall screamed out again from inside the black bubble. "He's Fine, He's in good hands", Darren said turning to Chandi, "I'm heading back to Vinchi before he kills Simmie and Poonta by accident, too. Take care of our guy, fair"? He started off back down the walkway and out through the doorway, closing it behind him as he went.

Randall had lost all track of time in the bubble. Mostly, it had become a blur of hands: re-coding, manipulating data, uploading, downloading, plus having multiple seizures, owing to his photosensitivity. At best guess, about forty minutes had passed and he was almost finished. The disk had been a Godsend, so had the cards. They had provided access to information that would've taken him much longer to compile by hand and now he was on the home stretch. All the way through this, he had a nagging feeling that something wasn't right. This was the main

371

reason for making a secondary back up on his RED card. This alternative exit strategy he had developed when building 'The System', he figured one day he'd need a safeguard. Crypto-currency had all but taken over, replacing real cash and credit when he started the build, so he'd created a safe haven. There were still a small number of countries that still acted as sanctuaries for the uber rich and those who needed to just, say, vanish. AntarctiGates, the islands of New Jackson and the Chilean Elon Islands, had all been now amazingly transformed into liveable paradises given the immense amount of global warming. New Jackson was his pick of his 'Eden', but if necessary he'd change and adapt if it became compromised to AntartiGates. This crypto-currency was embedded into everyday life and extremely hard, if not impossible, to counterfeit. It was securely monitored and enforced, but if he was careful 'The System' would just see this as a normal component of a recently-uploaded version update and a simultaneous back up. Easy for him, just time consuming. He'd opened an account under an alias only he could access and was backing it up to a cold site that would only come on line for updates when his DNA was verified.

Now Randall was simultaneously siphoning off and mining monumentally massive amounts of small percentages of cryptocurrency from millions and millions and millions of accounts including the Families' hidden accounts. They were small enough not to be missed, and set off alarms, but the tally he was racking up exponentially was enormous. Given these arseholes had stolen it from the current population, there was no way they could openly demand it back without compromising their own existence. Yet, it would also act as a bargaining chip against the Ancients along with the secondary copy of the 'The System' core codes on his cold site. He'd set it to a timer. He had a week to have it reactivated and be verified or the whole world would know. This was his insurance policy. It was called, 'Staying alive or I'll expose you all along with dumping every piece of information into open source channels'. By the time anyone noticed anything was wrong they'd be long, long gone and untraceable. As soon as this was moved offgrid, it would become untraceable and irretrievable to outside sources, except himself. If he got out of here he'd need a substantial amount to vanish and bribe his way into anonymity. The difficulty now was creating an alias for all his friends and erasing their original profiles as they stood on 'The System'. Essentially, after he was finished, none of them would have ever been officially born, let alone existed, or had families. Since he didn't have long, they'd just have to live with the persona and identity he created. He allowed himself a small amount of latitude and sarcasm, just enough to ensure it would be believable and unable to be contested.

For their part in Randall's operation, Simmie and Poonta had made their way down another level, when Simmie's wrist coms went off. "Crap, not yet. Damn, I thought we had more time. Poonta babe, I need you to do a favour for me. I need to level this place once we're done. Get down to level four and make your way up to level two and the water treatment room, planting our cherries as you go. Wait for me there. Get all the others up out of there if you can. It's going to be our only way out". Simmie moved over and handed Poonta her bag of bombs she'd lovingly prepared earlier. Poonta tilted his head to one side and asked, "Whats yous mean, yous gotta come with mes. Mes need yous to come wif mes". He was distressed as he urged emotional blackmail onto her. "Not this time, babe. I need to slow these drones down and we've just had another thirty land. No time for heroics. Get the job done and I'll meet you on level two", Simmie chimed back. "Besides, I saved your cute arse back there and you owe me one, and I always collect. Now come on babe, move, go!" She used her hands to signal the importance of her words.

Not long after, Simmie watched as Poonta raced off to carry out her orders. 'Now the fun begins', she speculated. 'Time to set a personal best and get the hell out of here'. Simmie began readjusting her gear and setting out markers on her wrist coms. She flicked a button on her wrist screen and knew that anyone listening in on that frequency which she already blocked would lose their hearing just as the coms shorted themselves out. She also rechecked the Greaser, as she'd seen these working and couldn't figure out why this one wasn't. That's when she, too, spotted the hidden safety, 'Dicks, who the fuck would design it like this?' She clicked off the safety and made her way across to the next encounter. By the time she was finished, Santos would regret making the decision to send his pawns. He was the reason she was out here and on point. He'd been a thorn in her side and now she'd been given orders to erase the entire family, every single bloodline connected to The Merovingians, security force and all. It was going to be a pleasure and extremely personal when she finally separated his brains from his skull. Once she'd gotten what she needed from Randall that would be the end of 'The Merovingians' for good.

Simmie had also been given free rein to do with Randall as she pleased, although it had been made abundantly clear to her that the powers that be wanted him erased before he could cause irreparable damage. She'd witnessed a glimpse of what her mentor was capable of and it wasn't pretty. Given the opportunity, he was made of pure rock-solid ice. She'd witnessed him erase an entire platoon, three hundred soldiers with four drones he'd hacked. It was a bloodbath, no one walked away and the equipment he hacked levelled an entire city, including the population that inhabited it, close to two thousand, when he dropped the bombs. Randall could be a loose cannon now and she knew it, given his health, there was also the danger he could compromise the whole mission. She needed his help to obtain her results and to do that she needed to be seen to be helping him.

You scrub my back and I'll scrub yours, problem was she'd seen more than Randall's back in the past and she wasn't real sure if she could carry through all her instructions, given her exposure to, and experiences with, her mentor. She had another shot here, she just needed to decide what to do about it. That was something she would need to wrestle with and live with the outcome should that time or event eventually come to pass. No need to decide now, procrastination was the best course, a decision could be made later, much later…

VALLEY OF DEATH…

Now acting alone, Poonta raced down the fire stairs to level four. He bolted out of the exit and zipped open the bag Simmie had provided him, slinging it over his shoulder so he could set to work laying the cherries. He'd make sure he got this done for Simmie, plus he could reunite with the others helping them gain ground to level two. He'd never experienced anything like this as he gawked at the servers all lined up in a methodical grid pattern. He knew Randall said the level was large, but he had no idea of the power computers had on his and everyone else's life until he saw this. He realised at that moment this was only one server farm throughout the world. Knowing he had limited time, he worked his way methodically up and down each corridor across the huge room. After he was roughly three quarters done crisscrossing the room, he thought he heard familiar voices, but he couldn't be sure. Poonta rounded a corner not expecting the greeting he received. As he turned the corner, he saw two hooded figures and some kind of barricade. He watched the figures react, levelling their weapons at him. Instinct took over, his body went prone just as they fired. Two blue dots zipped overhead missing him by inches. As he was going down, he flung away the bag and drew one of his XVR 460 Magnums. His street smarts and experience kicked in. Hitting the floor, he swivelled into position and fired off three successive booming rounds. The third shot belted one of the figures squarely in the chest and he went down like a rag doll. He then scrambled for the cover of the corridor he'd emerged from to get out of the line of fire. A silence descended over the firefight and it felt like hours passed.

A voice then broke the void, "Poont, it's Vinch mate, you just shot Darren. Get down here! NOW!". It took a fuzzy incoherent amount of time for this to actually register. "That yous, Vinch?", Poonta screamed back. "Yes mate, get over here, now". Vinchi's voice sounded desperate. Poonta heaved himself up off the ground, gathered his gear and raced back into the corridor, heading for the barricade. He scuttled over it just in time to see Vinchi checking Darren's vital signs. "Oh fucks, eyes didn't means to kill him, oh shit!, oh nose, nose, nose. Darren, I'm so sorries", Poonta howled, utterly distraught, now on his knees next to Darren, not knowing where to look or what to do physically. Darren's body finally came out of shock. He spasmed and coughed, clearing his windpipe. "Oh, shit, I fucking hurt", he mumbled as he opened his eyes slowly taking in his surroundings. He was completely dazed, "I'm alive, I think", he winced in pain placing a hand on his chest very gingerly, "What the, arrr!", he groaned again. "Stop whinging, you're alive, the body armour stopped the bullet, it just knocked the wind out of you. I thought you were tougher than that", Vinchi advised harshly, trying to get Darren to think more cohesively and get his mind off the pain.

"You try getting shot. I heard something go crack", Darren whined, sitting up as he groaned again. He looked directly at Poonta, "Nice shot. I'm on your side remember. The good guys?", he winced again. Poonta helped Vinchi place Darren against the wall and opened his cloak. He then checked him over for any major damage, announcing, "Yours sternums cracked. It's nots fatal buts its gonna take months ta heal. Sore too fours a while. Can't carries heavy shit", Poonta enunciated slowly, providing his own diagnosis of the situation. "Great, at least get me back on my feet". Darren demanded, "Just don't do it again, ok?". Vinchi lost it a little, "Oh, stop whining. Poonta had a tree hit him, I had my foot and chest shot, Randall was almost killed with a head shot and you're whining about a little bit of a bruise". They heaved Darren up to his feet. Assessing the situation and obtaining a quick debrief from Poonta, both Darren and Vinchi agreed they needed to start moving. Even if Randall hadn't finished, they needed to get out now if they stood any chance of survival. But according to Poonta if Simmie couldn't hold the horde back a while longer they would soon be overrun and rumblings above them didn't sound very encouraging.

Once the vending machine doorway closed, Chandie realised she had been left alone to man, scratch that to 'wo-man', the fort. Darren and Vinchi had gone off to ensure that they could all make it back safely to the planned escape route, while she being a woman had been given baby-sitting duties. She remembered when her brothers had treated her like this, until she showed them she was much more capable than they had once thought. Having put up with that amount of bullshit in her youth she wasn't going to go through this again. Maybe it was about time her friends really knew what she was capable of. Chandie stared at the bubble for what seemed like an eternity. There was nothing she could do about Randall's seizures inside and he was trapped in that infernal machine until either it let him out via his commands or if she blasted her way in. Time passed excruciatingly slowly, this provided her time to think about what was really important to her right now and mull over how she had gotten to this point in her life. She had spent years plateauing along just fine keeping to herself. Blinkers kept her from making any real important decisions, except how to stay alive. She liked being alone but the friends she'd made to date at the park were lifesavers.

Chandie had found a real sense of belonging. But it wasn't until Randall crashed into their little safe haven one night, finding his way onto Darren's back porch, bloody, bashed and pissed from alcohol. Darren had cleaned him up and over time the two of them became good friends. It'd taken roughly six months for Randall to settle in, become an integral part of park life, a person anyone could trust and rely on to assist wherever he could. She hadn't really liked him at first, but his sense of humour and unique perspective on life, given the hand he'd been dealt, intrigued her. He had on occasions become the park's practical joker. Neville, to everyone's delight, was his main victim. She realised at this moment he'd made a major impact on her life and was rather pleased she'd really gotten to know him. They had so much fun together and Chandie knew they were close, just not sure how close. But given how she felt about him, she was now entering unknown territory, especially since this bloody Simmie had arrived on the scene. There was obviously more going on here then Randall was letting on, and more background story to Randall yet to be revealed. She would never have believed herself to be the jealous type, but this bitch now seemed to be encroaching on her man and was presently her direct competition, this made her blood boil.

This copper haired 'Rambetty' had better watch herself or Chandie would enlighten Simmie to the secondary uses of a rotor rooter. The hissing gas in the room broke that train of thought. After all that screaming and thrashing about there was finally silence inside the bubble. The humming and whining coming out of the bubble was slightly ominous, but Chandie stood her ground, waiting. Then the bubble went clear. She instinctively placed her hand over her mouth at the sight that confronted her. Randall was slumped in the sling seat and blood was all down his neck. The hissing coming from the glass bubble slowed and it began opening, the seat slid out with Randall still in place. Chandie struggled to get him out of the machine. Using all her strength, she carefully placed him on the floor next to the doorway. His breathing was shallow and he appeared to be unconscious, until his eyes opened rapidly, waking with a start. Randall looked up at Chandie's eyes and mumbled, "We need to get the hell outta here, NOW!". That was all Chandie needed. It was the time to take charge. Anyone who got in her way as she

tried to get Randall out alive, in one piece, was going to cop it —
literally.

Darren, Simmie and Ponta turned abruptly to see Chandie
doing her best to keep Randall vertical as they shuffled forward
towards them. Randall, as white a sheet and fresh blood all down
the left side of his neck. "What happened to him?", Vinchi blurted
out as he left Darren in Poonta's capable hands. "The node he was
in bit him, he's lost some blood", Chandie explained, as Vinchi
assisted her with Randall, and, sat him down against the wall on
top of a server to take a look at Randall's wound. Coming back to
his senses and latching onto some form of vague coherence,
Randall told Chandie to go back and grab the pouch, gear and
close up the vending machine. Chandie looked at Vinchi
hurriedly, who consoled her by saying, "He's fine, I've got him,
go, if he needs it go, go get it, now, don't muck around, go, go,
go!". Chandie was off like a shot racing away to retrieve all the
articles Randall had requested. Vinchi turned his attention to
Randall, "Gees, Mate, you really know how to make an entrance,
don't you, bloody attention-seekers, both of you. Darren's just as
bad", he accused jokingly. "Let me have a look-see. We may need

the field kit. What actually happened in there?", Vinchi asked, "You've lost a fair bit of blood, you'll be woozy, mate". Vinchi grabbed the field kit and took a more serious look at Randall's throat. "A couple of stitches and you'll be fine. It could've been a hell of a lot worse. You could look like Darren. He's gone and got himself a cracked sternum", Vinchi mused, trying to make light of it all. By the time Chandie returned from her mission, Vinchi had stitched up Randall's neck. Chandie handed the pouch to Randall, who instantly opened it, removed a small red electronic-looking cigar-like object, lifted the lid and pressed a button. The explosion that followed rocked the whole structure and its foundation. It blew the banana vending machine off its hinges through the glass partition opposite, slamming into a bank of servers. "Won't be needing that, anymore", Randall breathed out. "Time to make a move out of here I think".

The resounding chorus was one of uniformity, "Yes, Yup, Yeah and Fuck... Yes", echoed his friends eager to leave here in one piece. "We need to get to level two... the sewerage pipe", Randall exhaled, in an excruciating amount of pain. "You bet, boss. It's all blasted out, ready and waiting for us", Vinchi agreed

with Randall enthusiastically. "You're ok to move... You ready?".
"Of course, he's ready. He's got me to support him", Chandie chided, butting in harshly. "Poonta can look after Darren if needs be and Vinchi you can clear out the obstacles in our path. If it moves kill it... Let's get the hell outta here, NOW!". Everyone looked at this woman who now barked the orders. This whole adventure had changed her. She was more confident and now that the group's Alpha males had taken a beating, she was stepping up to take charge until further notice. No one questioned her and everyone prepared to move out. The gear was sorted and weapons readied, they moved forward back to ground zero, their only escape route. They would throw everything they had at any attempt to stop them. The pace was now reduced to a slow stilted shuffle, rather than a normal walking speed. Poonta kept an eagle eye on Darren as they both laid cherries, making their way up through level three. Chandie assisted Randall who had another seizure as they moved. As Randall collapsed, grabbing Chandie on the way down, she thought 'fuck no, not now' making her more determined to drag him out of there, along with everyone else, if she had to. The only way to get to level two from where

they were was either via the fire stairs or a service elevator. Given the condition of the group, Chandie chose the path of least resistance, heading for the elevator.

As the five shuffled into the elevator, the dishevelled group of friends heaved a sigh of relief. As the elevator raised to level two, the entire building shook, the electricity wavered, lights blinking on and off, the elevator stopped briefly to reset before continuing. Unfortunately, as the elevator stopped and the doors opened it was clear that it had halted three quarters of the way up between floors. "Shite.... Not now", Vinchi yelled as he looked at the opening and again at his friend's faces. Chandie didn't hesitate. Turning to Poonta, she issued orders, pushing the others physically into position, "Come on, no dicking about, let's get everyone out. Poonta, give me a hand with Randall, then Darren, Vinchi and me. We'll haul you up last Hun, ok with you?" She placed a hand tenderly on his right arm. "Do it, lets go, nose wasting time", Poonta engaged back, hauling Randall upwards and pushing him through the opening. He waved a hand at Chandie, "Yous next, needs to protect us all, if goes south... No, no arguments, moves sweethart". Poonta wasn't mucking around.

He was deadly serious and Chandie wasn't about to abuse or argue with him. She just jumped into his enormous hands for a boost up and out. Upon getting out of the elevator, she stood up and unholstered her new weapon. She moved Randall away from the opening and took up guard duty over his body.

Vinchi and Poonta heaved Darren out, followed swiftly by Vinchi, when the elevator shook. It dropped twice about three inches in quick succession, the look on Poonta's face was one of absolute desperation. He launched himself up, arms locked onto the floor, which was now a ledge to haul his huge frame up onto. Darren and Vinchi scrambled to assist, locking hands and pulling back with every ounce of strength they could muster. Darren winced in agony, but didn't flinch as the elevator dropped yet again, Vinchi used both his feet and dug in, heaving backwards, tugging with both hands. They had only just pulled Poonta out onto the floor when the whole complex rocked with another explosion. The elevator cable snapped, hurtling downwards rapidly as gravity took over. The next scene was one right out of a Mission Impossible movie. Vinchi lost his grip on Poonta. His hands slipped off him completely due to sweaty palms. Vinchi wound up thumping back onto the floor on his backside, the look of horror on his face said it all, Poonta was dead and now was he to blame for not holding onto his mate? Poonta slid backwards down into the elevator, dragging Darren with him. Darren hadn't let go, but did the only option available to him. In the very last seconds he'd noticed large brass urns either side of the elevator door.

Darren flung his legs out sideways and forwards, catching the urn on the right with both feet. Knocking it over he used his whole body, slamming it into the elevator doorway, jamming the elevators roof and downward momentum. The elevator bounced on the urn and landed back into place, then stopped. Darren was in no condition to help. He was writhing on the floor screaming, trying not to black out. Vinchi leapt up and grabbed Poonta instantly, having latched onto his mate again there was no way he would let go. This time he'd go down with Poonta if he had to. Poonta's reaction was pure adrenaline. He wrenched himself up and onto the floor between the urn and the elevator roof, Vinchi pulling him every step of the way. Explosions rocked the complex again and this time part of the ceiling came crashing down.

Regrouping they assessed the damage, "Anyone dead, yet?", Chandie barked. The simultaneous reply she heard was, "No, Nope, Nah", giving her all the confidence she needed.

"Alright, let's go", commanded Chandie. "No one dies on my watch or I'll kill you myself!" They started off again, the point of escape was etched into their psyche. 'Get to the Pipes'. Vinchi once again took the lead chuckling to himself, he was the dwarf being followed by Bashed, Bloodied, Broken and Bimbo. So much for that fractured fairy tale he grinned and mused to himself, this seemed more like a bizarre horror story. They rounded a corner and walked out behind a squad of death Ninjas headed in the other direction, approximately ten metres away. Everyone dropped into position and let rip with a barrage from the new toys Simmie had provided. The resulting chaos wound up disseminating the squad. They were entirely caught by surprise and were now a gooey mess even that video game plumber, 'The Dalai-Lama' of Waste Management, would balk at cleaning up. Carefully stepping around the puddles that had been the five operatives, they left behind the stench of entrails, bile and bodily fluids. Moving with haste, they headed for the safety of the sewerage pipes and freedom.

By now, well on her own, Simmie wasn't exactly making the headway she thought she would. She'd been cut off twice, blasting her way through using everything in her arsenal. She'd uploaded the schematics of the media station and used the weaknesses of the structure against them. Just having narrowly escaped some falling debris, she scarpered over the remaining rubble and body parts heading for the fire stairs doorway. Dust and debris was all over the place, bullet holes riddled the walls and she could hear the frustration building in her pursuers. 'Gotcha, you pricks, keep coming, have I got a gift for you', she smiled, as she leaped over a pile of smashed furniture. She was being followed in hot pursuit by at least eight black clad Ninja crows armed to the teeth and randomly returning a hail of bullets. 'Fuck me, if these are the best of the best money can buy. I'd want a fucking refund boys if you worked for me, dumb arses', she thought skidding under a falling doorway. As Simmie burst through the fire door and began hurling herself down the stairs of the concrete interior, she pressed a switch on her wrist coms and kept going as fast as she could. It sounded as if every mine (one million at last count) in the demilitarised zone between North and South Korea had gone off all at once. One would have not liked to have been outside or at ground level as the cherries Simmie and Poonta had laid detonated simultaneously. These were deadly little suckers.

The explosions rocked the very foundations of the media station, cracking structural pylons and load-bearing walls. The surrounding walls had been reduced to a huge pile of rubble, making them unrecognisable. The gantry level that held the guard towers exploded upwards as if hit by an ICBM. It collapsed through level one's roof structure, as the load-bearing walls beneath them blew out. This subsequent massive amount of weight collapsing all at once then gathered momentum, collapsing through the floor structure of level one into level two, below ground level, crushing everything in its path. The flying debris of the towers and lower levels expanded out in all directions simulating the Big Bang Theory. The electricity grid and sub station that had been erected in the courtyard then disintegrated into a million pieces, cutting the power to the whole facility.

Everything went dead and black, and above and below ground level resembled a morgue. It was cold, it stank, the smell of rubble and stale air soon filled your nostrils and the sense of impending doom that you were now trapped like a rat in a drain pipe, settled spookily into the minds of the still coherent.

'Panic would set in soon', Simmie smiled, flicking on her night vision visor, 'You're mine, now'. She was banking on her co-conspirator Poonta carrying out his task she'd set him. By the time this was over, part one of her job would've been completed, media station of The Astors destroyed, tick. 'But, to think the Ancients hadn't known about this place...fuck-wits', Simmie chided to herself. Her next thought turned to Randall. She hoped he'd had enough time to complete his end of the deal. Knowing her mentor the way she did from her previous experiences with him, as well as the fact he'd re-grasped his past, having had the disk reactivated, he was probably already way ahead of her. She was just hoping he was too befuddled to know he was being doubled-crossed by the Ancients. This didn't sit well with her, at all, as this was her mentor. Further given the last few days, she believed given enough time Randall would realise who she was and just maybe... That's when she realised a grenade had been thrown with accuracy from well above her. It bounced at an angle off the railing in front of her and landed on the concrete platform before her at the end of this flight of stairs. She reacted just as the grenade exploded.

INTO THE BREACH...

Santos's operative, Moretti, was absolutely seething he was losing men left, right and centre. The delivery of thirty new operatives was a brilliant relief. That meant Santos wasn't the idiot he believed him to be. He'd have to play this game more carefully. Once the RFID could be removed safely, he would make his move with Taigon to usurp that prick. The main concern now was communication had been severed, satellite coms were down and there was zero way to report back to Home base now that this bitch they were tracking had levelled the place. He had zero idea of how many operatives remained. There was no way to tell how many were dead, missing or even if any had deserted. They were all trapped underground, under the rubble and would run out of fresh air long before help arrived. They would need to complete the mission soon and find a way out no matter how many operatives he'd lost. Failure was not an option, so if he failed this mission he was a dead man, no matter how you sliced it. The main priority now was to kill these bastards and get out alive.

Having had to switch to night vision to even see his way around was a pain. This was going to be difficult at best, for Moretti, but not impossible. He had eight operatives with him now after a ceiling collapsed cutting the others off. Those particular operatives would have to make their way down and around the long way, before catching up and regrouping. Now it was a matter of finding at least this Chimera and eradicating it for the reward. Being stuck on level two underground, he started examining the schematics he'd downloaded prior to entry. Barking out orders, he directed four operatives to the sewerage and water treatment area, "Once we're done, that'll be our way out. Kill anything that moves, that's not me". Breaking off from the main group, the four operatives moved off down the now blackened corridor, to bunker down and guard the escape route. Moretti's batch of mercenaries each began scanning the way ahead, weapons raised. If the enemy wasn't on this level, they'd have to make their way down to the server farm, searching level by level, corridor by corridor. Having no power anywhere was a nuisance and being so far underground required being self-sufficient. These two in combination with each other would make for interesting confrontations. Making their way through one of the fire doors, they edged down the stairs to the severs on level four underground to confront their quarry.

Back at the Hexagon of Death, Santos was pacing in his office. This mission was going to shit at an alarming rate. The techs couldn't work out what was jamming the system, they couldn't even find a 'work around'. Whoever had crippled their system was not only intelligent, they'd done a brilliant job of covering their tracks. Given the whole screen had gone blank in his office and communications had been taken out by this unknown force, he was losing his cool. Vapour was pouring out from under his door at an ever-increasing rate, the mood in the operations room was deathly silent. Taigon raced up the stairs as Santos had summoned him for a face-to-face. He made his way through the mist in the office and found Santos staring at a photo on his office wall. "You ok, chief?", Taigon queried. "No, I'm not okay. 'The Head' wants to know why he just received a summons to meet 'The Head of the Astors'. What the fuck is going on out there? We can't get online, yet 'The Astors' are unaffected. Why Taigon?" Santos fumed, the veins in his neck popping out prominently. "It's clear we've been targeted and the data feeds as far as we can make out are phishing data, completely false. Even I can't get a response back from the redirect team we sent in". Taigon sounded utterly bamboozled and was doing anything he could to avoid being held responsible. "Can we contact Mizrah and the team he's leading to redirect them to the others?", was the statement barked back at Taigon. "Yes, I think so. I'll get on it straight away", Taigon answered, as he started to leave as quickly as he entered. "Hang on, there's one more important addition... This time you're going to meet them on site. I need someone competent out there on the ground. You're in charge. Don't fuck it up!" Santos demanded. He eyeballed Taigon. "Get it done, or don't come back, now get out!"

The dust and noise had settled, metal shards had gone everywhere. Picking herself up off the stairs, Simmie went to move and realised she had been hit, for the first time in five years she'd taken another injury. Her armoured clothing had protected her from death, that was a bonus, she couldn't really complain about her injury. She'd deal with it the only way she knew how, ignore it and move on. The fragment had penetrated the only chink in the armour, a fold between the back part of her calf armour and boot. It hurt like hell, but now was not the time. She uploaded a pain management info pack and used this to block the nerve pain. Right after that she constructed a temporary tourniquet and used QR blood clotting spray to seal the wound and finally assessed her weapons.

Simmie could hear someone running down the stairs. She suspected it was her hunter who'd thought he'd finished her off and was coming to procure a trophy. This prick was in for one hell of a surprise. She detached a small drone like object from her top pocket and placed in on the stair in front on her. Flipping open her wrist coms and by entering some commands it whirred to life. It looked like a flying wasp with one hell of a stinger attachment. Tilting at a specific angle, it took off rapidly up the stairwell. The next noise she heard was a gurgle and sounds of a body falling down the stairs, job done. Raising herself to her feet, she tried to stand, it still hurt so she downed a painkiller. 'Damn fool', she chastised herself, 'You're better than this, Simmie. If Randy ever found out he'd...', she caught herself, 'Oh my God', it'd been over twenty years and she still couldn't stop herself from wondering what her mentor would think about how she'd let herself be caught off guard like that. It was at that moment she decided she wouldn't carry out the orders of her superiors. In fact she decided that for once in her life she'd had enough of taking orders. She would let Randall go as long as he assisted her to finalise her mission and if at all possible, would pinch what she needed from the Ancients' armour cache and disappear along with him. Locking that thought into place, she positioned her night visor and launched herself down the stairs, hobbling as she went, determined to get them all out of here. She'd deal with any unforeseen problems later, even Candy.

Randall's rag-tag group made their way along the quiet forbidding corridor with Vinchi leading the pack, everyone had now switched over to night visors to make their headway much easier. This was going to be the worst game of laser tag ever. If you lost, it was game over, permanently. The media structure moved again, shaking dust, plaster and fragments from cracked glass partitions around them. It was a less violent rumbling, but enough of a reminder that the structure was now completely unstable. Time was now against them, air would eventually run out and the only way forward was through an approaching death squad. Vinchi reached the end of a corridor which turned left. He stopped and peered around slowly. Then he raised his hand for the others to stop, and held up three fingers. Poonta moved forward and handed a couple of spiky echidnas to him, silently indicating the red switch. Tension filled the air. Vinchi flicked the switches and then lobbed these balls of death at the three targets as hard and as fast as he could. Three seconds later, two explosions shook the area and razor sharp blades flew passed the company, burying themselves into the end wall. Vinchi slowly looked around the corner. He saw one body lying crumpled on the floor, the two others were missing. He turned to his followers and held up one finger and shrugged with his hands, confused as to where the other two had gone.

This was when Randall switched his visor from night to thermal. He stepped away from Chandie's protection and walked across the width of the hallway. Turning, he raised his Sonic Railgun, the humming coming from it was a high-pitched squeal. Randall waved Poonta and Darren to duck and once they were out of the way, he set off two successive blasts three metres apart. The concentrated blast ripped through the glass partition wall, into the rooms opposite, through the servers it hit and kept going until there were two very audible distinct screams. Holding up two fingers to Vinchi so the others could see, he grinned, "Still got it, come let's move". They slithered off around the corner moving down the corridor with all the stealth of a group of wounded elephants. There really was no way to disguise the noise they made. Stealth was not an option. They resigned themselves to the fact that they were going to have to blast their way out. The biggest issue however, was Randall, given he'd taken a wound to the neck his body was stressed and anxious. Adrenaline was now pumping through his body at an abnormal rate. This lead to him having more seizures than normal, with each becoming subsequently more and more severe, including expletives. Eventually, they rounded the fifth turn with Vinchi leading and Randall providing verbal navigation as he'd now detached himself from Chandie, arguing he was fine and that he'd be the rear guard.

The small bunch soon closed in on the sewerage room. This was when Vinchi abruptly stopped. He adjusted his visor and whispered as quietly as he could over his shoulder, "They've barricaded the sewerage room, both ways, thermal shows eight. Christ, what do we do now Randall, we're running out of time mate?". No answer. "Randall?", Vinchi whispered, "Chandie, where's Randall, weren't you supposed to be looking after him?". "I... he... oh Christ, I don't know, he was right behind me". She seemed perplexed, more importantly she was angry, she'd trusted Randall that he knew what he was doing, and he seemed coherent when they were quietly arguing. "I'm gonna kill him... I don't know. I'll backtrack and see if he's fallen down somewhere", she vented. "Don't be so stupid...", Darren barked softly. "Randall's a big boy, he knows what he's capable of more than any of us... Besides we would have heard him fall down, he's not exactly quiet". "Whadda we do's now Vinch?", Poonta whispered. "Wes runnin outta time. Shouldn't Wes keep going?". Vinchi looked up at his big friend, "We need a plan, mate, we can't just go in guns blazing, we'll all wind up dead... Thoughts anyone?". That's when they heard the firefight breakout. This caused a normal reaction in all of them. So they flattened themselves against the wall.

Randall had heard a sound behind them and stopped to investigate. It was a shuffling sound, bipedal and getting closer. So he decided to confront this threat to allow the others to make their way into the sewerage room and out to freedom. He moved in through an open doorway and stood behind a vertical set of servers. Ten seconds later an armoured figure smoothly shuffled passed the door. Moving swiftly, Randall landed the first punch and hit so hard he heard a rib crack. Feeling the resistance, he adjusted for the armoured vest and then landed a second as he struck like lightning to crack another. He moved in to take out the legs from under this threat, just as he received a knife to the thigh that glanced off. Randall disarmed the entity and the two were then locked in a close-quarter combat death grip. This wraith had knocked Randall's visor off, so he was as blind as a bat and that's when pure instinct, and training, kicked in. He closed his eyes. Randall resorted to using the disks upload-able martial arts training and all of his other senses, ensuring that this would be a close combat encounter because if they got away it was all over. It turned into a brutal wrestling match. He took blow after blow and gave as good as he got. It wasn't until he had the upper hand that he hesitated, from a now-standing position, he'd grasped a right arm, preparing to break it at the elbow and then snap their neck. He kicked out at the ankle to collapse this combatant, preparing to follow through on his actions when she screamed in sheer pain. He pushed away as hard as he could toppling this nemesis, spread eagled onto the floor, face first, before he could finish her off.

"Simmie?", he yelled, "Shit, stop, stop, stop!!!". There was an awkward silence that followed. Simmie grimaced in agony, "Oh fuck", she blurted out, spat out a mouthful of blood and spun around to face him, "Randy?, Argh... Oh Christ, I hurt... You arse hole!". Randall moved closer until he could feel the side of her boot and moved his way up slowly in the dark, gently feeling his way until he was right next to her. Before he could speak, Simmie announced, "That's not my leg honey... Oww". She flinched, but didn't push him away. All Randall could feel was regret and fear, "Oh shit, Simmie, I didn't know it was you", he revealed as he put his arm around her shoulder and leant in. "Oh God, I'm sorry, I'm really sorry. Can you move, how bad is it? What can I do?". Simmie shifted herself so she was sitting further upright. "Well, for starters you can remove your hand, uhhh.... owww...", she flinched again. "I knew you were good, honey, but.... No, come on, I've had worse. Help me get to my feet". Randall complied, lifting her as gently as he could to her feet. She winced in pain, given her cracked ribs. Simmie leaned in against him softly and sighed in pain as she hugged him back. He had his arms around her, holding her up gingerly, trying not to hurt her anymore, feeling extremely guilty he'd inflicted pain and had almost snuffed out her lights. He was just about to apologise again when she came out with, "Oh, my hero...", she said sweetly, snuggling in closer.

Randall couldn't work out if she was taking the micky out of him or if she was just glad to still be alive. "Yeah, well, I don't feel like one... I could've killed you!, Damn you. Are you able to move?. We really don't have time for this". Randall was trying to extract himself out of this situation as delicately and as diplomatically as he could. "I suppose so if I have too, argh....", she said as she winced again, "Seriously, it's not that bad. I'll recover, but I'll need nursing back to health", she murmured and touched his face. Randall was now the one that flinched. "Seriously... Our lives are in danger and you want to muck around. You're hurt and we need to get out of here. I need to get you out alive...". She cut him off, "Oh, he does care, I was wondering how long it'd take you... Arghhh". This time she lost some strength in her legs and went down. Randall supported her and held her upright, "Simmie... Stop the sarcasm, I'm being serious here, I need to know if you're capable of holding your own, still?".

Randall was scolding her as he held Simmie up. "Where's my visor?", he said, looking around. "Funny boy, I know you can't see anything. I could really take advantage of you", Simmie chided. "Simmie!", he squeezed her upper arm, "Come on sweet, give me a hand here, we need to get back to the others in one piece. They're going to need both of us if possible. Play later, fair?". Simmie grabbed a handful of Randy's 'family jewels', "I'll hold you to that". She let go and bent over to pick up Randall's night visor. He put it back on immediately as Simmie grabbed him again. He looked her up and down and grinned, "Your turn to let go, hey... You seem fine to me... Come on, let's go, partner, the Chimeras have a job to do". Placing his hand gently on her shoulder, he turned and led the way. Randall set his mind to the task ahead. He was going to make sure they all got out. He was now utterly pissed off and Simmie saw it all over his face. She had only ever seen him this enraged before, that time he actually eliminated an Ancient. The moral of that story was never ever inflame a weapon that can turn on you if you can't control it. That scenario was a whole other story, one she wasn't in a hurry to revisit, so Simmie clammed up and prepared herself for what was yet to come. Randall was now completely unpredictable.

CHAPTER TEN

BENEATH GROUND ZERO...

Having reached level four, Moretti's crew fanned out. They crisscrossed the level of servers looking for intruders. As they moved, they ensured that they kept at least one of the others in sight at all times. This quarry was not going to get the drop on them. Eventually, they arrived at what was left of the banana vending machine. Moretti stared at the rubble that was once the hallway which led to the node. There was no determinable way to know what this hallway led to or what was now entombed. This was also another family's infrastructure and not being familiar with it, didn't help any. As the operatives gathered they saw a mixed look of confusion and intense focus settle into place as Moretti started barking, "Has all this level been scanned?". One operative who thought he was next in line replied, "Yes, nothing unusual to report apart from this anomaly right here". He was pointing directly at the destruction around them. "Any sign other than this of activity or breaches?". He scanned everyone as he said this. The reply was one in unison. "No". Moretti was sure he was right, he was sure they'd make their way down here. He had banked on the fact that the servers were what these people were after. He couldn't be that wrong, could he? If he was, he was a dead man. Moretti walked a couple of steps back and forth pacing up and down the corridor, staring down at his feet thinking, shaking his head from side to side, as he mulled over his thoughts.

This prey Moretti was stalking, had levelled the entire complex. They'd taken out the Astor Family's sentries to get in here, so what the hell was it they were after and why blow up a section of the server level. Were they trying to get at something or destroy a critical part or information, surely they weren't that dumb? The Astors would have backups everywhere so they could upload at a moment's notice. Was it information they wanted to steal, maybe for blackmail? It just didn't make any sense. It was a huge amount of trouble to go to just to steal information, and the whole facility was useless now given that there was no electricity and with no power there was no access to information. It was while he was mulling over these thoughts one of the group interrupted, "Ah chief, you were right". Moretti looked up perplexed at what was said, and why, "What in God's name are you on about, Jacobs?". Jacobs pointed as he explained, "Over there. There's something blinking. I hadn't noticed until now. The blinking is getting faster". Moretti followed the line of sight towards where the operative was pointing. He glanced at the little black ping pong ball. It's little red deadly eye was blinking on and off rapidly in succession. Moretti then surveyed the corridor both ways. These 'mini balls of death' were scattered everywhere. "Holy Mother of God, they've land-mined the place, they're set to destroy the complex. Get to level two, NOW!". In the split second that followed, everyone who had surrounded Moretti was off and running. All of them were praying they'd reach the sewerage room and out to breathable air without getting blown up along with the facility.

Simmie now followed Randall at a slow pace. He made sure that his partner was quite able to keep up with him as he wasn't going to leave her behind. There were way too many questions left unanswered at this point. Additionally, he needed to sort out the tension that he was sure would arise when the others found out his full background. That was one conversation he wasn't looking forward too, but had seriously considered needed doing. He had no intention of going back to work for his previous employers and had decided to enlighten his friends, no matter what the consequences. Before they moved off, he readjusted his weapons and took the lead, indicating for Simmie to be as quiet as she could. She gave him a farcical look, as if to agree, but wouldn't guarantee anything, pointing at her ribs and leg. It was a pantomime routine he'd never let her forget, he laughed and grinned silently. Moving down the hallway, Randall was busy accessing the disk, providing him the best route towards the sewerage room and other schematically correct data. At the next corner he stopped. Switching from night to thermal, he slowly peered out at the sewerage room. Scanning the room, he was grateful that the hunters weren't using heat masking armour and that the partitions were made of glass. He silently indicated back to Simmie and with his right hand, four fingers then another four. "Cool, let's roll!", Simmie whispered, setting her weapons and steadying herself.

Randall turned and voiced in a low manner, "Like hell, you're severely injured and will only slow us down". Simmie grabbed Randall's left shoulder and forced him to look at her as she retaliated, "Listen to me, you arrogant prick, if it wasn't for me you'd still be wallowing back in that cess pool of a park. I've been taking care of business since you bloody left. I was ordered to stay put... I've just got my beau and mentor back, I'm going in whether you say so or not. I don't need your protection. If anything, it's the other way around!". Randall softly placed his index finger on Simmie lips to keep her whispering as she was starting to raise her voice. "Fine, you'll be pleased to know I remember now...", he replied and tapped his head. "Thanks to you, I have my memories back. We'll talk later, about everything, fair... For now, all I need to know is, are you ready, partner?". "For you honey, I'm always ready. Let's roll. See you on the other side", Simmie leaned forward and placed her head on Randall's chest. Standing up straight, they both began to ready themselves. Pulling the hoods and electronic HUD's into place, Randall swapped weapons with Simmie. Each held two weapons, Randall dual Sonic Railguns, Simmie dual Greasers.

Zahed, who was just a pawn in Moretti's game, had joined the Merovingian Family for easy money. He was a typical armed forces recruit who had major attitudinal problems, especially with authority. Upon dishonourable discharge and release from the brig, he found employment as a mercenary for the highest bidder. The past two years had been extremely profitable. Unfortunately, that was all about to change. On this mission he'd seriously considered going missing-in-action, as this operation was going to shit. Now, he was trapped underground with limited escape options! The moment he saw two armour-clad fast-moving figures rounding the corner towards the sewerage room, dual weapons in both hands, his only thought was, 'Run'. Their movements were extremely well choreographed. This was a deadly ballet they had done before. Randall moved right in a sweeping diagonal action across the corridor, Simmie went left. As they moved, Randall let loose with an insane barrage of automatic Sonic Bomb Shells. These smashed into the glass partitions, shattering glass everywhere, servers that were hit erupted into metal shards, plastic bullet-like objects and razor sharp pieces of cable. The blasts detonated with such explosive force on anything they struck, turning objects into murderous confetti. The combination of sweeping the whole entry into the sewerage room forced the enemy back further trapping them. The mercenaries weren't giving up without a fight. The hail of bullets unleashed was incredible.

Being well-prepared, highly-skilled, experienced and equipped with state of the art armour gave Randall and Simmie the advantage. They'd also been here before. This was second nature to them. As trained assassins they moved with all the grace and fluidity of ballet dancers and the lethality of a modern day Gatling gun. Bullets glanced off their specialised armour as they raced forward, taking substantial heavy hits, slowing them momentarily. They trusted their armour to do its job as they did theirs. Having expected this retaliation, Simmie simultaneously sprayed the entire area Randall was demolishing with carnivorous little blue dots. Whatever infrastructure wasn't blown away to oblivion, the rest was melted away as their atoms dissolved. Upon hearing three different succinct screams, Randall scanned the room as he prepared to enter what was left of the entryway. Simmie stopped beside him, glancing around at their handiwork. She looked up briefly at Randall and nodded. The anti-room had been obliterated.

After recovering from his initial reaction, Vinchi peered out from his hiding spot, not far down the same corridor in absolute awe at what he was witnessing. Poonta yelled from behind him, "Whatcha seeing". Vinchi was trying desperately to extract any information at this point that would help their survival. "It's Randall and Simmie", was all he conveyed back over his shoulder, "They've cleared a path and need our help. Come on, move". He didn't even wait for a response. He was off and around the corner, headed straight for the sewerage room. "Oh, for Christ sake, another hero", Darren yelled. "Let's go get him before he gets himself killed". Chandie took off after him. Poonta not wanting to be left behind ran as fast as his legs could carry him. Vinchi was quick and using all his speed, closed the gap, screaming, "Randall, it's Vinchi!". He used this phrase, thinking it was being helpful. However, Vinchi soon found himself diving directly at the floor as a blast hurtled just over his head. After his tuck and roll he came up in a kneeling position, weapon at the ready thinking he'd made a mistake of identity. Darren passed Chandie, pushing her to the ground in case she was next and let loose with his Eagle forgetting completely he had a

Greaser attached at his hip. Accurate to a tee, it was a direct hit to Randall's left side thigh, which struck square-on. Randall buckled ever so slightly, then stood up with ease holding his thigh, smoothly composed himself and flipped the bird to Darren.

Satisfied it was Randall, Darren had halted behind Vinchi, stood upright and shrugged with his hands, indicating his somewhat lousy apology. Staring straight ahead at the leading figure, Vinchi saw Randall wave a hand in his direction urging him on, like Neo urging on Agent Smith. The two figures then disappeared into the rubble. Chandie touched Vinchi's back as she reached and crouched down next to him, "You, ok?", genuinely concerned that he had almost been ripped to shreds. Turning to face her just as Poonta arrived, Vinchi's confident demeanour was self-evident, "It's them. Darren tried to shoot Randall... We need to cover them. Let's go!". Moving as quickly as he could, given his injuries, Vinchi shuffled off. Poonta placed a hand on Chandie's back to encourage her to follow him. Chandie cuffed Darren in the back of the head as she passed him. Soon all four were standing in what was left of the sewerage room entrance way, the sound of gunfire and explosions echoed from inside the room. Each looked a little dumbfounded as to what happened now. Chandie spoke first, "Let's move in and find a spot to dig in. I gather there's more coming this way. Come boys... You wanted excitement, Poont honey, will here it is". Moving from the anti-room into the maintenance and staff changing area, all three noticed a gooey blob, a hand and a lower left leg, foot included. "I've counted four", Poonta said, "Mores coming, can feel in mes guts. We needs to follow them and locks the door, an barricades its". Feeling the room rock and shake with the blasts from the sewerage and water treatment room, Vinchi knew the mercenaries didn't stand a chance. "Where to now, Vinch?", Chandie urged. She knew he knew these rooms and where to go. "This way", Vinchi answered, as he moved towards the metal door where the sign indicated, '*Staff Only*'. Entering through the door, Vinchi knew he had originally come out of, he started feverishly searching the room. Amazingly he only now just realised that this was the only room with a self-supporting generator and emergency lighting was on.

The others also having realised this, lifted their visors to see more clearly, blinking as their eyes adjusted to the lighting.

Vinchi had taken about eight steps inside, followed by Chandie, Darren and Poonta, when they found three more very distinct gooey blobs on the floor. An appropriate end to some very violent people. Bullet holes had riddled virtually everything in the room, floor, ceiling, pipes, chairs and control panels. Moving deeper into the room towards where Vinchi had surfaced through the sewerage pipe, they found Randall cradling Simmie in his arms. They leant up against the section that Vinchi had cut open with the thermite putty. Randall was obviously in distress. Chandie was first on the scene pushing past Vinchi, "Oh Christ, what happened?". Randall looked up as Chandie approached, "High impact explosive. She's alive but unconscious". "How the hell is she alive still?", Chandie urged, sheer desperation in her voice. "Body armour and luck. No time to explain now. Poonta, Darren, Vinchi, barricade that door, use anything heavy you can find. GO, NOW!," Randall looked up at Chandie with remorse, pain and a huge amount of regret in his eyes, "I'm going to need your help to get her out of here. I can't leave her here. You up for that?". "Of course, I am, we all are. We need to get out of here, now. Keep her safe, I'll go help the guys, we'll be back, don't go anywhere, promise?". Chandie placed her hand softly on Randall's cowl-covered head and smiled back at him, "She's an important part of our crew now, there no way we'll leave her here, back soon, Hun". She then rapidly shifted off to assist the guys.

As Vinchi and Chandie searched for items that could block the doorway and hold the security door in place, Darren had levered a computer console off its table top and Poonta had found a crowbar. Poonta gently moved Randall and Simmie out of his way. He then used the crowbar in his hand to lever the section of pipe out of its current position that Vinchi had cut through to get into this room. This then gave all of them proper access to it so they could exit out that way. The next feat of human endurance was even more incredible. Bracing himself in a steadfast position, Poonta lined up with the section of pipe as he would have when lifting weights and heaved upwards. Using his sheer bulk and muscular agility, he raised the pipe section above his right shoulder, moving it over in front of the doorway. Standing in position, he released the section of pipe to the floor with an ear-shattering crash. Vinchi, Darren and Chandie then helped to restrain the door with anything they could find heavy enough to delay entry and create time. Poonta then forced the crowbar through and around the horizontal door bar, locking the mechanism in place.

All four made their way over to Randall still unaware of how Simmie was going. Poonta looked physically upset and was fidgeting with his hands. Darren looked like he was only just now sobering up. Vinchi, whose eyebrows which already had been singed off previously, now had forehead furrows so deep, they resembled a freshly ploughed field. Chandie just couldn't contain herself, "Come on you lot, she's not dead yet. Vinchi, this is the way you came in, right?". Vinchi nodded followed up by, "Huh, um yeah, it is. It'll fit all of us at a squeeze. I just don't know how we're going to get Simmie inside and then out in the state she's in?" Vinchi was looking completely perplexed. "Well, guess what sunshine, you get to lead the way", was Chandie's chastising response, "Randall will go next, followed by Poonta, Simmie and me. Darren you bring up the rear, ok, great. Poonta honey, we've got the hardest task. You most of all. You're going out backwards dragging our poor Simmie as you go and I'll help. Think you can handle that big boy?".

"Yes", was Poonta's only response. "Right so, let's move people. We're about to run out of air and the last scenario we need is to die in this shitty pipe, let's go, come on, we can shower later", was the encouragement Chandie provided. Everyone began to move, Chandie's plan seemed solid enough. Vinchi was convinced, Poonta did some stretching exercises, Darren yawned and Randall began to get Simmie's body into position with the help of Chandie. The lights started to flicker on and off. "Ok people we're running out of time here, let's move", Chandie yelled. Everyone was soon inside and all headlamps were activated. Chandie yelled out again, her voice echoing off the pipe walls, "Vinch Hun, how far do we need to go?". "About two hundred metres, two football fields, maybe less", came the response. "Ok, you're our eyes, just make sure you provide accurate info and don't go too fast, we've got Simmie remember?", was Chandie's recourse, trying to summon as much confidence as she possibly could. She certainly wasn't going to tell the boys now, that she was highly claustrophobic.

It was a long arduous task. They couldn't move very fast given one of them was unconscious. Poonta and Chandie took every precaution and care to make sure Simmie wasn't hurt any more than needed, given that they were escaping out through a pipe only a metre and a half in diameter. Every ten metres or so Vinchi would yell back roughly how far they had travelled. They had only gotten about eighty metres when they heard banging on the sewerage room door. The hammering continued for another thirty and suddenly stopped. "Oh fuck, we're trapped like rats in a drainpipe", Chandie admitted stating the blatantly obvious. "If they start firing in along here, we're all dead". Vinchi was the first to reply, "Chandie my dear, when are you ever going to realise that I'm a devious little prick, and always, always, have a second and third option to get myself out of trouble!". "Cover your eyes people, this is going to get loud, noisy and a bit smelly", Vinchi smirked, as he dived his right hand into his top trouser pocket. He retrieved a small detonator switch and yelled, "One, two, three, close your eyes!". The next instant a section well and truly behind them erupted in an immense glare as the thermite burst noisily into flame. The smell was horrible, but at least they didn't get singed like Vinchi did the first time around, as the pipe had been open long enough for the vapours to escape, so the only point they needed to be aware of was to not look at the glare. Even with their eyelids closed, all of them knew when the thermite had done its job.

The glare behind closed eye lids died out to black and there was an almighty crash as the pipe collapsed in on itself, blocking the entry back into the media station. Breathing a sigh of relief, the little group forged ahead as quickly as they could to escape this death trap. Emerging out of the end of the pipe, everyone gasped, taking in a huge breath of sweet fresh air. They moved off to a small opening in the scrub, carrying Simmie as gently as they could and settled her onto the ground. Standing up, they dusted and wiped themselves off. Everyone smelt like shit, literally. It was just too much, given they'd almost died in there and had emerged covered in faeces. "Oh, Holy Shit, what a crappy experience", Vinchi burst out laughing. The others couldn't help themselves. They all followed suit jubilantly as well. As the others celebrated their escape, Randall bent down next to Simmie, zipped open a pocket, reached into her trousers and pulled out a black box. He flicked open the top cap and pressed the button. The explosions that followed knocked everyone off their feet. Everyone looked shocked, then, realising what Randall had done, burst out laughing again. Randall joined in, he'd just destroyed the remaining levels of the media station, each level collapsing downwards, crushing the sewerage room and floor along with it. 'That was one group of vile hunters who won't be following us', Randall mused. Their foes were now completely entombed. The plumes of smoke, dust, dirt and grit flew into the air about twenty metres, enough to be seen from the ridge where the group were now located. Unfortunately, it was also seen by Taigon, who had arrived on the scene with another twenty operatives, as well as the other ten who had accompanied Mizrah to the server farm inside the city.

THROUGH THE JUNGLE....

On Randall's command, the five gathered up their gear and Poonta heaved Simmie up as gently as he could onto his shoulder. As he began carrying her, the rest of the gear was shared among the others as they started their escape. Randall had advised his friends they would be making their way to the rusty tin shack where he and Simmie had parked the ATV. There would be plenty of room for everyone, plus Vinchi could spread Simmie out in the back and perform proper first aid and attend to her wounds. He also confessed that he'd cracked two of Simmie's ribs and possibly her ankle, so he asked Poonta to be extremely gentle with her. These comments didn't go unnoticed by Chandie. However, she shook this off, chiming in sarcastically, "Remind me never to piss you off, Hun". To which Randall responded by glaring at her while holding up his fingers in a display of importance as he added a harsh inflection to his words, "It's not funny Chandie. Two seconds, two... if I hadn't recognised her scream when I fractured her ankle, I'd have snapped her neck and she would be dead at my hands... what if it had been you I'd killed? I couldn't live with that... I want both of you out of here alive, along with everyone else. I'm responsible for everyone being here and so far I've nearly gotten everyone killed. So, let's find the ATV and get outta here, once we're safe and free we'll all sit down and have 'that' conversation, all of us". He then gestured to everyone in the clearing, "Fair?".

The others nodded back in unison. Chandie was taken aback as she'd not seen this Randall before, he was serious and

425

terrifying all at the same time. He was beating himself up because he'd dragged his friends into danger and so far they'd been lucky, very lucky. "Fair Hun, I was just joking", she said trying to defuse the tension. "It's okay Chandie. I just don't want anyone hurt any further, physically or emotionally, but it is probably already too late, if I could've done this alone I would have. We need to roll, I surmise we're not alone out here, we're yet to strike the main force. Everyone gear up and be ready for anything, I'll lead". It was at this point Randall patted Vinchi on the shoulder, indicating he'd take over the lead as he moved off. Everyone followed Randall's commands and soon the group was forcing its way downhill, away from the media station. Randall touched the back of his head and appeared like he was in a trance, then they shifted direction sharply, making a direct beeline for the ATV. There was no way Randall would take any chances now, he made it very clear he'd get them all out or die trying. After about thirty minutes of hiking through the scrub, they eventually came across the tin shack Simmie had hidden the ATV in. Looking at it in the light, Randall was surprised that this rusty edifice hadn't collapsed.

As Randall opened the shack door he saw the ATV was still there and breathed a sigh of relief. Jumping into the driver's seat, he placed his hand on the biometric scanner and the engines roared to life. T-Rex was back and ready for some major carnage. Randall drove the ATV out and underneath the largest tree ensuring they were out of satellite view. He flicked a switch and raced around to the back as the hatch opened automatically. Poonta and Darren lifted Simmie onto the flat, sliding floor panel. Vinchi rifled through his backpack for the medikit, readying himself to play field doctor. Randall walked up beside Chandie, leaned in close and muttered, "I need you to ride shotgun, and man the side weapons. This lot can take care of Simmie and man the back hatch's Sonic turrets. You fine with that?". Chandie smiled, put her arms around him, squeezing the life out of him, then she let go. "Sure, I can help with navigating. I was great at orienteering". Randall hugged her back and grinned, "Cool, thanks Hun. You also get to play with the onboard weapons controls, too, come on, let's move". As they boarded the ATV Randall gave everyone a quick rundown on the weapons layout, seating, ammo, medical equipment and harnesses. Vinchi started checking on Simmie's wounds and vitals while Randall plugged in their destination to the onboard GPS. He fired up the engines again, slammed his foot onto the accelerator and engaged the other dash screen to scan for the enemy.

The huge four wheels bit into the ground, hurling gravel into the air as it launched forward, gathering speed, all eight hundred and seventy-five horsepower growled like a demon awakened from hibernation. As they raced along through the bush on what looked like an old dirt road, Chandie opened up a conversation with Randall, "So where are we headed sweet?" Randall kept an eye on the road as he answered her, "I took the liberty of arranging passage via a ship while I was in the bubble. I lifted Simmie's communicator a while back so I could make contact with my previous employers, 'The Ancients'. She wants out, too, so I decided she's coming with us and I've negotiated passage for us all. They've agreed to organise a private ship for our disappearance, provided I give them complete access to 'The System'. We agreed in theory because I've also an insurance policy to keep us all safe. I've agreed that if they require my specific skillset in the future, they have it. But if they decide to erase us, and, if I don't activate my personal broadcast beacon at very specifically timed intervals, every single piece of data and proof I have on them and other elites gets dumped simultaneously. It'll be uploaded to open source and all multiple media sites, globally. The underlying condition was they let all of you live and leave me and Simmie alone unless it's absolutely necessary. So, to answer your question Hun, we're headed for a safe house at the base of the world in New Jackson. This will be via private first class transportation where we'll never have to want for anything ever again, so as promised — our Eden".

Darren couldn't control himself, "Excellent, so we're talking rain, cold, wet, snow, wind and best of all no government interference, that's been declared a neutral tax free safe haven and an independent sovereign state for decades... Whoa, whoa, whoa hang on. How? That's an exclusive ultra-wealthy state, how the hell did you arrange that? I gather this beast has autopilot. I think it's confession time before we all rip out some of your vital organs, individually. I think you owe all of us a complete explanation pronto, Icarus!". The others chimed in angrily, all at once, also demanding to know what Randall was hiding from them, who he really was now and why all the secrecy. The only one not being demanding was Chandie. She told the others to stay silent and let Randall explain. She turned to Randall offering him a lifeline, "The stage is yours Hun, make it count". Randall swallowed, coughed then called back over his shoulder, "You happy, with that Simmie? You're not the only one who can play possum. You've been conscious for a while now, you even enjoyed the ride on Poonta's shoulder?". Vinchi looked down at Simmie confused. She then opened her eyes and winked back up at him and blew him a kiss. Sitting up gingerly with Poonta's help, she moved to one of the back seats, "Go for it, they deserve to know the vipers we're dealing with. Moreover, I think they've earned it". She let her head fall onto Poonta's shoulder and stretched a hand out to Vinchi who took it as she mouthed the words, 'Thank you'. "O.K.", said Randall, "Buckle up kids this is going to be one scary story".

Everyone remained silent, listening without interrupting, as Randall began to explain everything. He began with the history of 'The Ancients' and their intervention across time, to the rise and fall of every civilisation, their interference and introduction of selected technologies to the masses and the wars they initiated. Then he disclosed how the thirteen families or the one World Monarch was created and that they were in control of the world's population. They had been provided that position by 'The Ancients' to maintain obedience and control of everyone. The scary bit was that their hunters were from a lower class family trying to ascend up the ladder — 'The Merovingians'. Randall provided their entire history and background. This is when he advised Simmie that her mission to eradicate them was in hand and she was relieved of her duty for this task. Their bloodline would be 'history' by this time next week. He then explained the committee of three hundred and its distinct control mechanisms of each continent, from politics to banking to commerce and the ruse of the Government-enforced pension fund that went bust and that all funds were really just siphoned off electronically.

The funds had been globally transferred off for the elites as they needed it for another war between India and China. It wasn't a stock market crash. Then he expanded on this to include the control reasons behind the crypto-currency which made up today's cashless society. He recalled that the Think-Tanks were created as Big Brother spy agencies to monitor people, breach one's privacy, and keep closely guarded secrets to maintain the ultimate deception. Upon Randall's highlighting of every individual elite position from politicians to Kings, Queens and wealthy entrepreneurs, Darren took in a deep breath, but remained quiet. Randall then explained that all of these pieces fitted together to manipulate the population to do their bidding as pseudo-slaves and not with free will as everyone thought. Since no one interrupted, he elaborated on how these factions kept their own wealth and power intact and accumulated more, all while others struggled under the perception that all people had free decisions and choices while becoming more and more interconnected. Going on, Randall de-cloaked why social media had evolved and why the interconnectivity of technology was paramount as a way to maintain surveillance and invade a person's own privacy and control all the people's behaviour. Randall went on to verify that all of it was true, that the 'conspiracy theories' were real and completely hidden from the general population. The confirmation also included the names of people murdered and eliminated who threatened to expose the truth, but didn't have the leverage to back up their threats.

Randall recounted how he, like Simmie, had been genetically crafted by special DNA as Chimeras and what that actually meant to be the ultimate human weapon to maintain the peace and balance as others had before them. The silence persisted, so he elaborated about his newly-found skillset and how the disk in his head enabled him to download his new multiple talents. This and the ability to upload information seamlessly as these disks were imbedded into the neuro-cortex of the brain allowing him and Simmie to perform super-human feats as a global peace-keeping force. The fact that there were exactly four thousand of them across the globe was news to Simmie who looked stunned when Randall explained all of this. She was about to interrupt when she thought better of it and waited for him to finish. Randall went on to outline how the Ancients were the real power and that some of them may have heard the myths or folklore tales of them and Chimeras as 'the bogeyman', going on to explain the stories behind these 'legends', to which Vinchi and Darren just nodded. Randall also touched on the creation of 'The

System' and how he was one of the main architects with ultimate access granted via the Astor Family or the top of the tree of the World Monarch elite.

By the time Randall had recounted all that he knew, each of his friends sat in stunned awe. They then sat in silence, taking it all in, trying to make sense of what they'd always been told was once the truth, or real life. Seeing that no one was about to speak, Randall continued on. He explained again how he was selected to create the overarching parts of 'The System' to keep control of the masses, but how he'd also created multiple back doors should he ever need to access them one day, like today. He had taken advantage of the node to transfer funding to himself in an encrypted account only accessible in the New Jackson node or AntartiGate. Randall provided information about the last twenty years of his life and that he'd taken on a voluntarily induced selective amnesia to maintain his cover. Simmie went white knowing she'd been the one to reactivate him, a point which Vinchi witnessed silently. She also listened quietly as he recounted what the life was he thought he was living, not knowing it was all a lie until his medical condition overtook his own abilities to control his mind and how it all fell apart. He'd fallen from grace with no safety net, disavowed by the powers that put him there. Simmie could hear the hate resonating in Randall's voice, the venom was unmistakable. Randall reiterated that he'd accessed 'The System' to shift funds belonging to the elite families and copied 'The System' access codes for the Ancients and himself as blackmail or a bargaining chip for their lives. He then went silent.

Darren was the one who spoke first. "So how much are we talking here?". Vinchi punched him in the shoulder, causing Darren's ribs and sternum to move and he winced. Vinchi piped up next, "You're a dick, Darren. Randall's put his life on the line for all of us with the powers that govern whether we live or die and that's the first question you ask? Our apologies, Randall, please continue, mate". Vinchi glared at Darren, but then turned his attention back to Randall. Randall looked at Chandie before he continued. He noticed she was looking at him with a new-found respect, fully appreciative of what he'd done and been through to get this present result. Randall grinned, glancing at Chandie as he spoke. "It's no problem Vinch. I'll take Darren's question as a 'thank you', considering we all know it's all bluff and blow. Let's see: how does eight hundred billion in untraceable crypto-currency or one hundred and thirty billion each sound? Well, I figured we'd buy our way into New Jackson with another ten billion. That's already been transferred and in place so 'Eden' actually awaits. We just have to get there in one piece". Randall turned his attention to Simmie. "Simmie, partner... You've been taken off active duty. You're officially retired, for now, like me, but you need to come with us to stay alive. The Ancients aren't pleased, but I cut us a deal. We've got another mission once we're bedded down and have a home base, that was part of the agreement, I hope that's ok? There's two hundred Chimera now fully activated globally to wipe out the Merovingian blood line, but you and I have been tasked by the Ancients with something else entirely. You're not gonna like it, but at least we're alive, so that can wait. There's only one other small wrinkle in the plan now people".

Randell continued, "We need to get to the Fortress Islands of New Jackson to be safe and we've not only the remaining ground forces of the Merovingians hunting us, but the Astors aren't happy, either. We actually destroyed their access to 'The System' and it'll take time for them to rebuild it. No one knows I still have access, but we'll meet an Ancients' contact that I'll pass the Chimera Card on to once we hit the transport. It's all good though. I've kept a copy, just in case. We've also been deemed fair game with shoot-to-kill orders in place. Since I'm blackmailing the Ancients, our allies won't interfere, but we're on our own until we get to New Jackson. Even the transportation may not be totally safe from being sunk, that's the silver lining people. If we get to New Jackson in one piece then our safety is guaranteed. That's it, did I miss anything, Simmie?".

Simmie groaned as she moved and straightened up, "Not that I can add. I do have one thorn in my craw though. That prick Santos, head of the Merovingian troops, I want his head on a spike. I can't do that from inside a secure compound". Randall tried to ease her mind as he added, "Well, that can be a side mission once we create a base of operations. Word is he escaped the initial Chimera onslaught when they destroyed the Hexagon of Death. The Merovingian Head was taken out by the Astors, trying to usurp his power, leaving the Chimeras to clean up the rest. I also had contact with Vance, you remember Vance, Simmie, strategist to the Ancients, cranky old fart! They found and are sending me an encrypted file they can't break. Vance was smart enough to stop before it destroyed itself. It appears our Merovingian Head sent an encrypted message to an unknown source, so there is a possibility we have others now also on our tail. Maybe if I can crack it, we can find out what else we're up against? The other issue is the ground troops still out there looking for us and God knows how many the Astors have already activated heading our way". Randall slowed down a bit as the ATV lurched out of the bushes off the dirt trail onto a tarmac road. "Anyone else got questions? We're all still in danger people, so we're headed for the docks and taking the ATV with us, as we've got a timetable and deadline to meet. If there aren't any yet, think about them. Both Simmie and I will be happy to enlighten you all on the trip. The main part now to concentrate on is staying alive". Everyone remained silent as Randall continued to wrestle with the controls and keep the ATV on the road at the speed he was travelling.

As Randall breathed a sigh of relief, Chandie broke the silence, "I can't speak for everyone here, Hun, but thank you for getting us this far". The others then chimed in one after the other in agreement, to which Randall replied, "Don't thank me, yet. We've gotta get to New Jackson first and that isn't going to be easy. There's a whole militia after us now and God only knows what else. I suggest everyone harness themselves down tight as this isn't going to be an afternoon walk in the park. The Astors are more powerful than the Merovingians with greater resources and 'The Ancients' made it very clear they wouldn't be touched... yet". Randall punched the accelerator as they came out of the bend and T-Rex roared forward. They weren't far from the privately-owned dock and given the imposing deadline he wasn't wasting any time they didn't have. An hour later, they were on the final straightway that led to the next left and the highly secure gates of the Ancients' dock. As they made the final bend for the dock gates at speed, Chandie glanced over at him and saw fear all over Randall's face. He wrenched the wheel, punched the accelerator and turned the ATV violently onto the grass. T-Rex tilted over onto two wheels at high speed just as the heat-seeking guided missile struck the underside of the vehicle. Randall screamed out for everyone to hang on to something. The ATV was designed for this type of impact underneath and Randall knew it, hence the wheelie. The explosion was so massive it rolled the ATV over four times until it came to rest surprisingly on its wheels. The grass, dirt, fauna and gravel thrown up into the air with the impact was spectacular. It would have made any rally driver proud to have been able to walk away from. As the cloud settled Randall shook himself back to reality and bellowed, "Fuck, even James Bond doesn't put up with this much shit. Is everyone OK!, sound off!".

As they did, Randall reactivated the biometric scanner and T-Rex roared to life once more. He turned to Chandie and said, "You're weapons control, Simmie... driver's seat, NOW!" With that, Randall opened the driver's door, grabbed the weapons located in the door panel and was off and running towards the gates. Simmie moved like greased lightning. She slammed the driver's door as she identified her hand on the scanner to T-Rex and gunned the power. T-Rex limped to life, one back wheel locked in place, but thankfully there was no further damage, they could fix it later. Simmie looked at Chandie with sheer and utter determination as she stated, "Come on, Candy girl, let's go give our boy a hand shall we, time to unleash hell on these fucking Astors". Chandie scanned the weapons' console screen and flashed her hand over them. T-Rex's weapons lurched from their housings as the humming inside the cab intensified. Darren and Poonta unlocked their harnesses and took up positions at the back turrets as they activated the three sixty degree monitor screens. Vinchi jumped into the small seat that raised him through the now-open skylight, 'Time for the 'Drop Bear' to bare his teeth again' he thought as he took hold of the Sonic Railgun turret located on the roof. He then swung the turret around facing the front just as Simmie punched the accelerator again and turned right. They were getting into these docks dead or alive, and, with Randall now annihilating and lighting up the defences, they roared into the fray to provide the Devil incarnate the support he needed.

THE DEAD ZONE...

Simmie followed Randall's path of destruction as Chandie activated the side and front weaponry. She was eventually gaining on him, given the locked back wheel was slowing them down like a dog with a broken back leg and the gears were grinding away, T-Rex would definitely need some work done if they extracted themselves out of this. Simmie could see Randall was specifically targeting the ground forces outside the locked gates. For some reason he wasn't firing at the sentries lining the front gantries, gate or the complex itself. That's when it hit her, this was an Ancients' privately owned dock, if they were inside that was the guarantee of safety. These others were the Astor's private mercenary forces. She also realised that the remaining Merovingian forces would be bearing down on them any time soon. Upon this realisation, she yelled over her shoulder, "Concentrate your fire on ground forces only, don't shoot the ones in the dock, the're on our side!". She gunned the accelerator again and T-Rex shifted up a gear and begrudgingly roared and lurched forward, digging a shallow trench with the back locked wheel as she fought to follow a straight line. By this time Darren and Poonta had worked out that the mounted Sonic Railguns they were seated at could swivel and fire in an arc of two hundred and seventy degrees. This provided them an all-encompassing spread to cover blind spots and cross over with Vinchi's and Chandie's line of fire. All of them had noticed the hail of bullets raining down around Randall. He was either ignoring the barrage that bounced off his armour or dodging the rest. This man they thought they knew was clearly the Angel of Death in a previous life or a wraith capable of unimaginable destruction.

The solitary thought Randall's fellowship all shared was that they were glad they were friends with him, however, now it was their turn to assist him. It seemed so surreal as they watched Randall move with all the fluidity of water, delivering his own lethal fire. By the time T-Rex had caught up with him, he had successfully blasted three assault vehicles into shrapnel and sent fifteen mercenaries to the nine circles of Hell. The Astors' forces had ten assault SUV's lined up outside the docks along with a full brigade of sixty mercenaries. Simmie could clearly see now that the Ancients' forces hadn't moved. They were visibly entrenched watching the Dance of Death going on below them. Vinchi was blasting away at the armoured SUV's lined up, blocking their path into the docks. The Sonic Railgun mounted to the roof had an automatic mode and he was taking full advantage of its insane capacity. While he was busy turning these vehicles into Swiss cheese, he began yelling at Poonta and Darren to focus on the ground troops. Chandie was screaming at the top of her lungs at a group of mercenaries she was firing at with front and side weapons. These were completely different weapons to the ones the others were dealing out destruction with. These specific weapons were high intensity lasers and had a very distinct three-barrel arrangement to them, allowing these lasers to cover a wide spray area, slicing down anything they hit. Bodies were turned into gooey blobs and limbs were flying in all directions.

It wasn't all one sided though. T-Rex was taking an absolute hammering, parts of its armour were coming away in small, but valuable, pieces. This firefight would need to end soon or there wouldn't be much left to keep them tucked away safe inside the belly of the beast. Thankfully Randall had taken out the mercenaries with the guided missile launchers, but there were still more to get through and annihilate before they were safe. The scene in front of the docks was unfolding like the beginning of the Apocalypse. Bodies were piling up as drastically and as fast as they appeared. Pieces of humans and vehicles exploded into thousands of shards, all leaving for the Afterlife to be repurposed. Explosions from grenades shook the earth and all the while Simmie was wrenching T-Rex all over the place, avoiding the more lethal barrages, but copping others that shook T-Rex violently. Randall took a hard blow to his chest plate and went down heavily. Upon hitting the ground and trying to resurface he had another major seizure. As his legs went out from underneath him, with his outstretched right hand clamped down tight onto the trigger mechanism, locking it into place with the force of his grip. Unfortunately, this was bad news for the three mercenaries who thought they'd finally snuck up on him as all three had their heads blown away from their shoulders as he fell backwards, his arm and weapon outstretched. Simmie pulled up to a sudden stop in front of Randall, shielding him from the approaching onslaught.

While everyone returned fire Chandie opened the door She was about to get out and assist, but Randall now on his knees screamed at her to stay inside the ATV, that he was fine and

Simmie should know better. Randall went ballistic, "Stay inside and keep moving. I'm fine, we need to get inside that gate!" As Simmie gunned T-Rex away from Randall, a dust cloud of grit and grass rose before him. Randall used this opportunity to throw a grenade-like item the size of a large wine glass forward at the blockade. He launched it into an arc as high as he could into the air. As it reached its apex, the object exploded into several smaller drones which locked onto their targets and sped forward along the barricade of remaining vehicles, spewing out small metal shards as they went. These sliced unforgivingly into any person standing in their way. Another ten mercenaries fell to their deaths, the shards ripped their torsos and internal organs into blood-gushing strings of flesh. The drones then unleashed their last payload into four more of the Astors' SUV's. The detonations and resulting explosions tore more mercenaries to pieces. Simmie by this time had avoided the aftermath of Randall's destruction. She'd completed a full circle on two wheels, proud she'd kept this beast under control. She then lined T-Rex up and came from behind Randall as both man and machine made one final parallel push in tandem for the gate and ultimate safety of the dock. All screaming in unison, racing towards certain death, they unleashed another unearthly barrage of deadly projectiles.

That's when their luck changed. The onlooking forces that had been standing at attention as solid as stone gargoyles on the dock sentry towers, gate and gantries, finally opened fire. The crystal blue lightening that erupted from their weapons slammed into the remaining Astor forces, blood, guts, brains and machinery were all eliminated. The remaining barricade was torn apart and the earth was scorched beyond recognition. The smell of burning flesh and melting metal filled the air, the sensation was a new experience for Chandie who began to gag. The lightening evaporated as quickly as it began and the sentries stood back at attention, weapons by their sides. Both Randall and Simmie came to an abrupt halt, not wanting to get caught in this hellish fire from these alien demons who previously had not even moved a muscle to intervene to save them. As the smoke and haze dissipated, everyone could see that they were the only ones still left alive and breathing. The Astors' mercenaries were gone, utterly disseminated, their armoured SUV's destroyed, back to the depths of Hell from whence they came, and, a clear path had been made to allow access to the gates on the dock. The gates that stood before them cracked open, the bright lights which illuminated the dock area and sentry towers flooded through them, highlighting a single solitary figure, standing right in the middle. As the gates slid open, the figure lifted a hand and waved them forward, beckoning them onwards. It then turned and walked away back into the bowels of the delivery area. Simmie pushed T-Rex to the maximum. It lumbered, forward gears grinding as they went, it really needed fixing as it was in a bad way. She wasn't getting rid of the 'old boy' now 'he'd' saved their lives. The least 'he' deserved was a complete makeover.

Randall kept pace with the vehicle as he limped beside the ATV. He had a sense of the familiar as they approached this unknown figure. As they pulled up and were now stationery, the figure turned as the gates closed behind them, cutting off any other forces hunting them. Randall recognised the old man who stood before him, it was his and Simmie's old ally, Vance, strategist to the Ancients. Randall limped over to him, "You old coot, why are you here, friend?". He leaned forward and the two men embraced, then Randall backed up, respectfully. "Why the intervention? I thought the Ancients weren't going to touch the Astors, that we were on our own?" Curiosity was all over Randall's face. There was no way to hide it, so he didn't bother. Vance was much, much older than Randall. Rumour had it that he was as old as the Ancients themselves. That would have put him at close to six thousand years old. He looked every bit that age. He was at one stage Randall's mentor. They had got on so well, Vance accelerated Randall into elite Chimera training, pushing and moulding him into the weapon he was now. He had long grey hair then and it had gotten longer since Randall had seen him. Twenty years was a long time. Vance's face and hands were so badly wrinkled it was virtually impossible to determine his real age. He looked like a prune that had been left out in the sun to dry and had been forgotten.

All Randall knew was that he was of Mongolian descent and his deep green eyes had a way of penetrating your soul. As Randall had advanced, outmanoeuvring and out-performing every other Chimera who had been genetically engineered before him, Vance had become Randall's best and only friend. When the disk was implanted into Randall brain, Vance was there to ensure he survived and then moulded his training to become the ultimate weapon. That's when Vance decided he needed a mate, an ally, even a companion or partner to stand side by side with him, as they undertook the most dangerous and deadly missions any Chimera would be ordered to do. Each and every suicide mission Randall and Simmie went on they survived and passed with honours. Vance's number one crew had been the most successful pairing of all time. He was proud to see them back together. Vance's voice crackled as he spoke, "I was on vacation. You think I'm going to let rules confine me. I helped formulate the rules. There's no way I'm letting my best student perish when I have overriding authority to intervene". Randall looked at him quizzically, as Vance coughed. "You took a vacation? You've never had any down time that I remember. What's so important that you would come and see us off personally, let alone save us from that ruckus outside? Come on Bagsh... Mentor, what gives?". Vance looked solemnly at him and offered, "I'm coming with you to New Jackson. You and Simmie need to be debriefed along the way about your next mission. However, I won't be staying on once you're settled, you'll be on your own. That and the fact I'm your contact to obtain the card to 'The System' that's in your possession. More later, so let's meet your friends, I need to see my okhin, 'my daughter', Simmi, again". He moved past Randall as the others began to disembark T-Rex to meet their recent saviour.

Simmie was the first on the scene out of T-Rex She hugged and squeezed Vance as hard as she could, considering she had two cracked ribs. Randall began introducing all his friends and had just gotten through this when the sentries sprang to life again, releasing another round of crystal blue lightening. Vance touched the back of his head and explained. "It looks as though your Merovingian hunters think they can just barge in here and take you out. Parasites all of them, I don't know why the Ancients put up with these families and don't just take control themselves. It'd save all the smoke and mirrors rubbish. Why don't we leave the guards to eradicate these vermin and we'll board the Nebuchadnezzar? We can go through the introductions further. I'd like to get to know you all. Backgrounds and all that, then we can feast and relax. We've got a long trip ahead of us and I've organised a couple of armed escorts. Be insane to go with you to

New Jackson and put my life at risk, besides they need the training, so it should be a fairly uneventful trip". He turned his attention to Simmie and announced, "Simmie, it's okay my dear, I'll get them to load what's left of your precious T-Rex, don't fret he'll be safe on board soon. The mechanics will set him right while we sail. Randall, my honourable apprentice, we have a contracted exchange to conclude as well. Let's get safe and sound shall we"? Vance turned, headed off and called over his shoulder, "Let's move shall we? There's a fair amount to cover before we get there. From the look of you all, I gather a good bath and meal is paramount". The little troop exchanged confused, but relived looks, then stared straight at Randall who explained, "We're safe here folks. You've entered the next level of your existence. The debrief will explain a lot. Vance is as high up as you can get without being one of the Ancients. Some of the missing pieces you're searching for will be explained. Once that's done, we can concentrate on creating a home base and enjoying our well-earned freedom. Come on let's get onboard".

Randall turned and followed Vance. They walked around the corner of a building to the boardwalk that led to the ship at the docks. Darren's voice sounded like he was in physical distress, "Holy shit, that's the ship we're taking?". Randall chuckled to himself as he answered him, "Yes Mate, that's the Nebuchadnezzar, King of Babylon. Or, in our case, Queen of the Sea, impressive isn't she? If I'm right, we'll make the crossing in twenty four hours". Chandie squeaked out a reply, "She's enormous. She's almost as big as one of those huge luxury cruise liners that used to sail the world". Vinchi chimed in also, "Um, what are those weapons on the side there and on the top deck. Are they cannons?". Simmie answered him almost immediately, "Yes Vinchi, they're Sonic Cannons, the largest in the world. This ship is bristling with weaponry. I very much doubt we'll see any problems getting to New Jackson. Especially since Vance has organised an armed escort to assist this gargantuan hulk. Oh, I can just smell retirement now, can't you Randy?". Randall just locked eyes with Simmie, as he did so the whole group looked with him. "Simmie, look, I know you trust Vance. But I'm keeping my assessment of the situation to a realistic level for now. It's been quite some time since I've seen him and if the Ancients sent him as the errand boy to retrieve the codes, there is more going on here than is being divulged. I'm sorry, but I'm a little more realistic and have better access than you".

Randall tapped the back of his head. "No offence, Simmie, but I'm responsible for everyone here. If Vance turns out to double cross me, I'll blow him to kingdom come and anyone else who puts us in danger. My hair on the back on my neck is bristling and on edge. Do you remember the last time I said that when we worked together?". "Yeah I do... If I recall properly, the end result was extremely ugly and you sent a whole country back to the Stone Age, killing millions. Surely Vance isn't intending to misdirect us?", Simmie seemed genuinely scared now. Randall glanced at everyone, making sure to gain eye contact before he added, "We will play along for now, until we have enough information to make an informed assessment. New Jackson isn't under the Ancients' control, and if we get there we won't be either. Be ready for anything, we're dealing with a master of manipulation here, he wrote the book on it. One false move and we all need to react in sync. Come on, let's move, and stay armed. We've kept him waiting long enough. God... I need bath".

Within thirty minutes, everyone was on board and had been shown to their lavish quarters on a ship that was most definitely the best money could buy. While in the hallway, Vance had ordered the onboard tailor to take everyone's measurements, promising them new clothes. Randall advised Vance they would be keeping their armour and advised everyone to keep their cloaks, armoured clothing and weapons separate and within reach at all times. Vance seemed a little offended by this, but offered, "Randall, you're safe on board, if you like I can get the assistants to clean the armour and return them to your quarters. You've nothing to fear from me, my friend. I've been advised you hold the advantage and negotiated a deal with Hondorus himself. Even I can't get an audience with him, even in all the eons I've been advising them all. So it appears that for once the student has now surpassed the master, it's a shame you won't take over from me. Yes, I'm no fool Randall, I know what you're capable of, I trained you". With that Vance headed off to arrange the chef and the meal. As Vance disappeared from view, Randall explained to everyone that new clothes were fine but if they were headed for a fire fight on board they'd need all the protection they could get.

The comrades then headed for their allocated suites and luxuriated in the magnificent bathrooms provided. Once bathed, they surfaced to find the newly-tailored clothes laid out on their beds. They changed and donned their armour, weapons and headed out into the hallway to wait, going together as a group. They then felt the ship lurch slightly, the engines had started and she was gaining speed, they were now underway. Making their way to the dining deck, Randall encouraged his companions to be wary of anything and stay on alert. They needed to get off this ship before they could really find freedom and this was just another test, another step above what the families could throw their way. They were definitely swimming with sharks now, apex predators who'd eat you for dinner and not even think twice. Chandie didn't like that thought. She took Randall by the arm as they headed off to dinner with their new captain. Just as she grabbed hold of him Randall blacked out, another major seizure taking hold of him.

CHAPTER ELEVEN

SWIMMING WITH SHARKS...

As Chandie and Simmie tended to Randall, the others stood on guard. This time he was unconscious. They were all worried now as they would most definitely need their leader should something go south and if Randall was on guard they all decided they would be, too, until they docked. Darren grabbed Vinchi gently by his arm and led him from the ladies and indicated for Poonta to come with them. They moved a little out of earshot with Darren when he whispered, "Look guys, this place might look all safe and cuddly, but if Randy's not at ease then we need to be on alert. Keep your eyes out for anything unusual and memorise the security systems you see, no telling if we'll need to know this later. Stay on edge boys until we've safely docked, fair?". Poonta responded first, "Yous bet, Darrin, eyes keep on guard alright. Mees smells funny stuff since wes go on board". Vinchi echoed the same, "No dramas, if any of us see anything wrong, we tell Randall and confront this, Vance. I'm not dying now we've got this far and neither is anyone else. Simmie might trust this guy, but I'm the same as Poont, I smell something off".

457

Darren placed a hand on each of their shoulders, "Come on, let's update the ladies before Randy comes to. We need to all be on the same page".

They moved back to the others and Darren explained what they had been talking about. He apologised to Simmie, but she agreed with him wholeheartedly. Vance, she said, seemed a little too at ease. Randall eventually came to. Chandie and Simmie eased him to his feet and both held on as they made their way to the elevator and up to the main dining deck. The ship itself was impressive. Everywhere they looked there were marble Roman columns, rare timber furniture and cornicing, pure gold and silver trimmings, Renaissance masters' paintings, sculptures, and Persian rugs in these ornately-decorated State rooms. The crystal chandeliers in every hallway brightly lit their path towards their destiny tonight. This ship was most distinctly the best money could buy. This wasn't a six-star cruise liner. This level well surpassed ten or even twelve. Every piece of the collection on board this ship was priceless. Vinchi was thinking if this was the condition of the ship, the meal would be one to die for. That's what he was afraid of. He would now be more alert than anyone.

Once during his career they'd tried to poison him. He was only saved by his keen sense of smell.

Moving into the dining room, they met Vance who had changed into what seemed to be ceremonial robes. In fact, as he welcomed them into the room, he explained he was wearing the robes of his station, The Grand Strategist. He waved them towards the massive red Bubinga timber dining table, the second most expensive timber worldwide and certainly the rarest nowadays. He asked if they were happy with their new clothing, to which all agreed they were the best they'd ever owned. Vance seemed genuinely pleased that everyone was at ease and happy. The table was laid out with gold cutlery, rare crystal glasses, pure silver candelabras and rare cream silk place mats for the food-laden plates to be laid out on when they arrived. The rare orchids and flowers that adorned the table gave off a stunning and glorious scent. Vance explained that each chair had been hand-cut from a single Bubinga tree to keep its rigidity and natural grains. As each of them sat down Vance placed himself at the head of the table. Obviously this was a regular seating arrangement that followed a unique protocol.

Once they were settled, Vance explained that the meal they were about to eat was prepared by one of the best chefs he'd ever known. He went on trying to put his guests at ease and that the menu they would be enjoying would be divine as its contents were extremely rare. For starters, there would be Almas caviar, followed by Soup de jour, Wagyu steak, Golden Tigerfish with Deamchi-style mixed vegetables and Madagascan Vanilla gold ice cream, all accompanied by Chateau Lafitte 1787, to chill their throats as they ate. As Vance finished explaining the meal ahead, three waiters started serving the first course of Almas Caviar and wine. Vance opened the conversation, "I'm pleased you've all made it here to the dock and are now on board. I am extremely pleased to meet you all. It's nice to know my two best protégés are surrounded by people of quality and exceptional skills. But where are my manners? For starters, let me welcome you on board properly". Vance stood while indicating the others to remain seated. He raised his crystal goblet and made a toast before he was seated again. "Welcome on board the Nebuchadnezzar my friends, the King of Babylon, the flag ship of the Ancients, your divine hosts for this trip". Vance raised his goblet to the large painting at the end of the dining room, 'The Devine Eight Ancients — The Annunaki".

Simmie watched Vance sit and then, as per usual was direct, and to the point, "So father... My apologies, Grand Strategist, why are you here? I was under the impression you never left the Devine Sanctuary, and, please no bullshit, I know you better than anyone here". Vance raised an eyebrow. He responded in a clear and precise manner. "Oh, I knew using DNA from Celebra's genetics for you was a mistake You're every bit as sharp and intellectual as she ever was... How I miss my Ekhner. Maybe, more so my young one, but I do love you all the same... Now, if everyone will allow and indulge an old man I shall not over vacillate how I came to be here. So, in your own terminology, my dearest daughter, no bullshit". The wine and caviar flowed freely. Darren and Poonta asked for more as they'd never tasted anything like this. Chandie chastised them and told them to be polite, and that they were guests. Vance saw this and just smiled. He raised a hand, palm forward, to indicate to Chandie that it was alright and to eat up. Vance began his long recollection, "Where do I start...? Let me see. Well, for starters the Nebuchadnezzar is one of a kind. It's a fully self-automated armed vessel that only needs minimal staffing requirements and controlled by me where remotely required". Vance pointed at his wrist, where an odd looking bracelet was located. "The vessel is fully armed and capable of destroying an entire fleet of any war ships should they decide to attack. It has an onboard launch-able submarine inside the main hull should it be breached, but we won't be needing that on this trip with an armed escort. The staff on board are all handpicked by myself so you are all definitely safe from harm. So to answer your question, daughter... I'm due for... retirement!". Vance turned his attention towards Randall, "You were originally reactivated by Simmie on orders of the Ancients to be my replacement. She probably didn't pass on that memo, or selectively forgot, given your past history together. I'm a hundred and fifty eight years old and I'm feeling very weary. Randall, you were to be my logical successor, a huge honour. That was until you went rogue and blackmailed Hondorus. You know The Ancients aren't too pleased about that, but you've covered yourself from every angle, so well done my boy, you've exceeded and surpassed even my training and intellect, you would have made an excellent Grand Strategist." Vance shifted in his seat, it appeared that he was tired, but he continued with the explanations best he could. "Retirement is not what you would normally expect. I know too many secrets, that makes me expendable. It would have been the end of a very long life for me, would've been a beautiful ceremony and all, I suppose it's overdue given my age really, but I do digress. I too, like you, my boy, used my negotiating skills to bargain my way to a non-execution existence. If I bring the closed encrypted codes for 'The System' back to the Ancients I get to die of old age. So you see, we're both self-centred really, we like life. Besides who else would you have trusted to meet you and to take possession of and convey these highly precious codes back to our superiors. You'd have killed anyone else should you have suspected a trap. So I was the logical choice. The bonus is I can get you safely to New Jackson with no interference. But honestly, there were other reasons, I wanted to see my Simmie again".

Vance gathered his thoughts and stared more intensely at Randall. "I gather you've copied the codes for yourself as well, I would have too. Keep them, I've a feeling you're going to need them down the track". The main meal then entered just as the entree dishes were being carried away. Vinchi's eyes lit up, the meat, fish and fresh vegetables looked and smelled exquisite. He looked up and noticed everyone had the same expression, as it had been a very long time since anyone here had enjoyed a meal like this. Vance again turned to Randall seated next to him. He extended a hand towards him, palm upwards with a small black and gold-lined container. "Why don't we get the exchange out of the way, so we can enjoy the rest of the meal and my further explanation to your friends. This, dear boy, is the drive the Ancients want you to crack. The Head Of The Merovingians' personal data drive. It appears he had an ally, maybe one of religious origins. That could be a real hornet's nest, if it is, religion has become a difficult field to control. Find that out and all will be forgiven. The Merovingians will be wiped out by the end of next week, so no need for Simmie to get involved now. The bargain is, as agreed, you provide 'The System' codes so the Ancients can keep subversive control of the thirteen families and subsequently the masses. This then leads to you and your friends getting to live very long lives, uninterrupted and with luck, to die of old age. But you, my boy, with Simmie's assistance can be reactivated when required for any mission necessary. Trust me, your blackmail of Hondorus didn't go unchallenged, but it was agreed that the information in your possession to expose them and the elites was too valuable to go public. You're now too valuable to them and must be kept alive at all costs".

Randall took the black box and opened it. He recognised it immediately. He'd used this type before, or, more specifically, he'd used one for the Head of the Astors' family. "I'll take some time to crack open and ensure the information is still intact. Once done, I'll convey it by the secure regulatory channels", Randall replied. He was being very careful not to give too much away. He reached into the vest pocket of his newly-cleaned armoured suit and pulled out the hermetically-sealed mirror finish Chimera Card. Randall reached across to Vance and as Vance took hold of it in his fingertips Randall responded in a low Alpha-male, confident growling voice. "You and I've been friends for a very long time, Vance. But if you cross me or my friends I'll end you here and now and then I'll go after the Devine Eight and obliterate them back to the stars. Am I making myself clear?". Vance's smile disappeared and he became serious. "Crystal, my boy, crystal clear. That's what they are afraid of. They know very well what you're capable of. They know you have gotten stronger, too. What they don't know was that the re-activation Simmie put you through was also an upgrade from me. You're now the ultimate weapon my boy, Death personified. You now have complete and unrestricted access to all of the Ancients' data. If they cross you now, they know their extinction will be moments away. I made sure to reinforce that message, my boy. For once, just once trust your old mentor". Vance placed his other old wrinkled hand on top of Randall's and patted it softly, as he grinned cheekily. They each pocketed their priceless treasures and all returned to eating the main course. The rare wine flowed as the meal progressed and everyone wondered if this was going to be the norm, given they were now on their way to a better life.

Vance watched everyone and they seemed quite settled now. "So now, dear friends, with the main business concluded and dessert soon on its way, how about a story?". Vance relaxed as his guests responded positively. "It's been a long time so bare with me... Long ago, the Annunaki came into being, they are a superior race to the humans that populate this Earth and as you've probably heard from both Simmie and Randall they've been sitting behind the scenes pulling all the strings. They've supported and destroyed both the rise and fall of every major Civilisation since roughly four thousand BC. The main reason for placing the World Monarch in power was to control the masses. As humans became more intelligent, there needed to be a mechanism of subterfuge and manipulation so deep that no one making up the general population would realise that they were pseudo-slaves, free will and choice is an illusion put in place to maintain balance and restrain behaviours. By having an overarching body governing the creation of laws that confine commerce, trade and banking, they could freely introduce technologies, specific governing social structures, such as law and order, politics and social classes. It would leave them free to create this world as they needed for their own purposes.

The Chimera were developed by mixing human DNA with theirs and thus they created their own deadly security militia. So why are new governing families over time exterminated? Well, if these families choose to usurp power and manipulate the hierarchy such as creating a system that the Ancients cannot access to maintain control, these families are eliminated by the Chimera as they became a threat to the Ancients' plans. So, as a sideline the Ancients had to misdirect the masses with individual self-centred goals like the arts, and dumbed down education, jobs disguised to look like they had a purpose, but keep the masses minds' numb and sedate. Poverty was a creation to restrict the population, but unfortunately human breeding has become unchecked as they breed quickly. Recent years saw Aids introduced which was a manufactured disease to kerb the population as was cancer. However, the current overbreeding has become so bad the Ancients have decided to let natural attrition take place. In approximately ten years, the world will be so overpopulated that the manufactured diseases that the Ancients are now introducing into the water and food sources will finally eradicate the species to the edge of extinction. Yes, I can see your emotions, and no, the food and wine you drank is pure with no contaminants. What Randall and Simmie have done is try to extract themselves from a life of servitude, manipulation and killing for what one would call a higher purpose — freedom. In my eyes at my age, I still believe it's murder, but I've grown too old to argue and that's why I also want out. Hence, the reason I'm here to see your little troop to some sort of relative safety".

Vance looked a little drained, but he continued onward forcing himself to divulge a little more. "That drive, Randall, if you can crack it, will lead you to part of your next mission. My initial feelings and instincts tell me that the mission you've been tasked with by Hondorus and agreed with him to eliminate the Bundy Family is only the tip of the iceberg... Simmie you're involved whether you like it or not. The Bundys are ancestors of your mother's, you'll be called upon to wipe out your own surviving bloodline on her side. That's why Randall said you wouldn't like it... yes, Randall I know I'm sorry, Simmie needs to know sooner, rather than later. I was monitoring your communications. The real problem is the Bundys are well connected, especially within worldwide religious aspects. If that drive leads to religion undermining the Ancients to usurp them... Judgement Day and Armageddon will become real for everyone on this stinking planet". Vance fell silent. Dessert soon replaced

469

the main course and everyone was quiet. No one knew really what to say, including Vance. When the meal was over, the table was cleared and Vance announced he was retiring for the night. Due to his advanced years, he wasn't as nimble or as energetic as he used to be. Before he left, he explained that they'd be docking in ten hours and then bid everyone a good night's sleep.

"So what now, this seems all a bit surreal?". Chandie sounded emotionally drained and confused, "Does all that mean we're safe?". Randall, seated opposite, looked her square in the eyes and opened up, being as honest as he could be. This was for everyone's benefit. He needed everyone on top of their A game now. "Well, some of that was a surprise, I must say... But, given we're now currently underway to build a base of operations, I think we all need to be ready for any encounter. We may be safe on board for now, but that could change at any moment. The Ancients need those codes and with everything I have on them they shouldn't be in a hurry to eradicate us. I can't speak for Simmie, but I'll do what I can to keep everyone safe. We may need to stick together as a group for a bit longer for now. Simmie and I will need a support group if we're going on active missions as we can't trust our previous employers. I know this is asking a lot, but would you all be interested sticking together for a while longer?". Darren jumped in on the end of Randall's last sentence, "You know, mate, I knew you were special, but I was not exactly sure by how much, until now. Are you serious? This is the most fun I've had since I left Israel. I don't know about anyone else, but fuck it, I'm in boots and all. Besides that, we're all fucking rich thanks to you, we owe you everything and more and if I get to blow more shit up I'm your support team all the way. Whadda you reckon, guys?".

The resounding positive echoes of agreement from all his friends was all the reward Randall needed. Now all they had to do was get to NewJackson in one piece and begin to rebuild a base their formidable team could operate out of without restrictions. Randall rallied his friends by stating in agreement with them, "Excellent, I'm so proud of you all. How about we get some sleep? Tomorrow is going to be a huge day and we need to be rested and ready for whatever lies ahead". Randall turned and used both his hands to hold onto Chandie and Simmie's arms as they started off for their luxurious suites and a good night's sleep.

As they moved off he pulled them close and said, "Thank you, ladies, I couldn't have got this far without either of you". With that he gave them both a kiss on the cheek as they headed off for the elevator. Darren, Poonta and Vinchi walked behind the trio and mimicked them. Poonta and Darren held Vinchi between them, his legs dangling from the ground as they went. Randall and the women turned around and everyone burst into a fit of laughter. It felt good to feel so safe, even for a little while…

ACROSS THE SEA…

As they arrived below deck, at the stateroom level, Chandie and Simmie saw Randall to his door. Darren, Poonta and Vinchi had finally finished making fun of Randall and his dilemma with two women. They, too, decided it would be safer to go to bed before they got into any more trouble. This left Chandie and Randall in his doorway as Simmie had already said her goodnight and wandered off to bed, stating her ribs were giving her grief, and she would pay Randall back one day, should she ever find the opportunity. Randall stood there looking at Chandie and offered, "Well, almost there, didn't think we'd get this far after everything that's happened... Did you want to come in? I'm pretty sure there is no coffee in here". He flashed a brilliant smile and ran his fingers through his hair, hoping. Chandie poked Randall in the stomach as she whispered, "Not tonight, Hun, let's wait until we're all safe on dry land. I think I'll go for a walk around the ship to clear my head a bit, there's a lot going on here I need to get my head around. It's all good, Hun, just need some time to myself. We'll catch up in the morning for breakfast before we dock, ok?". Randall replied dejectedly, "Fair call, just don't stay up too late, it's going to be a huge day tomorrow. We've only got about nine hours before we land". He gave her a bear hug and they both moved off. Randall went to have shower to calm his head before bed and Chandie wandered back to the elevator. Waiting for it to arrive she heard Randall scream. She sympathised with him as she thought, 'Another seizure, poor bugger, he really needs me. I can only imagine how he holds it together'. Something didn't sit right with her, the part about an onboard submarine and the two armed vessels either side of the ship had her having disturbing visions. Time for a walk and check out this so-called automated ship. She'd never been a fan of computers let alone autonomous ones, and she'd read the book 'Skynet'. Stepping into the elevator, she eyed off the level buttons. Looking down to the bottom row, she saw a button labelled SubDock. She pushed this one and settled in for the ride, even if this led nowhere she'd get to see a submarine for the first time.

Randall couldn't sleep. He tossed and turned, but refused to get out of bed as his body needed the rest. They'd soon be landing in New Jackson and upon arrival they'd set out to build up a small home base of operations and the best part was everyone was coming with him. Finally, he'd be able to pay back everything his friends had done for him, tenfold. As he wasn't sleeping, every so often he'd check out the clock on the wall. Time had flown by quickly, there was only three hours left before they docked. He stopped leaning on his elbows and lay back, closed his eyes and began running over the priorities they would need to put in place, plus the contacts they'd be required to make. This was short-lived because as he was just about to drift off to sleep when the ship rocked violently and he was thrown out of bed, hitting his head against the base of the night dresser. This ship had the best navigation on board. Surely they hadn't hit a reef. Trying to stand, he was thrown to the floor again as the ship rocked, and this time it sounded like explosions were going off below decks. Something big was attacking the ship and he was determined that he wasn't going down with it. Thank God he hadn't changed clothes. He slipped on his armoured shirt and shoes, picked up his weapons holster and clipped everything he could find into place. He tried accessing the disk in his head and all he got was a scrambled feedback loop. Something was definitely off here, he just wasn't sure what. He had another seizure and went down hitting the floor hard, but he soon collected his thoughts, and gained his feet, while stabilising himself. It was at that point Chandie barged in through Randall's Stateroom door, her hands covered in blood — hers — and collapsed onto the floor. Just as he got to her and held her up in his arms, Simmie also burst through the doorway, yelling, "There's a trail of blood all down the hallway... Holy Shit, is she okay? What happened?". Randall lifted his head, looked at Simmie and screamed back, "No idea, but she seems badly hurt".

The ship lurched and rocked again twice. "Grab Vinchi, we need to stop the bleeding, he's our best field medic. Get the others, gear up armour and weapons only, we need to get the hell off this ship!". Simmie turned to go as the others all arrived behind her at the same time, armed to the teeth. They'd stayed prepared for any eventuality. As they pushed their way into Randall's room, questions started flying. Randall put his hand up and halted the barrage with, "Enough people... Vinchi go get the medikit. I'll try and stop the bleeding. Darren, Poonta guard the hallway, Simmie give me a hand here". Simmie raced over and kneeled down next to Chandie as Randall laid her out, "Who would do this, has she said anything?". Randall was busy holding a towel to Chandie's stomach to stem the blood. She was a white as a sheet, "Chandie, Sweet, stay with me, I need to know what happened, who did this? Come on stay conscious, Sweet, we need you, fight it, Sweet. What happened?". Chandie looked Randall directly in the eyes. She pushed to open her mouth and fought to get the words out, "Vance... Viktor was yelling orders at Vance... Angry... Near the Sub... Tried to get a closer look.... Shot me, came from behind", she closed her eyes again. Randall screamed at her, "No, no, no, no Sweet stay with me, come on, you're a tough cookie, hold on, we'll get you outta here. What about Vance, what happened?". Chandie wasn't responding, but she was still breathing and her heart beat, though erratic, was stable. By this time Vinchi was back and helping Randall and Simmie as they set to work on Chandie. The ship lurched again, something huge had slammed into it and now it was listing to one side. "We've gotta move people, we're outta time, Vinchi, you Simmie and Poonta look after Chandie. Darren, you're on point with me, let's get to the sub level, NOW!".

The friends made their way to the elevator. Poonta was carrying Chandie in his huge arms, everyone was on edge. She seemed to have stabilised thanks to Randall's quick thinking and Vinchi's skills as a surgeon. Darren piped up as they waited, "So Vance betrayed us and we're now sinking. Someone sure wants us dead". Randall responded, "No, I don't think so. I know Vance it's not his style. My guess is The Ancients want to renegotiate. Big fucking mistake!". The elevator arrived and they all embarked for the bottom level and the submarine. Randall began barking orders, "Get ready, people, this could get very ugly,

Darren you're on point with me, kill anything that moves. You lot follow up the rear, stay close. Simmie, Vinchi, cover the others, we're getting the fuck outta here!". They reached the lower deck and exited the elevator in armed formation and on full alert. Moving towards their target, they could see the giant mechanisms that held this gargantuan submarine in place. The level seemed eerily vacant, only the emergency lighting was on. Randall had expected a full complement or at least a welcoming reception of battle-tested Chimeras, but there was nothing. Water was flooding in steadily from a large tear in the side of the ship and it was listing even further. As they made their way to the submarine boarding station, Darren and Randall scanned the floor space and cargo loading area, nothing. They scanned the gantries around the submarine, nothing.

Everything down here was or appeared to be vacant. As they moved closer to the submarine boarding area, Darren caught sight of a pair of shoes protruding out from under a camouflage tarpaulin. He stealthily moved over and lifted the sheet, it was Vance. Upon further investigation Darren noticed the back of his head as he turned him over. It looked like something had exploded out the back that had been imbedded, maybe his disk? As the others stood on guard, Randall kneeled down next to Vance besides Darren. He started sifting through his pockets and clothing. "Fuck!", Randall spat furiously, "The card's missing... My bet is the Ancients took it, eliminated... retired Vance and are trying to bury us at sea to remove us as a threat. What better way than a burial at sea, flanked by two armed carriers". He turned to the others as he touched the back of his head, "Great, it works, thanks Vance". Randall's eyes glazed over for a moment, he seemed like he was about to have another seizure. He soon came back to his friends and noticed they were still scanning the docking area, expecting bullets to come from anywhere. "They're not here", he informed them, "They've disabled the launch mechanism for the submarine, so she won't escape out through her hatch". Darren stared straight at Randall, "How do you kno...? Scratch that, I don't wanna know. So what now, that means we're trapped with no way out. They've finally won, we all go down with the ship. Fuck, we were so close!". Darren slumped against the railing, "At least I get to die amongst friends, thanks for the adventure, mate, it's been fun". Randall looked up and gave his attention to everyone who now looked as drained and emotionally upset as Darren, even Simmie, she'd lost her 'father'. Tears welled in her eyes, they'd almost made it, they had come this close and now it was all but over. Death by drowning.

Randall looked at Chandie still cradled in Poonta's arms. He stood up straight and walked over to her. Placing a hand gently on her chest, he could see she was still breathing at regular intervals and her heartbeat was more regular. The blood had stopped oozing out of her wound and had already started to clot. She opened her eyes and looked up at Randall. He smiled and placed a hand on her cheek, rubbing it softly, she was going to be fine. She lifted a bloodied hand to hold his and as she did so he squeezed it gently. Randall didn't look away, he simply took one long deep breath, exhaled and smiled cheekily at Chandie. She'd seen this grin before. Randall was up to something. She mouthed the words, "What are you up too?". Randall patted her hand looked up at Poonta, then touched him on the shoulder saying, "Take care of her Poont". Extracting himself, he turned to the others and with every ounce of encouragement he could muster, chided each and everyone of them. "Well, I don't know about you lot, but I have absolutely no intention of dying today. You get this close to our goal and when it all get too hard you're giving up, just like that?!".

The water was pouring in through the gaping hole in the side of the ship, and with the roar of the water getting louder Randall spoke up. "Christ, do I have to do everything around here? Darren, Vinchi, go to those cabinets over there, they are full of C4 explosives. Place them on the anchor points that look like this all the way around the submarine and as far up that back wall section as high as you can go. We're going to blast our way outta here. Come on guys, MOVE, GO, GO!". Turning back to Simmie, Randall grinned, "We've got the best job Sim, help our Poont onboard with Chandie. Poonta find the med deck, it's one flight down, bunker down and keep Chandie safe. We'll all be along shortly. Simmie get them in place and get back to me. I'll be under big Bertha here we're going to blow the other anchor points from below. With the hammering they are giving the Nebakanezzar, there's no way they'll notice additional explosives. We'll get on board and wait for the pressure to equalise, we're in deep water here, roughly three kilometres. If we blow the restraints prior to sinking and we detonate the electrics we can cover our escape. As the ship sinks, she'll roll slightly. We use that to our advantage and use the submarine to escape unnoticed. Ok, let's move, you lot, go, go ,go. Simmie catch up with me, hurry".

A few minutes later Simmie joined Randall underneath the submarine, placing the C4 he'd collected onto the metal grips that held the submarine in place. They could both hear Darren and Vinchi scurrying about and clambering over the holding arms, planting their remote bombs. Simmie confronted Randall with, "You really think this is going to work? I've been running the calculations over and over and...". Randall put his finger to her lips to silence her. He said as quietly as he could, "You know, Simmie sometimes you just have to take a leap of faith, it'll work, come on, let's get these done and back inside. I want to fire this puppy up as soon as we blow the clamps and exit. We need to time this just right". Simmie was silent. This was her old Randy, full of himself, confidence overflowing and always right, it was nice to have him back, even if she had to share him for a while. Soon everyone had completed the tasks Randall had set them and they boarded the ship together. Closing the hatch, they made their way to the Captain's bridge. Randall took pole position in the Captain's chair while the others sat where the navigator, sonar and engineer would have been. The whole area looked like the architect had been a Star Trekkie fan as this resembled the bridge of the Enterprise. Well, they were all about to go where they hadn't been before, so it seemed only fitting if they were about to explore the unknown, why not do it in style. Randall began the countdown, "One, Two, Three". He pushed the detonator controls and could hear everyone take a deep breath in and hold it, hoping. The submarine rocked as the explosions shook the hull. Randall's hand flashed across the control screen which lit up showing the monitors where they had planted the explosives. Each arm holding the submarine in place had disintegrated and the huge hatch beneath them was blown outwards.

All they had to do now was launch into the ocean below them. Randall barked more orders to Vinchi, Darren and Simmie. He explained which buttons and levers to press and the submarine began to hum loudly. Every interior light came on and they could feel the vibrations of the engines, even though they couldn't hear them from here. Randall kept an eye on the monitor scanning the submarine berthing area, it was filling up with sea water rapidly. The instance it was full, he hit the controls and the 'Vernian' slid out of its cradle and into the depths of the Pacific Ocean. As they pulled away, Randall adjusted the ballast and the nose of the bridge rose. The massive clear bridge screen gave them a whale's eye view of what lay in front of them. As the submarine shifted slowly backwards, they watched silently as the Nebakanezzar sank slowly into the depths in front of them, on its way to what was supposed to be their final resting place. Randall cut the engines as the Nebakanezzar faded into the dark distance. He wasn't taking any chances they'd be spotted on sonar or any other deep penetrating satellite. Bringing the surveillance systems online, he announced to his newly-present crew that the two armoured scouting vessels were moving away. No depth chargers or other weaponry was after them, their ruse — on the surface — had worked. He stood up out of the Captain's chair and turned to Simmie, "Ok, first officer you have the Con, don't do anything until I get back". Simmie stood and moved over to Randall and seated herself in the chair as Randall turned to leave the bridge.

He opened the hatch leading to the hallway and turned back ordering, "I mean it Simmie, don't turn the engines on just yet, I'll be back soon".

Randall made his way down towards the next deck and the medical infirmary. He wanted to make sure Chandie was still okay. As he entered the medbay, he noticed she was sitting up and that Poonta was hovering over her like a mother hen guarding her little chick. "Well, we do like the attention, don't we", Randall said sarcastically as he smiled. Chandie bit back, "Oh, shove it, I almost got myself killed for you lot. A little appreciation wouldn't go astray". "Ok, calm down, put kitty back in her box. I just came to see that Poonta had been taking care of you properly and that you were still alive... In all seriousness though, I wanted to say thank you personally. If you hadn't been sleep walking and found out what was going on, we'd all be dead by now. By the way, everyone says thanks". Chandie went to get up off the medical bed when Randall ordered her back, "Oh hey whoa, where do you think you're going? You've taken quite a beating young lady, you're not going anywhere until you've healed properly. Whatever it is can wait. Poont, you're in charge. She doesn't leave this room without my permission or until Vinchi clears her for active duty, okay big guy?". Chandie's face went red, "Who the hell do you th...". She never finished Poonta as placed his hand softly over Chandie's mouth and ordered, "Mes the nurse, yous is sick. So shoosh. Bed rest until yous get better".

Randall backed out of the medbay, grinning wildly, as he retreated. He saluted Poonta and left heading for the bridge again. Chandie glared at Poonta with all the anger she could muster, "Who's side are you on anyway, Poont?". Poonta didn't even answer her, he just bent over and kissed her on her forehead, "Better nows, come on, get intos bed, baby". Randall re-entered the bridge and Darren stood up and sarcastically announced, "Officer on deck". His friends all followed his lead and each of them saluted. Randall wandered over and sat back down in the Captain's chair. As he did so, Darren said, "So where to now, Captain?". Randall tried to be serious, but he just smiled, "New Jackson, second mate, we're headed for New Jackson. We should get there in about three hours underwater, south end of the world. Pack your woollies, it's going to get real cold real soon, looks like you're gonna get to see your snow, Darren. Simmie, punch in these coordinates, please my dear, let's make some headway, shall we".

BRAVE NEW WORLD...

Randall was sitting in the Captain's chair staring into the distance smiling. They'd passed some southern migrating humpback whales heading north as the submarine was making good headway underwater to New Jackson. The 'Vernian' was one hell of a machine, the onboard weaponry was insane and state of the art, there was plenty of room for ten people inside and wasn't cramped, the best feature, however, was that this monster was a hybrid and nuclear, which meant it used its own waste by-product for fuel to produce a top speed of sixty knots. This steel and titanium leviathan could outrun anything on the planet, that and it could blow anything chasing them off the face of the Earth. He'd just finalised communications and arrangements for their final destination and their estimated time of arrival was roughly twenty minutes away. The feeling he got when he concluded the ten billion cyber-currency transaction fee had his endorphins racing, talk about retail therapy. Darren was being his normal sober self.

He was whining about why would Randall ever choose somewhere so cold, wet and miserable. Randall reminded himself he needed to ensure the nearest liquor cabinet was fully stocked for Darren. Randall looked around the bridge, it really was like being on the bridge of the Enterprise and everything looked new. That's when Simmie announced they were passing through Foveaux Strait at the southern end of New Jackson and would be entering Colac Bay, on course and on time. That was good news as Randall could see that everyone was suffering from cabin fever and really needed to get out of here sooner rather than later. Well at least the place they were headed for was going to be one hell of a surprise and a perfect fortified base to begin any operations.

Randall knew they had some unfinished business out here, but they needed to get settled first. He had already decided what their next mission was and before he unleashed another World War on this unsuspecting planet, they'd need to be well prepared. The door to the bridge hissed open and a battered and bruised Chandie walked in, followed by nurse Poonta. Randall jumped up out of his seat and announced, "Well, well, well... Everyone up, let's welcome our Chief Navigator and Head Security Manager to the bridge properly. How are you feeling, Sweet? Our head medic taking care of you...? You're just in time. We're almost at our new base. We're about to dock very, very soon, may as well take a seat, you two. Speaking of that, Simmie, according to satellite data, we've got a three hour window, plenty of time to surface and take in the view properly so everyone can see our new home. The 'Vernian' surfaced, slowed and turned right towards Colac Bay. From the bridge, all anyone could see was green as far as the horizon, there was one amazingly long beach to their right and the inlet bay they were headed for looked like one big fortress. Randall advised that, in the previous decades, this whole area had been purchased, bulldozed and developed by a wealthy Asian multi-billionaire, who purchased everything in Colac Bay, including its peninsula and adjacent beach, all completely isolated and fortified. As they grew closer to the small peninsula, they noticed the whole area had been dredged and built up to accommodate a huge dock that they could fit into quite easily with room to fit much, much more.

Randall flashed his hand over the Captain's chair touch screen and the huge dock began to open. All his friends just stared, no one said a word, even Darren was lost for words. Randall smiled quietly, that was definitely a first for Darren. Randall would chisel that win into the stone wall near the dock, one for the Home team. As they slowed and prepared to dock, they could see part of their new accommodation. Vinchi let out a whistle, "Holy Shit, this place is huge... Yet it looks like new". Randall chuckled and used a poor Italian accent as he replied, "You have no idea, Vinchi... Let's just say I made an offer no one would be game enough to refuse. It's large enough to be a perfect fortified team base and far enough away to remain anonymous and isolated. I can be very persuasive and charming when I want to be". That was when Simmie chimed in, "Yeah and lethal when you're pissed off, does it have a full time doctor? We're all still sporting some war wounds here, my dear Randy". "No, but we can buy one who doesn't ask questions", Randall mused. "So how big is this place, Hun?", Chandie asked. Randall elaborated and smiled as he cradled his chin in his thumb and index finger, then turned and gestured out the front of the glass bridge screen, "Well, let's see... The house is over two and a half thousand square metres, with every facility and technology known to humans, all we'll ever need really... It's got all the latest toys and includes some military high-grade surveillance and satellite systems.

This fortification's weaponry includes automated surface-to-air missile batteries, a few newly-installed fully-functioning ICBM's and is surrounded by a fully-walled electrified armed reinforced perimeter to repel intruders. The entire facility has an autonomous weapons system that covers every square centimetre. It comes complete with biometric scanners so it will automatically kill anyone that decides to intrude or infiltrate unnoticed. Which reminds me, we all need to go through a bio-scan at the house once we arrive. The armoury is fully equipped with whatever you'd want and Simmie... We even have a replacement T-Rex. Don't ask, it's complicated... It'll be waiting for you in the underground twenty car garage along with a few big boys' toys for everyone else. Mine's the one with the number plate 'GROWLER'. This is just my way of saying 'thank you' for sticking by me. The downside is we need to all live together off the grid for a while, just until things cool down. But, if you lot want to stay, Simmie and I could really use a good support team?". All Randall got was a resounding agreement. Again, he openly smiled as the 'Vernian' began its automatic docking procedure. "Well friends, I guess once we dock, we get ready to make ourselves at home. I'll explain the house plan, its idiosyncrasies and personality over a good meal and drinks, we've deserved a bit of a break. It's been well earned, so let's meet up in say five minutes at the exit hatch... Let's go, people, our new life awaits — Eden — as promised". Randall led the group off the bridge and towards the elevator and their suites. The mood was now one of relief and Randall breathed more easily too. He was more than pleased they had travelled this far. He honestly thought they would be long dead before they arrived here. No need to confess that, not now, there was more important information to own up to.

About an hour later, the meal had finally been prepared, drinks were being handed out and the friends all wandered into the large sunken lounge area and made themselves at home in the cream leather lounges around the marble coffee tables and a huge polished lava-stone fireplace. Chandie made herself comfortable and snuggled in next to Randall. Simmie paired off with her new best friend, Poonta, and Darren sat down disgruntled near Vinchi. Randall looked at Darren as he asked, "So what's wrong with you, grumble-butt?". Darren couldn't help himself as he was stone-cold sober, "It's cold, it's wet and it's rainy. We're at the bottom end of the world... Why couldn't we have found somewhere tropical? Besides that, I'm sure that bloody bio-metric scanner hates me. I still think I was personally violated". Vinchi laughed, "Maybe it'll buy you a drink and take you out to dinner later. Oh, get a grip Darren, we're alive, mate. Honestly, this is the best outcome we could have asked for. Look around you, be grateful, for once. We're safe, isolated and theoretically we're all dead. If Randall and Simmie do go on any missions now, we become their 'A-Team'. How cool is that? As for me, thank you, Randall. I'm here for as long as you need me, thank you, mate". Poonta turned to Randall and asked, "Me knows it not me business, mate, but what deal dids yous make to keep us safe?". Randall squared off against his big friend and made eye contact as he explained as honestly as he could, "You deserve that much, Poonta mate. To keep everyone safe, I had to agree that Simmie and I would go back and do some of the Ancients' dirty work for them. One specific family within the one World Monarch is trying to usurp the world order and unbalance everything. It's called greed. We were tasked by the Ancients to take them out, completely, the entire bloodline. However, it appears Hondorus took offence to the fact I was also blackmailing the Ancients. He's their Head honcho so to speak. I used the node to my advantage to take what I needed which they can't get back and that pushed Hondorus over the edge, which is where he made his big mistake. The issue is they thought they could take me out and get rid of their problem. They took the Chimera Card with the access codes to 'The System' off Vance's body and Hondorus obviously believed if he killed me it was all over. He called my bluff. Unfortunately, for him I wasn't actually bluffing, I actually have enough information on them and all the elites to bury them, it would expose everything. They would lose control of the world, literally. By calling my bluff and killing me off, they think the problem has gone away. It's worked in our favour that they now think we're all dead".

Now it's was Chandie's turn. She placed her hand on Randall's right knee and queried him, "So, what happens now, so... They think we're all dead, that's a good outcome, right? I mean they killed Vance, took the codes and then destroyed the ship to kill us. Does that mean we can just disappear now and stay safe here? We are safe here, aren't we...?". Randall looked at Chandie, then at everyone else in turn, trying to gauge their feelings before he spoke, "We could if we wanted to, we've got everything here we need. We have a roof over our heads, a palace to live in and we can buy anything we'll ever need. We actually pulled it off! Even I thought we'd be dead by now or at least some of us. We could live here in perfect peace and harmony for the rest of our lives if we want to. The powers that be think we're all dead and they get to play out all their absurd power games. However, we have one small thorn in our side, one we didn't expect, plan for or see coming".

Randall fell silent for a second or two trying to gather his thoughts as he shook his head, slightly bemused. That's when Simmie raised her voice, "What Randy, what's up? What the hell is going on?". Randall sighed, heavily, something no one had ever seen him do. Something had him exceptionally frustrated and they could see his anger building. Soon he was seething as he looked up and answered Simmie, "I found these when I was rifling through Vance's pockets. I never even saw this coming and didn't even get a warning with all the access Vance provided me along with the upgrade", he revealed as he tapped the back of his head. Randall produced a little piece of round black plastic and a hermetically-sealed purple card. He tossed the piece of plastic to Darren who caught it and rolled it over in his hands, utterly puzzled and confused. He then looked up to Randall, querying, "I don't get it, what the hell is this thing, Randall?". Randall took his time to explain to Darren, "I didn't get it either until I used the purple card in our own personal node here while everyone was going through the biometric scanners". Randall paused then continued, "There's a message on the card for me. No video, just a message. He killed Vance and took the Chimera card, so he was on board the Nebakanezzar somewhere. He's involved somehow with the Ancients, I'm just not sure how, yet. I'm now being blackmailed and he wants everything we took, all eight hundred billion or the Chimera card goes missing and Hondorus gets duped and we'll be staring down the barrel of a whole Chimera contingent coming directly for us. The message was very specific with transfer instructions attached". Randall fell silent again. Seeing this, Darren couldn't contain himself, "I still don't get it Randall, you've obviously worked it out, so spit it out, we're all here to help, so let us do that. Who is it?".

Randall composed himself and shook himself back to reality, "Take a closer look Darren at that little piece of plastic you're holding. It belongs to a very specific piece of equipment. It's Viktor's boom box". Darren exploded, "You're shitting me!!! Ichabod Crane, that little dweeb is connected to all of this, how the fuck can that moron be an evil mastermind? He's flat out not falling over his own feet, let alone being part of some World Monarch conspiracy or part of some ancient death cult". Simmie cut off Darren and was next to interject, "That explains the purple card. Vance always used to say that the Ancients had a long line of spies in the ranks watching the Chimeras. Their own personal rats or 'snitches' within the system. Vance used to joke they were just phantoms, those who walk unseen, you know the ghost in the machine, a reference back to those old historical comics and Japanese manga". Randall sat still and just nodded, he was letting his friends put the pieces together for themselves. Vinchi now put his hand up to jump in over Simmie, "That explains the interference in communications back at the media station. It wasn't Simmie jamming all of the coms frequencies, the rest was the boom box of which Viktor was so possessive. He was ensuring all communications went black, he was following us. Thinking back he never let anyone touch it, ever, he carried it with him everywhere he went. I knew there was something off about him, he never really fitted in, he always seemed out of place". Chandie asked the question that was on everyone's mind by now. She turned to Randall looking him squarely in the eyes as she said, "So, Hun, what do we do now? Surely we can't just cave into this little arsehole? We've all worked so hard to get to this point, some of us nearly got killed getting here. We can't just give up, we've earned the right to be here!". Randall put his hands up in submission and to indicate he wanted to speak. "Whoa, Whoa people, it's all good. Think about it logically for a minute. We've got ourselves a low level rat who's bitten off more than he can chew. If Hondorus gets wind of his double cross, he's screwed. We've got the advantage here. Not only do we have all the resources, but we've got the most lethal Chimera team ever created and trained. Simmie and I now have the best backup support team we could ever need. As well, I have no intention of ever being used by 'The Ancients' ever again. Once we get organised here and have a plan formulated, we're going after them, all of them. So when I say all of them, I mean all of them, we're going to take down the whole 'Pyramid". The Ancients, The World Monarch and along the way we get to eliminate Vance's killer, Viktor. So, get some rest while we can because tomorrow I intend us to be the last ones left standing, period". Randall stood, lifted his glass of wine and everyone around him followed suit to make a toast, "Here's to the best friends I could ever ask for" Their leader then made a statement, as their glasses clinked, they'd never forget. "Time for our A game people. We're going hunting...!"

www.ingramcontent.com/pod-product-compliance
Lightning Source LLC
Chambersburg PA
CBHW071932130726
47908CB00015B/126